EXTRAORDINAR[illegible]

STAR[illegible]

"Promising new author Laura Baker [illegible] debut with this uniquely spellbinding tale. STARGAZER focuses on the internal and external conflict of those torn between the ways of the past and the reality of the present." —*Romantic Times*

"STARGAZER is a lovingly crafted tale of the great Navajo nation—past and present. Mysticism, mystery, mayhem, and sweet romance; they're all here in this unique time-travel page turner."

—Nan Ryan, bestselling author of *Outlaw's Kiss*

"STARGAZER is absolutely magical. Laura Baker has created a wonderful hero, and a tale to savor. Don't miss it!" —Megan Chance

"STARGAZER is an adventurous debut blending surprise, desire, and fascinating Native American lore. Laura Baker's powerful story holds more than a few unexpected twists and is guaranteed to keep you up until the wee hours."

—Christina Sky, author of *Season of Wishes*

"Laura Baker sees the stars of the Navajo sky and gazes the true belief of the Navajo culture from the old ways."

—Ben Silversmith, Navajo Medicine Person and Philosopher

"I was fascinated by the Native American lore and the beauty of the Southwest as seen through Ms. Baker's eyes. If you like time travel and Indian mysticism, STARGAZER is the book for you!" —Kristin Hannah

Willow found herself facing the most fearsome Navajo she'd ever seen. Hair, so black it looked almost blue, swept back from a high forehead and fell free past his broad shoulders. His furrowed brows and piercing black eyes made him look as if he were squinting into the sun. The only soft line of his face was the slight arch of his upper lip. Even that was raised on one side in half a snarl.

His eyes narrowed at the plastic barrier. She thought she saw a flicker of confusion, but then it was gone. And in the next instant so was the tape. With a broad swipe of his arm, he stepped free.

''Stop right there.'' Willow leveled the gun at his chest.

He stood, legs braced apart, like a warrior ready to do battle. Like a relic from the past. . . .

fth

Stargazer
Laura
Baker

STARGAZER

ISBN: 0-312-96316-5

Printed in the United States of America

St. Martin's Paperbacks edition/January 1998

St. Martin's Paperbacks are published by St. M
Avenue, New York, NY 10010.

To the memory of my father,
who loved music most of all—
Con Brio al Fine.
—Warren Henry Schuetz—

WITH WARMEST THANKS:

to Karen and Larry McCartney for your stellar advice.

to Evelyn Lopez for gladly answering any number of my questions about the Navajo Tribal Government.

to Ben Silversmith for patiently matching my written Navajo with your spoken language.

to Kathy M. and Roberta S.—you know why.

to Sandy Elliott for every one of those "just one small" questions—first I cringed and then I thanked my lucky stars for your insight.

to the late Bill Auble, whose knowledge of the Navajo was surpassed only by his love for their unique presence on this earth. I will always miss your companionship and humor.

and to Robin Perini because you make me the best that I can be—in writing, in friendship, as a person.

PROLOGUE

Canyon de Chelly, August 1863

Shadows cut across the ring of warriors motionless at the edge of the towering canyon. The air hung still and heavy, laden with the grim talk of battle.

"You are not welcome here."

Jake Lonewolf searched the faces in the smoky campsite until he found the piercing gaze of Black Horse—the one the white men called Defiant One. Though weak from four days of fasting, Lonewolf stood his ground.

The old warrior's wizened eyes hardened. "Are you deaf, *Ma'ii*? Leave now. You do not belong here."

Lonewolf fought his instinctive reaction to the slur. Mischief-maker. Bringer of disorder. Words of fear hurled at him by people afraid of their future.

But the stars had spoken true to him. Visions so black and powerful, he had wept. They had told him Rope Thrower would kill every Navajo. Once a friend, the white man Kit Carson now led the army into the womb of their homeland. Every rock in the canyon whispered to Lonewolf. Leave *Dinehtah*. Or die.

"No, Black Horse," he said at last. "I am not deaf. It is you who do not listen."

"I should listen to you say the People will die? Here in the canyons made by Changing Woman? You think the white man is more powerful. Did you forget all you knew of us when you lived with them? Fifteen years is a long time."

Lonewolf stepped from the shadows. White-hot embers sparked from the fire, like tiny fireflies shot into the night sky. Nervous murmurs rose and mingled with the cedar smoke.

"I did not forget you, nor have I forgotten them. The white men will not give up. They are not driven by honor or revenge like the marauding Utes. They lust for our land. And that greed will not disappear as long as the People live here. You will not win—just kill more of the People."

"You dare to mock us here?" Black Horse waved his arms toward the canyon wall. The fire's flickering plumes illuminated the massive war painting. "*That* is what we did to the Utes. And what we will do to any enemy. Have you forgotten you are a warrior? Those brave soldiers burn our orchards and hogans. How many treaties have we signed? And *still* they let rancheros and Utes steal our wives and children."

Black Horse stood and moved in for the kill. "You will let them do this? You would surrender to the ones who protect the murderers of your wife and son?"

Lonewolf summoned all his strength to keep from striking the old warrior. He hated the word "surrender"—the thought ate away at him now, even as he fought to make these warriors understand that staying in the canyons led to certain death.

He let the celestial spirits fill him. The canyon hummed with their voices. A chorus of desperate cries that echoed from every rock, until the sounds became one and filled Lonewolf with a sad harmony.

The swirling smoke carried Lonewolf's words like a prayer. "I have seen a land scorched and barren. Black smoke rising from burned-down hogans. Cold, harsh winds blowing through canyons and across the mesas, silent and empty. The only sound the harsh screams of death's owls. Above all, the Sacred Mountains covered in a black cloud so dense it captures the Holy Ones. The *Diyin Diné'e* can only look down and mourn."

His voice rose above the fire's spiraling tendrils. "No, I do not fear death. I am not afraid to fight. But you are afraid to hear the truth. The white man's army leads a powerful nation. How many thousands of soldiers wait beyond our fires to invade *Dinehtah*?"

Distant thunder rumbled, like thousands of galloping hooves on the mesas above.

"We have two choices, Black Horse. We can send scouts to every part of *Dinehtah*, gather all the People, and find refuge in *Naatsis'áán*. They will not pursue us to Navajo Mountain. They do not want us. They want this land, *Naat'áanii*."

"That is not a choice! We could never gather everyone. Or would you leave hundreds to die? *Do tah!* We will not run like rabbits chased from their burrows."

"The rabbit who outruns his enemy lives, *Naat'áanii*." Lonewolf paused, then continued. "The other choice is to talk peace with Rope Thrower. Walk with the white man to their reservation. At least the People would survive."

Black Horse's eyes filled with contempt. "Retreat or surrender? That is your counsel? Leave now, Lonewolf. You have stolen my patience. And now we have less time to plan their defeat."

Lonewolf looked at the faces of the councilmen. Friends. Clansmen. They knew his powers of vision but they would never fully accept him or believe. Anger welled in Lonewolf, unbidden and with sudden force. "You would scorn me for what I learned from my white family. Would you also dismiss what I know? Are you so proud you would lead our people to a sure death?"

Black Horse faced Lonewolf across the campfire. "Who are your people? Who do you fear will die? Are you Lonewolf, clan of Lone Tree? Or are you Jacob Tallman, *adopted* son of the *Bilagaana*?"

The cutting words sliced through to Lonewolf's heart and he suddenly understood they saw him as the enemy.

Already he could hear the whispers of witchcraft. His visionary powers would be questioned or used as evidence of his evil magic. And why? Because these warriors—men he respected and would die for—could not consider leaving *Dinehtah*. They were the Lords of the Land. They would die here.

"I am neither." Saying this, Lonewolf knew he was a dead man for he could not let their pride kill more *Diné*. He would go to Rope Thrower and find a way to peace.

"You are both."

Lonewolf froze then turned toward the familiar voice. From shadows beyond the campfire stepped Grey Feather, his old frame lean and tall. Lonewolf longed to smile at his grandfather. But a gnawing emptiness consumed him. He managed the slightest nod.

Grey Feather nodded back, solemnly. "You are well, *shi yázhi*?"

At the term of endearment, something plucked at Lonewolf's heart. He saw in Grey Feather's eyes what he truly asked. *Are you safe?*

"Yes." Lonewolf lied and knew instantly by the glint in Grey Feather's eyes he had not deceived the wise man. He felt the old man's gaze probe deep. Before Lonewolf could conceal his intentions, Grey Feather's eyes widened in understanding. Then they shuttered closed.

His weathered voice, soft as well-worn leather, filled the small cove. "Your power alone cannot save the People, *shi yázhi*."

"The stars guide me, Grandfather."

Grey Feather opened his eyes. Lonewolf nearly staggered back from his intense look. "The stars tell you what has been or what will be. One is as certain as the other. You can fight against the future of the People, but it will come just the same."

For a moment, Lonewolf was speechless. Never had his grandfather's voice held defeat. He scanned each man's face. He saw the sad eyes of Zarcillo, haunted by the loss of his three sons. He saw the hard jaw of Tunicha, who had nearly been killed in an ambush at the fort. Their faces, and those of all the other warriors, were set with grim determination—resigned to fight until the bitter end. If not for the celestial message, he would be beside them. But this fight against the white man was futile.

Lonewolf spoke past the clutch at his heart. "If you stay and fight Rope Thrower, *Dinehtah* will run red with the blood of the People. Thousands will die. And still you will lose. *You cannot win.*"

Harsh grumblings rose from the circle of men. Lonewolf looked to Grey Feather. The old medicine man had never questioned Lonewolf's visions. The right words from him now could sway the council.

Moisture filled the old man's eyes until they looked like black stones lying at the bottom of a clear pool. "Hear me, *shi yázhi*. The stars speak true and so it will be. But not for you."

Thunder rolled across the distant plateau. Coldness shuddered within Lonewolf, like an icy breath through his veins. "And now hear me, all of you!" Lonewolf moved closer, his toes touching the burned earth near the fire. Flames jumped to the sky. "The soldiers will push through *Dinehtah* and destroy everything in their path. And when they are done, *Dinehtah* will be dead. The Holy Ones will mourn from the mountain peaks. But we will not hear. We will be gone!"

"*Do tah!*" Grey Feather's emphatic response struck Lonewolf in the heart. "By all that is sacred, I say to you now, go from here. Your future is not here, Jacob Lonewolf."

Lightning cracked above the canyon, but Lonewolf could not hear past the pounding of his heart. When he turned from the campfire, from all he held dear, he did not hear the whispered goodbye.

Shadows engulfed him. Twilight pulled at the darkness, untangling it from the jagged cliffs.

He did not look up to his beloved stars. He knew they were shrouded by rainless clouds. Instead he kept his eyes ahead as he tread carefully, soundlessly along the dry wash through the canyon. His ears strained for the slightest noise. Black Horse would send someone. Kee Nez, maybe. As if killing Lonewolf would change the truth given by the stars.

Grey Feather's words haunted each step. *The future of the People will come just the same.* A vision of a silent, black *Dinehtah* filled Lonewolf's mind. He staggered ahead, not seeing where he set his feet.

Had he read the stars wrong? Misinterpreted the message? No! The sky was not just a Navajo sky. He had learned that among all the books of his white family.

Lonewolf clenched his jaw against the memories. He had spoken the truth to Black Horse. Lonewolf had no one, now—Navajo or white. Black Horse had been right about one thing. Fifteen years was a long time to be with the whites. Half his life.

You are not welcome here. The words of Black Horse echoed through his mind.

Wrenching sadness seared his gut as he neared the peach orchard, the pride of the *Diné*. A sweet, sticky fragrance hung in the boughs of thousands of trees, beckoning him, reminding him of his long fast. With gratitude, he plucked two handfuls of the ripe fruit and stored them in his bundle.

He left the trees and trudged up a talus slope. Centuries of debris lay beneath his moccasins—broken pottery tossed from the ancient cliff dwellings above him, covered with sand and gravel. The slope steepened. Lonewolf bent close to the ground the last few yards. He did not bother looking behind him. The rocks told him he was not alone.

The mouth of the cave yawned black in the gray

dawn. He stood just inside the entrance and let his eyes adjust to the outline of the ancient dwelling.

He bent to clear the pueblo doorway. The blackness closed around him, but he could find what he sought without his eyes. He knelt and dug in the rough earth until his fingers closed around the soft buckskin. He pulled the bundle loose and spread the buckskin on the hardened dirt floor, deftly laying the contents out evenly. Everything was as he had left it. He knew it would be. No other Navajo would dare enter a home of the ancient ones. Too many spirits of the dead.

Lonewolf did not believe in ghosts—something else he had learned with his white family. It served him well here. He never feared leaving his medicine bundle and masks buried.

Thunder boomed outside the cave. Lonewolf peered out the door of the ruin and looked across the canyon to the mesa top. Night had retreated, but not without a fight. Jagged streaks of lightning, like witches' fingers, danced across the plateau. A feeling of loss passed over Lonewolf.

Your future is not here.

What had Grey Feather meant? A chill ran through Lonewolf. Did death await him beyond the canyon?

Not since he had been torn from the lifeless arms of his mother by raiding Mexicans had he known fear. That small boy had sworn then he would die before the *ladrones* would see him cower. That small boy now told him he had nothing to fear if he followed his visions.

Grey Feather was right—you cannot escape your destiny.

Lonewolf whispered his star way chant. He called upon his starborn ancestors to give him guidance. His eyes half-closed, he used his hand to seek his painted handprint on the cave wall. Filling the painted silhouette with his palm, he raised his eyes to the ceiling for the comforting scene of his familiar star pattern.

You do not belong here.

Constellations swirled before his eyes. The ceiling shifted as if the cave had opened up to the heavens. A noiseless thunder roared through him, pounding in his chest. He tried to pull his palm away from the handprint, but his arm would not obey.

By all that is sacred, go from here.

The roar increased, echoing off the walls of the small cave. The air vibrated and crackled. And, in that instant, Lonewolf wondered why Grey Feather had called him Jacob.

From far off, Jake Lonewolf heard a scream.

ONE

Canyon de Chelly, August, Present Day

Willow screamed.

She hadn't meant to, but then she hadn't expected the shadow to move. Right away she felt silly. Wide yellow bands of undisturbed crime-scene tape blocked the small doorway to the ruin. Only an animal could be on the other side. The boy's body had been removed yesterday.

A low groan filled the cave's dark chamber, echoing off the pueblo ruin walls. It droned deep and constant, like wind moaning through the lonely canyon. But she knew it came from within the cave, from the shadows in the ruins. Like someone in pain.

"Who's in there?"

She stepped closer, her eyes riveted on the blackish shape. The air felt at once electric and heavy, as if the magnetic pole had shifted.

"Are you all right?"

No response. Even the moan ceased. Yet something *was* in there. She could hear faint sounds of movement in the thick, charged air. She reached reflexively for her holster.

"I'm Officer Becenti. Whoever is in there, I want you to move into the light where I can see you."

"What are you doing here?" The low, labored voice reverberated through her like the tolling of an ancient bell. Her heart pounded in her throat.

"That's my question and you'd better have a good answer. You're trespassing on a crime scene."

The man paused. Willow could make out a tall figure with long hair. Her pulse quickened in apprehension. Had she stumbled across the murderer? She eased the revolver out of her holster. She was through playing games.

"Raise your hands and walk into the light."

A long moment passed before the shadow moved. The cave's air practically sizzled with electricity, raising the hair on her arms. Willow stepped back until she bumped into the cave wall. A mere five feet now separated her from the pueblo doorway.

First blurry, like a figure arising through heat waves on the desert, the form suddenly coalesced. With only flimsy tape between them, Willow found herself facing the most fearsome Navajo she'd ever seen. Hair, so black it looked almost blue, swept back from a high forehead and fell free past his broad shoulders. His furrowed brows and piercing black eyes made him look as if he were squinting into the sun. The only soft line on his face was the slight arch of his upper lip. Even that was raised on one side in half a snarl.

His eyes narrowed at the plastic barrier. She thought she saw a flicker of confusion, but then it was gone. And in the next instant so was the tape. With a broad swipe of his arm, he stepped free of the small ruin.

"Stop right there." Willow leveled the gun at his chest.

He stood, legs braced apart, like a warrior ready to do battle. No Pueblo blood in this one. A full-blooded Navajo. Like a relic from the past.

His clothes had endured plenty of wear, yet she had to admit they fit him well. A chamois shirt fell loose over deerskin trousers, which in turn were tucked into dark buckskin leggins. From shoulder to ground, the reddish-brown leather matched the color of his sun-warmed skin.

She suddenly noticed a leather pouch he held in one

hand. His fist flexed possessively, and she looked up to see him glaring at her, his face a mixture of anger and defiance.

"Did Black Horse send you?"

With no clue as to who Black Horse could be, she ignored the question and got to the point. "What were you doing in there? What's in that bag?" She gestured with the gun barrel.

He seemed to consider her before he spoke. "No, not Black Horse. Rope Thrower sent you. And what I have in the pouch will be of no use to him without me."

"We'll see about that. Drop the bag."

The Indian didn't move.

"Set the bag down."

Still he didn't move. He stared at her, his features set with determination, his intense gaze never straying to the gun she had leveled at his chest.

"Whatever you're thinking," Willow said with meaning, "won't work. Now drop the bag."

His arm rose slowly, as if independent from his steadfast stance. The pouch dangled only two feet from her reach. Then it dropped. Willow stretched a leg to the bag, toed it closer and reached for the pouch.

An electric shock jolted through her.

In the next instant, he'd pinned her arm behind her back and wrenched the gun from her hand. Her body was pressed between a cold cave wall and a strong, rock-hard Navajo.

He spoke close to her ear. "Rope Thrower was foolish to send a woman to spy. Did he think we would not notice you? Did he think this long black braid would hide your *bilagaana* blood?" He ran his hand down her braid, grabbed the end and wrapped it fiercely around her neck.

"I am half white!" she choked out. "Half *Diné*." His hand brushed her skin, and Willow felt a cyclone of images fly from his fingers into her. Never before had the visions come so fast. Burning hogans filled her mind. *Darkness. Impending disaster.* She bit the inside of her cheek with enough force to cause pain and stop the maelstrom. *Not now! Don't get swept away!*

He pulled the braid tighter around her throat and leaned into her ear.

"Now you will tell me where Rope Thrower is."

Willow swallowed past the bitter taste of fear and spoke evenly. "I am an officer of the law. Unhand me this instant, or I'll arrest you for battery on an officer."

"You speak brave words for one so far from friends."

She struggled beneath his weight. "That's where you're wrong. Now let me go!"

"You bring the enemy with you?" He spun her around with such force she knocked her head on the cave wall. But it was his fierce look that left her weak. His dark eyes were lethal and compelling. Like a hawk. His glare impaled her. She mustered her will to break the trance.

"Do you consider the Navajo Tribal Government your enemy?"

Again she saw wisps of confusion cloud his eyes. Was he high on something? Willow thought fast through her years of crisis training and decided to take a chance.

"Why don't you let me take you to Fort Defiance, and I'll get you some help?"

"I have seen the help you give. Our People who go there do not come back. Some are shot. The rest we never see again." A bronze hand captured her wrist and drew it up to her chest.

Willow steeled herself from his touch. But she couldn't stop a sudden rush of desperation coursing through her, as if time were running out.

"You have taken holy ground and turned it red with blood!" Rage flamed in his eyes. "Have you no shame? *Do tah!* I will not surrender to your *siláoo yázhi.*"

Little soldiers. Willow fought to understand what didn't make any sense.

"I have words for Rope Thrower. You will take me to him."

"No." She stared, unflinching, at the man towering above her, his face set with purpose and determination.

"You will come with me. Test your courage with Black Horse. You will tell him what you know about Rope Thrower and what awaits the *Diné*."

A firm hand gripped her shoulder and shoved her to the ground. She watched as he carefully set down his bundle. He untied the buckskin strap that bound it and pulled it tight as if testing its strength, stood and approached her. Suddenly, she realized his intention and sprang to her feet.

"Wait! Stop! You can't do this!" She backed away from him.

He captured her hands and, despite her struggles, swiftly tied her wrists together.

"Officer Becenti, come in." The noise crackled from the radio at her hip.

"I'm a cop! Don't you hear?"

He pulled a knife from his moccasins.

The ground shifted. Willow stared at the lethal steel blade and fought for breath. A tug at her belt and the radio was gone.

He stared at it—the look of an intelligent man trying to decipher a cryptic message—then flung it across the cave. Willow winced involuntarily at the crack of stone and metal.

"Officer Becenti." His deep, quiet voice pulled her eyes up to his. "I do not plan to harm you. But you *will* talk to Black Horse. Do not fight me." The last was given as a warning.

Without taking his eyes from hers, he put one of the leather straps dangling from her wrists between his teeth, pulled it taut, and sliced through it with the knife.

He put the other strap between his teeth, along with the knife. Then he crouched and pulled his bundle together. Willow watched, noticing the special care he gave to placing each object within the bundle. A gourd rattle with a star pattern drilled on its face caught her eye before it disappeared within the buckskin. His long fingers deftly tied it with the strap he'd just cut.

"Is that why you trespassed onto the crime scene? For the bundle?"

"What is your interest in this?" His voice carried a possessive warning.

"Because if that bundle came from in there, it could be evidence. It might help us find the murderer." She weighed her next words carefully, knowing she was taking a dreadful chance, but one that might knock some sense into him. "You wouldn't want to interfere with that. Unless you had a reason."

He stood swiftly, in one quiet, lithe motion. "You are worried about one murder." His voice was deadly calm. "What of all the others?" He tied the bundle to his waist, slid a quiver of arrows over his back, and picked up a broad bow.

Through it all, he had not looked at her, though he held the long strap connected to her wrists. Now, he stepped close.

"The truth, Officer Becenti, is that you do not care. You have already betrayed your people."

The accusation wasn't new and Willow had thought she was immune to the misjudgment of her career—until now. Why should the words of a total stranger make her heart pound? She wished she could retreat from the cold contempt in his eyes.

Without a word, he pulled her out of the cave and down the gravelly slope to the dry riverbed. She fought down her emotions and tried to think as he led the way across the broad sandwash.

"Where are we going?"

"Where is your horse?"

"I came by foot." She didn't mention she'd left her horse on the mesa above. "Just tell me why you're doing this and maybe I can help."

Silence.

On each side of her, four hundred feet of sandstone cliffs blushed red in the morning sun. At any other time, she would have gazed in awe at the majestic beauty. Right now, all she could feel was vulnerable, deep in wild country with a madman.

She had to get him talking again. Get him to let her go before they disappeared into the canyon's labyrinths—where no one would find her.

"Look, you don't want to do this. Kidnapping an officer is a federal offense. Let me go before this gets out of hand."

No response.

Anger edged out the fear. "Others will come looking for me. You can't get away with this!"

His abrupt yank on the strap stopped her in a skid, his face within inches of hers. His tone was cool, matter-of-fact. "If you scream, no one will hear you. If you run, I will find you. There is nowhere you can hide. The canyons are mine. And if you do not stop talking . . ."

He broke off and walked to the canyon wall. He reached out his fingers and touched the inscription scratched into the rock: "W. E. Dodd. Co K 1st Cavy. N. M. Volts." His hand stopped at the date. "Aug. 1864."

Time froze.

Willow knew the Dodd Inscription had been etched by a cavalryman during Kit Carson's campaign to force the Navajo to surrender. What no one had accomplished through warfare, Carson had accomplished through starvation, deprivation, and exhaustion. And on the date inscribed, he had ordered the destruction of the Navajos' prize orchard of five thousand peach trees. But, for the

Navajo, the worst was yet to come in the Long Walk to Bosque Redondo in New Mexico.

Willow watched as he stared at the date. All was silent save for the sound of her own breathing and the trill of a mockingbird from a mesa-top piñon tree. Willow stared at the leather strap dangling in the sand. She took a small, quiet step backward.

He suddenly turned from the cliff wall, his face twisted in torment, his eyes a rage of anger and something else Willow couldn't name. She staggered back and would have fallen, except he grabbed her upper arm hard and yanked her toward the dry bed wash.

She stumbled, trying to keep pace with his long strides, not daring to protest. One look at the fierce, rigid lines in his face made her swallow her words. He looked like a warrior in battle. Set for revenge. At that moment, Willow had no doubt he would kill whatever got in his way.

The next instant he turned and roared at her, "What have you done?"

Willow's breath caught at the savage look in his eyes. "What are you talking about?"

"Where are they?" he demanded through clenched teeth.

Willow stared at the canyon valley, frantically trying to figure an answer for his question, but all she saw was a goat peacefully browsing on the roof of a summer hogan.

"Is your magic so great you could make it all disappear?"

Willow rounded on him. "Are you mad? I didn't make anything . . ." His eyes stopped her. Their torment was so palpable she felt a stab of pain in her chest. He looked beyond her down the canyon. Something in his face pulled at her heart. She'd never seen such a lonely, confused expression. She was simultaneously angered and touched by the crack in his invincibility.

In an instant it was gone. Without another word, he set off through the canyon, pulling her along by the leather straps trailing from her wrists.

He led her up Canyon del Muerto. Caves yawned from high above them. They passed Kokopelli Cave, Ceremonial Cave, Stipple Cave.

The late morning sun warmed the surrounding cliffs and probed into its crevices, crags, and burrows. Soon the canyon would soak up all the sun it could hold, then release it in shimmering waves of choking heat. Already, Willow wished she could roll up the long sleeves on her uniform.

They'd walked for an hour in silence when they passed a small pueblo ruin, its rooms huddled beneath a rock overhang nearly fifty feet above the canyon floor. Willow gazed with longing at the high shady shelter. She imagined a breeze circling round her as she rested her tired legs. But the constant tug on her wrists kept her moving.

Around the next point, they suddenly halted. Below a protruding ledge, a massive painting covered thirty feet of canyon wall. Indians against Indians. The Ute Raid Panel.

The Navajo approached the brutal scene and reached his hand toward the figures. Then he walked a circumference of ground beneath the painting, kicking tumbleweed aside, sweeping his toes across the sand. He looked for all the world as if he were searching for something among the stately yucca and gray sagebrush.

A low moan, deep and mournful, filled the rocky cove. The primal sound sent shivers down her spine.

He sank to his knees and clutched at the earth. His inexplicable grief tugged at Willow's heart.

But her eyes focused on the gun he'd dropped at his side.

Willow moved with stealth and patience, a step at a time. Her toe nearly touched the discarded weapon. In one movement, she crouched and touched its handle. A bronzed hand flashed before her and grabbed the gun.

Willow swung with all her might and connected with his chin. He fell with a groan. She scrambled around him and ran for all she was worth.

She knew she couldn't get far. She couldn't get any speed with her wrists tied together. He had to be right behind her. Gaining on her. Taking aim with her own gun. Or maybe she had done him at least some temporary damage. She didn't dare look back to see.

She just ran.

Willow gave thanks for all the years of rock climbing and prayed her legs would hold up. She focused her eyes on the dry wash ahead, picking a path among the rocks and deadwood deposited during the last flash flood.

Where was he? He should have caught her by now. *Don't give up. Think, Willow. Remember where the caves are!*

She fought through a dense stand of tamarisk trees. Their spindly limbs whipped her forearms and face. She swiped at moisture on her forehead only to find blood on the back of her hand.

Willow broke free of the trees and half stumbled through a ravine. Ancient ruts gouged the earth, twisting her feet. She stole a glance at the canyon wall and saw the black holes of the Four Hole Site, a labyrinth of caves thirty feet above the canyon floor.

Pellets of sand and gravel shot from her shoes and pelted her legs as she scrambled up the talus slope. Her tied wrists like a vise, she grabbed at jutting rocks, scarcely noticing her torn and bloodied knuckles.

Willow pulled herself onto the rocky ledge and collapsed at the mouth of the caves. Her heart beat at her throat, squeezing the air out of her lungs. She looked down into the canyon, half terrified she'd see her captor climbing toward her. But he was nowhere in sight.

Cool air sighed from the cave, washed over her and

enveloped her. She wanted to lie there forever, but didn't dare. After a moment she hauled herself into the welcoming darkness.

She stumbled over fallen boulders and rubble, her fingertips brushing the rough walls for guidance. In the northernmost cave total blackness engulfed her. Like a sightless mole in a burrow, Willow crept along the wall to the back of the cave, where she settled in a corner.

Cuts stung on her face and arms, but Willow ignored the pain and dug her teeth into the strap binding her wrists. In her haste, she pulled the leather tighter, cutting off blood to her hands. Her fingertips throbbed as she worked slowly, agonizingly, to loosen the knot. Sweat beaded on her brow.

How had this happened? What the hell was she doing here? Her instincts had always served her well as a cop. Boy, they'd really stunk today. A possible murderer had gotten her gun, kidnapped her, and nearly gotten away with it. *Still could,* a sarcastic voice goaded her.

No way, she countered and tugged so hard on the strap her teeth hurt.

Unbidden, the warrior's words of warning came back to her. *If you run, I will find you. There is nowhere you can hide.*

"We'll see about that," she muttered, and with a final tug, she loosened the leather at her wrists and flung the strap across the cave. Something scampered in the shadows.

Willow rummaged through her backpack, pulled out the flashlight and flicked it on. She let the light sweep the cave floor and wall. Its beam shone on a chalk painting of a bird hovering over a horned shaman—an ancient drawing of a powerful medicine man capable of magical soul flights. Legends told of gifted medicine men, sent by the starborn ancestors to lead the *Diné*. The medicine man would be known by the sacred mark of the horned shaman.

You're a fairy tale. Just one more myth in the line of superstitions.

The artist had neglected to give the shaman any eyes, yet Willow felt his gaze on her: an accusing look, as if questioning her presence deep in this small, rocky confine.

"I wouldn't be here if I didn't have to," she rasped out, her breath still ragged and shallow from running.

Willow cleared away the stones beneath her and settled down. Still something poked her in the leg. She shoved a hand in her pocket and fingered the pottery shard she'd pried from the lifeless hand of the dead Navajo boy. She wouldn't be here if she hadn't been assigned to investigate the young *Diné*'s death.

She would be in Fort Defiance, beside Manuelito. She *needed* to be there!

How could she have let that "throwback" take her by surprise? He was trespassing a crime scene, he was obviously a suspect. Why hadn't she been more on guard?

She saw him as he had stood in the cave—arrogantly tall, impossibly rigid. A man not given to compromise. Or bluffing. There was no doubt he was the most fierce Navajo she had encountered. Why hadn't she reacted faster?

The simple answer, one she hated to admit, was what she had seen in his eyes. They'd been defiant, even challenging. But they hadn't held a trace of guilt. Whatever he was doing in that cave, he figured he had the right to do it.

Like stealing a medicine man's *jish* bundle. It couldn't be his. If he were a medicine man, she'd have heard of him. Experienced *Hataałii* were well-known and sought after. And she'd *definitely* never seen or heard of anyone like him before. He wasn't someone you'd easily forget.

She saw his face twisted with rage when he'd yelled,

What have you done? The guy was absolutely delusional. No grip on reality.

And what about you? You call your visions normal?

"I call them gut instinct and nothing more." Willow glared at the silent shaman on the wall as if he were the one taunting her. "It's easy for you to act superior. You're safe here. You don't have to go out and live in the real world. And if you did, those horns would have to go."

You have betrayed your people. She felt the Navajo's hot words at her ear and unconsciously raised a hand to her neck. "How dare he! I don't have to justify my job to anyone!"

But the warrior's words hung in the air, as if spoken aloud. The accusation wasn't new to her. Willow's own grandfather considered her job as no more than an arm of the white man's power.

But he was wrong. The old ways, full of legends and magic, kept the Navajo weak. Grandfather could keep his visions and superstitions. Willow had a better way for the Navajo.

Willow drew her knees close and wrapped her arms around them. Cold air leached from the jagged rocks cutting into her back. In a few hours, it'd be dark enough for her to sneak out of the canyon, ride to Chinle and radio for help.

By morning, she'd see the Navajo locked up and answering *her* questions.

Lonewolf ached.

The thunder in his head had abated, leaving in its stead a hollowness. The emptiness filled him with immeasurable sorrow. Like gazing up at a sky devoid of stars.

But the stars could no more disappear than . . . five thousand peach trees . . . or the council of headmen.

He rubbed one source of pain—his chin. He had underestimated her. That would not happen again. The blow to his head had knocked out the noise. Perhaps he would thank her.

But who was she? She dressed like a man and carried a gun. Her hair and features were *Diné*—but that was all. Her skin was pale brown and her eyes bright green, like a cougar's. And like the stealthy mountain lion, she did not give up, and she showed no fear. He respected that—and that she had caught him by surprise. That would not have happened if his head had not been filled with thunder.

He touched his jaw again as he looked up at the cave. She was in there. Though he had not followed her, the rocks had led him to where she hid.

Lonewolf crouched against the opposite cliff wall and pondered her choice. Maybe she sought safety in the presence of the magical singer. She would be disappointed. *Ha'tanii* belonged to Lonewolf.

He bit into one of the peaches and waited for the night. He could be patient. Soon, his stars would shine and speak to him. Tell him where to find the others. And where Rope Thrower hid.

Then he would go for her.

TWO

Willow edged through darkness to the cliff opening. Though the canyon slept, its pitch-dark night was shades lighter than the obsidian depths of the cave. She focused so hard on the mutating blackness her eyes ached.

When she finally emerged from the cave's mouth, she drank the cool, crisp air into her dusty lungs. Dense clouds hung low, nearly resting on the shoulders of the broad plain above the canyon.

It took Willow longer to descend from the caves than it had to climb up. The full measure of her senses strained for the slightest untoward sound. Every muscle in her body tensed for silent movement. When she finally set foot on the sandy wash at the bottom, her knees nearly buckled from the exertion.

She gave each thigh a brisk rub then quickly moved on, staying close to the canyon wall. She had a mile and a half to cover, then up the opposite cliff face to where she'd left her horse tied on the mesa.

With each determined step, Willow felt compelled to go faster. Her legs wanted to run and the fine hair rose on the back of her neck. She didn't fear the night in this canyon, where she'd wandered with Grandfather as a child. But she had excellent animal instincts. She knew when she was being stalked. Every muscle in her body tensed, ready for flight.

Was this how her father had felt? He'd run for his life, alone in the jungle, pursued by an unseen enemy. Her father had died in that jungle, terror in his throat.

Willow's heart pumped loud and fast. She thought she'd scream from the roar in her ears.

She stopped and pressed her back into a crevice. Night hid the opposite canyon wall, with nearly a quarter mile of canyon floor in between. All she could hear was her shallow, ragged breathing. She willed her heart to slow, took several deep breaths, then closed her eyes and concentrated on her surroundings.

The air stirred around her, like wisps of ghosts brushing past. Willow opened her eyes. The canyon held its shadows close.

She could feel the menace.

The Navajo.

A tendril of fear curled in her stomach. She calmed herself with the knowledge that he hadn't seen her yet. If he had, Willow told herself with forceful logic, she wouldn't be standing here wondering where he was.

She stole down to the dry wash coursing through the canyon. She could walk more easily here and with more coverage from the high, mud-packed walls of the arroyo.

But the banks also blocked her view of what lay beyond the next turn. If only she had her gun, or even a knife. All she had was the useless flashlight. She couldn't very well turn it on, which left throwing it as a weapon. Somehow she didn't think he would stand still long enough for her to aim.

The sense of dread built within Willow, knotting her stomach. Twice, a sound behind her gave her a start. When noises came from the ground above, she would halt mid-step, not daring to put the other foot down. Always, when she stopped, the air surrounded her with silence. Still the knot twisted deep in her, prickling her sides, and sending warnings through her veins.

Willow knew she needed to climb out of the arroyo and cut across the canyon to the trail. What would be facing her on the ground above? Had he followed in silence, waiting for the moment to capture her?

It was now or never. She grabbed and pulled at roots, jamming a boot hold into the hard bank for leverage. She caught hold of an overhanging juniper branch and swung herself over the top.

She was alone. Willow released the breath she hadn't known she'd been holding. She could barely discern where the opposite canyon wall curved in to form Deadman's Cove. White House trail would be directly across from her. Just fifty feet to the canyon wall and she could start the hard climb up.

Willow let her senses travel—close by around her—then over surrounding areas. She heard the tiny paws of deer mice as they scampered for cover. She felt the air subtly shift from soaring wings. She smelled the sharp, musky aroma of piñon burning in a distant hogan. Nothing unusual.

In a crouch, she scurried between squaw bush and service berry, their pliable stems whipping across her arms. Kneeling at the bottom of the cliff, she took a moment to catch her breath, then started to climb. Loose dirt and gravel shifted beneath her feet. She grabbed at jutting rocks, clumps of sage, exposed roots. With every step her panic increased. She tamped down the fear, scolding herself for acting like a child who feared the monster's hands would shoot between dark basement stairs to grab her ankles. And she cursed every unstable foot that slid through the dirt.

She reached a plateau where the real trail began. Halfway there. Even when she got there, it wouldn't be over, she thought miserably. She had a long ride ahead of her to get help. Then back to the canyon.

Closer now to the top. Cool air wafted down to her, but it did nothing to ease her struggle. The steep trail strained her calves. She pressed a hand on each leg, forcing them to bend and climb. Every muscle ached. But she couldn't slow down. She couldn't shake the feeling of being pursued.

Then she heard a rock fall far behind her. Panic leapt into her throat. She scrambled off the trail, taking the shortest route up. Scraggly, tenacious junipers grabbed her pants and shirt, tearing at them as she rushed past.

Another rock crashed down the side of the canyon wall. Willow risked a look over her shoulder and gasped at the figure of a man not twenty feet behind her, scrambling after her over the unforgiving rock face. She couldn't let him take her again!

With a surge, she rushed for the top. Frantically, she grabbed for strongholds, clawing at the bare rock. Suddenly an outstretched arm appeared over the top.

"Take my hand."

Him! No! He couldn't be ahead of her. Panic and confusion choked in her throat. Who was behind her? Willow shot a frenzied look over her shoulder. Her feet shifted and suddenly she was slipping. She clutched at the stone wall. Her fingers dragged along the rocks, her boots scraped, pebbles crunched beneath her. Jagged stones slashed through her shirt as she slid down the sandstone wall. She saw hands reaching for her from below.

A hard yank on her outstretched arm broke the downhill plunge.

He had her.

A shot rang out from below.

She felt herself being pulled over the top, then unceremoniously dropped. She shifted her weight and tried to sit up, but had to bite back a scream of agony. She collapsed on her left side, her arm limp at her side. Spasms of pain shot from her neck.

She lifted her eyes to see the Navajo towering over her like a tree. In one motion, he unslung a bow from his back and slipped an arrow into place. Willow watched, hypnotized, as if it were all happening in slow motion. Faint moonlight shone on his face. Primitive and fierce. He arched the huge bow with ease.

Another shot rang out. She thought he flinched, but she couldn't be sure. Black spots blurred her vision. In the next instant, the arrow flew with such power and speed all she registered was a whoosh of air over her head. Then the blackness encompassed her.

Willow tasted clay. She opened her eyes to see a pottery canteen at her mouth. The cool water sluiced down her throat and washed away the dust. She gratefully licked her parched lips, only then noticing warm fingers examining her neck and shoulder.

His touch, though light, found every wound. He let his hand rest on her shoulder. Heat emanated from his fingertips and swirled through her. Excruciating pain coursed through her arm, building, pumping through her veins, drawn to his touch.

Just when Willow thought she would pass out from the agony, the pain rose to her shoulder and escaped. Only a dull throb remained.

Willow's breath caught at the unexpected relief. Before she had time to speak, to offer any thanks, strong hands supported her back, folded her upright and pressed her against the Navajo's chest. She felt soft chamois against her cheek. She opened her eyes to bare skin at the neck of his shirt. Her senses filled with leather and earthy male.

"I need to remove this bag on your back. Can you move your good arm?" his low voice whispered in her ear.

At first Willow didn't comprehend. Then she felt the Navajo's fingers tug slightly at one of the straps of her backpack. Willow crooked her right arm and worked it through the opening. She felt the other strap slipped gently off her injured shoulder.

Steel arms braced her back, then carefully settled her on the ground.

"Thank you," she rasped. "I'm all right now."

She tried to shift, but another spasm of pain attacked her shoulder.

He arched a skeptical brow. ''Your shoulder is injured.'' He rose to unstrap the bundle from his waist.

She braced herself on her right arm and tried to rise. Searing pain sent tears to her eyes. She closed her eyes to the agony.

''What about the man below?'' she managed to ask.

''He is gone.''

His words brushed on her cheek. She threw her eyes open to see the Navajo bending close, his gaze intent on her.

''Watch me. Here.'' He pointed to his eyes with his first two fingers. ''Do not be afraid, *shi yázhi.*''

Willow looked into his ebony eyes and felt pulled toward him. His eyes steadied her, mesmerized her. Humming came from deep within him, an ancient song meant for healing.

The song lulled her. Each monotone distanced her from the throbbing pain.

Lonewolf shifted and Willow felt both his hands at her shoulder. She didn't have time to brace herself. In the next instant, Lonewolf yanked on her arm. Bones grated. Muscles screamed. Waves of pain threatened to drown her.

Incessant humming droned in her ears. It annoyed her, grated on her nerves. Willow pulled herself from the depths, fought through the daze. The noise rose and Willow followed it up, out of the haze.

Then it stopped.

''Open your eyes, little one.''

Willow stared with lazy focus at the warrior bending over her. She felt him cup her head with a large hand. In the other, he rolled something between his fingers. A roundish white bulb that looked like an onion. Without taking his eyes from hers, he put the small root in his mouth and chewed on it.

Willow's gaze fell to his lips. She watched spellbound as his mouth worked the root. His strong, masculine lips moved in a rhythm.

Slowly, his mouth lowered to hers. His firm lips covered hers, flooding Willow with a myriad of sensations. Circles of warmth spiraled through her. More than a mere ministration, his touch penetrated deep, to the core of her. To something so deep she didn't know it existed. She sighed a small moan.

He parted her lips with his tongue and cupped her head closer to his. Warm liquid rushed inside her mouth. She drank from him, drowning on the sweet taste. The potion coursed through her languidly. She could feel it drawn to every part of her, leaving her limp and deliciously warm.

His lips pressed against hers. He moved his tongue beside hers and sent more nectar down her throat. The liquid pooled at her shoulder and worked its magic. She felt not only instant relief from the pain, but more. She could almost feel her muscles mending, knitted together by the medicine.

She felt magic in his lips, in his long, lean length pressed against her. The Navajo's power coursed through her, healing her. *With a medicine man's powers of control.*

The knowledge flooded her with anger. He'd overtaken her again! This time with the smoothness of a trickster. She pressed a hand against his hard chest. Awareness shot through her, angering her even more. She pushed harder. Beneath her fingertips throbbed pure strength. A shudder passed through him, and suddenly she was awash in visions. Fragments of scenes surrounded by blackness hurtled at her, like snapshots thrown in the wind. A blur of images. Until only one remained.

A man stretched on a fur blanket, his bronzed back glistening in firelight. His body naked save for a square of scant dark cloth, meager covering for his flexed buttocks. Beneath him lay a woman, her eyes full of longing. Feminine fingers kneaded his shoulders in an urgent, timeless rhythm. Warm fireglow played on their bodies, flickering shadows across limbs moving in tender caress.

Willow gasped. Her heart filled, overcome with emotion until she thought it would burst. Never had she felt such love.

Then, from the darkness beyond, she felt sorrow, unforgiving, unrelenting. The feeling built, threatening to choke her. Her eyes flew open only to meet the Navajo's dark, brooding gaze. She was caught, like a deer in headlights, unable to comprehend the onslaught of emotions. Where had the image come from?

She studied the man above her. His eyes were narrowed, his features taut, his mouth drawn back as if in pain. Then his lips moved.

"Your grip has power, little one."

For a confused moment, Willow merely stared. Had he spoken? Was this still the vision?

"I believe you have your strength back." He nodded toward his shoulder.

All of a sudden, Willow comprehended. She had dug her fingers into his back. She pulled her hand away, her fingers sticky with something. In horror she saw they were covered with blood.

"Oh, my God. Did I . . . ?"

"No. Your hand found the wound, but did not make it."

"What wound?"

Without a word, he gathered his pouch and moved to stand. Willow stopped him with a tentative hand to his back. She found the wetness, even now oozing. She knelt beside him and pulled the flashlight from her backpack. The instant she flicked on its beam, he sprang to his feet, dropping his bundle.

"It seems your power is very great."

Willow tested her shoulder. "It's *your* medicine that's powerful," she admitted, reluctantly. "My shoulder feels much better. I'm grateful," she said, her voice quiet. She reached her hand toward him. "Please, let me see your wound."

He stared at her hand. "You can . . . control the light?"

His tone was skeptical and Willow immediately thought of the man with the gun. "Oh! You're right." She flicked off the flashlight. "Please hold still and I'll try to see how bad it is."

She laid her hand on the wound again. The chamois shirt stuck to his back in such a wide swatch, she had trouble finding the source of the blood. Then her fingers passed over a hole near the top of his left shoulder.

"You've been shot!"

"Yes. But did it go through?"

His matter-of-fact tone annoyed her until she remembered he must have been hit *before* he shot the arrow.

"You saved my life. And then you ignored your own pain to . . . to give me . . ." Suddenly, Willow's emotions were a tangled knot, lodged in her throat.

"We will go to Rope Thrower now." He cupped her chin with a slightly unsteady hand. His gaze, however, was certain as he looked into her eyes. "The killing must stop."

His words made her remember who she was. A policeman for the Navajo Tribe, investigating a murder. Add to that, a shooting.

He released her and used one hand to fold the deerskin pouch. He kept his left arm bent, close to his side. In the partial moonlight, wetness glistened on his shoulder.

Could she overpower him? Willow dismissed the idea almost before it was fully formed. Even if she could get her gun, how would she get him back to Window Rock? He'd never make the forty miles. She wasn't sure she could even make it.

On the other hand, Grandfather's hogan was only a few miles away. The trick was, he'd have to come willingly. An idea started to take shape. She realized he hadn't mentioned Black Horse recently, only Rope Thrower. Perhaps if she played along?

"I can't take you to Rope Thrower. That is, not right now," she added matter-of-factly. "But I can take you to someone who can help."

"I do not need help."

He still hadn't managed to secure the deerskin into its pouch.

"I can see that." She knelt beside him to assist, but before she could touch the leather his hand stayed her with a light touch to her wrist.

"I must do this," he said quietly.

She *knew* better than to touch a medicine man's *jish*. Each item was hand-selected by the medicine man. Some were acquired. Most were handmade by the owner. All were imbued with the medicine man's own magic. Only a fool would chance unleashing the powers contained.

It dawned on her then that the medicine bundle was his. She watched as he, with labored care, folded the deerskin into the pouch. Who was he?

"Hash Yiniłyé Ha'taaii?" Belatedly, she realized she'd posed the routine question in formal Navajo.

His shrug surprised her, as if he would dismiss the respect accorded a medicine man.

"Lonewolf *Yinish'yé.*"

Lonewolf. Figures.

"Well, *Hastiin* Lonewolf, you—"

"Just Lonewolf. Or Jake." He rose, a bit awkwardly, obviously trying not to use his left arm, and tied the bundle to his waist.

"I should have known you wouldn't go in for formalities." Willow stood and walked to her horse. "Anyway, as I was saying, you are in no condition to find

Rope Thrower tonight. The man I know can bind your wound and ease the pain—''

''I do not feel any pain.''

Willow knew without a doubt he was lying. His flint-hard eyes effectively masked whatever was going on inside his head. But the vein pulsing on his forehead and the small beads of sweat across his brow belied his stoic determination. This throwback would die in his saddle before giving up.

For the first time, Willow questioned her own assumption that Rope Thrower was merely a figment of Lonewolf's imagination. No one would risk his life for an imaginary person.

''Lonewolf, listen to me. You won't accomplish anything if you die first. You must take care of that wound.'' She paused, then added, ''The man I have in mind can answer all your questions.'' Not quite a lie. She smiled inside. Grandfather would agree he knew everything.

Lonewolf paused, his hand on the saddle horn.

In a last ditch-effort to convince him, Willow threw all pride aside. ''He will also have a place to lie down. I could use the rest.''

Lonewolf narrowed his eyes at Willow. She thought he was about to argue. Instead, he pulled his shirt out from his leggins and, in one swift move, tore the shirt over his head.

Only a hiss escaped his lips, though drops of blood splattered his chest and back from the wounds.

''What are you . . .'' Her question trailed off as he approached her, his shirt dangling from one hand.

''You need to keep your arm still. This will have to do.''

He wrapped the shirt under her arm and elbow, moving with such care Willow barely noticed her arm now bent snugly to her waist. As he fastened the shirt sleeves at her neck, Willow stared at a trickle of blood trailing from his chest wound over his nipple and down.

Lonewolf finished and stepped back. With an approving nod, he turned, picked up her backpack, and tied it to her horse. "What is this man's name?" he asked over his shoulder.

All Willow could try was the truth. "*Natsé na táá.*" She gave her grandfather's warrior name and silently prayed Grandfather would forgive her. To speak his secret name was to rob some of its power. But the name held honor and respect for all those who had inherited it. She hoped Lonewolf would respond to that.

The ploy worked. In one fluid movement he mounted her horse. He held his good right arm toward her and swung her up with such ease, Willow felt as weightless as a child. That playful image dissolved the instant he nestled her back against his hard chest. Their legs seemed as one, both wrapped around the horse's belly. He pulled her close with his left arm, leaving Willow to wonder how much more strength he would have if he weren't wounded. As it was, she felt trapped.

With a click of his tongue, Lonewolf caught the horse's attention. He turned the horse away from the canyon and started across the rocky bluff. "What is your horse's name?"

"Red Wing." At the sound of Willow calling his name, the chestnut horse raised his head.

"And where is the hogan of *Natsé na táá*?"

"At the rim, near Bear Trail."

Only the clip-clop of Red Wing's hooves on the bare rock filled the night. After a few moments, Lonewolf spoke again. "I am glad you lied."

"About what?" she answered cautiously.

He smiled against her hair. "Do you tell so many that you cannot explain one lie?"

Willow fell silent. As much as she hated lying, she couldn't deny she'd told him a few. Furthermore, she didn't know which one he was talking about. She decided the best course was to attack his logic. "Why would you be glad I lied?"

Lonewolf drew in his breath to keep from laughing, and was instantly sorry. Her musky scent filled his senses. He exhaled in a hiss. "Because I would not like to walk."

"Yes, well, I've had plenty of that myself, today."

Red Wing veered right and onto the path that led to Indian Road 7. Willow hadn't felt Lonewolf's muscles flex to guide the horse in that direction. But then Red Wing wouldn't need any coaxing to head for home and some fresh straw at Grandfather's corral.

Willow knew the feeling. But, for her, it was more a case of a relentless pull, much like a rubber band stretched taut—it always snapped back.

As they neared Grandfather's hogan, her stomach tightened in the familiar coil of anxiety. What would he find to lecture her about? One look at her and he'd know she'd had her share of problems today. Not that that would get her any sympathy. She could hear him say that adversity was no reason to lose focus. A ripped shirt, cut face, and a shoulder in a sling didn't exactly give evidence of staying in control.

She couldn't hide her appearance, but she didn't have to tell him what really bothered her—the visions. He'd be delighted if he knew. The old medicine man was sure she had it in her. He wouldn't understand visions made her feel *less* in control, not more.

He would take one look at her and purse his lips. He would tell her she had to get in touch with the world around her. She must tap into her natural power. And she would let him talk, though his words would feel like salt in her wounds. For she would never succumb to her weakness. Visions were for old men and children.

Red Wing's abrupt stop jerked Willow from her thoughts.

"Why did you stop?"

"I sensed your uneasiness. Is this place we go to safe?"

"Of course," Willow replied. The truth was, between Lonewolf's deep voice resonating through her back and Grandfather's hogan before her, she felt more like the captive than the captor.

"Then why are you tight here?"

His broad hand flattened across her stomach and pressed her against his hard chest. Awareness spread through Willow. She felt the length of each finger, the pulse in his wrist, the leather sash at his waist. His heat seeped through her. Willow braced herself against unwanted images. None came. Gradually, she let her muscles relax.

"Maybe I'm just hungry," she offered, then realized it was probably true. She hadn't eaten anything since the small snack she'd had while in the cave.

"You feel as if you have not eaten in months. You are too skinny. Here, have some of this."

Lonewolf pulled a peach from his bundle. Her first bite into the large, fuzzy fruit evoked the last memory of harvesting peaches with her father. By dusk, she, along with every other child, had been covered in sticky fuzz, smelling of peaches and sunshine. She had ridden alongside her father, his peach crop packed onto another horse, and fallen asleep in his arms as he sang to her. He had left soon after that, and died without ever holding her again.

A lump harder than a peach pit formed in her throat. She tossed the unfinished peach onto the path and brushed Lonewolf's arm. She realized she'd been leaning against him. Self-contempt rose within her.

She had no right to be comfortable in Lonewolf's arms, moving with the gentle sway of Red Wing. The man was dangerous. She could never relax. Not until she got her gun.

* * *

Lonewolf felt the woman stiffen. She raised a hand to wipe juice from her face and her fragrance, mixed with that of the peach, enveloped Lonewolf. The scent was both fresh and musky—like a cougar's coat in winter.

He smiled at the comparison. She might be quiet at the moment, but without much provocation she could bare claws and draw blood. A warrior like himself. Yet she had not fought when he had given the datil to her. She had lain beneath him and taken the dangerous potion from his mouth. For a moment, in her trusting look, he had thought he was gazing at Corn Flower. He had even felt his wife beneath him, her slender body moving with his.

But Corn Flower's eyes had been black, not green. And Corn Flower was dead. What powers did this woman have to bring on images so strong? He had already dismissed her as a spy. No spy would let an enemy give datil—too much of the poisonous root could kill.

Yet he knew she lied. She said she was raised in the canyon, but she dressed in clothes no woman would wear—clothes more suited to a man. And the bundle she had carried on her shoulders—now tied to the saddle—had no opening he could see.

He would not have to trust her for long—just until his wound was tended and his questions answered. Then he would seek Rope Thrower and either find a way to peace . . . or steal Rope Thrower. Maybe if he captured the hated soldier, the army would talk treaty.

A light flickered ahead through the head-high piñons. The trees blocked any view across the mesa, surrounding them with the scents of pine and earth. Lonewolf could also smell cedar smoke, then he heard dogs barking.

Nothing prepared him for the sight before him. A small Navajo man ran toward them, shouting and waving a metal pan in the air. A small white skirt tied over his breeches flapped in the air, as did his long white hair. Shirtless and barefoot, he charged toward them, a tangle of yapping dogs close behind.

"Get him!" the little man yelled.

A flash of red darted between Red Wing's legs. The horse snorted and stepped to the side as an hysterical rooster scrambled out from under the horse's hooves.

Before Lonewolf could speak, Willow slid from Red Wing, just missing the bird. "You want him dead or alive?"

"Alive, of course!"

The half-crazed rooster flew a few feet, then landed, then flew again into the dense piñons. Lonewolf watched as Willow crouched beneath the shaggy piñon canopy. The old man raised a hand and the dogs, nearly as one, stopped barking and turned back to the hogan. Suddenly, all was quiet and Lonewolf could hear Willow whispering to the hidden rooster.

"So you want to fly away, like your brother the eagle? Would you soar over the mesa, your wings lifted on the wind?"

Willow's soft voice rose to Lonewolf. He could picture the rooster, riveted by the gentle tone. Lonewolf couldn't take his eyes from Willow.

"But what of your wives? They would wither without your proud look. You must think of them."

Fascinated, Lonewolf watched the bird walk into Willow's outstretched arm.

"Thank you, my child." The old man took the rooster from Willow and, in the blink of an eye, snapped its neck.

"But I thought you wanted it alive!"

"Yes, I did. Thank you."

"But . . ."

"I had to have him alive to kill him." The old man chuckled and started down the path. "Now, I can invite you to dinner!"

"We didn't come for dinner, Grandfather," Willow

called ahead to the old man, now yards ahead, making his way agilely back to the hogan. Lonewolf slid from Red Wing and walked beside Willow.

Willow called out again, "He needs your attention."

The old man walked on, chuckling to himself.

"Grandfather! He's been shot!"

"Well, then, child. You cook dinner." With that, the old man handed Willow the limp bird and led Lonewolf into his hogan.

THREE

Lonewolf stepped inside the hogan door and froze.

Nothing was as it should be in this place. Instead of bare adobe walls, colorful objects crammed every available space—covering the walls, hanging from the roof beams, and spilling onto the floor. Mexican serapes vied for space with spirit masks. Portraits and black and white photographs peeked from behind Osage headdresses and Pawnee fringed shirts. A cabinet threatened collapse under the weight of books jammed haphazardly on the shelves. Not even in the house of his white family had Lonewolf been surrounded with so many *things*.

He stared at the rugs beneath his feet, layered so that no bare earth showed through, except for an area in the middle for the fire. None of the rugs held the subdued colors of the weavings by the *Diné*. Reds, pinks, blues, and oranges danced around the small, circular room.

The explosion of color assaulted his senses. What was a Navajo doing with all these things? How had he acquired this wealth when the *Diné* suffered such hardship? Were these people witches?

Unable to take his eyes off the crazy quilt of rugs on the floor, he bent to touch one.

"You like my rugs? Some are Zapotec. Some are machine-made. You know the ones at the gas stations? Anyway, none of these are Navajo. They're good to walk on, no?" Grandfather chuckled.

Dazed and suspicious, Lonewolf ventured into the room. He ducked Hopi kachina dolls and baskets which hung precariously from the roof beams, then took the chair offered by the old man. Across the table, Willow stubbornly grappled with the dead rooster's body. She used her left arm to hold the bird, while her right fingers pulled and yanked, twisted and tortured, until the hapless bird no longer resembled anything you would want to eat. Lonewolf grimaced. He had never seen such a mess made of the simple job of plucking feathers.

Just then, Willow looked up. Her eyes—so green, they defied comparison—dared him to speak.

"The bird is already dead. To kill it twice is not good manners," he said.

"You're right, of course. It's not this bird's fault I've had a lousy day. I'd give anything for a simple bowl of green chili stew." She made a face at the fist of feathers she held in one hand. "Besides, I think it's all I could manage."

Lonewolf looked at the mangled mass of feathers on the table. "I believe the rooster will forgive you."

She chuckled and the brief sound left Lonewolf wanting more. For the first time, he studied the woman who had so complicated his life.

Her face was smudged with dirt and laced with fine cuts. Her hair held twigs and bits of other debris. She had cleaned her hands somewhere outside before tackling the bird, but now they were covered with feathers and blood. Lonewolf stared, enthralled.

For all that, she looked like the Desert Willow of her name—her strong cheekbones were the flower's rosy pink, her glistening eyes were the leaf's misty green. All were framed by a cascade of ebony hair.

Now he recognized her musky scent—heavy and sweet like the fresh blossom.

Their eyes met. She did not look away, but neither did she smile. Her eyes held questions, demanded answers. She sat there, dirty, exhausted, wounded. And she held every fiber of his attention. He could not help but smile.

Willow lowered her eyes and the next look she shot him made him wish he could read minds. More was going on in her head than curiosity.

She rose from the table and he watched her move across the small room, the man's pants she wore not able to hide her slender body. By all that was sacred, this woman could lead him to distraction.

Then she lifted a hanging rug and disappeared behind it. A hidden room behind the rug? Only in the white man's houses were there several rooms. Who *were* these people?

Willow let the tapestry flutter closed behind her before she drew a long breath. Damn her fickle body! Her insides were in a knot. She didn't want to like him. So what was she doing laughing with him?

Actually, he'd never laughed. He'd barely even smiled. The hard lines bracketing his mouth had never eased, as if chiseled over years of relentless sorrow. His eyes, however, had lost any hint of sadness. They twinkled like young stars teasing the early night sky.

Willow tossed her head in disgust. The only thing *starry* about this guy was that he was keeping her in the darkness. That was about to end.

Through a simple window, moonlight played across a single bed and a wooden desk overcome with books and newspapers. Silvery fingers of light touched cans on the pantry shelves. The one of green chili stew was straight across from her. She ignored it and walked to the bed, crouched, and pulled a small trunk out from under it. Inside, she worked her hands through the layers of her clothes, school papers, and other keepsakes, until her fingers touched the cold steel of her gun. She checked the cartridge. Full and deadly.

Grandfather's singsong chatter and Lonewolf's deep voice drifted to her, their words unintelligible, caught in the dense weave of the heavy rug.

She didn't know if she could use the gun on

Lonewolf. That thought brought her hard up against her feelings. He stirred something deep and powerful within her. Confusing and unsettling. The heat of his healing passion still coursed through her. But she sensed a determination, a purpose stronger than his life. Something for which he would die. She didn't believe he was involved with the death of the young Navajo. Yet she had nothing on which to pin her belief, only her instincts—and the visions.

They disturbed her most of all.

Whatever this mysterious man's mission, her investigation of the murder took priority. She tucked the gun between her blouse and pants at her back and grabbed the can of stew.

Lonewolf knew, without looking, that Willow had reentered the main room. The air shifted, as if to make way for such a strong presence. She smiled, but the warmth never reached her eyes. They assessed him and Lonewolf wondered what this stealthy cougar planned.

The old man's hand lightly touched his shoulder. "Sit back now. Let me look at your wounds."

Lonewolf complied. Weariness and a welling confusion plagued him. He had the unsettling feeling there was something he should know. Something he should understand.

It was the bullet wound, he told himself, and these strange surroundings. Perhaps he had left the datil in his mouth too long—the poison could cause hallucinations.

Stinging pain told him that Grandfather held a rag of something against Lonewolf's shoulder. Lonewolf pressed his back into Grandfather's hand and felt the medicine absorb into his open wound. He closed his eyes to the alien room. The torment brought comfort. Soon he would be bandaged. Then with information from the old man, Lonewolf could find the traitor Rope Thrower. He would make him listen.

"What do they call you?" Grandfather asked.

"Lonewolf."

"Ah, a good name. An old name. I haven't heard it used for a long time. What is your mother's clan?"

"Lone Tree. I was born for the Bitter Water clan."

"Your people aren't from here, then?"

"No," Lonewolf lied. What did the old man want?

"Interesting. I know many from Bitter Water. But I have not met any from the Lone Tree clan. Interesting," he said again.

Lonewolf glanced at the small table beside him. A white metal basin held the cleaning rag. A glass bottle with clear liquid stood alongside. The alcohol, he surmised. Then he noticed a small tube. Crinkled and folded at one end.

"What is this?" he asked, as he picked up the tube and squeezed it. The soft container molded to his fist. He squeezed harder and white cream snaked from one end and oozed between his fingers.

"That *was* medicated salve. Don't smear it! That was all I had. Just hold still a moment."

Lonewolf heard a tearing noise. The next moment the old man handed him a square white cloth. Yet it was not a cloth. He stared at the thin material.

"You're surprised to see paper towels here? I have my weaknesses." He shrugged. "Besides, they are so convenient. I buy only the white ones."

"You buy rags?"

"You see anyone here who would make rags for me? My granddaughter, the policeman, she's too busy arresting our people. Making them criminals. Is that how you were shot? Did she make you a criminal?"

Lonewolf felt Willow's gaze on him. He looked up and caught her eyes on him. She quickly diverted her attention to the can she was opening.

"Grandfather, you're chattering away while he bleeds!"

"Let me see if I can salvage any of the medicine."

Lonewolf shifted in his chair and untied his medicine bundle. "You have no spider flower?"

"Not for many years. Mostly, it grows in Kansas and Texas, not Arizona. Too far for me to travel. The last I saw came from a Kiowa from Amarillo. He was going to a peyote ceremony. I traded him some feathers and rattles for the spider flower."

Lonewolf reeled from all the words. He knew of Kansas and Texas. Places that had joined the mighty nation of the white man. What were these places arizona and amarillo? He set the bundle on the floor before him and pulled out his herb bag. He sat up and blackness encroached on his sight.

Rugs he did not recognize, words he didn't understand. Nothing the same.

I do not belong here. The words echoed in his head.

He focused on Willow crouched in the corner, pouring the contents of the can into a metal pot. Now and then she glanced his way, not really looking at him, though. She set the pot on a small green box made of metal and moved knobs at the front. Suddenly flames licked the sides of the pot. He jumped from his chair. The whole room went black. He grabbed for the table, but caught only the corner. The table tipped and he fell to the floor.

"Ha'ish'aa!" Grandfather yelled.

Lonewolf felt spindly, but strong arms pulled him from the ground. He dared not open his eyes. What would assail him next? He had to get his information and go. This place could be the death of him!

Settled in the chair, he waved off the helping arms.

" *'Ahéhee'!* Leave me be. I am fine. Just too hot."

"Granddaughter, get him some water. Granddaughter!"

Lonewolf slowly opened his eyes, half sure that, though the voices of the old man and Willow were the same, they would now appear in their real forms. Coyotes? Or perhaps wolves?

He relished the sight of their human bodies. Grandfather pushed a glass of water into his hand. Lonewolf barely registered how cold the water was, for he realized Willow was staring at the spilled contents of his medicine bundle. There, for all to see, was his sacred necklace, the Ha'tanii. The horned shaman, cut from shell, intricately inlaid with turquoise, malachite, and serpentine, hung from a delicate braided-hair necklace—a gift from the ancient star way ancestors. Its power illuminated the room. No one could look on it without knowing the celestial beings held the answers. No one *should* look on it but the one ordained to wear it.

Lonewolf snatched up the bundle, then threw the spider flower liniment on the table.

"You may use this. Please be fast. I have no more time for idle chatter. You will tell me now what I need to know. Where is Rope Thrower?"

The old man fell silent. He froze, his hand in midair, about to pick up the herbal pouch. Lonewolf grew increasingly irritated. Already, too much precious time had been lost! He moved to rise, fighting back the dizziness that threatened to overtake him. Then, a slender hand with quiet strength pressed down on his shoulders.

"Grandfather, hand me the pouch."

Crushed herbs and cool fingers soothed his shoulder, yet stoked his anger. Willow's methodical movements tore at his temper. Still no one answered his question. Impatience ripped through him, followed by a tremor.

Willow's hand stilled. Inexplicably, Lonewolf felt his blood rise to her fingers, as if called to her. All his anger welled to her touch, like poison sucked from a wound. A whirling haze filled him. From its shadowy depths, a shivering image walked to him. A young boy held out his hand, in his palm a broken turquoise necklace.

Suddenly the image disappeared. Willow's hand had flown from his flesh, as if burned.

Lonewolf pushed away from the table and stood.

Though he towered over Willow, she did not flinch. Her eyes, however, could not mask her alarm. Widened and dilated, they stared back at Lonewolf.

Grandfather broke the silence. "How were you shot?"

"A man."

"A man? That's all you know?"

"These are dangerous times."

"Have you made someone angry?"

Lonewolf laughed. "*Natsé na táá*. I am your guest. But, right now, you make me angry. You answer my question with more questions. It does not matter how I was shot. A man was sent for me. By Black Horse, by Rope Thrower. It makes no difference. He failed, is all that matters. But I must not. I *must* find Rope Thrower! Did your granddaughter lie? She said you knew everything."

Lonewolf did not miss the look between the old man and Willow. He just did not care what it meant.

"Aie! Enough! You waste my time!"

"Do you mean Kit Carson?" The grandfather's voice, quiet and solemn, stopped Lonewolf.

"Yes! And none other. What can you tell me of him?"

"Please forgive my hesitation, Lonewolf. I'm old, and I haven't heard that traitor's Navajo name in many, many years. What do you wish to know?"

"By all that is sacred, I am tired of your riddles! If you know where he is, tell me now!"

"He is dead."

"You lie! That cannot be!" The image of a darkened *Dinehtah* filled Lonewolf's mind. What if one of the People had killed the traitor? The image would be reality. No one could stop General Carlton. He was more insane than Carson. Lonewolf fought down the panic. "Who killed him?"

"I don't know." Grandfather paused. "I think he just died."

Lonewolf sank down to the chair and buried his face in his hands. *No! It cannot be!* Again, scorched canyons and smoking hogans filled his mind's eye. Was all lost before he even had a chance to try? He felt his energy flow out of him, each throb of pain at his shoulder another heartbeat of his lifeblood, draining away. With Rope Thrower, he had had a chance. The old scout had once been a friend to the Navajo. General Carlton wanted nothing more than a land rid of all the People.

What could Lonewolf do—one man against an entire army?

"Why do you care how the soldier died? Lonewolf! Do you grieve for the murderer?"

"Be careful, old man, what you say."

"Explain yourself, Lonewolf. Why does your spirit sink? What did Kit Carson mean to you?"

The old man's quiet tone did not escape Lonewolf. He heard the suspicion, the accusation. The old man could think what he liked. Lonewolf was past caring what anyone thought about him. "It does not matter now."

"Now! Why should now be any different from five minutes ago?"

"I said it does not matter. If you are done with my shoulder, I will go." But it did matter. Even now he was thinking about how he could get to Carlton and beg for more time. Carlton's rage with the People would be fierce. If Rope Thrower had been killed by a *Diné,* Carlton's army was probably already on the way—with orders to kill all the People. Lonewolf had to stop the massacre.

A haunting feeling swirled through Lonewolf, whispering, *You cannot change what is to be*. The air felt stifling and clammy, a roar thundered through his head. Like in the cave! What had happened to him there?

He fought past the crashing noise in his head with all his strength. He could not lose control. He rose slowly from the chair, bracing himself against the consuming blackness. He had to escape this place.

The old man took a step back from him. Willow stood her ground and stared in silence. Not like her to be so quiet, Lonewolf thought. But then she would realize that he knew of their scheme to keep him away from Rope Thrower. They would say anything. Do anything.

He stared back at her. Questions filled her eyes. Then they hardened with purpose. She would try to stop him. How could someone so beautiful be so evil?

"Your plan will not work," he said. "Whoever you are, *whatever* you are, you cannot stop me."

"What I am, Lonewolf, is an officer of the law. You *will* stop for me!" She raised her arm and pointed a gun to his chest.

"Granddaughter! This man is wounded and confused. Is there a law against that, too?"

"He certainly is confused if he thinks he will walk away without answering any questions. Have a seat, Lonewolf."

"No." His actions belied his words, for he moved to sit in the chair. In the next instant, he rolled from the chair, kicked out his foot, and caught her legs, throwing her to the ground. With lightning speed, he got on his feet. He stopped her fall and grabbed the gun from her hand.

"Now, *shi-siláoo yázhi,* you have your job, but I have mine."

Willow twisted against his grip. "I'm not *your* little soldier!"

Lonewolf tightened his hold on her wrists. "You should be. You have the courage and fire of many warriors."

"Navajo warriors are a relic of the past. Where it seems you've been living!"

She emphasized the last with a swift jab of her elbow to his side. Lonewolf grunted but held tight.

"Do not dare my powers! *This* warrior will not be stopped!" A strange feeling swept through Lonewolf, swirling and spiraling. It called to him. *You cannot stop what is to be.* "Your words are in vain, witch! I swear to the Holy Ones, the killing will end. You cannot stop me!"

He flung Willow to her grandfather, nearly throwing the old man off balance. But the haunting feeling continued. He knew, with deadly certainty, he had to get out of the hogan, or risk losing his sanity to the swelling maelstrom of images in his head.

Yet, now, everything in the small round room seemed determined to trap him. The baskets above his head swung, knocking into the kachinas—eagle dancers, shalakos, and ogres swirled, as if alive with mystic energy. A roar of sound filled his head. Lonewolf ducked and dodged until he reached the door, where a spirit mask faced him, its fierce expression leering. Did its mouth move? Voices sung to him, like those of the rocks and trees. The celestial spirits had not abandoned him. Yet they were muffled, stifled.

He hurled the mask aside, turned back to the door and gasped. A photograph hung before him. He staggered back from the picture. There, on the door, hung the image of his beloved *Dinehtah,* laid to waste. Ghostly cliffs rose above a charred, empty canyon. The same as in his vision.

The singing rose, filling his head, surely filling the whole room. A multitude of voices, sweet and sad, as if bidding him goodbye. The precious sound was agony.

"When did Rope Thrower die?" Lonewolf spoke, yet he did not recognize his voice. It sounded far away, low to the ground, defeated.

"In eighteen sixty-eight. The same year our People

came home from *Hwééldi*. They were freed, he died. The Holy Ones were happy."

Lonewolf dropped to his knees. He understood. Moments from the last day played again. The strange yellow cloth in the cave, the peach orchard—gone; the war council—disappeared; the death of Rope Thrower, this enchanted hogan. Most of all, the woman, Willow. Her strange dress and manner. Lonewolf could not ignore the truth any longer. His throat constricted with the certain knowledge he would never see his people again.

He pressed a hand to his chest, to the mark he would forever wear as ordained by the star way ancestors. The mark that now banished him to another time. Out of reach of his people and the only way to help them.

Too late, Lonewolf sensed movement behind him. Bright pain exploded in his head at the impact of something large and heavy. His last thought was, "*Ha'tanii,* do not abandon me here!"

FOUR

The skillet dropped from Willow's hands and hit the dirt floor with a thud. The old man looked at his granddaughter and his heart lurched at the myriad of emotions he saw drawn on her face. Concern creased her brow as she beheld the half-naked man slumped on the floor before them. She looked ready to help him, yet the thin line of her lips bespoke her restraint. Even unconscious, he commanded her interest.

Good. Perhaps this one holds promise. At least he will not bore her. Grandfather smiled to himself as he picked up the skillet.

"You have good aim, Granddaughter. Maybe you should trade your gun for the skillet. You could stick the handle in your holster." He demonstrated by letting his arm hang straight down, then he cocked his elbow and brought the black pan up swiftly.

"Great idea, Grandfather," she replied dryly. "And handy. After I bashed a criminal's head, the next morning I could cook eggs for breakfast."

"With a gun, all you can do is kill." He knelt next to Lonewolf and took the gun from his hand. Then he feathered his fingers through Lonewolf's hair, delicately feeling for the rising lump on the back of his head.

"Don't touch him!"

"Why not?" Grandfather looked up for her answer, but Willow just stared past him at Lonewolf. For a moment, he saw his son reflected in her face. The way he'd looked after a night's vision quest—his sleepless eyes red and weary, yet brimming with the stars' messages.

Though starving and exhausted, he would not rest until he'd delivered the answers to the patient. Visions did not let him rest.

Willow's eyes held the same look of obsessed enchantment. Grandfather felt his heart skip with realization. Willow had visions.

He had known she would. Try as she might, she couldn't escape inheriting the power carried to her through her father.

A skimmering thread of excitement traipsed down his spine even as he saw the look of pure dread on her face. Whatever the vision, she hadn't liked it. Well, that was the way with the power. It didn't choose to reveal only pleasant, comforting visions.

And for all the years she had denied the power, this vision must have been particularly strong to make her see. Already he could see logic masking her eyes, forcing the vision to recede.

Abruptly, she turned away, removed the pot of bubbling soup from the small stove and cut off the burner. He smiled inwardly at his willful granddaughter.

"If I can't touch him, how do I move him?"

"Just leave him there."

The cold force of her words milked away some of his satisfaction at her predicament. He could almost feel sorry for her. Almost. Poor thing, she was truly beside herself.

"Granddaughter, he has been shot in the shoulder and hit on the head with a heavy skillet. Did you have more punishment in mind?"

She stared at him and he caught the dying flicker of remaining magic in her gaze. Without a word, she left the room and returned with a length of rope which she dropped alongside him.

"Tie him before you move him. I don't want any more surprises."

"You're the policewoman. If he is your prisoner, you should tie him up."

He stood and made a bowl of soup for himself. Willow didn't move. Grandfather watched with interest as she sat unmoving and stared at the Navajo sprawled at her feet.

"What did he do?" he asked, finally.

Willow nearly laughed aloud. Should she tell Grandfather Lonewolf had kidnapped her, or that he'd saved her life, or about the haunting visions that possessed her at his touch?A manic impulse bubbled within her to blurt out all three.

She rubbed her temples to relieve the tension and caught a glimpse of him watching her with worried eyes, patiently waiting for an answer.

"I'm taking him in for questioning."

"He is a suspicious person, then?"

"I just have some questions." She masked herself in authority and let him regard her. The ploy didn't work.

"And so you get his attention with a skillet? I think he will have questions for you, too."

"I couldn't let him go, Grandfather. Just leave it at that."

"Then tell me this, Granddaughter. If he is so bad, why is he without a shirt, while you have one wrapped around your arm?"

She turned her back on Grandfather to close the issue, which left her staring at Lonewolf. She was immediately sorry.

He lay on his side, one arm stretched above his head. Powerful muscles bunched at his shoulder. The muted light from the kerosene lamps cast him in partial shadow and accentuated the strong muscles of his back. He had the body of a warrior. And the scars to match.

Old wounds latticed his brown skin; the white lines and blotches were eternal reminders of forgotten battles. The width and length of some of the scars made Willow wince at the thought of the original wound. How had he accumulated so many?

The gunshot looked almost appropriate, as befitting a man who bore so many wounds. In time it would be just another part of his back.

Right now, though, his body fought the newest injury. The skin surrounding the wound was purple fading to red. A small amount of blood oozed from the hole. She told herself it served him right. He's the one who'd crashed around the hogan. Her own shoulder throbbed from when he'd pushed her into Grandfather.

But she couldn't let him lie there.

"Can you help me move him to the bed?" Grandfather's quiet voice didn't surprise her. She'd known he was watching her. "And then you will let me see *your* shoulder."

Willow looked up at Grandfather and found him smiling at her. He rose and came around the table.

For a second, she considered grabbing some gloves. But then she'd have Grandfather's questions to answer. She decided she would rather face touching Lonewolf.

"What are you waiting for, child?"

Him to vanish like a bad dream, she wanted to say. Instead, she grabbed her gun from the table and tucked it at her back.

"Good idea, Granddaughter. He might try to crawl away."

"Let's just get this over with."

They each took one of Lonewolf's arms and pulled him from the floor. The man was a ton of rock-solid muscle—all of it dead weight. Willow tried to avoid touching Lonewolf with her fingers. She used the back of her hands, her forearms, even her damaged shoulder. But when Grandfather stumbled over one of the rugs, Willow instinctively grabbed Lonewolf around his waist. The only unsolicited response was a groan deep in Lonewolf's belly.

Still wary, but feeling less threatened, Willow kept her hand at his waist. She suddenly wondered about the woman she'd seen in the vision. Had Willow witnessed a real moment between two lovers? Was she, at this moment, thinking of Lonewolf? Worried about him?

Willow frowned at her irrational concern. None of it mattered. None of it interested her.

They reached the bed and lowered Lonewolf to the mattress. His broad shoulders pinned Willow's arm. She knelt beside the bed and eased her arm out.

"Tell me this, child," Grandfather said. "You don't suspect him of murdering that Navajo, do you?"

Willow's gaze flew to Grandfather. "You knew of the murder and didn't tell me?"

"What was there to tell?"

Just then she realized how mad she was at Grandfather. Why hadn't he called her about the murder in the cave? Why hadn't he sensed she'd been in trouble? "That's never stopped you before."

In answer, Grandfather just smiled. Willow looked back at Lonewolf. "I don't know what to suspect him of, Grandfather," she said. Without thinking, Willow ran her hand over Lonewolf's head, until she found the lump she'd caused.

Willow let her hand rest on the knot at Lonewolf's head. She felt the rhythmic pulse of life in the lump. Her fingertips tingled, as if blood rushed to her hand. Her pulse beat in time with Lonewolf's. He wasn't the murderer. She knew it in her core. But how could she explain that to the station? She couldn't.

"It's not for me to decide what he's done. He needs to be questioned at the station."

As she uttered the words, a flood of sensations overwhelmed her. Her body grew heavy, she couldn't lift her hand from Lonewolf's head. Her head swirled and the room darkened. She felt balanced on a precipice, the edge of a void.

Excruciating sadness floated through the blackness and enveloped her. A deep voice resonated through her. *Do not abandon me.* Fear of betrayal laced the words.

With great effort Willow pulled her hand away from Lonewolf's head. Had he spoken to her? One look at his unconscious form dispelled that notion. She shook her head, trying to throw off the lingering hopelessness from the vision. A dull ache pulsed at the back of her head.

"I've got to let the station know where I am," Willow said with effort as she pushed herself up from the bed. "Is there a phone at Many Goats' trailer?"

"Yes. Curtis, the boy, is probably still up." He put his arm around her and led her back to the main room and to a chair. "Now you will let me see *your* shoulder."

"Grandfather, that can wait." She tried to shrug him off, but his leathery fingers held strong on her.

"It's not polite to argue with the medicine man," he said sternly.

"Since when have you been big on manners?" she replied, but couldn't help smiling.

Grandfather's humming effectively eliminated any more conversation. He untied the shirtsleeves knotted at Willow's neck and let the shirt fall to her lap.

Willow fingered the soft chamois. She stuck her first finger through the ugly hole at the back and out through the hole at the front of the shirt.

"Lucky it was a clean exit," he said.

"Yes," she said, absently.

"Interesting that Lonewolf chose to stop the man with an arrow instead of a gun."

"My gun," Willow said.

"Yes, and why not use it? Certainly would be faster to shoot a gun. Odd, don't you think?"

"Who knows?" Willow heard the annoyance in her

voice. Why wasn't Grandfather concerned Lonewolf had her gun?

"And you say that, with one shot, in the dark, Lonewolf stopped the man shooting at you."

Willow relived the moment at the cliff. It all came back in a flood. Her chest was tight with terror. Her shoulder screamed with pain. She saw Lonewolf towering above her, the arrow poised to fly, his face fierce with concentration. The warrior had risen to the attack.

It hadn't seemed odd at all.

The moment had been like a slice of life from another time. Everything about Lonewolf seemed out of place; the clothes he wore, the way he talked, his whole manner. Hell, her first impression of him in the cave was of a warrior.

And there were the visions. They had no place or time. The throb in her head pounded with more force.

"Grandfather," Willow said quietly. "What do you learn from your visions?"

Grandfather's hand stilled at her shoulder. "That depends, my child, on what you are seeking."

"You've never had visions just come to you?"

The old man pulled a chair up to Willow and sat down facing her. "All visions 'just come.' Whether you have fasted in a sacred place and prayed for guidance, or whether you are picking tomatoes in the field. They just come." His eyes glistened and his lips formed a soft smile. She couldn't tell if he was looking at her, or past her.

"But if one comes unexpectedly, you weren't seeking anything. So, why the vision?"

"Ah, child, you think if you do not ask for a vision, it should not come?"

"It would be a lot less troublesome," she said, then added quickly, "At least, it would seem that way to me."

Grandfather's chuckle filled the small room. "Yes,

well, like real life, visions are unpredictable."

"But you said you learned from them, depending upon what you were seeking. But if you didn't ask for the vision, how can you know what you were seeking?" Willow heard the frustration in her voice. She tried to temper it by adding, "I mean, isn't it confusing for you?"

"Not at all. The question and the answer lie within the vision."

Willow had the almost overwhelming urge to yell at her grandfather to speak straight. But then, she hadn't been exactly forthright, either. She kneaded her neck and massaged her temples. The throbbing had swelled to a full-blown headache.

She'd wanted to know about the visions, what they meant. She couldn't bring herself to say any of that. So she fell silent. Much to her surprise, Grandfather didn't pursue the subject. He gave her a smile, then fetched some clean cloth to sling her arm. One more question itched to be asked. Why hadn't Grandfather known she was in trouble today? As the unofficial guardian of the canyon, he would've sensed the trouble. Murder certainly rated. So would kidnapping his granddaughter, she would think.

She was about to ask, when Grandfather spoke.

"Could the bullet have been meant for you?"

"If it had, wouldn't you have sensed something terribly wrong about the canyon?"

Grandfather said nothing. Willow immediately felt a pang of guilt. It wasn't fair to throw that in his face. Maybe the old man was slipping.

And who was she to question his visionary powers? She'd never given visions much credence. Not until today.

Grandfather stood before her and raised her chin so their eyes met.

"I'm sorry," she said. "I didn't mean it to come out that way."

"Of course I sensed there was trouble." His glistening eyes held her gaze. "But the visions told me you were in good hands."

"What do you mean? Do you mean Lonewolf?"

Grandfather ignored her and finished tying the cloth at her neck.

"But he caused a lot of the problem!"

"Then I guess you better call the station and tell them about him, too."

Grandfather busied himself cleaning off the table. He was right, Willow thought. She needed to make that call. But for some reason, it seemed much less urgent. She forced herself to stand and walk to the door.

"I guess I'll go to Many Goats' and use their phone."

"That's fine, child. You do what you have to do."

"So, I'll be back soon," she added.

"I'll be here."

Willow walked into the chilly night. It occurred to her she hadn't taken a last look at Lonewolf to be certain he was still unconscious. The lapse in security didn't seem to bother her. Perhaps she hoped he wouldn't be there when she returned. She really didn't know what she hoped for.

All she knew was that she had to call the station. She had to report the gunman. But what would she say about Lonewolf? If she said she'd found him in the cave, she'd have to bring him in for questioning. Why did that notion now bother her?

In the ten minutes it took to reach Many Goats' trailer, Willow still hadn't found an answer. She'd walked the horse to give her time to think. But the incessant pounding of the headache drove off any thinking.

The dogs started barking before she was even in sight. Willow dismounted fifty feet from the trailer and stood patiently. If Curtis watched from the window, he could see she brought no witches with her to sneak through the open door. They might live in a trailer, but Many Goats' family believed in the old ways.

She stood quietly for five minutes before the trailer door opened. A skinny young man in shorts and a T-shirt stood passively on the top step. Though they were neighbors for all her childhood years, Willow never had become close to Curtis. As a boy, he'd been sullen with a harsh laugh. The gaunt man before her didn't seem to have gained any humor.

She approached the trailer slowly.

"Hello, Curtis. It's Willow Becenti. I'm sorry to bother you so late, but could I use your phone?"

In answer, Curtis merely stepped back into the trailer and left the door open.

Willow climbed the metal stairs. Only the glow from the small television kept the inside of the trailer lighter than the night. Willow could just make out Curtis slouched in a corner chair facing the set.

"I really appreciate this, Curtis. I have to make two calls, but I'll try to be quick."

He didn't respond. Willow stepped quietly to the phone and dialed the station in Window Rock.

"Tribal Police."

"Sergeant Lopez, this is Officer Becenti."

"It's about time you called in, Becenti. Where the hell are you?"

"I'm at de Chelly. At my grandfather's."

"You were due back this afternoon. What happened?"

"Sergeant, I was at the cave—" Blinding pain stopped her words. She couldn't think. She couldn't speak. Her head threatened to explode.

"Officer Becenti, are you there?"

"I—yes—hold on."

Do not betray me. As if riding on the pain, the words pierced her mind. In that moment, Willow knew she wouldn't tell the sergeant about Lonewolf. She wasn't surprised when the excruciating pain in her head immediately subsided.

"Officer Becenti!"

"Yes, I'm here. I had to check my notes." Willow cleared her voice and stole a glance at Curtis—his silhouette lined in blue television light. "I spent the better part of today in the canyon. I checked several caves for possible clues. I'll deliver my report on that tomorrow." Willow silently promised herself she'd get answers from Lonewolf.

"Is that it?"

"Not entirely. As I left the canyon, I was pursued by someone. The person, a man, shot at me. A Navajo on the cliff pulled me to safety. He shot the assailant with an arrow—"

"An arrow?"

"Yes, Sergeant. The assailant fell down the cliff. He's at the bottom of White House trail."

"Do you have an ID on him?"

"Who?"

"The assailant, Officer."

"No, Sergeant. It was dark. I didn't get a good look at his face."

"Sergeant Carejo will meet you there tomorrow morning at eight-thirty."

"Yes, sir."

"Becenti."

Here it comes. Willow took a deep breath.

"Yes, sir?"

"Are you all right?"

"Why . . . why do you ask?"

"You sound strange. Were you injured?"

"Just a pulled shoulder, Sergeant. My grandfather has dressed it. I'll be fine. Thanks, Sergeant."

Willow hung up and let out her breath. She glanced

at Curtis. He looked at her over the rim of a tilted beer can.

"I just have one more call to make, Curtis. I really appreciate this."

Curtis averted his gaze back to the television.

Willow punched in the numbers for the hospital. She pictured Manuelito sleeping soundly, his hand curled under his chin, a comforting night-light softly glowing.

But with every staccato ring of the unanswered nurse's phone, the warm scene receded to the reality of a distant, cold hospital room. He was so small and helpless and she was stuck here.

"Answer the phone, dammit!"

She checked her watch. It was midnight in Fort Defiance. Which meant two nurses held watch on the critical-care floor. Where were they? Gossiping? Reading magazines? Or were they both at Manuelito's side fighting for his life while she stood at a phone forty miles away?

Three minutes passed and still no answer.

"Where are you?" Willow yelled into the mouthpiece.

"Critical Care Unit, may I help you?" The young, pleasant voice registered in time for Willow to rein in her temper.

"This is Officer Becenti and I'm calling about Manuelito Begay. Can you tell me how he is and how the tests went today?"

"Just a minute, please, while I check his chart."

Willow waited impatiently, one hand gripping the receiver, the other briskly rubbing her arm. She was suddenly cold, chilled to the bone.

"Officer Becenti, what is your relationship with the patient?"

"I'm his guardian," Willow said.

"I see. Does he have any immediate family?"

"Yes, but they're not available. Is something wrong?"

The nurse paused. Willow felt her chest tighten.

"I'm sorry, Officer. Manuelito has slipped into a coma. I'm sorry," she said again.

Rage swept through her so quick and fast her eyes burned. She wanted to hit something or somebody.

"How can he be in a coma? How could that happen?"

"I'm sorry, I wasn't on duty."

"What does the chart say? Did the seizures worsen?"

"The night nurse noted a series of prolonged convulsions."

Willow wished she could reach through the phone, grab the chart and read it for herself. She forced her breath out and tried to talk evenly.

"Did the specialist come today? Could his tests have brought more seizures on?"

"Yes, Dr. Voorman was here. I can't answer your question, though. You'll have to ask him."

"Do you have the results?"

"No, Dr. Voorman said the lab work will take a few days. Would you like him to call you?"

"Yes . . . no. I can't be reached right now. I'll call you again in the morning. Wait. Before you hang up, can you tell me when he became unconscious?"

"The chart says at six-thirty this morning."

"Thank you." Willow replaced the receiver in its cradle and rested her head against the refrigerator door.

At dawn. Manuelito had slipped from this world at dawn while she'd been poking around a murder site and unearthed a very live Navajo. At the thought of Lonewolf, resentment filled her. It was all his fault she wasn't with Manuelito.

The pull to get to Manuelito's side consumed her. She could jump on Red Wing, ride like the wind, and be there by early morning. Not that Red Wing could run nonstop for forty miles, even if she could ride off and leave Lonewolf at Grandfather's hogan. Which she couldn't.

After a moment, she straightened from the refrigerator and squared her shoulders. She pulled her wallet from her back pocket and left a ten-dollar bill on the kitchen table.

"Thank you, Curtis." She forced a smile on her face. Not that it mattered. Curtis didn't look up from the television.

"I've left money on the table to pay for the calls. I'll just let myself out. Tell your mother hello for me."

With a need to be somewhere—anywhere—fast, Willow coaxed Red Wing's speed back over the rocky path to Grandfather's. Stars spread across the blackness, a glittering jacket on Father Sky. The sparkling sequins stretched to all horizons, embracing the earth. Enveloped, guided, horse and rider moved as one through the night, as if carried by the stars.

Willow sensed the hogan before she saw it. Millions of twinkling lights danced above her, welcoming her home, and Willow had the feeling she could not have gone anywhere else. They wouldn't have allowed it.

The brisk ride had also calmed her temper. She couldn't do anything about Manuelito tonight. She would be with him tomorrow. Right now she had to get Lonewolf to talk, explain his actions today. And she had to do it without touching him or looking him in the eyes.

If she let him hold her gaze, she'd believe anything he said. And if he touched her, she'd question everything she believed about the known universe. She didn't believe in magic, or powers. She believed in the here and now, facing it, dealing with it, and moving on. And right now *she* was the reality Lonewolf had to deal with and he'd better adjust to that, because she wasn't wasting any more time with foolishness about Rope Thrower or Black Horse.

FIVE

“You think I would choose to be here? I tell you, there was no warning.” Lonewolf stared at the blackness beyond the cliff where he and Grandfather sat. The canyon hid in darkness, as did any explanation of why he was here. The only light was the intermittent red glint from Grandfather’s cigarette.

“Will you be missed?”

“A man followed me from the council. He will find only an empty cave.”

“That doesn’t answer my question, Lonewolf.”

“I argued with the council before I went to the cave. They sent me away.” Lonewolf thought of the irony. “Missed? No, I will not be missed. They will think I have gone to Rope Thrower. And when I do not return, they will be glad not to see the ‘traitor’ again.”

Grandfather chuckled.

“You find this funny, *Naat’áanii*?” Lonewolf looked in amazement at the old man.

Grandfather tried, unsuccessfully, to sober his smile. “It was not enough you were banished from the council and then traveled through time one hundred and thirty years? You decided to also anger my granddaughter?”

A wry smile escaped from Lonewolf. He touched his head, remembering Willow’s determination. “That was not my plan. The stars took me to her.”

“You are a stargazer?” Grandfather broke into laughter, then quickly clapped a hand to Lonewolf’s arm. “Forgive me, Lonewolf. I’m not laughing at you. But the stars must be very angry with you to send you to

Willow. She hates anything to do with stargazers."

The words fell on Lonewolf like flakes of snow on a summer's day—stunning him and leaving him unreasonably chilled. "And you? What is your opinion?" he finally asked Grandfather.

Grandfather became solemn. "My son, Willow's father, was a stargazer. He died in Vietnam. A war," he added, obviously seeing Lonewolf's confusion.

"So, he died a warrior," Lonewolf said.

"Oh, my boy, this was not an honorable war." Grandfather pulled on the cigarette and the red glow at the end illuminated his thoughtful face. "My son divined the cause of many illnesses. He is still missed."

"If Willow's father was a stargazer, why is she so against stargazing?"

"Willow was just a child. She blamed the stars for taking her father away. And then—" Grandfather broke off his sentence with a shrug of his head. Lonewolf knew there was more to the story, but Grandfather did not seem willing to talk about it.

Lonewolf followed the old man's gaze to the sea of black beyond their feet on the white sandstone. He could not see the canyon, but he could sense it, as he could any presence. He let his senses embrace the canyon—his *Dinehtah,* the one thing familiar in this unfamiliar time.

Except that it was not the same. The red walls and white sand floor might be the same, but it was a living testimony to the life of the People. It carried in its womb their joy and suffering. And it was no more at peace now than it had been in his time.

But what could be the problem? For what reason was he sent? His only clue was the woman. He was certain it was no coincidence the stars had sent him to her. Add to that the visions they had shared . . . or had she?

Lonewolf replayed both images in his mind—both when he had given her the datil and then again when she had been applying medicine to his shoulder. He saw her face at the moment the vision had ended—startled, confused, even fearful. Yes, she had shared the visions. But would she admit it?

Locked within the visions was his purpose and Willow held the key. He would make her admit them. Only then could he do whatever he was sent for and return to his time.

Whispers, more quiet than the shush of a velvet skirt, made Willow stop. She didn't hear voices, but more like the *promise* of voices carried on the wind.

Willow let her feet lead the way away from the hogan and straight for the seemingly impenetrable juniper grove—an improbable direction to anyone who didn't know the path through the thicket. She emerged on a bare ledge—a huge sandstone boulder which led to another and another and another. The gentle curves flowed straight to the edge of the cliff overlooking the canyons. There, on the edge, silhouetted by the dancing stars, sat Lonewolf and Grandfather.

Grandfather was fine. Willow could tell from his soft chatter that he was at ease. She stood in the shadows and watched the two of them. She didn't know why, but it filled her with peace just to look.

Their intimate voices drew her closer. All her senses reached toward the two men. They talked in low, steady tones, engrossed like friends in an old conversation, or rather, an old argument. While Grandfather's singsong voice rose and fell, Lonewolf's voice held an edge.

"Why would you want to go back?" Grandfather asked, his voice incredulous. "At least here, the People are not at war, under attack from all sides. That time is past."

"For you. But for me, it was just this morning. My people are suffering, but they will not surrender. For you, this is all history. But it is happening right now.

As I sit here, *Naat'áanii.* It happens right now.'' Lonewolf punctuated each word. *Somehow, I will get back,* Lonewolf vowed to himself.

''Perhaps here is where you belong,'' Grandfather said. ''After all, the horned shaman brought you here.''

''And he will take me back.''

''I saw the horned shaman,'' Willow said. Lonewolf and Grandfather both looked up with surprise. Willow noticed that Lonewolf quickly masked his expression. Grandfather, on the other hand, looked delighted.

''Why didn't you tell me, Granddaughter? I just saw it myself. Isn't it wonderful?''

''It's just a drawing. Why the sudden interest?''

''That's all you have to say about it?''

''He had no eyes.'' Willow paused. ''Which makes sense. That way, he doesn't have to see the trouble he causes.''

''No eyes, you say. I didn't notice. Lonewolf, could you—''

Lonewolf interrupted Grandfather. ''Where did you see this drawing, Willow?''

''In the cave, this afternoon. And why are you so impressed with a sightless shaman?''

''In the cave? But we are talking about—''

''*Naat'áanii,* may I be alone with your granddaughter?'' Lonewolf spoke quietly.

''Yes, I can see the two of you have much to talk about.'' Grandfather chuckled. ''An exciting day for you, Willow, no?'' He chuckled again as he made his way across the moonlit rock and disappeared into the juniper grove.

Willow sat on the sandstone, a few feet from Lonewolf, and looked at him. He wore one of Grandfather's flannel shirts. Though short, Grandfather was stocky, so his large shirt fit Lonewolf. Yet it didn't look right. Like paint on a hardwood floor, the shirt didn't belong on

Lonewolf. Natural, unfettered—that's what suited him, she decided.

He sat at a slant, his arms braced on the rock behind him, his head tilted back toward the sky. As if impervious to the chilly night air, Lonewolf had rolled the cuffs up on the sleeves. Sinewy tendons stretched taut on his forearms. Only his hair, blacker than the night, moved.

He stared at the stars. Willow knew he awaited her questions. In that moment of stillness, Willow accepted what her heart had told her earlier. He was not a murderer. And he wasn't crazy. She suspected, however, he held his share of secrets.

"Your shoulder must feel better," she offered. "It doesn't hurt to lean on that arm?"

"Some, but I am used to it."

"Yes, I saw your back. How did you get so many wounds?"

He studied her for a moment. "I would think, that since you are a policewoman, my scars would not seem unusual."

"Not unusual, just plentiful."

Lonewolf looked up to the sky and Willow knew the subject had been dismissed.

"And your shoulder?" he asked suddenly.

"It's still there." When he looked her way she added, "The pain, it's still there. Though the sling helps take the pressure off."

"I have some more datil," he said. His tone was matter-of-fact, but his eyes seemed to say something more. They held her tight, as if in an embrace.

Willow felt her insides warm, as they had when the medicine had drifted through her. She remembered his lips against hers, his tongue guiding the potion. The sense of liquid power that had coursed through her veins.

And the vision.

Willow broke her gaze. My God, he affected her even

without touching her! She would have to be careful with this man. She stood, trying to assume some command of the situation.

"What were you doing in the cave?" Willow asked without preamble.

"I was getting my bundle. I buried it there."

"But how did you get past the crime tape?"

No answer, and then, "I did not get past the tape."

"What do you mean? You were on the other side of the tape. You had to tear it down to get out the doorway."

Lonewolf chose his next words carefully. "The way I came, the tape was not a barrier."

"You mean there's another entrance?"

Lonewolf looked her in the eye. "Yes."

Willow's face was a mixture of stunned disbelief and confusion. Lonewolf longed to tell her the truth. But the woman did not believe in the power of *Ha'tanii*. How could she believe in a traveler from another time?

"Tell me this, Lonewolf, if you had nothing to feel guilty about, why were you so hostile in the cave?"

"*You* were the one who pulled the gun."

"Yes, and then you took it away."

"I thought you had been sent to kill me."

"By whom? Who would want you dead?"

You are not welcome here. Black Horse's words came back to him over and over.

"My visions have angered some men."

"Enough to kill?"

Willow's tone drew Lonewolf's attention. Concern creased her brow, yet the hard focus of her gaze said something else. Lonewolf knew she was thinking through the implications of a man accustomed to violence. Otherwise, why so many scars?

He saw the question forming in her eyes even before she spoke.

"Did you murder the Navajo boy?"

Lonewolf stood and walked to her. "Tell me, Willow, did you sense any violence in the visions we shared?"

Stars arced from Willow's eyes to Lonewolf. Lonewolf had to know her answer. He had to hear that she had shared the visions with him. He crooked a finger under her chin and raised her head. When she finally met his eyes, Lonewolf lost a breath at the power of her steady gaze.

"What visions?"

The urge to simultaneously laugh and strangle Willow nearly overwhelmed Lonewolf. She took the choice away by turning and walking to the edge of the cliff.

Lonewolf strode after her. He had to make her talk of the visions. And if she would not talk, then he would force another vision. This woman would not stand in his way.

"Willow," he said, and heard the threat in his voice.

She turned halfway to him. "Yes?"

Lonewolf ignored the sudden questioning look in her eyes. She might be determined not to submit to any visions. He could not let himself care.

She stood there stoic, unwavering under his advance. A gentle rise of wind lifted her hair and swept it forward, half covering her face. She looked at once strong and vulnerable and Lonewolf's mind suddenly cleared of any thought but touching her.

She had the power to take him home. Even if only within the images. A need gathered within him so strong and demanding he could not stop himself.

He laid a hand against her cheek and spoke quietly. "You cannot deny you have seen things when we touch."

"You forget I'm an officer, Lonewolf. I'm trained to rely on facts."

He captured the side of her head with his other hand and held her face before his. "You felt nothing at all?"

"Gut instinct. Nothing more."

"I think perhaps you are afraid, Willow."

"I'm not afraid of something that doesn't exist, Lonewolf."

"What of things that *do* exist?"

"How can I be afraid of something that's not there? The gods aren't there. The visions aren't real." She stopped talking and just stared at him. "I'm not even sure you're for real."

Her eyes reflected the stars, lights of life charged with energy.

"Then this should not frighten you, little one."

Lonewolf lowered his mouth to hers. Softly, he pressed against her lips. Scents from the past filled him. He tasted musk and wildflower, cedar smoke and earth. New tastes assaulted him, things he could not name, tastes he had never known.

The old and the new rolled through Lonewolf, churning and spinning, until he felt caught in an endless spiral with no past and no future. Panic welled within him. He had been so sure that she'd be the one tasting fear, not him. But he was the one caught dizzy and off balance. Yet he could not let her go.

Nothing was familiar.

Nothing was right.

Except for the woman in his arms.

Lonewolf pressed her closer and felt her hands at his back. She slanted her lips ever so slightly. She gave herself into the kiss and that knowledge pulled Lonewolf over the edge.

His hands circled her back, his mouth sought more. He drew her with him into the swirling tempest. Around and around, down and down. A shattering of stars exploded all around them.

Suddenly, the world calmed—as if they had stepped off the cliff and now drifted, weightless, with the night.

He heard children laughing and adults singing. He felt the sun's heat on his face. The image unfolded and

Lonewolf found himself surrounded by trees, the scent of ripe peaches filling the air.

A man's voice drew his attention. Lonewolf searched the image and found a man holding a little girl. She had been crying and peach fuzz glistened in a trail down her cheek.

"Do not be afraid, *Naa glen ni baa,*" the man said. "The stars will always protect you."

The child whispered to the man and, though Lonewolf stood far away, he felt every word at his ear. "Please don't go, Father."

The child hugged the man fiercely and Lonewolf felt the desperate embrace. The child looked up and Lonewolf stared into glistening dark green eyes. He brushed a kiss on the child's forehead and tasted peaches and salt.

Then the child became a woman. Lonewolf now looked on from a distance.

The woman cradled a boy's pale, lifeless body. She hummed and rocked, holding him close. Tears traveled down her cheeks and fell to the boy's head. But, as they landed, they turned to stars. Soon, his head was crowned with lights. The woman cried out and the boy, now only stars in her lap, drifted into the sky.

Lonewolf reached for the stars to bring them back to the woman, but his arms were not long enough. He tried desperately to run to her, but every step he took toward her somehow took him farther away. Old fears pounded against his heart. The boy's life depended on Lonewolf, but he could not reach him! Just as he had not been able to save his own son.

"No!"

Caught for a moment between the vision and the present, Lonewolf was not sure where the yell had come from. His breath in gasps, he still felt the struggle of reaching the woman. He did not want the vision to end. He still had not learned enough!

A hard thump on his chest brought him fully back to the present. Lonewolf took a deep breath and tried to calm himself.

He had been a part of her vision! They were entwined—their visions becoming one for each other. Never before had he felt the power in another mingled with his own. What did this mean for her?

One look at Willow told him she had shared this vision, too. Her eyes shimmered with unshed tears. He could also see a fight if he asked any questions. Would she deny this vision, too?

''Let me go,'' she demanded.

''No.'' Lonewolf held firm to her shoulders. ''Willow, who is the boy? You must tell me.''

''Who *are* you?'' Her question was more like a plaintive cry.

For a moment, Lonewolf considered telling her the truth. He needed her help, of that he was sure.

But the truth posed too great a risk. She was, as she liked to keep reminding him, a policewoman.

''I am just a man, Willow. A man who might be able to help. Can you not think of me as a friend?''

''A friend? What right do you have to call yourself a friend?'' She shook loose of his grip.

Lonewolf watched in desperation as the magic disappeared from Willow's eyes. And in the next moment, she walked across the rock ledge and into the juniper grove.

He had to make her see!

''What are you afraid of, Willow? What did you see?''

''Nothing that concerns you,'' she said over her shoulder, as she disappeared into the thicket. ''I don't know who you are or what you're doing here. Why don't you just go back to wherever you came from and leave me alone?''

Laughter split the silence. Willow had never heard

such a sound. It started as a chuckle and grew, until booms of laughter filled the air. The deep sound echoed through her. She felt it low in her stomach.

Suddenly, the laughter stopped.

"I am afraid that is not possible," Lonewolf said and he walked to her.

His voice still held the shimmer of laughter and Willow stared at the immense transformation the smile had on his face. When he was serious, his features were a rugged study of sharp planes and angles. But now, those same harsh lines radiated from his eyes. Then, before her eyes, his face sobered.

"Do not run from me, Willow."

"I wasn't running, Lonewolf." She paused. "I've had enough of that for one day."

A callused finger raised her chin until her eyes met his. Against her better judgment, Willow held his gaze. The stars shone in them. She wanted to stand there and stare; to get lost in those fathomless eyes. They held a promise of help and compassion. She wanted to believe. Oh, how she wanted to believe that he could help.

She forced herself to look away. She could use a friend, no doubt. But not one who turned her inside out. She couldn't trust herself—or what he could make her see.

"Willow, is the boy your son?"

"No."

"What is your attachment to him?"

"I'm all he has." Overwhelming futility, fueled by her fatigue, coursed through her. For a fleeting moment, she wished the burden wasn't hers. She couldn't bear to lose Manuelito. But a familiar voice, calm and full of strength, reminded her she was not a quitter. She could always count on herself.

She left Lonewolf in the thicket and walked to the hogan. As she raised the rug to enter her room, she heard the door to the hogan open.

"Our paths crossed today for a reason, Willow," he said, his voice serious.

Willow looked over her shoulder at the tall, proud Navajo silhouetted in the starlight.

"I can hardly wait to find out what that is," she said and let the rug drop behind her.

Willow lay down on her cot. Finally, she was alone. But, instead of relief, frustration filled her. A whole day gone and she had accomplished nothing. She was no closer now than the beginning of the day to solving the murder or helping Manuelito. She had, however, managed to lose touch with reality three or four times.

The most notable when she'd allowed Lonewolf to kiss her. She'd known it was coming. She'd seen it in his eyes. And then she'd practically dared him.

Why in the world had she let him? Some vain attempt to prove she was fearless? What a laugh. The minute his hand had found her neck, her pulse had quickened.

But not from fear, she told herself sternly. She just didn't want the visions. She had no control when they came. Maybe this time, she'd finally learned that lesson.

Willow sat up, her legs curled under her, and gazed at the stars through the small, unpaned window. The sky twinkled and blinked at her, alive with millions of lights. No city lights dimmed the dance. Out here, deep in Navajoland, the stars ruled. They held all the answers. Every good Navajo could tell you that was the way.

Her father had believed. Unbeckoned, the vision replayed for her. Once again, she was a child, sticky with peaches, cuddled in her father's arms. *The stars will protect you, little one*. Those had been his words when he left.

But all his faith and all his star power hadn't been enough to keep him alive. And it had not been enough for her mother. Her mother, who had mourned her father, cried every day. Willow could hear the muffled moans. Then her mother had left.

Willow shook off the immediate feeling of loss and concentrated on the second half of the vision, when Manuelito lay in her arms. Why should this vision come, full of grief, longing, and helplessness. And why now—with Lonewolf?

She hated that it didn't make sense; that the answer was out of reach. She didn't need to be reminded of her shortcomings. She hadn't been prepared for Lonewolf; not when he kidnapped her, not when he kissed her, and not when he evoked the visions.

Maybe that was the answer: to stay in control. She hadn't trusted her instincts today, and then she'd gotten the bad news about Manuelito. She'd let herself weaken. And the weak could be manipulated.

What if she could work some of that manipulation on Lonewolf? He wanted to help. He'd practically insisted. Maybe he *would* have an idea about Manuelito's sickness.

Her injuries did not equal Manuelito's coma, but doing *anything* for Manuelito would be better than the nothing she had done for a week. Doctors and nurses poking at him didn't count.

There was a time—just this morning—when she would have said a medicine man didn't count, either. But she was desperate. Desperate enough to even admit the importance of the visions?

The thought made her pull the covers closer.

Yes, was the simple answer. She would do anything for Manuelito. She had seen Manuelito and so had Lonewolf. She didn't want to know why. But she couldn't argue with the obvious anymore: Manuelito was a connection between them. So be it. Let Lonewolf help.

Willow turned her back on the star-filled night. Maybe their paths had crossed for a reason.

SIX

Willow awoke to the aroma of coffee cooking over a cedar fire. The fragrance took her back to times when she had camped with Grandfather and she lay there, her eyes closed, drinking in the memory. She shifted toward the scent and the throbbing soreness in her shoulder brought her fully awake.

Willow massaged the ache and cautiously manipulated her shoulder. Really, it was only stiff and she marveled at how quickly the injury was healing. Thanks to Lonewolf.

She rubbed and thought about the decisions she had made in the night. First she and Lonewolf would go to the cave and he'd show her the other entrance. Then she would take Lonewolf to see Manuelito. Today would be different than yesterday: today there would be no surprises.

Willow could hear someone moving about the next room. Any minute, Grandfather would raise the rug, show his much-too-cheery face, and chide her from bed. She might as well get moving. It was not good Navajo form to ignore the blessing of a new day. Willow rose with optimistic purpose.

She was right about the coffee, but wrong about the person. Lonewolf crouched in the center in the room, bent over a small fire on the dirt floor. The fire's flames reached upward, pulled by the draft through the smokehole at the top of the hogan. A saucepan balanced on two red-hot sticks.

At his side was a can of ground coffee, its plastic lid

still in Lonewolf's hand. He turned the lid over and over and tapped it with his finger. Willow watched with amazement as Lonewolf held the plastic before his face and moved it side to side. What in the world was so doggone fascinating about a coffee-can lid?

She opened her mouth to ask when he thrust his arm wrist-deep into the can of coffee. He withdrew his hand, letting the coffee sift through his open fingers. A brown film of coffee grains clung to his palm, which he raised to his nose.

By this time, Willow wondered whether Lonewolf considered himself some sort of coffee connoisseur. His next action dispelled that notion. He bent the lid in half, scooped out a "lidful" of coffee from the can and dumped it into the saucepan. The water level doubled to accommodate the extra mound of coffee. Though it'd been a while since Willow had shared cowboy coffee with her grandfather, she knew the concoction wasn't equal parts coffee and water. Just the thought of the potent brew woke her up.

Lonewolf held the saucepan over the fire and swirled it in slow, steady circles. Willow's gaze drifted to his shirtless back. The rhythmic motion of his arm worked every muscle in his shoulder. She watched, nearly hypnotized.

He looked quite at home by the fire. Willow could imagine the hogan and all its contents vanishing, leaving just Lonewolf and his fire. The picture suited him—alone, wild, and a little primitive.

In fact, he seemed so fully focused on the pot and the fire, Willow felt sure he didn't know she stood behind him, staring. For the moment, she was content to do just that, watching the graceful movement in such a powerful back.

She leaned against the doorjamb. That slight movement gave her away. Lonewolf looked over his shoulder at her, his keen eyes quickly hiding a trace of surprise.

"You are as quiet as a Ute."

"Is that a compliment or an insult?"

He quirked a brow. "Are Utes still so unpopular?"

"They are in this hogan," she said, slightly embarrassed. "Grandfather holds grudges for all enemies of the Navajo. Where is he, by the way?"

"He was not here when I awoke." Then, "He still battles the Utes?"

"Well, not so he'd draw blood." Restless, she moved around the room. She hated conversations about her grandfather's beliefs. As far as she was concerned old hatreds were ancient history. It would be better for all Native Americans if they could learn to work together. Unfortunately, plenty of *Diné* agreed with Grandfather—once an enemy of the Navajo, always an enemy.

She stopped opposite Lonewolf, with only the fire between them. "Let's just say Grandfather keeps old battles alive with words. Not that he runs into many Utes out here, anyway." Willow's gaze settled on the fresh entry wound on his shoulder. Other scars, small white lines, hugged the muscled curves of his bronzed chest.

"Those battles were long ago."

Something in Lonewolf's voice drew Willow's attention. She looked at him, expecting him to say more. Instead, he set the pan aside and swiftly rose. He turned his back to her, grabbed his shirt, and pulled it on, tying the leather strap at the neck before taking his seat again at the fire.

The swift maneuver left her speechless. Was he modest? She started to make a light remark when it occurred to her that maybe he'd wanted to cover his scars. Out of embarrassment or a sense of privacy? She recalled how he had denied the wound even hurt. Denying pain was common enough for a man, but not hiding scars. Most men she knew, even Navajo, wore old wounds with pride. Every bit she learned about Lonewolf only added to the mystery.

"I think the coffee is ready," he said. "Would you like some?"

"I think that's what woke me up," she said diplomatically. "Why didn't you use the Coleman?" She nodded with her head toward the camping stove.

Lonewolf grunted. "I like the smell of cedar in my coffee."

"So do I." Willow walked to the homemade wooden cupboard and pulled out two mugs and the sugar bowl. The pungent aroma of cooked coffee so filled the small room, Willow was surprised the hogan didn't lift off the ground merely on the power of the fumes. She ladled a heaping teaspoon of sugar into her cup, thought about it, and added another teaspoon.

Her nose hadn't deceived her. She nearly gagged on the first bitter sip. Lonewolf wasn't so polite. He spewed his mouthful of coffee on the fire, making it sputter and hiss.

"Anh! This is disgusting."

"It's not so bad with some sugar." Willow handed him the sugar bowl.

He ignored it. "How can you drink this stuff? And where are the coffee beans? We never had to scoop coffee from a can. It was always beans, and we knew how much to grind!"

He'd gotten louder with every pronouncement until the last sentence, which he punctuated by slamming down his cup and standing up. None of that bothered her, and not just because the cup hadn't made much of a sound hitting the dirt floor.

She couldn't name exactly what bothered her. Only that, for a moment, he sounded like Grandfather, who liked to complain about modern conveniences and extol the virtues of the old days.

Willow looked over at Lonewolf. He stood at the hogan door, each arm braced on the mud-packed opening.

He seemed to be staring far off, beyond whatever she could see.

"Where are you from, Lonewolf?"

"Far from here." Lonewolf stared across the red earth, past the juniper thicket, toward the canyon. His home. Only a few miles and over a hundred years away. Why was he here? Frustration roiled within him and only through conscious will did he keep it from boiling over. He forced down his emotions and tried to think.

"If you aren't from here, why did you keep your medicine bundle in the canyon cave?"

Willow's questions were like tinder to his temper. "Because it was safe," he said tightly. "I was safe."

"Is someone after you?"

Lonewolf took a deep breath.

"I am safe from my enemies for now," he said, without turning his head.

"A man shot at you last night. If someone is out to hurt you, the police can help."

"I did not know that man." He looked over his shoulder to Willow. "He was shooting at you."

"You sound disappointed, even angry."

He was—both disappointed *and* angry. *Why am I here?* His only clues were the visions and the murder Willow was investigating. "Perhaps there is a connection with the murder?" Lonewolf asked.

"If that's the case," she said, "that's still no help. We don't have a motive for the murder. There are no priors on the dead boy. He was just a canyon kid, living here year-round with his family."

"If he knew the canyon well," Lonewolf ventured, "maybe he knew something others wanted kept a secret."

"We can't get a lead on that, either. Nobody knows what he was doing that day or where he'd been. All we know for sure is that he didn't die in that cave."

"What do you mean?"

"He was dumped there, already dead." Willow got up and paced.

"Where was he killed?"

"Who knows? It's a big canyon. Hell, it's a big reservation. It could've happened anywhere. Plus, there's no sign of how the boy's body got into the cave to begin with."

Every question led to more questions. Lonewolf clenched his jaw to keep his scream of frustration within. He gazed out the door, letting his vision travel over the juniper forest, to the rim of the canyon and down. It was not so far back to the cave . . .

"That's why," Willow continued, "I'm very interested in your information about another entrance to that cave."

"I see," Lonewolf murmured.

Willow stopped in front of him. "Where is the other entrance?"

"It is not easy to describe." Lonewolf turned from the door. He would ask one more question.

"Who is the boy, Willow?"

Two beats passed before she answered. "His name is Manuelito."

Her straight answer surprised him, but he quickly asked another, "And what is he to you, Willow?"

At this, she looked away, out the door, as he had done just moments before. And Lonewolf wondered what secrets *she* held.

"He's all I have," she finally said. "His mother hightailed it off the res years ago. His father is never sober enough to comprehend he *has* a son. I'm it."

"But you said he is all *you* have."

"Did I?" She walked past him, picked up the sugar bowl and coffee can and carried them to the cupboard. For all her movement, Lonewolf still detected a trace of sadness in her voice. Without reason, he needed to know *why* she felt this sadness.

"You have Grandfather. And your job. Tell me, Willow, you are proud of your job?"

"It's not so much pride as it is a way for me to make a difference for some people." Willow looked away from Lonewolf as she spoke, which told him her answer held more meaning than she wanted to admit.

"Why did your grandfather accuse you of making criminals out of people?"

"Like I said, once an enemy of the Navajo, always an enemy." She shrugged. "I guess to him I'm just a pawn of the white man's laws."

As she talked, she went to the fire and lifted the saucepan of coffee.

"Are you?"

"Am I what? A pawn?"

She stood there for a moment, the pan of hot coffee bending her wrist. Then she walked up and stopped right in front of him. Her cold stare cut right through the rising steam. Lonewolf expected a lecture or, at the very least, some cutting words in her defense. He did not expect her tone to be curious.

"Do you play chess, Lonewolf?"

"Yes. I learned . . . a long time ago."

"And what do you consider the most important playing piece, with the exception of the king?"

"That depends on the game," he answered. He fully expected her to claim that the pawns did the hard work.

He was wrong.

"Precisely," she said, then brushed past him and dumped the coffee. Her actions drew the interest of several dogs, who, after one sniff, looked disappointed as they returned to the spots they'd been warming. "As far as I'm concerned, any part I can play to help my people win against the odds—well, I'm glad for the chance. I do what I have to do."

That he would have given the exact same answer did not escape Lonewolf. He also would do what he had to do. More and more he saw Willow as someone like him, another warrior.

''Is that what you are doing for Manuelito? Helping him win against all odds?''

Willow set the pot on the counter and turned to Lonewolf. ''Yes, I am doing all I can.''

''You are saving him from his parents, then?''

''No, he's sick and no one knows why. A specialist saw him yesterday, but . . .''

Willow's words trailed off as she turned her back on Lonewolf. But he heard the pain.

''You have consulted a *Hataałii*?''

''Medicine men are not allowed in the critical ward.''

''You allow this?''

''I don't make the rules, Lonewolf. Besides, I'm sure they have their reasons.''

Lonewolf watched her walk to the counter and pour water from a jug into the pan. How could anyone deny spiritual guidance to a Navajo?

Willow approached the fire but stopped and looked at him. ''Just as I'm sure you have your own rules during ceremonies you perform, right?''

''Yes, but those rules protect the patient and ensure the correct use of the power.''

''Just as hospital rules protect their patients and the doctor's prescribed therapy, perhaps?''

''And so you are happy with the treatment your *doctors* provide?''

The fire in her eyes matched that of the one at her feet. For a moment he thought she might even ask for his help. But then she tilted the pan and poured some of the water on the fire. It hissed in anger.

''I'm happy with the results, Lonewolf,'' she said. ''And what about you? Are you always happy with your results?''

''Like you, Willow, I do what I have to do.''

''And what is it you *have* to do, Lonewolf?''

"Go home." The words fell from his mouth before he could think.

"Where is your home, Lonewolf?"

"The canyon." Once again, his heart answered.

He watched Willow douse the fire. In a last gasp, the fire belched smoke and a few flakes of ashes. And in that moment, Lonewolf made a decision. He would try to get back to his time and place right away. If the Holy Ones had had a plan sending him here, that reason was lost on Lonewolf. He was not needed here, not even wanted. The boy was a possibility, but then the visions of him could easily have been caused by the power of Willow's concern for the boy.

No, he could not waste any more time trying to determine any good reason for being here. He would go straight to the cave.

He gathered his bundle and tied it to his waist. He glanced at Willow, who also seemed ready to leave. He would miss this one. Her calm determination and fiery spirit had given him an anchor.

"Are you ready to go to the cave?" she asked.

"Why are you going back to the cave?"

"So you can show me that other entrance, of course."

Of course.

Willow saddled Red Wing and Lonewolf rode one of Grandfather's horses. She let him lead the way to the cliff—better to contemplate the man while watching his back.

He rode straight and tall . . . and bareback. His legs molded to the horse's belly. His hips sat tight on the horse's back. He was made for the horse. Both their bodies—Lonewolf's and the horse's—lean and muscular and primitive.

Primitive. The word hung in her mind. Lonewolf's bow and arrows swayed against his back, in rhythm with the horse's strides. His chiseled face looked cut from the canyon rock: hard, uncompromising. So much about

Lonewolf set him apart from other Navajo men. And from other *Hataałii*.

She could expect a *Hataałii*'s indignance with the hospital's policies. But Lonewolf's reaction was more than indignant, he had looked appalled, as if he hadn't ever heard of such a thing.

She had been tempted to ask what Lonewolf would suggest for Manuelito. But she'd felt cornered and misjudged. If relying on doctors had been a mistake, how much harm had she done? She couldn't go straight from that accusation by Lonewolf to asking for help. She just couldn't. She would find another time to ask his opinion. Perhaps while they were in the cave, where she would be in charge, gathering information. She would be on duty, as would the other policemen who would join her.

She hadn't told Lonewolf about them, either. But then, that wasn't any of his business, or concern. If he was truly innocent of any crime, he had nothing to hide.

They followed the trail to where she'd left Red Wing the day before and left the horses tied at the top of the trail and descended the rocky slope. Willow looked for signs of the man who had chased her up the cliff. When she spotted some crushed sagebrush the man had rolled over, she crouched to take a better look.

''No blood,'' Lonewolf said, as he walked past her.

''Perhaps you missed,'' she said.

''I did not miss.''

''You don't have to snap at me. It was night, he was moving, and, if you recall, you had been shot. How could you expect to hit him?''

Her words galled him, though Willow had only been stating the facts. Still, Lonewolf knew his arrow had found its mark.

He glanced at the cliff above and figured the likely course of a rolling body. He veered off the path Willow had chosen. Within a few steps he had his proof.

''Here, on the boulder.''

Willow joined him and they both looked down at a swatch of red. Lonewolf let his gaze travel farther down the cliff.

"And over there." He pointed to another rock about six feet away. The man's path back down the cliff was now obvious. In silence, Willow and Lonewolf retraced his fall. But at the bottom, where a battered body should be, there lay only sand, rocks, and flattened service berry.

Parallel ruts in the soft earth told him he'd been dragged for a bit, then slung over someone's shoulders. Single, deep footprints walked in one direction, then disappeared over boulders.

"He had a friend," Lonewolf said.

"An accomplice, you mean. Whoever carried him off had to have witnessed him chasing me." Willow felt like kicking something, but she knew better than to disturb a scene. She still didn't know if the man was alive or dead. There was no doubt, however, that Lonewolf's arrow had connected.

The sergeant wasn't going to like this one bit. Hell, she didn't like it. How much more complicated could things get?

As they neared the cave, Willow was not too surprised to find they were the first ones there. It was only eight o'clock, which would give her time to scope out the other entrance Lonewolf had mentioned and maybe do some quick thinking about the murder. Her spirits started to lighten.

Though the climb up the cliff was strenuous Lonewolf's pace never eased. At the top of the talus slope, they stood before the cave housing the ancient pueblo ruin.

"Where is the other entrance?" she asked, her voice raspy from all the dust.

"I cannot show you."

"What?"

Lonewolf's hand encircled her wrist. His grasp, though firm and unyielding, didn't annoy her. Instead, it felt oddly protective, as if she were standing on shaky ground.

"When I came here, I was not myself. I do not know how I got here."

"Lonewolf, you're not making any sense."

"Willow, please listen to me. I was on a vision quest. I had fasted for four days. I was hungry and tired. I came to this cave . . . I came to seek some answers. But I honestly do not know how I entered."

"Let me get this straight. You were on a vision quest—in a cave. What kind of vision quest?"

"I am a stargazer."

The air in the cave evaporated. Willow's chest tightened. Her lungs struggled to breathe. She backed out of the cave.

"Willow, what is wrong?"

"Some air—I need some air."

A stargazer. He was a stargazer, just like her father. Willow stumbled over the rubble toward the opening of the cave and gulped at the fresh air. The vision of her with her father flooded over her. All the old feelings bubbled to the surface: the anger, the frustration, the *betrayal.* She clamped the lid down on the boiling cauldron and focused on the canyon vista, letting its majesty calm her.

She, of all people, knew better than to let the past disrupt the present. She was stronger than that, she told herself. Her fears were in the past.

Her mind began to clear and she regained her equilibrium. Fortified, she turned and saw Lonewolf staring from inside the ruin. Embarrassed, she strove to regain control. "Since when does a stargazer seek answers *inside* a cave?" she asked.

Lonewolf reached a hand out and drew her to the entrance of the ruin and pointed to the ceiling. Willow stared at the stars overhead. How had she overlooked them yesterday? The pecked symbols—chalk crosses, diamonds, and circles—were at once simple and compelling. So carefully etched by a hand long since gone from this earth.

Lonewolf led Willow into the small chamber. He dropped her wrist and pressed his palm against a handprint on the ceiling. His hand perfectly fit the painted silhouette. She glanced at Lonewolf and found him staring at her. The desperate look in his eyes sent a shiver through her.

"What are you doing?"

He didn't answer. He had to have heard, but he had closed his eyes and now leaned his weight against his one hand pressing on the roof of the cave.

"Lonewolf, please answer me." She had the overwhelming urge to pull his hand from the ceiling and make him face her. But the sound of voices traveling up the cliff drew her attention. She looked out the door of the ruin and saw Sergeant Carejo climbing the slope. Trailing behind was Deputy Chavez, grunting like an ornery pack mule.

"Hello," she called down.

The sergeant waited to reply until he'd reached the top. "Good morning, Willow."

"Morning, Cal," Willow answered with an easy smile.

The sergeant eyed her shoulder. "What happened to you?"

Willow tried to shrug but was rewarded with a shooting pain up her neck. She smiled weakly. "A pulled shoulder, that's all."

"But how?"

"I reported it last night, Cal. A man chased me out of the canyon. Lonewolf pulled me up the cliff."

The sergeant looked into the ruin. Willow could see Lonewolf past the sergeant's shoulder. He still had his hand against the ceiling, but now he was softly chanting.

"This, I take it, is Lonewolf?" asked Cal.

"Yes. We found the trail of the man who shot at us last night. Evidently, he had someone waiting in the canyon who carried him off."

"Shot at 'us'?"

"I'm not sure who he was shooting at, Cal. His bullet hit Lonewolf just before Lonewolf shot him with an arrow."

"Mr. Lonewolf?"

Lonewolf didn't look to be in any mood for introductions. His hand remained pressed to the ceiling. Though his eyes were closed, there was no doubt about his intense concentration. His whole face was rigid, the lines bracketing his mouth etched even deeper.

"You say Lonewolf, here, shot the man with an arrow?"

"Yes."

"A man with an arrow wound was found dead in the Embudo Arroyo this morning." Deputy Chavez's first words held a note of suspicion. He was a career cop at the ripe age of twenty-two. A Navajo boy who made his family proud and the cops he worked with uncomfortable with his arrogance.

Willow accepted the news in silence. So much for questioning the guy.

The sergeant interrupted her thoughts. "So Lonewolf, here, just happened to be at the right place at the right time?"

Willow suddenly saw how unexplainable the whole situation was. But then it was her job to make sense of things. She took a deep breath and started again.

"I met him in this cave yesterday morning."

"Where in the cave, Willow?"

"In this room."

The sergeant noticed for the first time that the yellow

crime tape trailed on the floor. "Was the room sealed then?"

"Yes."

"You found him in this room, behind the crime tape?"

"Yes, Cal. He was on a vision quest and came to this cave to seek answers. He's a stargazer." Since the sergeant was full-blooded Navajo, Willow added this last, hoping to lend some credibility to what sounded like an awfully lame explanation.

"Can Lonewolf talk for himself, or is he stargazing now?"

Willow didn't miss the note of sarcasm in the deputy's voice.

"Lonewolf, this is Sergeant Carejo," Willow said, deliberately ignoring Chavez.

For a moment, she thought he wouldn't talk. Then, "Tell . . . him . . . of . . . other . . . entrance."

"There's another entrance to this cave?" asked Cal.

"It's . . . behind . . . the dwelling." Lonewolf's words came forced through gritted teeth.

"Let's see about this entrance, Deputy."

The sergeant and deputy walked out of the ruin and disappeared around the corner. Willow laid a hand on Lonewolf's shoulder.

"What are you doing? Are you okay?"

Save for the beads of sweat on his forehead, Lonewolf's face could have been sculpted of stone in the image of a fierce warrior. Then he turned his head slightly and Willow gasped at his ferocious gaze.

"You . . . did . . . not . . . trust . . . me."

"What do you . . ." was all Willow got out. The next instant the sergeant stuck his head through the door.

"I don't see any entrance back here."

Lonewolf's eyes narrowed and Willow understood exactly. He thought she called the police to turn him in. He turned to stone again, facing the cave wall.

"You say Lonewolf here shot the man we found dead in the arroyo?" Chavez slipped by the sergeant and approached Lonewolf.

"Deputy, we don't know that's the same man," Willow said, doubly annoyed with his attitude and arrogance.

"Well, how many Indians you know run around with a bow and arrow?" The deputy flipped the bow on Lonewolf's back with his finger.

"Officer Becenti, we need to question this man."

Willow didn't miss Cal's reversion to the formal. "I understand, Sergeant." Willow turned to Lonewolf. She felt like telling the deputy to get his arrogant hands off Lonewolf, but she resisted. "Lonewolf, please, answer me."

He didn't move.

"Lonewolf, you've got to stop."

"Officer Becenti."

"Lonewolf, stop what you're doing. Now!"

His grunt sounded like a no.

"Officer Becenti, get this man moving right now."

"Lonewolf!"

"Do-tah!"

The sudden, loud exclamation from Lonewolf echoed in the small chamber.

"You're coming with me right now." The deputy pulled on Lonewolf's left shoulder.

Willow realized too late it was his wounded shoulder. But Lonewolf didn't budge, as if he hadn't even noticed.

"Now, Long Hair!" The deputy pulled harder.

Lonewolf spun, his arm out, catching Chavez off balance. "*Do-tah!* Go! I must get home!"

Sergeant Carejo grabbed his arm and slammed Lonewolf against the ruin wall. A flash of metal descended on Lonewolf's wrists.

A primordial sound echoed off the ancient walls, and enveloped Willow with unbelievable sadness.

SEVEN

"Why are you arresting him?"

"For trespassing a crime scene, assaulting an officer . . ."

Willow opened her mouth to protest.

"And murder," the sergeant finished.

"The Navajo boy?"

Lonewolf caught the tone of disbelief in Willow's voice. She believed in his innocence. That fact meant more to Lonewolf than it obviously did to the sergeant. But why, if she had called the police here, did she now defend him?

"At this point," continued the sergeant, "he's a suspect in two murders."

"Two murders? First of all, he shot the arrow in self-defense. Second, you don't know that his arrow killed that other man. Furthermore, I questioned him about his presence in this cave. He was stargazing."

"In a cave?"

Willow pointed up to the ceiling. The sergeant did not bother to look up. Instead, he turned his gaze on Lonewolf. Lonewolf stared back. Neither man shifted his gaze and Lonewolf saw, in the older man's eyes, not arrogance or stupidity. He saw a patient, relentless quest for the truth. And, perhaps because Lonewolf knew his eyes held only secrets, the sergeant finally looked away and shook his head.

"I'm taking him in for questioning, Willow," he said quietly. "If you've got a problem with that, take it up with the captain."

Willow stared at the sergeant. Lonewolf could not see her eyes clearly in the dark, but he could feel the tension and Willow's frustration. Why should she care if he were arrested? Had that not been her plan? If not, why did he now sit here handcuffed?

"Come on, get up."

A jerk on Lonewolf's collar brought him to his feet beside the deputy.

"We all calm now, Long Hair?"

Lonewolf looked down at the deputy. The officer's eyes shone white in the dim light.

"No. One of us is still nervous."

The deputy grabbed the bow and arrows from off Lonewolf's back and shoved him out of the pueblo chamber.

"Let's go," the sergeant said behind Lonewolf. The sergeant led the way down the talus slope. Willow followed and the deputy stayed at Lonewolf's side. Though his handcuffed wrists made the steep slope more of a challenge, Lonewolf managed to keep his balance. He focused on Willow's back and followed in her steps.

Once, when the deputy slipped and sent rocks skittering, Willow turned, her eyes wide with concern. Lonewolf smiled. She did not smile back, but looked at him for a moment before continuing down the slope.

What was on this stealthy cougar's mind? Did she wonder why he had lied about the other entrance? Was she now adding up all the odd pieces from their last day together? Or perhaps she just appreciated the picture of his wrists bound, as hers had been yesterday.

Lonewolf let his mind wander behind him, past the junction of the two canyons, up the more lush, shaded main canyon, and farther, along the mazelike canyon fingers full of hideaways and caves. He knew he would not find those from the past—the council, the warriors, the mothers and children. Lonewolf's chest tightened with grief. The battles were over, many had undoubtedly died, and through it all, those who mattered most to him would have thought he had abandoned them.

He twisted his wrists within the handcuffs. He was surrounded by people he did not know, in a time he could not yet comprehend, yet Lonewolf could not believe his destiny was to stand accused for a murder he had not committed.

Except he had no one to prove his innocence, but himself. As the foursome left the canyon behind, Lonewolf silently vowed to return.

"Where is your jeep?" Willow asked the sergeant.

"Just up ahead."

Lonewolf tried to prepare himself mentally for the new world he was about to face.

Of course, that was impossible.

He soon saw what a "jeep" was. The strange box of metal sat above the ground, supported by four wheels, the like Lonewolf had never seen, even in his youth in Santa Fe. The wheels were black and wide and not of metal or wood. The whole contraption looked made for problems. It was too close to the ground to avoid boulders. Mud or quicksand would easily overtake the hubs and threaten the very inside. The most peculiar oversight was the lack of horses. There was not even a hitch at the front to tie on a team.

He stepped into the jeep and sat in the back, as directed by the deputy. At the front, between Willow and the sergeant's seat, was a rod with a knob on the top. The sergeant shifted his weight, moved the rod, leaned forward and turned something. Next thing, the jeep rumbled to life and Lonewolf nearly leapt from his skin.

He steeled his senses from the brutal pounding by concentrating on the passing scenery. Except that too was alien.

Trees that should not be there blocked his view. In a blur of spindly limbs, the jeep broke through the thicket and passed a family of *Diné,* working outside their home; except the dwelling was not a hogan, but a four-sided adobe.

With a lurch, the jeep left the rutted dirt and pulled onto a road. Black surface covered the rocks, boulders, sand, and gravel.

Like a snake, flattened, dead—to be avoided—the road wound over the mesa. Lonewolf had wondered at the lack of horses, but now saw they could never tolerate such a hard surface beneath their hooves.

The jeep picked up speed and only those things on the horizon did not pass in a blur. Lonewolf stared at the passing landscape—his beloved *Dinehtah*. Familiar . . . and foreign. He forced himself to look at what he did not want to see.

Wires strung from high poles interrupted the big sky. Cattle grazed on Navajo land. Now and then he would see a hogan standing alone. More often, he saw long, squatty metal buildings surrounded by dirt. All of it fenced in. When had the fences come?

He closed his eyes to the never-ending barrage of alien sights and suddenly felt overcome with exhaustion. How would he find, in all this vast newness, why he was here?

"This way, Long Hair."

The deputy escorted him into a low building, down a long hallway, and into a room busy with people. Lonewolf noticed an ebb in the bustle of activity as he walked through the room. People stopped what they were doing and looked at him. As he passed, talk ensued, until the room filled once more with noise.

"Have a seat, Long Hair. I'll be right back."

Lonewolf sat down next to the desk indicated by the deputy. Willow had followed the sergeant to another room. Lonewolf was alone, yet surrounded—surrounded by a roomful of new sights and a cacophony of foreign sounds. The room was alive with clicks, clatters, buzzes, door slams, whistles, and booming voices. Above it all, there was incessant ringing. A machine on the deputy's desk rang, then stopped, then rang again. The same sound came from several of the desks.

Lonewolf used all his powers of concentration to minimize the noise in his head. He was so absorbed, he didn't notice the deputy return to his desk.

"Okay, Long Hair, what's your name?"

"Lonewolf. Jake Lonewolf."

"All right, Lonewolf, empty your pockets."

"I do not have any pockets."

"You don't have any pockets." The deputy mimicked him. "Where's your wallet?"

Lonewolf just stared at him.

"Your ID? Where do you keep your money?"

"I left my money behind."

"You one of those renegades from Navajo Mountain?"

"Navajo Mountain?"

"Don't act stupid with me, Long Hair. You know what I'm talking about. You look just like one of those holdouts."

"I am not from Navajo Mountain."

"You're not, huh? Well, then, where are you from?"

"I am from the canyon."

"I need an address."

"I do not have an address."

"Where is your home?"

"Right now, I do not have a home."

"Listen, smart guy, I need an address. Do you have any relatives?"

Lonewolf thought back to his white family. An image that never left him for long came back full force. A child stood on the auction block in Santa Fe, alone, and faced a crowd of strangers who yelled words he could not understand. Sarah and Joseph Talman had bought him, raised him, let his hair go long. Lonewolf started to smile inwardly, then crushed the feeling. He had grown soft during those years, letting himself think all would be good. Then they were killed by enemy Utes.

"Long Hair, I need an answer."

"Sarah and Joseph Talman, Abiquiu."

"Abiquiu, New Mexico?"

Lonewolf gave a slight nod.

"What about a phone?"

"A phone?"

"Don't start with me again. What's their phone number?"

Lonewolf took a guess. "They do not have a phone number."

"They don't have a phone?"

"No."

"Look here, Long Hair, you want to make this hard? I can make it harder. I expect answers to these questions. We can sit here all day, but you *will* give me the answers."

The deputy shook his head in obvious frustration. He continued on the form, asking questions. Lonewolf studied the deputy. He knew this kind. He had lost respect and lost touch. The deputy's eyes were a dead giveaway to the hole in his soul.

Lonewolf glanced around the noisy room in an effort to catch a glimpse of Willow. He needed to see her. Her eyes were not dead. Her eyes held fire and life. Even more than Corn Flower's. The thought startled Lonewolf and he forced his attention back to the nagging deputy.

Lonewolf answered every question from the deputy, although the latter was obviously not always happy with his response.

He asked again and again about the cave: why had Lonewolf been there, how had he gotten inside, what was he doing there? When his questions zeroed in on the medicine bundle, Lonewolf felt a trickle of panic down his spine.

"Is that the bundle there?" The deputy nodded toward the pouch tied to Lonewolf's waist.

Lonewolf considered lying. He knew with horrible certainty what would happen next. He glanced around the room. He was outnumbered and nearly everyone had a gun strapped at their waist. He could never escape. But lying would only stall the inevitable. For the first time since he had entered this new time and place, Lonewolf knew fear.

"Let me see the bundle, Long Hair."

"This bundle is mine, Deputy. It is a part of me. It has always been with me."

Lonewolf held the deputy's gaze. In Lonewolf's unflinching stare, the deputy's gaze went from arrogant to curious. In that frozen, unblinking moment, Lonewolf swore he saw a trace of respect. He thought the deputy might actually let the subject drop.

Then the deputy's gaze hardened. In the next instant, the deputy stretched an arm over the corner of the desk and grabbed the pouch.

"Do tah!" Lonewolf yelled and leapt to his feet.

The deputy sprang to his feet, his hand still clutching the medicine bundle. With a sharp jab, Lonewolf broke the deputy's grasp. The policeman grabbed for Lonewolf's arms. Lonewolf blocked the deputy, then he turned and kicked. The deputy fell back across the desk, scattering papers and tangling his leg in the cord hanging from the ringing machine. He tried to lunge for Lonewolf but the cord tripped him. The deputy yanked at the cord, ending the incessant ringing of the machine.

Lonewolf heard a scramble of feet behind him. In the next instant, he was completely surrounded by policemen. They twisted his arms behind him and forced him to the ground. His cheek pressed against the hard, cold floor.

"What the—"

Lonewolf recognized the sergeant's voice.

''Let him up, Chavez.''

That was Willow and Lonewolf smiled into the floor.

''What happened, Chavez?'' asked the sergeant.

''He wouldn't let me have this.''

Lonewolf felt the knot loosen at his waist and the weight of the pouch lifted.

''That's his medicine bundle.''

''Officer Becenti, he has admitted this is what he was getting in the cave. It could be evidence in the murder.''

''I did not murder that boy.''

Lonewolf's voice, low and forceful, sent a frisson of awareness through Willow. The room quieted. Willow marveled at how the man even now, held to the floor by four hefty policemen, commanded attention. His voice had not held any threats, only a flat statement of fact. It was the tone of authority that couldn't be ignored.

''Let him up, Chavez,'' Willow said again. The deputy glanced at her for a second, but kept his knee firmly pressed to Lonewolf's back. She hated the look of enjoyment on the deputy's face.

Chavez looked back at Lonewolf and said loud enough so everyone could hear, ''You ready to cooperate now, Long Hair?''

Willow wanted to slug the snotty kid. Righteous anger surged through her. How dare he!

She reached an arm toward Lonewolf. The other policemen, except Chavez, backed off. He raised himself slowly from Lonewolf's back, as if reluctant to let him off the floor.

Lonewolf pushed himself up and stood in one lithe motion. Willow felt a surge of strength from him. Surrounded by the other men, Willow had the odd sensation he was bolstering her, instead of the other way around. She also saw that, without exception, he towered over every person in the room.

The sergeant took charge. ''Deputy Chavez, finish

your questioning. Nez and Lopez, stay with Chavez. Becenti, see me in my office."

"Yes, sir." But Willow hesitated. Chavez had untied the bundle and was already rummaging through the contents. Crystals, a fireboard, a carved male bull-roarer, rattles, and wood tsintel boards bearing painted pictures of Father Sky, Mother Earth, and Lightning fell from the pouch and littered the desk.

"If this is possible evidence, shouldn't you be wearing gloves?"

The deputy threw her a dark look. "There's no weapon here," he said. Willow heard disappointment.

She stared at the sacred items scattered among police papers, used coffee cups, and an overflowing ashtray. The incompatible sight choked her.

She looked at Lonewolf, expecting to see rage on his face. What she saw took her breath away. His face showed no emotion, as if he were chiseled from stone. His eyes were black and unreadable. Only a vein, pulsing at his temple, revealed his inner battle for control.

She laid a hand on his shoulder, hoping to give some reassurance. A fireball of anger, seething, yet focused, bolted through her. Her body surged at the violation, pumping adrenaline, prickling the fine hairs on her neck. She didn't pull back, but let his fury vent within her.

The violence subsided, pulling with it all her defenses, leaving her drained, as if she had been in a battle.

Thank you. She felt the words more than heard them—within her hands, if that were possible. She looked at Lonewolf and he managed a wan smile.

"Becenti!"

"Yes, Sergeant."

Willow moved around the desk and started to put everything back in the pouch. It didn't matter that she touched it now. The harm had been done. Everything would have to be reblessed before Lonewolf could do any ceremonies.

"Hey, I'm not done looking through that." The deputy made a vain grab for the pouch.

She tied the pouch and took it from the desk. "Yes you are." Willow walked to where the sergeant stood halfway out of his office door and handed him the medicine bundle.

"There's no weapon in here. Not even anything he could use for a weapon. Unless you think he might have tickled the boy to death with the feathers."

The sergeant closed the door to his office and took a seat on the corner of his desk.

"What's going on here, Willow? What's with you and that renegade?"

His tone held no derision, only curiosity. Still, Willow bristled.

"Your question would be better put to Chavez, Cal. He's treating Lonewolf like he's guilty. Whatever happened to presumption of innocence?"

Willow heard the sergeant sigh. "He's just doing his job, Willow. Who I'm worried about is you."

"Because I would care what happened to his medicine bundle? I'm not totally heartless, Cal."

"I was watching you over there. You looked like you were going to faint."

"I'm fine. I've just had a couple of long days."

"Why don't you take off? Rest up. A new cowboy bar opened on Highway Twelve. What do you say—"

"I'm not what you'd call a great dance partner, Cal." Willow gingerly lifted the sling away from her body. The pain she expected didn't come. She was tempted to test how far she could maneuver her shoulder. But now was not the time.

"We could just sit and talk, Willow." He looked at her with warmth in his eyes. "We've always been good friends. You know, if you've got any problems—"

"Thanks, Cal. And thanks for caring. But not tonight, okay?"

He nodded and moved around the desk to his chair.

"Now." Willow changed to a business tone. "Any more news on the guy found in the arroyo?"

"Not yet. I should have the report later."

"And meantime, you're going to hold Lonewolf? Because he had the talent to stop the pursuer with an arrow?"

"How about trespassing and assault, for now? We can always work up to murder."

"What assault? Chavez grabbed his injured shoulder." She gestured toward the window and glanced for Lonewolf, but he was gone. His absence stopped her and for a second she stared—as if the squad room now lacked something of importance.

"His injured . . . Willow, he threw a punch at Chavez!"

"I'd like to do that myself," she murmured.

"I'll ignore that, Officer Becenti." He took his chair and shuffled papers, without looking at her. "Take off, Willow. When I get the report, I'll give you a call."

Willow knew the sergeant better than to argue anymore. Truth was, she had to wonder about her condition, too. Why in the world was she defending the actions of a total stranger?

She left the station, climbed in a jeep, and just sat, staring into space. It was clear to her he wasn't a murderer. She knew it in her soul. But she didn't know *how* she knew it. The sensation was akin to looking at a complex math problem and knowing the answer without working any calculations. Without knowing what calculations to even perform!

What was driving her to defend Lonewolf? She reminded herself that just last night she had decided to let him see Manuelito in the hopes he could help. But that was before she discovered he had lied about the other entrance to the cave. Was she so desperate to help Manuelito that she would take a chance on an unknown medicine man? A man who had just yesterday kidnapped her and now sat in a jail cell? A man who looked more like a warrior from the movies than a medicine man?

A man who stirred such powerful images within her?

Willow touched her shoulder, squeezed it tentatively, then with more force. It ached, but the searing pain was gone. In less than a day.

She struggled with the knot, then finally pulled it over her head. She stretched and straightened her arm, expecting resistance, ready with a moan for the certain pain. But it never came.

Whatever Lonewolf had done, he'd done it well.

Willow jammed the keys in the ignition, found first gear, and tore out of the gravel lot. She flew down the two-lane highway out of Window Rock, through frozen sand dunes that eventually rolled into piñon hills. She drove as fast as she could, away from the man sitting in a jail cell and toward a boy—lying in a hospital bed in Fort Defiance.

Within half an hour, she was striding through the double doors of the critical care ward. She stopped short of the door to Manuelito's room and looked in the picture window. All she could see were machines. Stacked two high in places, they surrounded the bed, dwarfing the child who lay there.

Willow walked into the dim room. No windows to the outside let in light or life's noises. In here, all was quiet, save for a hum. The only movement in the room was a green line on the EKG monitor and drips of liquid through myriad tubes affixed to the small, utterly motionless boy.

A small, round face nestled on the pillow. Eyes closed, his lips slightly parted, his reddish-brown skin and shots of black hair in stark contrast to the surrounding hospital white. His small arms lay still atop the sheets.

Willow walked to his side and took one of Manuelito's hands in her own. It was warm with life, but so spiritless. She rubbed her thumb across the back of his hand and over his dimpled knuckles. She waited, even half expected his eyes to open.

More, she needed to see him smile. She thought of how they'd met—his face expressionless as his father was led to the jail cell. This child had sat quietly, already experienced in abandonment. Willow had given him paper and a pencil to pass the time until Child Services appeared. He had drawn a horse and left it on the chair when they came for him. It wasn't a sharp-edged stick figure like those pecked into stone in the canyon of the boy's home. His soft pencil strokes had caught the horse in flight, none of its hooves touching the ground. A horse free of any concerns.

Right then was when she'd fallen in love, Willow realized. She had taped the drawing to the wall beside her desk. And, after every one of his visits, she had another to add to the gallery. He never looked at the display, but then he always left on the chair whatever drawing he had made—except the one time she gave him crayons instead of a pencil. He took the picture with him and the crayons.

The next time his father was hauled in, the colored drawing appeared on her desk—a bright pink horse balancing on two desert stones. As she added this to the wall, she saw Manuelito leaving the room and she swore she saw him smile. His smile did not spread across his face with childish abandon. No, his was a small gift, and the more valuable—only a glimpse as he disappeared round the corner, taking the smile with him.

Even in the visions, he had not been smiling. Willow's heart clenched in her throat. She stroked his arm and stared at Manuelito, willing his eyes to open. Wherever he was, he was out of her reach.

She would give anything to see him smile.

* * *

A lone truck circled the block of stores in Gallup. After a second pass, the driver cut his headlights and cruised through the parking lot and stopped behind Khalib Trading Company. From the box beside him, he carefully lifted the pile of towels.

He unrolled the last one and let the lethal bundle drop gently into his palm. Twenty sticks of dynamite should do the trick. He snickered at the perfect plan.

It had been so easy to plant the drugs at the boy's home. A simple brown paper bag stuffed into a coat pocket, with part of the bag left showing. The mother should find it today, definitely by tomorrow. That would be the best—the boy's funeral scandalized by drugs. He snickered again. Would serve him right. That kid had almost ruined the whole scheme with his stupid curiosity. Now he couldn't ask any more questions. And soon, everyone would be asking questions of the Arabs.

He climbed from the cab and walked nonchalantly to the back door of the Arab shop. Everyone knew the Arabs dealt drugs. Now they'd think that poor, innocent Navajo boy had gotten taken in by the big, bad Arabs.

A perfect plan. He lit the fuse and walked back to his truck whistling.

EIGHT

Willow uncurled her legs from the too-small chair and moaned aloud at the pain from the cramp in her muscles. She looked to Manuelito, worrying about the noise she'd made. It seemed like only moments since the nurse had ended another of his seizures with a shot of phenobarbital.

Willow glanced at her watch. Two hours had passed. She'd fallen asleep, her hand still on Manuelito's. Willow stood—her wobbly legs making her lean against the bed—and studied the child. He lay still now. The sheet remained neatly tucked in on both sides—his arms resting quietly atop.

Only hours before he had thrashed and kicked. Without her weight, he would have thrown himself from the bed. His eyelids had fluttered, his mouth hung open. He looked as if he were battling for dear life. But he had not uttered a word. Not even a moan.

Willow had screamed for the nurse.

It was one of many, Josie, the nurse had said. And Willow had looked on, exhausted, horrified.

Now, he lay quiet. But for how long? The specialist's report still hadn't come back. She had the helpless feeling that everyone was puzzled, with no idea what to do.

Willow brushed a stray lock of hair from Manuelito's forehead, letting her fingers linger at his temple where life pulsed, slowly. She would not wait around for answers. Not anymore.

Willow pressed a kiss to his cheek and left, saying goodbye to the nurse. She drove fast, as was usual, except this time it wasn't mindless speed, but a need to get this done before she lost courage. She would do whatever it took to get Lonewolf out of jail. She didn't care what Cal said, what the rules said, or even what her better judgment said.

The station was still quiet when Willow arrived. Cal sat at his desk, his attention on some papers. Willow knocked on his open door and entered. Cal looked up and his eyes narrowed on her.

"I've come for Lonewolf," she said.

Cal just stared, taking her in from head to toe.

"I don't want any arguments, Cal. I know he didn't kill that boy."

"You look like hell, Becenti."

"Did you hear anything I said?"

"Where did you sleep last night? In your jeep?"

Willow ran a hand down her hair and felt tangles. She hadn't brushed it since . . . she didn't know how long. A twig fell out and dropped to the ground.

"If you must know, I slept at the hospital."

Cal opened his mouth to say something and Willow plowed ahead. "Cal, just tell me if you've gotten the report on that other man."

Cal pulled a sheet off the pile on his desk and handed it to her. "His name was Romero."

The heading on the stationery was that of the coroner's office. Willow glanced over the morbid details, the man's description, and the legal description of where the body was found, honing in on the bottom line.

PROBABLE CAUSE OF DEATH: A 38 MM PROJECTILE TO BASE OF SKULL CAUSING MASSIVE TRAUMA.

"Lonewolf didn't kill him," she said.

"That still leaves the Navajo boy."

"There's no evidence. No weapon, no motive. Lonewolf doesn't even know him."

"So you say. But there is the medicine bundle."

"There's no weapon in it. It belongs to Lonewolf."

"It's evidence, Willow, and you know it."

Willow heard a weakening in his resolve. "And you know you've got no probable cause. You can't keep him just because he retrieved his bundle from the crime scene."

"And what about the assault?"

Willow just stared at him.

"All right. He's all yours. I'm releasing him to your custody."

Willow reached for the pouch. The sergeant closed his hand around it. "The medicine bundle stays here. And keep him available, Willow. There's something funny about that renegade."

"I assure you, Cal, there's nothing funny about Lonewolf at all."

Lonewolf awoke and, in those first moments between dreams and the real world, he did not know where he was. A shaft of early-morning light—half beams, half mist—obscured the room and he thought he lay on a mat in Grey Feather's hogan.

He was home, with those who knew him. It had all been a bad dream. His mission, to find peace for the People burned within him, unobscured by any nightmarish distractions of a foreign world and a confusing woman.

At the thought of Willow, something deep inside him quickened, like the stirring of his soul.

In that instant, he returned fully to the present and the reality of the bars caging him. His brief respite ended, smothered in layers of frustration.

Lonewolf swung his legs off the cot; the tight muscles of his shoulder protested. He paced the cell, the way he had nearly all night, in a vain pursuit of answers. Why, if she wanted him in jail, had she defended him? And if she did not believe in his innocence, then why did she protect his bundle?

His thoughts, like his steps around the cell, only went in a circle.

Never, until today, had the sacred buckskin been out of his reach. He had to find a way to retrieve the deer-skin and all the sacred contents. Lonewolf raked a hand through his hair. He had lost control and now the deer-skin was gone.

Lonewolf thought of the spiritless deputy who had bested him. He either did not know the meaning of the things he had handled or he did not care. Lonewolf thought it was the latter. And here was a man of authority. From what Lonewolf could understand, these policemen now governed the People. Had the People forgotten that the stars govern their rules for living? What if the Holy Ones intended him to right this wrong, to set things back in order?

Lonewolf stopped pacing, stricken by the thought. That could not be his purpose. The task was too huge. Not to mention impossible—confined to a jail cell without his medicine bundle.

Again, his thoughts drifted to Willow. She and the boy were connected to his passage here. But how? And how did he find out when his one source, Willow, did not trust stargazers, denied her visions, and succeeded in caging him behind bars?

Lonewolf leaned his head against the bars. He had thought she believed him innocent. He now held in his hands the iron-bar proof of his misjudgment. Yes, his stealthy cougar was a worthy adversary.

He pictured her in her most familiar stance: green eyes wide and challenging. Layered on that image was one of her facing the sergeant in the cave, defending Lonewolf. And another, of her ordering Chavez off Lonewolf, and the pained look on her face at the scattered contents of his bundle.

Lonewolf pushed off from the bars and paced. Why did she defend him only to abandon him? The answer mattered more than he wanted to admit. From the moment she had confronted him in the cave, she had sparked to life something inside himself—something he recognized *within* himself. She had fought back with words and finally with strategy. The closest she had come to surrender was in his arms, taking the *datil* from his lips.

Suddenly, Lonewolf saw the answer to the circling question of whether she trusted his innocence or not. She was threatened by the visions they shared, and she sought to protect herself. He had to smile at her animal instincts—she had the heart of a warrior.

So, what would Willow do next? As in any battle, Lonewolf tried to think as the opponent. Would she leave him here? His gut clenched. He had to make her believe in the visions. He must make her believe in him. He *needed,* he realized with a start, for Willow to believe in him.

The sound of keys at the outer door interrupted Lonewolf's thoughts. His heart picked up as he anticipated Willow's face appearing in the hallway. Instead, an officer escorted a staggering Navajo man into the next cell.

"Sleep it off, old man," the officer said.

"Old man?" the Navajo yelled, and almost lost his balance. A thin, leathery arm shot out and grabbed a rail. "Who are you to call me 'old man'?" He spaced his words between breaths that reeked of alcohol.

The outer door shut on the officer without any response.

"No respect!" he yelled, then looked at Lonewolf and his face, softened with booze, drooped into a wan smile. "Hey, you . . . d'jou got a smoke?"

Lonewolf eyed the Navajo. The man was drunk, his

words laden with liquor. He weaved across the floor between the bars separating their cells.

"Or maybe . . . d'jou got a drink?"

"No. I have nothing."

"I bet'jou got some money. Right?" He tried to grin, but his face fell slack.

Lonewolf had seen his kind before, hanging around forts and trading posts, skulking like a timid, beaten dog. He wondered if this man received any spiritual guidance. "No, *Hastiin,* I do not have anything."

The *Diné* threw a hand up and made an insulting noise. "You have nothing! *I'm* the one who has nothing. All I want is a damn drink and I can't get that." He clung to the rails, his knuckles white, and stared at Lonewolf. "What do *you* care?" His tone, full of ridicule and suspicion, struck out at Lonewolf like a lance thrown at his feet. No Navajo would ask another if they cared, because it was a fact of life. Each one was responsible for the next—in their family, in their family's family, and ultimately to the whole clan. To ask was throwing that commitment in another man's face. Unless, of course, no one *did* care.

"Why do you drink, *Hastiin*?"

The man snorted, but his eyes softened, and Lonewolf got a glimpse of the Diné's soul—a black void echoing with anger. The sight weakened Lonewolf.

"What else do I have to do?" was the old man's only response.

Before Lonewolf could speak, the outer door opened. The air shifted and all of Lonewolf's senses came to attention. He knew, without looking, that Willow had walked in.

"Good morning," she said.

Lonewolf turned to her and smiled. His cougar had returned. He took in the welcome sight of her, noticing she wore the same clothes as yesterday. She looked no more rested than he felt and he longed to run a thumb over the faint shadows beneath her eyes. Instead, he greeted her. "*Yá'át'ééh, shi yázhi.*"

Willow nearly sighed. His quiet voice had the same effect on her as walking through her front door. Like coming home. She didn't stop to analyze the feeling, she just let it be and gazed at the man who evoked it.

How, in only two days, had this man become so much a part of her life—so familiar? From his long black hair, loose and tangled—like hers, she supposed—to his buckskin leggins, she knew him. Familiar, yet wild, like a wolf on the mesa. Except this wolf was caged. As he approached her, his long legs eating the ground silently, something inside her leapt. Not in fear, but in anticipation. He looked primitive and beautiful, perhaps even more so behind bars. Like something endangered.

"I've come to rescue you," she said.

"That will make twice."

"Yes, well, I'm not sure pulling Chavez off you or getting you out of jail equal a bullet in the shoulder. But I'm trying." She unlocked the cell and stood aside for Lonewolf to exit.

"Rescue him? What about me, Becenti?"

Willow registered the voice and a pit opened inside her. She looked in the next cell—at Manuelito's father—and smiled, though her stomach gripped. "Hello, Mr. Begay, I see you're visiting us again."

"This is no visit. Get me out of here." He shuffled to the bars and glared at Willow.

"You don't really want that," Willow said in a firm, gentle voice. "What you need is to sleep a while until you feel better."

"What I need is my son back."

His look of utter hatred choked Willow. His son lay dying—from what, no one knew. He should be with Manuelito, not here. But did he even remember Manuelito was in the hospital? In all Manuelito's eight years, how many days had his father been around? For all intents, Manuelito had been abandoned and the court agreed, giving Willow custody. But this was his father. What Willow wanted, more than anything, was for Manuelito to have a whole life, not one fractured by an absent father.

Willow walked to the bars and spoke evenly to the old man. "You're right, Mr. Begay. He does need a dad. Someone who'll teach him things. Someone who'll protect him."

"Protect him! From what?"

Willow almost screamed back, *From you!* She wanted to wipe the selfish look from his face and order him to *be* there for Manuelito. Didn't he care that this child was growing up without a father?

Old emotions constricted Willow's throat. She would be there for Manuelito. She could help him find his way into the white man's world. *He* wouldn't get lost like so many others. Like his own father. And he wouldn't face it alone, as she had.

She looked at the drunk beyond the bars and silently prayed he would listen. "Mr. Begay, you're not going to get your son back if you can't stay out of jail. The best thing you could do for Manuelito would be to get better and stop drinking."

He grabbed the bars with both hands and glared at her. "You can take your advice and go to hell, Becenti."

A hand at Willow's elbow led her from the holding area. She let Lonewolf lead the way out of the station as she struggled to get past the emotions that threatened to drown her. She couldn't dwell now on the pain Begay's words had caused, because if she did, she would only get tangled up in grief—his and hers.

She had to put the best face on what Lonewolf had just witnessed. She still had to ask him to help Manuelito, to at least take a look at him. What would be his answer after hearing those scathing accusations from the boy's own father?

Lonewolf broke the silence as they reached her jeep. "The boy, that is the one you care for? The one that is sick?"

Lonewolf felt her arm tense within his palm. "Yes," she said finally.

"And that man is his father?"

"Yes, that's Manuelito's father."

She walked to her side of the jeep and faced him over the top, her eyes swimming in sadness, yet not a drop spilled over her cheeks. Lonewolf knew, firsthand, the power of her love for the boy. And for all the father's words, Lonewolf had not gotten the message of love, but of anger. What *was* Willow's part with Manuelito?

"I did not steal his son, Lonewolf."

"Why do you say that, Willow?"

"Because of the way you're looking at me."

Willow slid into her seat and stared out the window, one hand on the rod separating the seats, though she made no move to bring the jeep to life. Lonewolf rested his arm across the back of her seat, his fingers within reach of her hair.

"Does he know the boy is sick?"

"I told him, but I don't know if he remembers." Her voice was full of unspent emotion. "He drinks so much . . ." Her voice trailed off.

Lonewolf stretched his fingers toward the braid. He wanted to loosen the plait, weave his fingers through the silky mass, draw her head toward his shoulder.

"You were right to take the boy, Willow. That man is not a father."

"But he is!" Her gaze flew to Lonewolf and he lost a breath at the grief in her eyes. "He is the father. He's also a drunk and unemployed. But he is the father. And if the world were right, he'd be with Manuelito. Manuelito needs a father who cares."

"He has you."

"Yes, he has me," she said, her eyes glistening with

resolve. With a start, Lonewolf saw that Willow's determination to help Manuelito matched Lonewolf's own to complete his purpose here.

"Will you tell me about the boy now, *shi yázhi*?"

"I came to the jail to tell you. In fact, I came to ask if you would see Manuelito."

She looked at him squarely, her eyes unwavering, yet her voice held doubt, as if she worried that he would say no. What she could not know was how much Lonewolf *needed* to see this boy—this child of their shared visions.

Taking his silence as hesitation, Willow gave up what little remained of her defenses. "He is the boy from the visions, Lonewolf."

She could not have anticipated his reaction. Another man, one who needed to hear he had been right, would have, at the very least, smiled with triumph. Lonewolf only held her gaze, his brown eyes deep, fathomless, and said, "Thank you."

Willow hated hospitals. She hated not being in control. Outside the hospital walls, she had the power, even if limited, to try to make things right. In here, she had to rely on someone else. A position she hated to be in.

A glance at Lonewolf told her he wasn't any happier about being in the hospital than she was. His eyes continually scanned the hallway, as if he half expected an ambush.

Willow wondered if he'd ever been in a hospital. After all, he had his own ways of healing. Which was what she was counting on.

When they reached the glass room housing Manuelito, Willow held out a hand to stop Lonewolf.

"There he is," she said quietly.

Lonewolf laid a hand on her shoulder and Willow reflexively tensed. No visions came, only a welcome spreading of warmth. She looked up and saw compassion in his eyes. But could he help? Every doctor she'd talked to had shown compassion, had become sympathetic. A few had even apologized for this act of nature they couldn't comprehend. They had all looked at Manuelito, but seen a *case*. She needed, desperately, for someone to *see* Manuelito, the boy with a life ahead of him.

"Tell me about him, *shi yázhi*."

The words were like keys to her heart. Emotion choked Willow's throat and she took a moment before speaking.

"It happened a week ago. It was night and we were walking to Grandfather's from the canyon. Suddenly, he just collapsed." She saw him, rigid on the ground, his fingers frozen grotesquely at his side. Willow felt a shudder grow in her belly and weaken her knees. Lonewolf's hand tightened on her shoulder and the sense of panic eased. "I grabbed a stick and shoved it between his teeth. It was all I could think to do. We were so far away from anywhere!"

Willow found herself focusing on Lonewolf's reflection in the window. He stared ahead, his eyes narrow, as if focusing on something far away. At his height, he could see over the vast array of machines which dwarfed Manuelito. So, she looked at Lonewolf as he looked at Manuelito. And she continued her story.

"I ran, carrying him, to my jeep and drove him to the clinic in Chinle. An ambulance brought him here. They've run all the tests. He doesn't have a history of seizures, no epilepsy. There's no aneurysm, no weird heart spasms."

Lonewolf's reflection stared back at Willow. Their gazes locked. As always, his eyes, so brown, so knowing, made her forget everything around her, as if he, alone, saw her standing there.

"And then, two days ago, he went into a coma."

"When we were in the canyon?"

"Yes." Then Willow added what had been eating away at her for those two days. "He went into the coma near the same time we met. In the cave."

She saw a flicker of something cross Lonewolf's eyes. Perhaps it was a reaction to the anger she knew shone in her own eyes—anger she hadn't quite conquered. And because she didn't want to deal with that now, but concentrate only on Manuelito, she turned from Lonewolf and opened the glass door.

Once inside, Willow knew immediately Manuelito had suffered another seizure. The sheets lay askew, the chair she'd slept in now faced the wall, as if hastily pushed out of the way. She took Manuelito's small hand in her own and bent close to whisper, "I'm here, Manny."

All at once, an alarm sounded on the EKG, a bell rang in the room, echoed by another at the nurse's station. Manuelito's body shook, his hand flapping within Willow's palms.

"Help! Someone!" Willow bent over Manuelito, trying to quiet his convulsions.

The door opened and shushed shut. Willow looked up to see Lonewolf cover the room in three strides.

"It's happening again! Get someone, please."

Instead, Lonewolf went to the other side of the bed and placed a hand on Manuelito's forehead. He reached to his side where his pouch usually hung.

"He doesn't have a fever! Get someone!"

Lonewolf kept his left hand on Manuelito's forehead and, with the other hand, pulled the sheet back past his chest. Another convulsion wracked the boy.

"What are you doing?"

"Be quiet," Lonewolf ordered.

Willow's gaze flew to him. "How dare you—"

"Find a way to turn off that noise."

"I'm getting a nurse."

"Please." He finally looked up from Manuelito. His

eyes begged her to act without questioning.

Without looking away—unable to take her gaze from Lonewolf—Willow flicked off the switch, as she'd seen Josie do many times. Then she watched the medicine man work.

Lonewolf had kept one hand on Manuelito's forehead. His other hand rested on the middle of the boy's chest. He leaned close to Manuelito and started to hum. Another spasm grabbed the boy, but this time it was more like a quiver passing through his body.

Willow stared, completely taken with the sight of Lonewolf bending close to Manuelito and chanting. She couldn't hear the words, and only a hint of the monotone reached her.

A different sight suddenly overwhelmed her. She stared at Lonewolf and saw the figure of her father, bending over a patient. She didn't know where the image had come from. She had no memory of watching him perform a ceremony. Yet she saw her father clearly, crouched on a dirt floor, chanting over an elder Navajo, the smell of sage and cedar heavy all around.

She heard a door open and the image evaporated. Two nurses blew into the room.

"When did the seizures start?" one nurse asked, all business, then she faltered a step at the sight of Lonewolf chanting to the boy.

"Just a minute or so ago," Willow said, her gaze also on Lonewolf. He had climbed onto the bed and now straddled Manuelito. His left hand was still on the boy's forehead and his right was pressed to Manuelito's chest.

Willow immediately noticed that Manuelito was calm. The seizure had stopped and his chest slowly rose and fell against the weight of Lonewolf's hand. Lonewolf had taken charge and the notion hit Willow with such force she almost backed away. He was in control, when it should be her.

"You'll have to move," the nurse said as she rounded

the bed. "Get the cardiac tray and the strap," she ordered the other nurse.

Lonewolf didn't answer, but he stopped chanting. With his left thumb, he gently raised one of the boy's eyelids, then the other.

Clanking metal preceded the other nurse pushing a cart ahead of her through the door.

"Sir! Get down from the bed. We have to strap him in." The first nurse glared at Lonewolf but got no reaction.

Lonewolf crouched close to the boy's ear and murmured in Navajo. Willow leaned in to hear what he said.

"Níká iishyeed."I will help you. As he climbed down from the bed, he said to the nurse, "He is fine, for now."

She quirked a brow at the other nurse, stepped in front of Lonewolf and proceeded to strap Manuelito to the bed.

"You do not need to do that."

"Sir, I'm going to have to ask you to leave so we can go about our job."

"But you do not understand."

"Officer Becenti?"

Willow barely heard the nurse. Because, for all their talking, they'd missed what she'd seen. Manuelito had smiled. She was sure of it, though the proof was now gone from his face.

No one would believe her. Except maybe . . . She looked at Lonewolf.

He stood in the corner shadows, legs braced apart, his hands clasped in front—a warrior sure of his skill, a healer sure of his power.

The world dissolved around her until all that remained were herself and Lonewolf and Manuelito. And she smiled.

NINE

The power was in his hands.

Willow stared at Lonewolf and saw him for the first time. She'd seen him as a murder suspect, a kidnapper, and a confused, delusional renegade. And when she'd felt the magic on his lips as he ministered to her shoulder, she'd known him as a healer.

But even that assumption had not been wholly correct. Any medicine man could conjure a potion for an ailment. At least, Willow assumed they could. She respected medicine men, but as a person would an elder. But how many medicine men could lay hands on a patient—a child whose body convulsed in seizures—and bring peace, even a smile? Excitement replaced the hollow hope Willow had been carrying in her heart. Lonewolf could help Manuelito. Where before, only a needle and drugs had managed the feat of calming Manuelito, Lonewolf had used only his hands.

Willow looked at those hands. In this frozen moment existing for only her, Manuelito, and Lonewolf—his hands seemed apart from him, radiating their own enchanted light, as if carrying a life unto themselves. In the way of shadows and light, she could see every detail: blunt fingernails—not manicured, but worn down—spoke of ability and persistence; his slender fingers, with broad knuckles, were confident, capable; and the large veins coursing from his wrists to his knuckles were testimony to a man who wielded strength with control.

Her gaze lifted, involuntarily, as if pulled by a magnet, to Lonewolf's eyes. He looked back at her, his gaze calm but assessing. Always alert, like a wolf in dangerous territory.

Unbidden, the memory replayed of Lonewolf leaning over her, cupping her head with one of those knowing hands, pointing to his eyes with his other and demanding her concentration. How could any person, any woman at least, defy that combination of strong hands and bold eyes?

A frisson of awareness shot through Willow—silent, yet powerful like the arrow from Lonewolf's bow. And in that instant, she knew why a deer froze before a hunter: it was the anticipation of the inevitable. Danger, laced with a keen sense of life, coursed through her. When she had slipped from appreciation of his powers to assessment of Lonewolf as a man, Willow didn't know. All she could have said was that the thought of being with him made her blood run hot.

And cold.

How could she be thinking of passion with Lonewolf when Manuelito's life might be at stake? With a brusque, scornful shake of her head, Willow broke the trance and her gaze with Lonewolf. With trained efficiency, she let her logical mind take over, study the facts. Yes, Lonewolf had calmed Manuelito. Between Lonewolf's talents and the doctors' skills, Manuelito had a better than fighting chance.

Willow suddenly remembered the specialist. "Is Dr. Voorman here?"

"No," the nurse said and moved brusquely between Willow and Lonewolf. "You both are going to have to leave."

Willow wouldn't be put off so easily. "I understand he ran tests on Manuelito two days ago. I'd like to see the report."

"If you'll just wait for me out in the hall, I'll see what I can do. Now, I have things to do." The nurse looked Lonewolf up and down. "Are you the medicine man?"

"Yes," Lonewolf said, without hesitation.

"You're pretty young for a medicine man."

Willow saw a flicker of amusement in Lonewolf's eyes.

The nurse turned her attention to Manuelito. "Well, you're not allowed in here."

"Why do you not allow medicine men?" Lonewolf's tone would've made warriors flinch. As it was, the nurse cocked a fist on her hip and stood her ground.

"Because you get in the way. And if you need to know more, you'll have to ask the doctor. I don't make the rules."

Willow held out her hand. "Lonewolf?"

He looked at her and Willow nearly stepped back from the fierce look in his eyes. She thought he might speak but then he simply took her hand and walked to the door.

When they reached the hallway, Willow pulled her hand loose. "Lonewolf, I need to talk to the doctor."

He gave a curt nod, but continued walking.

"Lonewolf! Don't you want to hear what he says?"

He looked over his shoulder. "I will be in the jeep."

What was the matter with him? He should want to read the report. He should want all the facts about a patient. Surely, even a powerful medicine man respected the laws of science. Why not take advantage of *all* the experts?

She stared as the swinging doors closed behind Lonewolf. Did he think he could just take over? And just what would she do if that was his plan?

She was a practical person, she told herself. She'd listen to the devil, if he could make Manuelito better. All in all, she considered, that's what she might be doing.

* * *

Lonewolf hummed an ancient chant to calm himself as he walked through the hospital. He ignored the curious looks of the people he passed. His thoughts were focused on that night, twenty-two years ago, when he had been touched by the celestial spirits. Lonewolf knew, without a doubt, Manuelito was experiencing the same body-wracking pain he had endured. He also knew, with equal certainty, the boy would die if the proper ceremony were not administered. And soon.

Already, the boy was almost beyond reach. It had taken all of Lonewolf's concentration to coax Manuelito from the numbing blackness. He knew how terrifying the sharp light of the celestials could be. If not for Grey Feather's wisdom and power, Lonewolf himself would never have survived.

Now *he* was the one to deliver the next Starway Shaman. Except the last boy who had laid his life in Lonewolf's hands had died. His son's small face, distorted by terror and pain from the Ute's arrow, leapt to Lonewolf's mind before he could protect himself. Emotions, as strong as when he had found Red Shell, stampeded through him: the violent revenge he had wanted to exact, the hollowing grief, and finally, forever, the guilt. He closed the door on the hole in his heart before the pain swallowed him, but not before his soul uttered the word "failure."

He would not fail this time. He was the Starway Shaman. And soon, Manuelito would own the same powers.

How much time Lonewolf had, was the question. He had to retrieve his medicine bundle. Willow would help with that.

Or would she? In Grandfather's own words, Willow did not trust the stars. Thinking Lonewolf was merely curing an ailment was one thing; what would be Willow's reaction when she learned who Manuelito was to become? Would she help at all?

Willow emerged from the hospital and Lonewolf

watched her walk across the grass toward the jeep, her thick braid keeping graceful time to the subtle swing of her hips. He thought of her beneath him when he had given the medicine. Willow had never mentioned that vision and yet he had felt the passion rise within her.

He wondered now about the vision. Had it been Corn Flower or had it been Willow? There had been no face to the female form, only intense desire let loose in a rush, like mountain snow melt suddenly flooding a desert arroyo. He knew she had felt it. And he wondered, as she neared the jeep, her cougar eyes keen on him, whether he could make her feel that way again.

Willow slid in beside him and looked at him a moment before she spoke.

"What you did back there. That was incredible."

"I only acted out of . . . habit."

"I want to thank you. What he was going through was terrible."

"I calmed him down."

Willow shifted in her seat and faced him squarely. "No, you did more than that. It was as if you reached into his consciousness and quelled his fears."

"I gave him a chant to sing in the darkness," Lonewolf said simply.

Willow studied Lonewolf. "Can you bring him out of the coma?"

Her directness threw Lonewolf off balance, though he knew his face held no emotion. This was the job he had been sent for. This was his purpose here and he felt the power of the celestials surge through him. Was this the time to tell her? Should he take the chance?

"Willow, we have to talk."

"Just tell me if you think you can help."

Lonewolf raked a hand through his hair. How did he begin?

"What did the doctor report say, *shi yázhi*?"

"Nothing, basically. He calls the seizures grand mal."

She gazed out the front window of the jeep. "He doesn't know what's wrong."

"And the specialist?"

She looked at Lonewolf and he had to steel himself from the frustration in her eyes. "His report isn't in yet. Either he's lazy, or too busy, or doesn't know. None of which is an excuse. He's a professional, damn it, the best. He should act like one!"

Lonewolf searched her stormy eyes. Flecks of brown sparked within the green, like fire in juniper. If she would give half the energy to her seeing powers that she spent on logic, the stars in the heavens would be outmatched. If she tried, she could even see what was in his eyes, what he was thinking.

Abruptly, Willow looked away from him and stared out the front window. Like any cougar, Willow did not like staring games. Nor did cougars like surprises. And what Lonewolf knew about Manuelito would be, he knew, past whatever Willow could imagine.

He sighed inwardly and chose his words carefully.

"A special ceremony will bring Manuelito from the darkness."

"Then let's do it." She opened her door and put a foot on the pavement.

"It's not that simple, Willow."

She sank to the seat and faced him. "Do you know the ceremony?"

"Yes."

"Then what's stopping you? Please, Lonewolf. I'm willing to try anything."

Lonewolf wondered if she truly meant that. By all that was Holy, he longed to tell her where he really came from. Her eyes challenged him to tell the truth, but she did not believe in the *Ha'tanii*. She did not even believe in her own powers. The life of the boy, the next Starway Shaman, now rested with a woman who feared her own powers. Perhaps he could push her toward those powers.

"He is waging a battle in here." Lonewolf placed his hand on her chest and was immediately sorry. He felt her pulse quicken beneath his fingers; her eyes widened and her mouth fell partly open. Her instant response to him was unmistakable.

"In his chest?" she murmured.

"In his heart."

"What . . . what do you mean?"

Her gaze had not wavered from his. In fact, she had not moved a muscle. Lonewolf knew he should break the contact, concentrate on Manuelito. He had not evoked any visions, only passion.

"His body is waging a battle. The battle is between Father Sky and Mother Earth. If they are not appeased, they will tear Manuelito apart. He will scatter like so many stars in the sky."

With that, he gestured with his hand, as if throwing stones in the air. When he looked back at Willow, she was staring out the front window again.

"And the ceremony is the cure?" Her voice sounded as distant as whatever she stared at.

He finally said what he knew she would not want to hear. "The stars will tell me the way, *shi yázhi*."

At the mention of stars, Lonewolf saw fire ignite in her eyes and, just as quickly, she extinguished it. She would not argue with him. Not yet.

"Of course," she said, finally.

She looked at him a moment longer then, without another word, Willow started up the jeep and pulled away from the hospital. She attacked the hard roads with fury and speed. And Lonewolf smiled. Perhaps she *would* try anything to help Manuelito.

The hard road changed to rutted dirt. Willow jammed the jeep into gear and roared up the dirt road to her house. She hit every hole in the road with force, with some violent need to jar loose the unsettling mood enveloping her.

She'd known it would come to this. She'd known from the moment Lonewolf told her he was a stargazer that they would be at odds. Now, Manuelito was dying and the only person who offered a cure was a damn stargazer. Like her father. She had vowed never to mix beliefs with reality.

Except, when she'd made that vow, she had never met anyone like Lonewolf. A stargazer who turned her world inside out. She had to conquer the feelings he evoked. Before yesterday, she'd been able to repress, even deny, the visions. Two days ago, she thought stargazers were hopeless dreamers.

But Lonewolf was not a dreamer. His chiseled face knew life's rough hand. When his dark, fathomless eyes held her gaze Willow knew a relentless force was at work. She was drawn to him with the same force that warned her to keep her distance. With only a small push, she could lose herself in his gaze.

Willow slammed the jeep to a stop in a swirl of dust. She had said she would try anything and she hadn't lied. She needed Manuelito back. Even if that meant staring at the stars all night. But she would *not* trust her feelings to a stargazer.

Willow threw open her door. "Coming?"

Without waiting for an answer, she walked the brick path to her small adobe and unlocked the wooden door. She shed her backpack and sat on the hallway bunko. She dropped one boot on the terrazzo floor and wondered, once again, how bright this was. Not that she'd had much choice. Lonewolf didn't belong in jail, behind bars, next to drunks. She couldn't have slept, thinking of him on that hard bench. Whether she'd be any more comfortable with him under the same roof was another matter.

A shadow fell across her. Lonewolf filled the doorway. The sun, setting at his back, threw him in darkness. Willow couldn't see his face, let alone his expression.

Her heart skipped a beat, as if in jeopardy for its safety.

She needed distance. Distance from Lonewolf and the feelings he evoked in her. The man had a way of simultaneously threatening her beliefs and driving her passions. Either way, she wasn't in control, and she didn't like that.

Willow pulled off her other boot and threw it on the tiled floor where it slid nearly to Lonewolf.

"You can come in, you know."

He closed the door behind him, but moved no farther into the room.

"Willow, why are we here?"

"You're in my custody, remember? No relatives nearby. No address. No phone. Where else would I take you?"

She walked into the kitchen and pulled open the refrigerator door, effectively cutting Lonewolf out of sight. *Some dinner, a bath, a good book, and bed. That's what I need.* She took a deep breath and counted to ten.

She rummaged through the refrigerator and came up with enough vegetables to make the bag of noodles she had more interesting. From the freezer, she pulled a bag of green chilies she'd prepared. Her arms full, she elbowed the freezer door shut, turned, and came up hard against Lonewolf. His scent, all male and somewhat primitive, enveloped her. Her knees weakened at the assault.

She kept her eyes at his chest, focused on the pattern in the flannel. His hands closed on her shoulders.

"Willow, we must talk."

"Not now, please."

"Now. Look at me." His hand caressed her jaw, moved to her chin and tilted her head so her gaze met his. Her heart pounded at the intensity in his eyes.

"I will help Manuelito, *shi yázhi*. You must trust me."

"Lonewolf, I . . ." She couldn't find the words, not

with his eyes on her. She glanced at the counter, as if searching a place to put down the food.

"Let me make dinner, okay?"

Lonewolf's hands dropped and the heat he had generated dissipated. Willow stared at the counter, not seeing it. She shook her head and set the vegetables in the sink, and turned on the water.

"We'll eat, we'll be calm. Then we'll talk. Okay?"

She slid a knife from its holder and sliced some tomatoes. She heard Lonewolf take a few steps out of the room.

"Why don't you call your family in Abiquiu?" she said over her shoulder, striving for normalcy. "You can use the phone on the table beside the couch."

"They will not be there."

"Oh, are they on vacation?" She glanced at Lonewolf, and was instantly sorry. He looked ready to explode.

"I have not seen them for a long time." His controlled tone contradicted the flash of pain she glimpsed in his eyes. Willow wanted to retreat from what was obviously a sore subject.

"Look, why don't you turn on the television? We can catch the news. This won't take me long." She waved the knife over the mound of vegetables.

Lonewolf raked a hand through his hair as if fighting for restraint. Suddenly, he turned and strode from the kitchen straight for the front door.

"I will be outside."

Willow washed and sliced vegetables—absentmindedly pushing them around the cutting board. Her eyes were on Lonewolf. She could see him through her kitchen window, leaning against the corral fence. Bandit loped over from across the field for some free affection and nuzzled his arm.

Willow almost called out a warning against the horse's reputation for nipping. Not that she'd have been heard through the windowpane. And she soon saw that it wouldn't have mattered. Lonewolf dug his hands into the horse's black mane and buried his head at Bandit's forehead. Remarkably, Bandit complied and didn't bite or pull his head back. In fact, though she couldn't be sure from this distance, Bandit seemed to lean toward Lonewolf, as if lending support.

Lonewolf climbed the rails and walked on the other side. Bandit loped alongside him, rubbing against him almost like a puppy.

Suddenly, Lonewolf straightened his arm to Bandit's back, took one step back from the horse, and in one leap and a roll of his shoulder against Bandit, he landed on top of the horse. Just like an Indian on the big screen. The watermelon sunset cast horse and rider as a single silhouette.

Bandit took off across the desert pasture, with Lonewolf clutching his mane, his long legs hugging the horse's belly. He looked so natural; riding bareback, his black hair flowing behind him. Wild. Primitive. Willow wouldn't have been surprised if he'd raised one arm in a war whoop.

She watched mesmerized. Maybe this was his way of driving out his personal demons. Some people got in their cars, others exercised themselves into a sweat. Lonewolf rode. Hard.

They circled the pasture, and Willow drained the noodles. They loped down the middle, and Willow mixed the vegetables and noodles together. Lonewolf dismounted at the fence, and Willow added the cream and green chilies to the mixture.

She walked outside just as Lonewolf jumped from the rails and started across her yard. His long strides ate up the ground. Willow felt an odd pull low inside. For a moment she wished she were welcoming him home. Her warrior. His long hair blowing, his eyes keen on her. He would grab her and sweep her inside.

He drew near and she cleared her throat. "You ride well," she said, quietly.

"You have a good horse. Fast. But different from the ones . . ."

His voice trailed off and he looked over her shoulder as if searching for the right words.

"Probably smaller," she offered. "Paints don't get as big as quarters. But he's a good size for me."

"Yes, I see he is meant for you. Full of spirit and drive." He looked down at her and smiled. In the light from the kitchen window she could see small creases pinch the corners of his eyes. The grooves alongside his mouth deepened. She wanted to trail a finger in one and test its depth. The wayward thought brought her up short and she turned back to the house, trying to dam another flood of emotions. Emotions she neither wanted nor needed.

"Dinner is ready," she said over her shoulder.

He caught her arm and stopped her. "You are angry again?"

"No, just hungry," she murmured. "And the food's getting cold."

He backed away from her. "Go ahead, then." He stood tall and straight, his face serious.

"You're not coming?"

"I must begin the fast."

"But I thought you said you'd just come off a fast? Why another?"

"Fasting clears the head." She could see in the dim light that his eyes were somber.

"I can see why there aren't many stargazers."

Lonewolf quirked a brow and she continued. "They end up starving themselves to death."

"I have to speak to the stars again," he said.

She knew, then, what his purpose was.

"You're stargazing for Manuelito, aren't you?"

"Yes."

A breeze picked up and she clasped her arms to her. Lonewolf reached out a finger and tucked strands of her hair behind her ear. He let his hand rest at the nape of her neck. His heat circled through her, warming her, drawing together every fiber of her being into one, pulsing cord.

"You can do it without your medicine bundle?" she asked, trying to stay on the subject. But her eyes couldn't leave his and what she saw fueled the fire building within her.

"I do not know. I have always had my bundle before. But I have to try." Though his tone brooked no argument, his voice sounded husky.

"You're doing this for Manuelito." She knew she repeated herself, but her mind wasn't functioning fully. What held Willow's attention was his thumb, moving in circles just below her ear. She felt her defenses relax. She wanted more than his hand on her neck. She wanted to feel his lips against hers, as before.

Willow's gaze fell to his mouth.

"Yes, for Manuelito. And for more, much more."

She watched his lips move and felt herself lean in. The spell was nearly spun.

"Do you believe now, little one?"

"Do I . . ." Suddenly, Willow realized his question and how foolish she'd been. "I believe you know how to spin magic, Lonewolf." She tried to take a step back from Lonewolf, but his hand tightened at her neck.

"So you are still afraid."

"Not afraid," she protested. "Just . . ."

"How do you feel about me?"

Heat spread from his fingers through her neck, down her back, like a trail of warm water until her spine tingled. He wanted an honest answer and all she could think was that he was not the right one for her. She didn't need another stargazer in her life.

"Don't waste your time, Lonewolf." Willow ducked away from Lonewolf's grasp.

"Ah, little one, time is a funny thing. I am not sure we have any choice in the matter."

TEN

His deep voice drifted on the air and settled between them. Willow's throat constricted. She hadn't come out to argue with him. She didn't want to leave mad. She hated unresolved emotions.

Willow waited a moment, hoping he would change his mind, then turned and walked back to the house. She took one look at the pasty noodles and limp vegetables floating in cold cream sauce and turned off the kitchen light.

Fasting one night wouldn't hurt her, either. She could use a clearer head. She went to the bathroom and ran the water. As the tub filled, she undid the tie at her braid and loosened the plaits, then sank into the tub and adjusted the faucets with her toes.

Dust from the last two days floated off her body and made swirling patterns on the surface. She trailed a finger through the water.

"This dust is from the first cave," she mumbled. "This is from the Four Hole Site."

The patterns broke apart and rejoined. Willow circled a finger around one and sent it spinning. "This dust is from the cliff, the first night." *From the kiss,* she thought to herself. She'd lain in the dirt, taken medicine from Lonewolf. From his mouth. The vision of Lonewolf and the other woman flooded over her.

She forced her head back under the surface and let the water cover her face, fill her senses. She emerged in a cascade of water.

The vision was gone and so were the patterns. But

the unsettled feeling inside her remained. She couldn't deny her body was drawn to Lonewolf.

Who wouldn't be? she thought with a smile. He was Hollywood's picture of the quintessential renegade. She hadn't been out of the action so long that she didn't recognize a great male specimen when she saw it.

She wished that was all there was to it. Mere attraction she could handle and walk away from. But what Lonewolf evoked from her went deeper than desire, even deeper than passion. Just his presence made her question what she believed.

She pictured him, beyond the wall alone in the darkness. How long would he stay there? How long would he go without food? All for Manuelito.

He truly believes in the power of the stars. The thought brought goose bumps to her flesh.

And what is it I believe? That stargazers have no powers? It was absurd for her to argue that anymore. She had witnessed too much.

And her father had had powers. She still met people, older Navajo, who quietly told her stories, their eyes shining with respect, of how he had healed them. The old familiar feeling of anger gripped her stomach. If he had been so powerful, then why had he died? Why hadn't the stars helped him, too?

No, the stars could not be counted on. Like Navajo gods, they too were mischievous and sometimes unreliable. Not to be trusted.

Except, maybe, just this one time, she could hope? If anyone could bring the stars in line, it would be Lonewolf. He knew what he wanted and he would do what he had to do. Sometimes when she looked at him, she could almost see her ancestors—the ones Grandfather would talk about. The Lords of the Land. Lonewolf was unlike any Navajo, any man, she had ever met.

Willow let the water drain from the tub and pushed the tab for the shower. If she had any sense, she'd make it cold and drive some sense into herself. She scrubbed shampoo into her hair, ruthlessly pulling at the tangles. With every yank, she cursed herself. *Damn the confusion!*

Truth was, not only her body was drawn to him, but her instincts, too.

Lonewolf searched the sky for Coyote Star and Slender First One. He had given up on finding Dilyehe, which hung near the horizon.

He pushed off the ground and paced to another spot. He had already moved twice, each time taking him farther from the house. Still he could not see the star patterns. The earth shone too bright.

It was the lights from the houses, from the towns, from the roads. So many lights that the magic of the stars was lost.

This world had so *much*—so many people, buildings, roads, so many things! But his world had more and he suddenly missed it desperately.

Every fiber of him yearned for the world he knew, the People he had been born to guide. People he might never see again. All because of the life of this boy.

Lonewolf's steps faltered at the magnitude of the power of the celestial spirits. They had chosen this child and delivered Lonewolf from the past to accomplish their mission.

They had deemed this boy's life more important than whatever Lonewolf would accomplish in his own time. For the first time in his life, Lonewolf hated the spirits and their cruel manipulation. What right had they to choose certain lives over others, to *condemn* the *Diné* who fought, as he stood here?

Lonewolf could not let that happen. He *would* not let that happen. But first he would fulfill his birthright and guide Manuelito through the passage.

This time he closed his eyes. He stared at the sky

through his eyelids, calling to the spirits to guide him. He tried to picture the star placement. Instead, Willow's image filled his mind's eye—her black hair loose, hanging over her shoulders, her green eyes flashing. She looked straight at him.

He wondered if Willow knew what a temptation she was. But, even that, he knew, was not what obsessed him. She was a warrior like him. What would she think of him if she knew he was a warrior from the past? What myths did she believe of her long-dead ancestors?

He shook his head at his musings. She did not even *see* him. He was not real to her. No more real than the *Ha'tanii.*

But he could *make* her believe. He could lay her palm against the sacred scar on his chest. He would hug her close, force the doubt from her, erase her fears. He would make the warrior within her join with him, believe in him.

His insides tightened.

As always, he knew without looking that she was near. She stood just behind him, maybe ten feet away. His mind cleared and his senses came alive.

He listened to her breathe. Her musky scent, now freshened with soap, wafted to him on a breeze and his heart quickened. Yet, she did not move.

"Come closer, *Naa glen ni baa.* I will not bite."

He smiled at her startled rustle. After a moment, she appeared at his side.

"How did you learn my warrior name?" she demanded.

He looked up and his earlier image of her paled in comparison to reality. Her shining hair hung free over her shoulders and past the curve of her breasts. Wrapped from her neck to her ankles in some white, fuzzy garment, she looked swaddled and warm. And ready to attack.

"I heard it in the vision. The one of you as a child

in the canyon,'' he said softly. ''She Who Rises Up and Fights. It suits you. I once knew a child with that name,'' he added.

She stood still, staring at him—her eyes, as always, unwavering. Then she looked to the horizon, as if she had made a decision.

''That was my Great-great-great-grandmother's name.''

Lonewolf's breath caught in his throat. ''Who did she fight?''

''Kit Carson.''

The air around crashed down with the weight of all time. He could not speak to stop her. And her words flowed.

''It was the winter of eighteen sixty-three and Carson's campaign had penetrated deep into *Dinehtah*. Carson knew the Navajo. He had been a friend. With his great knowledge of the *Diné,* he set into motion the systematic extermination of every Navajo. The warrior Black Horse led several skirmishes against the soldiers, but he could not stop the relentless pursuit by the army.

''Carson kept the Navajo in constant movement across *Dinehtah*. They had to abandon their crops, their livestock, their homes. They slept in caves and crevices, never staying longer than a few days in one place.

''He wasn't interested in captives. Any Navajo seen was shot on sight. Mothers suffocated their hungry, crying babies so that the family would not be discovered and slaughtered by the patrols. Close on their heels, Carson destroyed everything. He torched the hogans, butchered their cattle and sheep. He choked them off.''

Willow paced the ground before Lonewolf. And though he could not move, he was with her, in the canyon, with his People, the horror so real he could hear the cries.

''*Naa glen ni baa* was only eight years old. She fled

with her clan relatives to *Tse-ewa*. You know Fortress Rock in de Chelly?''

Lonewolf nodded. He could not speak. His insides felt like one big knot. He did not know if he could stand any more. But his heart made him listen.

''Navajo warriors dragged logs, eighty to ninety feet long, from the top of the canyon down to *Tse-ewa*. They made pole ladders, scaled the eight-hundred-foot rock, and hauled food, water, and supplies to the top. Then they pulled the logs behind them.

''*Naa glen ni baa* was a strong-willed child. She would wander the top of the rock and search for ways to get down. One day, she saw a patrol approaching the rock. She hid behind a boulder and watched in terror as the soldiers struggled up the craggy face, using crevices as footholds. If she ran to the others, she would be seen. And she knew better than to yell.

''As quietly as she could, she gathered rocks and sticks, anything she could throw, all the time watching the patrol get closer and closer to the top. She waited until they were near the top, then stood over them and hurled the stones down. The first soldiers to fall were too surprised to even pull their guns. But one at the rear took aim and hit *Naa glen ni baa*. Still, she kept throwing things at the soldiers.

''The warriors heard the shots and ran to *Naa glen ni baa*. They found her standing like a statue, a rock raised in one hand. The bodies of ten soldiers littered the side of Fortress Rock.''

She looked at him, her eyes too bright, a thin smile on her face.

''Other patrols came. The warriors fought them off in the same way. But there were always more. Carson himself camped at the rock and starved them out. He knew their food and water couldn't last forever. Finally, they were forced to surrender.''

''And *Naa glen ni baa?*'' Lonewolf managed to ask.

"She lived a long life and is buried on top of Fortress Rock." Willow looked at Lonewolf but he could barely see past his grief.

He had known Carson would be merciless. He had *seen* the tortured *Dinehtah* in his visions. And his vow to save the People still lived. Except they were dead, slaughtered. And he had no more existence in this time than he had in the past.

Lonewolf took Willow in his arms and pressed her hard to his chest. He sought consolation, something human, someone *real* to cling to.

Too fast, his senses swam with her: her cool hair, still slightly damp and full of her scent; her warm cheek, also wet with tears. He felt her heart beating against his ribs and he needed, right then, for her to know him.

He lowered his mouth and captured her lips. A shudder passed through her and into Lonewolf. His blood surged at the knowledge she wanted him. He pulled her to him, fighting to keep control of the urgent need to prove his own existence.

His hands slid up her shoulders and into her hair. Its silkiness caressed his fingers. He drove his hands deeper, pulled her closer, but he could not get enough. He touched his tongue to her lips and she moaned. That small sound of acceptance undid him.

He circled her back with an arm and they fell back to the earth as one. Mother Earth. Ground his People had walked. They had lived, died, fighting for their earth. He had lived. He was not a myth!

He slid his hands beneath Willow's robe. Found cotton. She arced toward him, the movement alive with passion. He battled the cloth sheathing her neck to ankle, shoving it higher, until her legs, warm, smooth, tensed beneath his fingers.

Words pounded in his head, in time with the hammering of his heart. He was alive. She would believe.

He slid his hands up her thighs, encircled her small

waist—his thumbs could almost touch across her belly. He worked his hands up her back, kneading her spine, the pressure pushing her closer, harder against him.

A groan escaped Willow. The sensation of Lonewolf's roughened palms brought her pulse to her throat. The hands he healed with, the hands he had laid on Manuelito and quelled his fears, those same hands elicited waves of pleasure within her. A corner of Willow's mind warned against unwanted visions, but she was past caring.

He inched higher, his thumbs brushed her nipples, once, then over and over. Involuntarily, shamelessly, she arced, seeking more, each graze of his thumbs hardening her. Then his mouth covered one nipple, and Willow thought she would die. As if she were his bow, she felt a cord draw tight within her, pulling deep in her abdomen, to the core of pleasure between her legs. He circled and licked and the bow string tautened as if he strummed her inside.

His magic enveloped her, coursed through her. And she spiraled with it, lost to the power in his hands.

Then cool air brushed her breasts, where his warm mouth had been. She opened her eyes to see Lonewolf shed the flannel shirt. Daggers of moonlight cut across his lean, strong chest. Long, midnight hair whipped over his shoulders. Every bit of him powerful, primitive, and beautiful.

Willow ran her hands up his naked chest. His nipples stood taut—iron disks against a sea of bronze. She leaned forward and traced each with her finger then sought one with her mouth, as he had done. She felt an answering spasm within Lonewolf. His taste, so unique, was like a new fruit, just discovered. Her whole body leapt to the experience, each of her senses seeking to detect the secret ingredient. She ran her hands around his back and pressed him closer, letting her lips and tongue savor.

Sun-drenched canyons and night breezes, juniper and cedar smoke. Earth and sky. She trailed her tongue to his neck, tasting, exploring.

Lonewolf's breath caught and Willow raised her head to meet his gaze. The moon and the stars. That's what Willow saw in his eyes. Dark and fathomless, they reflected the night sky—full of mystery and power.

As always, she could not look away from him. His eyes commanded her, stroked her, as he undid the leather lacing at the top of his leggins.

Willow's blood surged. His arousal pressed at her abdomen, kindling her heat. But his eyes stoked the fire. She felt his gaze deep within her, impaling her to the spot.

This man, like no other she'd known, knew himself and what he wanted. Right now, his mission was in his eyes. And it was her.

Lonewolf bent over her and his long hair lightly swept her chest. A thousand arrows of desire shot through her. He lifted and peeled off his deerskin. Willow touched him, felt his urgent pulse in her palm. Warm passion pooled within her.

Stars flashed inside Lonewolf. Constellations swirled. His whole body surged like a comet hurtling through darkness.

They fought for the same purpose. Hands gliding, breath panting, legs entwined. Warrior to warrior. Man and woman. Mother Earth below. Father Sky above. They throbbed to the beat of an ancient drum.

Willow shivered. This time Lonewolf felt a slight breeze on his back. He pulled the robe around her, grabbed his shirt and leggins, and, in one movement, lifted her in his arms. A strap from her robe floated free and caressed his leg with each stride.

Willow reached a hand to his face and traced the line

at his mouth, setting his insides on fire along the path of her finger.

"I knew I could talk you out of stargazing tonight," she murmured.

"Oh, I saw stars."

"You did?"

"Yes. And I plan to see more right now."

Lonewolf held her close and she snuggled to his chest. He walked without feeling the ground, with only a sense of wonder at the woman who fit within his arms. When she had taken him within her, closed around him with tight need, she had given him more than her desire, her passion. She had given him an anchor in this time.

A strange feeling of security passed over him—and a surge of pride at the miracle that she was drawn to him. She was strong, not fragile. Unlike many, she thrived on the truth.

He would miss her.

The cool night air settled on his shoulders and he hugged Willow closer. But the chill settled in his belly. He would return to his time and have only the memory of this warrior.

And what would she know of him? What would she remember? The coldness spread and gnawed at the pit inside him—at the place he buried his fears. She could not know he was a failure, a warrior of no tribe, a medicine man distrusted by his People and his powers manipulated by the stars.

Just as he had manipulated Willow. He had used her to prove his own existence—to prove he was alive. He had succeeded. He had never felt so vital. But that would fade, just as he would become only a dim memory for Willow after he left.

Once again, he would be alone. As it should be, as it was meant to be, he told himself and forced his heart to harden.

Lonewolf walked down the hallway toward the last

door. He crossed the threshold to her bedroom, strode to the bed, and settled Willow on the covers.

Willow looked at the man leaning over her, naked, vulnerable, and her heart surged. A warrior. Her warrior. With the eyes and hands of a healer. In those eyes, though, she thought she saw sadness, a flicker of pain. What could he be thinking, when all she felt was something extraordinary, as if a lost piece of her had been reclaimed.

She laid a gentle hand on Lonewolf's cheek and felt his quick breath.

"Why are you sad, Lonewolf?"

His eyes widened, then he looked away.

"I am fine, *shi yázhi,*" he said, tonelessly.

"You don't sound fine." Willow levered partway up and studied him, her hand tracing his stern jaw. "At least not as fine as I feel."

He stilled her hand, then brought it to his lips and kissed her palm. He held it there for one beat, two. Instead of warmth, anxiety rose within Willow.

"What is it, Lonewolf? Please tell me."

She pressed his cheek with her fingertips, urging him to look at her, to open up.

What would a man be feeling bad about? Her anxiety narrowed, focused, pointing like a laser, toward one thing. She thought of the first vision, the woman. And she knew.

"You're married." At the words, she withdrew her hand from his face.

"Married? What made you . . ."

Willow looked away, not wanting to meet his eyes. She didn't want to see the lie there. Lonewolf framed her face in his hands and forced her to look at him.

"You saw the vision with me."

"Yes. But that's not the point, is it? Are you married? Just tell me the truth."

He pulled her close and smothered her mouth with

his. "No, *shi yázhi,*" he whispered between kisses. "I am not married." He drew back and smiled, the light reaching his eyes. "That was you."

His words stunned her. "That wasn't me, Lonewolf. I hadn't . . . I mean, we hadn't . . ." She stopped. "There was a fire," she said, settling it.

"Your logic does not have all the answers. The vision came from our hearts, little one. It was colored by who we are, by where we come from."

"But I have never—" She cut herself off before admitting her experience did not include passion oblivious to hard ground. Until tonight, she corrected herself. "We had never met," she said.

"Perhaps our hearts knew each other."

"I don't believe in destiny," she said quietly, not wanting to ruin the moment.

"Yes, I know."

There it was, the sadness again. Before she could think of what to say, Lonewolf rose and, without a glance at her, began to put his leggins on. He slipped the deerskin up his long legs, over taut muscles, including one prominent muscle. Willow's mouth went dry.

Lonewolf laced the leather and bent over her for his shirt. Willow tried to see his face, but his hair shielded his eyes. She felt the mood slipping away—from intimacy to something estranged.

"I am sorry," he said, and turned to leave.

"For what?" Suddenly, she couldn't stand the nontalk, the backing away from the subject. She would make Lonewolf talk. "What are you sorry for, Lonewolf? For making love?"

"*Do tah!*" His exclamation matched the fierceness in his eyes. She registered the pain in his eyes and for a second wondered about it. But her anger was too great.

"Don't tell me to stop! Because I'm not sorry." With each word, his eyes glowed more fiercely. The anger flooded her, and the words flowed. "I made love to you—the man—strong, intelligent, powerful. Do you have a problem with that?"

"I am not who you think I am, *shi yázhi,*" he said.

"Then who are you, Lonewolf?"

He stared at her, his eyes black velvet, impenetrable. "*Shi'éi'táádoo biniyé hida nisin,*" he said, and left.

Never mind. Willow stared at the empty door, the sadness in Lonewolf's voice still hanging in the air. What had happened in the short time it had taken to get from the outside to the bed? One minute he was promising her stars, the next his eyes were colder than the night.

Idly, she fingered a portrait of her and Manuelito. It sat on her bedside table, the last thing she looked at at night. Had the picture reminded Lonewolf of his promise to help Manuelito? But why not just say that?

No, it was something else. Something he didn't want to talk about. But what? Something their passion had brought to the surface?

He was right. She *didn't* know him. What kind of secrets did a stargazer have? The thought startled her from her musings and Willow realized she hadn't thought of Lonewolf as a stargazer when they made love—but as a warrior. Funny that she would have forgotten.

She pictured him now and saw him surrounded by stars. She waited for the accompanying anger she always felt. But it didn't come. Instead, she saw the beauty and peace. Is this how her mother had felt about her father? But then why had she—

Willow cut off the thought with violent ease. She paced from the bed and settled in the chair by her window. Stars spread across the sky. The same stars Lonewolf watched.

Whatever Lonewolf's secret, she would discover it. But if she couldn't find the answer through logic, that left only her emotions. Could she trust them when right now all she wanted were Lonewolf's arms of steel around her?

Lonewolf left and kept on going. He followed the darkness, leaving the earth shine behind. He walked until the stars filled the blackness above. If only he had someplace to go, he would have gone there.

But there was no escape. No matter how fast he walked, he could not leave behind her musky scent. No matter how tightly he briefly closed his eyes, he could not wipe out the sight of pain in Willow's face.

But another moment with her and the hardness protecting his heart would have cracked. The words from her mouth had flowed through him without warning like music from a flute. Every fiber of his being had responded.

He had no doubt he would be sent back to his time. He had been brought here merely to right a wrong, to reclaim the balance from the past for the future. When his mission was done, the spirits would send him home. And he would have to leave Willow.

Better to leave her now. Except, of course, that was impossible. Because to leave her, he would have to abandon Manuelito.

Lonewolf suddenly stopped in his tracks.

He was trapped. With no way back and the path forward leading to ultimate despair.

For how long he stood there, Lonewolf had no idea. Eventually, he sat down and raised his gaze to the stars. Jet black surrounded him. Earth and sky were as one. He was alone with the stars, perched on a black cloud with millions of lights dancing just for him.

For a while, he just lay there, not really seeing the stars or their patterns. But he could not ignore their beauty for long. Like demanding children, the stars twinkled and teased. Some shot across the sky; one dove for the earth; until, finally, they had Lonewolf's full attention.

A part of him worried he might not recognize this new sky. He thought back to the books he had read as a child. He could see his white family's library, looming above him like a canyon of books. So much knowledge. Though he had been confused by the white man's names for the star patterns, he had managed to learn more about the sky than any other Navajo stargazer had ever known. He could see the depth of the universe, recognize unique features' names in the books. For all that knowledge, the white man did not see the power of the stars. But Lonewolf did.

He lay back, relaxed now. The sky was his. Its knowledge belonged to him.

More importantly, the secret lay there, and he would find it.

He got his bearings on the Bear, low, near the northern horizon. From there, he found the Coyote, and then Yei. Finally, he settled on the Seven Sisters. They clung close, hugging each other in the vast darkness, daughters of Changing Woman.

The cluster of seven stars spoke to him, winking, fading, then brightening again. Suddenly, one of the stars vanished. Lonewolf blinked, then focused again. Only six stars remained. He looked harder, widened his eyes and stared so hard the stars seemed to approach—becoming bigger, brighter, reaching for him.

In a shower of sparks, the sky descended on Lonewolf. The stars carried him, higher and higher, to their realm. He gave himself up to the familiar feeling of free-falling *up* into the glittering darkness.

The stars no longer were flat patterns named by some earthbound gazer. They surrounded Lonewolf, in no recognizable shape. Experience took him past the first moment of fear and the urgency of the stars gave him no time. The celestials whisked him through space until he thought he might reach the outer limits.

He felt before he saw the cold weight of a giant's hand. Black turned to red—the deep, cold red of old blood. Lonewolf stared at the awesome superstar, Monster Slayer. The legendary warrior raised his spear and hurled it. It flew straight at Lonewolf and found its mark. Lonewolf recoiled from the blow, his chest burned white-hot. Another spear appeared and tore past Lonewolf, searing his side. Yet another spear materialized in the hero's hands. A fierce shaft of hot air shot at Lonewolf. He grabbed the bolt of light in his hand and raised his arm high.

The hand beneath him let go and, in a gasp of pain, Lonewolf tumbled through the vastness. The fiery spear disintegrated. Millions of lights streaked past him. He fell in a rush of blackness and light, the breath crushed from his lungs, his body a leaden weight. His whole being threatened to shatter.

From a remnant of his consciousness, Lonewolf willed the vision to end. Soundless as a moonrise, easy as a bird gliding to the ground, he drifted until the sky and earth righted themselves. When the motion ended, he opened his eyes. High in the sky, the Seven Sisters looked down at him. The cluster was complete. As Manuelito would be.

He had his answer. And not much time.

ELEVEN

So cold, Willow thought. The ground's chill seeped through her. She reached for Lonewolf, to feel his sun-bronzed skin. He would warm her.

She brought his face close, his lips closer. If only he'd put his arms around her. She kissed him and his eyes twinkled with the promise of passion. She laid kisses up his jaw, trailing her tongue, tasting him, yearning for more of him.

She nuzzled his ear, burying herself in his neck, but his scent escaped her. And the coldness she had tried to ignore crept up her legs, numbing her. She couldn't concentrate. A blanket, that's all she needed. She groped at her side and found hard floor. The dream dissolved, but her body was unprepared.

Instead of the ground outside, she lay on the floor beneath her window. Instead of Lonewolf, she held a throw pillow from the chair. She remembered Lonewolf had left. The pang of loneliness and confusion returned.

Willow pulled herself into the chair and wrapped the Pendleton around her. The wool held in her body heat but couldn't reach the chill curling in her stomach, spreading from her center, like a hole widening and swallowing her.

She hugged the blanket closer, not to ease the shivers but to quell the gnawing void. Oh, she knew this sensation—the emptiness threatening to consume, the *need* to know why . . . Why had he left?

It's better this way, she told herself sternly, as she had forever, for as long as she could remember, ever since she was a child. Whatever need she'd had as a child, she had left in her childhood. *This* need was only lust.

You lie, her heart answered.

That may be, but it will have to do.

For whatever reason Lonewolf had left so abruptly last night, he kept it a secret. It was no less honest of her to protect her heart. She had nearly surrendered it to him last night. In truth, she would have if he hadn't left.

Willow looked out her window, past the juniper and sage, to the horizon. The familiar vista lent comfort. In the early-morning light, she could see past last night. If she were alone this morning, it was no different from hundreds of mornings before. And if she felt . . . left alone, *that* had happened before, too. She would survive.

Willow grabbed the robe from her bed, cinched it, and headed for coffee. She turned into the hallway and a brisk breeze of chilly air greeted her. The open front door surprised her, but it was the wafting scent of burning cedar that stole her breath. Her mind immediately leapt to when she'd awakened to Lonewolf cooking coffee at Grandfather's.

Anticipation grew within Willow as she neared the door. She stepped into the cool, clear morning air. There he was—on red earth beneath a perfect turquoise sky. He sat cross-legged on the ground and swirled a pan above the fire. Natural as could be.

"I didn't hear you come back." She sounded stupid, but she was occupied with the mere sight of him. His hair was wild, blown in haphazard array. His eyes, however, were keen and focused on her. They were full and dark, yet glittering in the early-morning light. As if he carried the stars within him.

An onrush of the inevitable washed over her and she stepped back from him. "You've been stargazing."

"Yes." Lonewolf expected anger or, at least, questions about why he had left so abruptly. He was not prepared for her quiet assessment or her sleepy beauty.

The moment grew and Lonewolf realized *he* was the one staring in surprise. The acrid smell of burned coffee broke the trance.

"Ah! I have ruined it again."

"I was just going to make some coffee."

A flutter at the door and Willow had retreated inside. Lonewolf poured the worthless liquid on the fire. It belched at the insult and died. Lonewolf found Willow standing in the middle of the kichen, the evidence of his search for a pan surrounding her. Cupboards stood open, cans of food sat on the counter.

"I was looking for coffee," he offered.

She shot him a sideways glance. "Do you keep yours under the sink?"

Her question stumped him, but thankfully she did not seem to need an answer, for she started putting everything away. Lonewolf crouched to return the pots he had scattered in his search for the right pan. A rush of water brought his head up sharp against the top of the cupboard.

He grunted at the pain and heard Willow chuckle.

"You deserve that for the mess you made."

"I am sorry if I woke you," he said, rubbing his head.

After a pause, she said, "I didn't awaken from your noise." She continued to move around the kitchen, getting cups, spoons, a bowl Lonewolf assumed held the sugar she liked.

He tried to stay out of her way, but he could not avoid the sight and smell of her. And he did not want to. He watched her every move, powerless to look away. The tilt of her shoulders as she poured the coffee; the way her thick hair fanned across her back and lightly swept the hand she rested on the counter; the wide belt of her robe hugging her small waist.

If he had stayed last night, he would have awakened to her, and he would have the courage now to wrap his arms around her, loosen that belt and run his hands through her hair.

But he had left. For good reason. And she did not ask why. She had last night, but then perhaps she too had reconsidered.

Willow handed him a cup with coffee and faced him across the narrow span of floor. Her gaze caught his mid-thought and the way she looked away made Lonewolf wonder whether she had read the desire, the regret, or the resignation—or all three.

"I have to get going," she said and walked past him to the hallway.

"Am I still in your custody?"

Willow stopped so suddenly her coffee sloshed and a trickle ran over her fingers. Lonewolf noticed she did not flinch at the heat. Neither did she look directly at him. "Technically," she said.

"Technically?"

"Yes." She faced him squarely. "You're in my custody.

A shrill bell rang behind Lonewolf and he jumped.

Willow reached behind Lonewolf for the wall phone just as it rang again. He walked quickly to the other side of the kitchen, but she'd seen the look on his face. It was the same look of confusion he had given the crime-scene tape in the cave. "Hello," she said, still looking at Lonewolf.

"Officer Becenti, this is Deputy Chavez."

"Yes—" She cleared her throat. "What is it?"

"We got a call from that boy's mother."

"Sammy Nez's mom? What did she say?"

"It's what she found."

Willow didn't like the excitement she heard in Chavez's voice. He thrived on intrigue.

"What did she find, Officer?"

"Drugs."

"He was a canyon boy. Where'd he get drugs?"

"She didn't know. She was pretty rattled. The captain wants you to go up there this morning and talk to her. You know the canyon people. Maybe you can find out where he'd get drugs."

"Okay, Deputy. I'll be in touch."

"Drugs," Willow said to herself as she replaced the receiver. "It doesn't make sense."

She gazed out the window. If it had been a Hopi or Zuni, maybe. But not a Navajo. Alcohol, yes. But not drugs. Drugs were communal, to be shared. Alcohol suited the Navajo solitary life. She frowned in thought.

Lonewolf liked the way her lips pursed. The look reminded him of the tiny bud of a squash blossom. Her gaze lifted to his and her pensive look cleared to one of purpose. "I have to go to the canyon to talk to Mrs. Nez—the boy's mother."

"That is good. There is something I need from the canyon for the ceremony."

"I see. I'll be ready in about fifteen minutes." She said the last as she turned away.

To the canyon. Lonewolf could not believe his good luck. The ceremony would be hard without his medicine bundle, but impossible without the Starway Chant skin. He could only hope *Ha'tanii* had protected it.

Willow pulled on a clean khaki shirt and tucked it into Tribal-issue slacks. With each layer of her official uniform, she regained a measure of control. She couldn't have stood another second in that kitchen; how was she going to stand a whole day in the jeep?

She'd lost all sense of how to behave around him. They'd made love, but they weren't lovers. He was *technically* under arrest, but she didn't consider him a suspect. Willow strapped on her belt, her holster, checked her gun and pinned on her insignia. The uniform was complete, but her composure wasn't. She needed to assign their roles, define his place.

He was a healer. She could accept that. He was a

stargazer. She could even deal with that. After all, he used the stars to devine cures. She was counting on him for that. She just didn't want to count on him for anything else.

All the way to the canyon, Lonewolf wondered how he would get to the cave where he had buried the Starway Chant skin. But when the jeep pulled onto the shifting sand at the mouth of the canyon, he could not think anymore. It had been only three days since he met with the council there. It seemed a lifetime ago. Yet, for all the time passed, the canyon had not changed. It stood silent and welcoming.

"You take the jeep into the canyon?"

"Not through de Che, but into del Muerto. There's no threat of quicksand there."

"Del Muerto?"

Willow threw him a quizzical glance. "Canyon del Muerto. Where you took me two days ago."

"Why do you call it the canyon of the dead?"

"Not just me. Everyone. It's had that name for over a hundred years." Willow stared at him. "It was named that by an archaeologist in the eighteen eighties after he discovered mummified bodies in one of the caves."

Lonewolf gazed ahead at the immense canyon forking off de Che. What had only been "the other canyon" in his time now had a name. "Canyon del Muerto," he repeated to himself.

Willow pulled the jeep onto the path and continued down the canyon. When they approached *Tse-ewa,* Lonewolf thought she might slow down, but Willow rounded the immense Fortress Rock without a sideways glance.

Ten more minutes of silence passed, then Willow pointed to ruins resting on a knoll within a high-ceilinged cave. "Mummy Cave," she said. "Where they found the bodies. They're gone now. In some museum."

Lonewolf felt her gaze. But he just stared at the ruins. The bodies of the ancient ones had not been disturbed since Changing Woman. Now they were gone.

The jeep bounced and lurched through a deep ravine. When they emerged, the place sacred to all Navajo loomed ahead.

"Two Fell Off," Lonewolf said, without thinking.

"What?"

"That is the name of the cave. Two Fell Off."

Willow stopped the jeep and just stared at Lonewolf. "Why do you call Massacre Cave 'Two Fell Off'?"

"It does not matter."

"No. I want to know."

Lonewolf sighed at his own lapse. Maybe he was just getting tired of pretending. "Hundreds of *Diné* holed up in the cave when the Spaniards attacked. One soldier climbed to the cave, shooting his guns. A *Diné*—a woman—fought him. The two fell to their death on the rocks below."

"So you call it Two Fell Off. But that doesn't tell the whole story."

"Neither does the name Canyon del Muerto."

Willow smiled at him. "You could get a job giving tours here, you know."

"I will remember that," he said, wondering what "tours" were.

Willow started up the jeep again, but did not travel far before they reached the end of the canyon. She pulled the jeep in front of a hogan, shaded by a huge cottonwood.

"Wait here. I think I should go alone."

Willow stood beside the jeep until the hogan door opened and an elderly woman stepped out, her gold velvet skirt and shirt the same color as the chamisa blooming in wild clumps. Lonewolf watched Willow approach the hogan slowly, with respect, and he smiled to himself.

She might live and work with the white man, but the old ways came to her naturally.

The two women talked outside the hogan. The *Diné* disappeared inside and came back out clutching a bag. She handed it to Willow. The two talked some more and then hugged. When Willow reached the jeep, she turned and waved to the old woman.

Willow set the bag at her feet. She hit the rod between the seats and the jeep lurched forward. "I'll kill the person who is spreading this here."

"You? Kill?"

"Don't tease me, Lonewolf. This cocaine is lethal. But the dealers don't care. His poor mother. She didn't even know what she'd found. Just that it wasn't right." Willow shook her head. "I just hope there are some fingerprints on the plastic bag."

What was cocaine? What could be in that bag that could kill? Lonewolf let his question die.

"It all seems so convenient," Willow said.

"For who?"

Willow looked at him and Lonewolf wondered at the consideration he saw in her eyes. "Good question," she finally said.

Nearly an hour passed before they reached the junction of the two canyons. Lonewolf touched Willow's arm to gain her attention.

"Willow, stop. I need something . . . for the ceremony," he added.

At his touch, Willow's blood had surged. All morning she had been conscious of him next to her. But the inches might as well have been a canyon guarding his emotions. Willow jammed the gears and slowed the jeep alongside a towering cliff. Before she stopped, Lonewolf was already out.

"The cave I need to see is right up here," Lonewolf said over his shoulder.

Willow fell in alongside him. "I assumed what you

needed were herbs, plants—something for Manuelito."

"No, this ceremony depends on the stars."

Willow knew so little about stargazing. Medicine men kept it wrapped in secrecy and legends of spirits. The mystery gave the belief power over the *Diné*. Just one more in the layer of superstitions that kept the Navajo chained to the old ways.

And here she was subscribing to the myth. But she did it by choice, she reminded herself, not *because* of the magic she saw in Lonewolf's eyes. She did this to help Manuelito. "I guess I thought all your ceremonies would depend on the stars, but the healing would come from medicines."

"Yes, that is true. But this ceremony is different. There is only one way to heal Manuelito and what I look for in the cave will help me find that way."

"One way—?"

Lonewolf's gesture cut her off. "Here is the cave."

Willow gasped. It was Four Hole—where she had hidden from Lonewolf. If he knew, it didn't seem to concern him. He was already climbing the talus slope. Willow watched for a moment, then followed. But with each step, she was bothered more with the coincidence. What were they looking for? When had he hidden it?

Vividly, she saw herself scrambling toward the cave, her heart pounding, desperate to escape—from the man she now followed. Then, he was a kidnapper. Now, he was a healer.

A healer, she reminded herself and took a deep breath before ducking into the darkness.

"This way." Lonewolf's voice, deep as the cavern she entered, guided her steps.

Within a few feet, the pathway turned again and they were engulfed in total blackness. The cold, dry air smelled of fresh dirt. Like a new grave. Willow shivered, trying to shake off the eerie feeling that had settled on her.

"Just a minute," she said. She reached behind to her backpack, pulled out the flashlight and flicked on the light. "Here."

Lonewolf stared at the flashlight. "Thank you," he finally said, "but I am more used to finding my way in the dark."

"Well, I'm not."

His fingers closed one by one around the casing, as if in slow motion. Lonewolf turned back to the path, but faltered a few steps and the beams waved erratically over the rock ceiling and walls, as if the flashlight were held by a child.

The passage narrowed to only a few feet and Willow had to walk sideways to clear the encroaching walls. The crags and crevices she had known before only by the touch of her fingers now danced eerily in the unsteady light. Her head spun and the closeness pressed on her lungs. A strange tension built in her chest.

Thankfully, the earth opened into a small cavern. They stood deep in the womb of *Dinehtah,* in the chamber of the *Ha'tanii.* Willow bent and gulped in air; closed her eyes briefly to quell the rising . . . what? Not panic. She couldn't be frightened.

Irritated with herself, Willow straightened slowly, willing back her control, and saw Lonewolf kicking aside stones, paper, debris that littered the dirt floor. The tension she had felt within now filled the air.

"It is not here." Lonewolf's voice sounded strangled.

"What's not here?"

He didn't answer but kept sweeping the light over the cave. Willow averted her eyes from the dizzying kaleidoscope and searched the floor. Her toe hit something hard and she bent down and dug her fingers through the earth.

"I've got something."

She felt Lonewolf bend close. Willow's fingers

touched cold metal and, from a shallow grave, she withdrew a gun.

"A thirty-eight." Willow held the weapon with two fingers at the barrel. A thirty-eight had killed the boy!

Lonewolf abruptly stood, shifting the light away from the gun. Irritation with herself refocused onto Lonewolf.

"Lonewolf, the light."

He ignored her and trained the beam on the cave wall. Willow fumbled for a plastic evidence bag. "I can't see what I'm doing." She heard herself snap the words out.

"What good are you?"

Willow's head jerked up. "How dare you—" But she saw he was talking to the wall.

"You failed me."

Willow shifted and saw the *Ha'tanii*. She looked at Lonewolf, his rough-hewn face uncompromising in the flashlight's reflected beam.

"What were you looking for, Lonewolf?"

"The Starway Chant skin," he said. "But it is gone."

Unease crept up Willow's spine like a spider. "There is no Starway Chant."

"There is, and I know the chant. But I must have the skin."

"Why? What *is* the ceremony you have to do for Manuelito?"

He turned and his gaze, harder than the age-old rock surrounding them, struck her to her soul.

"Do you know the legend of the horned shaman?"

"My father spoke of him. Supposedly, the *Ha'tanii*'s spirit could take flight from his body."

"What of his celestial powers? Did your father speak of those?"

Willow tried to quiet the quaking inside her. A horrible sense of foreboding was building within. "Yes, he told me the fairy tale. A gifted shaman, sent by the starborn ancestors."

"He is more than a shaman. He is the Starway Shaman."

"There isn't a starway shaman, Lonewolf. There isn't even a starway ceremony. Supposedly, the last stargazer disappeared before the Long Walk."

"The what?"

"The Long Walk," Willow said, exasperated and anxious for the conversation to end.

"No, I do not imagine the *Diné* have had a Starway Shaman in a long time," Lonewolf said thoughtfully. "He is a rare gift of the starborn ancestors."

With every word he spoke, Willow became more tense. "What is your point? What does this have to do with Manuelito?"

"The Starway Shaman is sent in times of severe strife. He holds all the powers of the celestial spirits. Through him comes the guidance for the *Diné*."

"I don't have a lot of use for myths and legends, Lonewolf. And you haven't said what this has to do with Manuelito."

"Manuelito has been chosen as the next Starway Shaman."

Willow backed away from him. "A stargazer." She could barely speak past the trembling consuming her. "Manuelito is not a stargazer. He's an eight-year-old boy, dying of something."

"The same age as *Naa glen ni baa* when she fought Carson's troops?"

"She battled soldiers. She wasn't answering any call of the stars. She was fighting for her life!"

Lonewolf could sense her fear, but it was not of him. She feared the unknown. Like a cougar in unknown territory, she looked ready to bolt. He would have to ease those fears.

Lonewolf walked to her and took her shoulders in his hands. He felt a shiver run through her then a hard push at his chest. Her eyes flashed a warning to stay away.

"Why are you concocting this story? If you can't help Manuelito, just say so."

"He has to have the ceremony, *shi yázhi,* or he will die."

"Die? What makes you so sure?"

"The stars. Manuelito has three days."

"How do you know that? The doctors don't even know that!"

"Do you so easily doubt everything? Must you always have proof?"

"Yes!" Stars flashed in her eyes, nearly blinding Lonewolf with their power. "When it involves a boy I love. Yes."

"And how would you have that proof?" He grabbed her shoulders. "Do you have another boy I can practice on? Someone who is also having seizures?"

Her eyes darkened. "Manuelito is not some messenger of the stars. He's not a mythological horned creature!"

Lonewolf felt her gaze deep within him: touching, probing, stirring a need he could barely control. "Neither am I."

TWELVE

The air sizzled. They stared at each other across several feet of ground.

"Who are you?" Willow didn't recognize her voice any more than she knew the man standing before her.

He paced, raked both his hands through his long hair. It fell in shadows on his shoulders. "I just want to help Manuelito, Willow. We are not at odds."

"Yes we are."

"I know you love him—"

"You know nothing about me!" The tremors threatened to return but Willow defeated them through sheer will. "Who do you think you are? You think you can appear out of nowhere and interfere in people's lives?"

"You are the one who is interfering, *shi yázhi.*"

Willow heard the dangerously quiet tone in his voice, but she was too furious to pay any heed. "I am not your little one. I am not your little soldier." She ignored the growing fire in Lonewolf's eyes. "I am not your little anything!"

She saw a flash of pain in Lonewolf's eyes. If she hadn't been so afraid of her own feelings and so angry at herself for becoming vulnerable—if she hadn't felt so cornered—she might have cared about Lonewolf. Instead, she advanced on him, with no concern for whether her words hurt.

"I should have listened to my instincts the first time we met."

"Your instincts have always been sound, Willow. What do they tell you now?"

His voice reverberated through her, amplifying the tremors. "That you're crazy."

Lonewolf clasped her upper arms. His eyes, black as the cave, bored into her. "You can tell me to leave. That has been done before. You can call me a liar, evil, a witch. *That* has been done before. But you cannot change what is to be."

"Don't be so sure," she said.

"I will not beg you to believe in me, *shi yázhi*. You either trust me or you do not."

How many times had Willow said those very same words to Navajo suspicious of her and her job? She knew, too well, the feeling of not being trusted. She lived with it every time she arrested a Navajo for breaking the law—white man's laws, some *Diné* would say. But she believed in what she did.

"You can believe all you want, Lonewolf. It doesn't change the fact that a small boy is lying unconscious in a hospital bed. That's reality."

"And what of the reality of the visions we have shared?"

A shudder ran through Willow and she felt Lonewolf's hands tighten on her arms. If a vision came right now, would it be of Manuelito? Would she see his death? She steeled herself against the possibility, but all she felt was Lonewolf's warmth circle through her. She couldn't deny the visions, she had already admitted them to Lonewolf.

"Reality contradicts visions," she said tonelessly.

He pulled her close, pressed her to his chest. His scent, earth and buckskin, filled her. "Think, Willow. Remember at Grandfather's when you were rubbing my shoulder? A boy walked to me, holding out a broken *Ha'tanii* necklace. That was Manuelito. And remember on the cliff? When we kissed?" His voice lowered, whispered in her ear. "You were a child with your father. Then you were a woman holding a boy, but the boy turned to stars. Remember, Willow?''

The magic. She felt it within and without. His strong arms around her, anchoring her. His heat coursing through her, relaxing her. She felt the tremors subside. All from his touch.

She was foolish! Foolish to let herself become vulnerable. She pushed hard on him. ''What's your point, Lonewolf?''

''The boy, Willow. You know the truth.''

''If he was in the visions, it was because I'm so worried. He's my family, Lonewolf. You can understand that. You got all upset when I mentioned Abiquiu—''

''I did not want to speak of them because they are long gone.''

''Gone?''

''I no longer have any family in Abiquiu.''

Willow stared at him in disbelief. ''But you told Deputy Chavez you have family there.''

''I lied.'' His voice held no apology.

''I see.'' Coldness, like an icy breath in her veins, spread through Willow. ''What else have you lied about, Lonewolf?''

''None of the rest is lies,'' he said.

''What about the cave? How did you get in there? What about the boy? The bundle? Is it really yours?''

''The bundle is mine. I never met that boy.'' He reached a hand to her and gently touched her arm. ''I told you how I came to be in that cave.''

Willow shook off his hand. ''Yes, another entrance. One we never found.''

He stared at her, his gaze not angry, but resigned. ''Did *Ha'tanii* talk with you the other night?''

''Did—?'' Willow shook her head at the abrupt change in the conversation. ''What are you talking about?''

''Here. The *Ha'tanii*.''

''You knew I hid here?''

"The rocks told me. *Ha'tanii* belongs to me."

A shudder ran down her spine. She thought about that night. Had he known where she was the whole time?

Willow backed away. She needed air. He really was crazy.

Lonewolf's eyes smiled. "Was he good company?"

Willow gazed at the Navajo before her. *Play along, Willow, until you can get away.* "Actually, he was kind of sarcastic. I told him he would have to lose those horns if he ever got into the real world. He's definitely a relic from the past."

"I made him."

He turned to the wall, put his hands in the places of the prints, and leaned against the drawing. For a moment, Willow lost her breath. His whole torso, his head, shoulders, arms, and hands, filled the *Ha'tanii.* He was one with the shaman. Lonewolf was so still, he seemed to become the drawing.

Willow took a step back, then another. She stuck one arm behind her to feel for the wall, the other hand gripped her gun. In just another minute, if he didn't turn, she could get out of there.

"Willow."

His low voice echoed off the cave, swept behind her. *He knew.* Somehow he knew she was trying to escape.

She drew her gun and leveled it on him. "Who *are* you?"

He faced her. "What have you known about me since we first met, *shi yázhi*?"

Willow tried to calmly breathe. But she couldn't fill her lungs. Sweat sprung out on her brow, though the cave's air was cool.

"I told you. I thought you were crazy."

"Why, Willow?"

The tremors increased, as if her world were shaking down to the ground. "Because you talked of men who don't exist. You looked . . . you looked strange."

"How?"

"You acted as if you were on drugs." Suddenly, Willow thought her legs would collapse. "You . . . the boy . . . it's been you all along!"

"*Do tah!* Stop it! I do not know drugs! This has nothing to do with that!"

"Prove it, Lonewolf! Tell me why I shouldn't take you back to the station right now!"

"The proof, *shi yázhi,* is on my chest."

Slowly, he walked toward her, tugging loose his chamois shirt.

"Stop right there."

"Look at the scar, *shi yázhi.*"

He shone the flashlight on his chest and, as if drawn by a magnet, her gaze followed the light to a small scar above his breast. Except it didn't look like a scar anymore. It looked somehow familiar. She looked closer. The shape was unmistakable. There, on Lonewolf's chest, was the perfect impression of a miniature *Ha'tanii*—the horned shaman crowned by the soaring bird.

The Starway Shaman carried the mark of the horned shaman. Her father's voice rang in Willow's head. Her vision dimmed, blackness encroached. In a swirl of dizziness she felt the all-too-familiar sensation of falling.

"Willow. Willow!"

Lonewolf's voice and his firm hands on her shoulders brought Willow back. She tried to focus, shook her head and felt Lonewolf's grip. Her gaze flew to his.

"No. This can't be." She tried to move away, but he held tight. He took her hand and placed it on the scar.

"Think, Willow. Use your logic. What does it tell you?"

She felt Lonewolf's heart beating beneath her touch. Unbidden, scenes of the last three days replayed in her mind: his confusion about Fort Defiance, his fury in the canyon over the inscription site, his relentless questions about Kit Carson. A man who died over one hundred thirty years ago.

At the time of the Long Walk.

The same time the last stargazer was to have died.

Then she saw him emerging from the cave ruin in a cloud of light. From the other side of the crime-scene tape.

"No," she said, but couldn't hear her voice.

Instantly, a dark void opened around her. She was surrounded by stars, with nothing but space beneath her feet.

Instead of being frightened, though, Willow felt free, unfettered, and protected. No visions came, no strange images. Just a sense of peace and safety. *The horned shaman brought you here*. Grandfather's words came to her—the ones he had spoken to Lonewolf on the first night.

Suddenly, she knew. The knowledge swept through her like a canyon wind. She opened her eyes to Lonewolf and saw the man she had made love to, now holding her. The dizziness was gone, the pain in her chest—gone. The air was cool, dry, and filled her lungs.

She breathed deeply and filled with the scent of Lonewolf. Red earth and cedar. The fragrance of her canyon. Whether now or a hundred years ago, the essence was the same.

Willow's gaze rose to meet Lonewolf's. His eyes smiled at her, his sinfully handsome face weakened her. She found strength the only way possible. She stared back, locking eyes with Lonewolf. Her fingers sought and found the *Ha'tanii* on Lonewolf's chest.

His gaze turned dark and serious. Unmistakable passion filled them. "I want you." His voice, husky with emotion, claimed her.

His arms circled her back and pulled her close. His mouth found hers and pressed, wanting more. His urgency matched that of last night, but now she understood. She could taste the question on his lips: *do you believe? Say you believe.* Willow obeyed the silent command of her heart and answered with open lips, wanting more of him. His tongue skimmed the inside of her lips and the need within her widened, like circlets in a pond, ever bigger, until the pulse beat between her legs.

Willow slipped her hand up his chest. His heartbeat jumped beneath her fingers. She pushed the shirt higher, and followed it with her tongue, sliding along his skin. She felt his groan on her lips, and it drove deep inside her.

Lonewolf shifted and, in one move, yanked his shirt over his head. He lay back and Willow straddled his hips, her need pooled where they touched. She pushed her hands up his chest, to his nipples. Her finger found the scar and she traced it, gently, watching him. His ebony eyes twinkled, like the night sky. In them she saw magic, a gift from the stars to the legend beneath her.

Willow straightened and undid the buttons on her shirt. She worked deliberately, his gaze following her fingers. His hands slid down and back along her legs, kneading her, caressing every inch. He stopped at her hips; his thumbs met below her zipper, where her pulse throbbed.

And then he rubbed her. The seam of her slacks pressed where she was most sensitive. Willow's breath shortened, she arched, her hands stilled at her shirt. And her blood soared.

She looked to Lonewolf, to his eyes. They were glazed with passion and need—a man's eyes, not a legend's. She gave herself to both—the myth and the man, to the magic and the passion.

His hands settled on hers and she felt the buttons slip, the shirt slide off her shoulders. Her buckle loosened, the snap popped, the zipper slid. And she felt warm fingers against her belly. She found the leather at his waist and desperately, fingers flying, undid the laces. In a breath, their clothes lay around them.

The cool cave air settled on Willow, but she hardly felt it. Lonewolf's hands, warm, roughened, glided over her, grazed her breasts and caressed down her sides, down her legs—leaving warmth in their path, and sheer anticipation along every inch. He slid a hand behind her, curved her bottom while his other cupped her. His palm ground between her legs. Both hands moved, pressing harder, faster, driving her pleasure deeper. Shameless, consumed in desire, she let the rhythm take her. Harder, faster.

Willow shivered to her toes. A finger found where she was already moist. Someone groaned. Him? Her? Willow couldn't tell. She was lost in the moment, in the rising beat of this ancient dance. She clutched his shoulders, bracing herself, working the tension, letting the intensity build through her.

She felt herself lifted as if weightless, then lowered to sit astride him.

She sank onto him with a shudder. They moved as one. Like a bow and its arrow with perfect tension and balance. He drew her tight, exacting more, taking all she had, giving all he was—

Willow looked into his eyes, at his chiseled face, at his lips pulled back, accentuating his natural snarl. A warrior. Her warrior.

"Please, Lonewolf. Now."

"Now?" he said, through gritted teeth.

"Now, you renegade," she whispered.

Lonewolf plunged into her full force. Willow rocked upright and rode. Power surged through her like a mighty starburst. In a shower of stars, she found her release. She felt Lonewolf stiffen, clench.

Willow fell to his chest. Their hearts beat furiously against each other. Ever so slowly, the throb tamed, their breathing lengthened. But, within her, Willow felt his pulse. The pulse of the last Starway Shaman.

Her eyes met the drawing of the *Ha'tanii,* the creation of Lonewolf—more than a century before. She lay in the arms of a nineteenth-century warrior.

A shiver ran through her—one of wonder.

"Are you cold, little one?"

His voice rumbled within her chest and she loved the feeling.

Lonewolf groped with one hand in the dirt beside her and Willow felt clothes pulled over her back and part of her legs. She snuggled against Lonewolf, content to lie here forever.

"Tell me about him," she said quietly.

"He is special, no?"

"He is special, Lonewolf. When did you carve him?"

"At the beginning of the Fearing Time."

"The fearing time?"

"At a time when we feared everyone around us. The Utes, the rancheros, the army. Especially the army. Everyone was an enemy."

He stared at the *Ha'tanii,* his gaze far away. "There are treaties, but only the Navajo honor them. They keep us boxed in and at everyone's mercy."

His haunted voice, cold and distant, rose the fine hair on Willow's neck. He was talking in the present, as if it were still going on. For him, this *was* all still happening.

Willow ran a hand up and down his arm, trying to ease the incredible tension she felt beneath her fingers. "Those enemies are gone, Lonewolf."

He looked at her, his eyes immeasurably sad. Willow realized she had not only dismissed his enemies but his whole life, the people he knew—and loved. He had a life, one he had been living with people he cared about. A life he would want to return to.

This wouldn't last.

Lonewolf must have sensed her sudden withdrawal, for he lifted a questioning brow.

"Are you all right?"

She let her fingers trace the lines in his face, gently, with no clue of the force she used to tamp down the growing ache in her heart. She would not ruin this moment with possessive doubts.

"I'm fine." She levered up and gazed at Lonewolf to emphasize, more to herself. "Couldn't be better."

She dropped a kiss on Lonewolf's lips. His arms hugged her closer, the kiss deepened and the ache within her disappeared, released. But was not forgotten.

The noise in the station stopped. Not all of it, of course. The phones rang, and the fax churned. But nearly all conversation stopped as Willow and Lonewolf walked to Cal's office. Funny, she hadn't noticed if he had had this effect when he was arrested. But then she had been noticing a lot in the last few hours she hadn't *ever* paid attention to before.

Seeing the world through Lonewolf's eyes was enlightening. The drive from the canyon, routine just yesterday, took on a new dimension. They had talked of fences, telephone poles, and trailers; then telephones, refrigerators, and flashlights; and she had to explain that not all cars were called jeeps. He had been saving questions for days and they poured out during the miles from the canyon.

And they talked about the Navajo Reservation. She could still see the look on Lonewolf's face when she told him the Navajo now numbered a quarter of a million. There was pride, but something else in his eyes. And Willow couldn't help but think of the few, only twelve thousand in Lonewolf's time, who had fought to preserve this land.

When he asked about drugs, alcohol, and the *Diné* he saw wandering the streets, Willow was glad they had reached the station. How did she begin to explain what the People of this time faced when Lonewolf had fought Utes, Mexicans, and the army? When Willow thought of all that had bombarded Lonewolf in the last three days, it was a wonder he had not actually *gone* crazy.

Three days. It was only another three days until the ceremony. If they could find the Chant skin. He had talked of stars, of alignments, of the Seven Sisters, until Willow thought she was taking an astronomy class, and not understanding a word. Except that they had only three days.

Would he leave? Even as they walked into the station and they were hit with silence and turned heads at their passing, Willow tried not to think what life would be like without Lonewolf.

She pushed open the door to Cal's office and found him as he always was, his head buried in paperwork. He looked the way she had felt yesterday: worn out and grouchy.

"Now you're the one who looks like hell." She plopped down in the chair opposite Cal's desk. Lonewolf stood.

"It's been hell. What are you"—he looked up and noticed Lonewolf—"doing here?"

"You sent me to the canyon, remember? To talk to Mrs. Nez?"

Cal ran a hand over his head and rubbed the back of his neck. "I forgot. Been on the phone with the Feds all morning. Had two bombings in Gallup and contraband pottery in Red Rock."

"Bombings?"

"One at Khalib Trading and another at the owner's house."

"Sounds like someone is taking the Indian trading business a little too seriously."

"Either that or drugs," Cal said.

They looked at each other across the desk. They both

knew the reputation of the Arabs for dealing drugs to the Indians.

"So, what did you find at Sammy's house?"

"Cocaine. She also swore to me her son wouldn't be mixed up with anything bad."

"Were there prints?"

"Don't know." Willow pulled the paper bag from the backpack. She also withdrew the plastic bag with the gun and placed both on the desk.

"What's this?" Cal poked the gun with a pencil.

"I found it at Four Hole Site. In the cave farthest back."

"What in the world made you look there?"

Willow knew this question would come and she didn't have any choice but to tell the truth. But maybe she could make it sound less suspicious.

"Actually, I was looking for something else. A chant skin."

"A what?"

"A Starway Chant skin," Lonewolf said.

Cal glanced at him and looked back at Willow. "Since when have you become interested in anything doing with the stars?"

"Lonewolf needs it. He seemed to think it would be in that cave."

"And did you find the skin?"

"No."

"But you found a gun."

Willow could feel the tension all around her. "I know what you're thinking, Cal."

"You do? Why don't you tell me?"

"You are thinking I had something to do with the murders," Lonewolf said.

"And did you?"

"He—"

"I have not *murdered* anyone." Lonewolf walked over Willow's words.

"Oh, but you have *killed,* haven't you? It's in your eyes."

"Cal, you don't know what you're talking about."

"Don't I? I had him checked out, Willow. Nobody's heard of Lonewolf."

"Is that so?" Willow heard the sarcasm in her voice, but she had finally had enough. "Then you haven't found a record on him, either, right?"

Cal didn't move, didn't move a muscle. "Not yet."

"He saved my life, Cal."

The silence grew until it was obvious Cal wasn't going to back down or apologize.

"Check the gun for prints, Cal. I guarantee you won't find Lonewolf's."

"We'll see," he said, but the way he went back to the papers on his desk told Willow he already knew she was right. He just didn't want to admit it. She was about to ask what she'd really come for, when Cal looked up at her.

"There's something else I want you to do."

"Sure."

"You know the contraband pottery I mentioned? We got a call from old Weatherbee at the Red Rock Trading Post. A guy was trying to sell him this pottery, but was vague on the provenance. And didn't have any papers. Weatherbee got suspicious and called us."

"Did you get the guy?"

"No. And we can't figure where he got the goods. I mean, it's really old stuff. Here's the sheet, with pictures. Do you recognize it?"

Willow gave the sheet a cursory glance. "I'm not a pottery expert, Cal."

"No, but your grandfather is. Would you mind seeing what he says?"

"You realize I'm going to have to listen to one of Grandfather's lectures on the sanctity of Navajo artifacts."

"All in the line of duty."

Willow folded the sheet, stood and stuck it in her pocket. "Now there's something I need, Cal." Willow braced her arms on his desk. "I want Lonewolf's bow and arrows and his medicine bundle."

"You can have the bow and arrows."

"And the medicine bundle?"

"It's evidence, Willow. We've been over this."

"Cal, he needs the bundle."

"Why, Willow?"

"He has to do a ceremony." She didn't want to say the rest—that it was for Manuelito. She didn't want to see his look of disbelief.

Cal looked at Lonewolf, then back at Willow. "Then it'll just have to wait, Officer Becenti."

"He didn't murder anyone, Cal. I know that. You know that. You saw the report on Romero."

"And Lonewolf was found on the other side of the crime tape. Remember?"

"I was there! And I *know* he had nothing to do with the murder!"

"Can't do."

"Cal, the ceremony's for Manuelito."

"Damn, Willow. You know I can't let the bundle go."

Willow glared but Cal didn't see, he was already back at his papers. "Like I said, Willow, we'll see. That's all I can promise."

Willow pushed off the desk, but didn't move away. Cal looked up and quirked a brow. "Something else?"

"The bow and arrows."

THIRTEEN

At the edge of town, Willow pulled the jeep off the road and onto the dirt. Dust blew up from the tires and swirled around the jeep, making Lonewolf squint to see the small white building.

"It's the Kinlichee Chapter House. We should find Grandfather here. Maybe he knows about the chant skin."

"A chapter house?"

"It's Tribal government on the local level. Like a council," she added at his glance. "Anyway, today is the monthly meeting and he can't resist putting in his two cents."

Lonewolf heard some annoyance in her voice. "You do not approve?"

"It's not that." Her pace slowed, then she stopped and stared ahead. Dozens of Navajo stood in groups or sat beneath the shade of the lone tree. "Everyone here has a complaint and everyone will be heard. Maybe it's a marriage dispute, or concern about neglect of a clan relative. Each side is heard, over and over, until they reach an agreement."

"No Navajo can tell another what to think," Lonewolf said thoughtfully.

"Yes, and I like that. Decisions coming from compromise. But, for some issues there is no way to compromise." She sighed and started walking again.

"And there is an issue that worries you or Grandfather?"

"I'm a cop, Lonewolf. I'm always an issue." She

gave him a smile, but it was forced. "Never mind. Have a look out here and I'll see if Grandfather's inside."

Lonewolf nodded and wandered through the groups of Navajo. As expected, people cleared a path for him. He was a stranger and, therefore, suspicious. The sing-song chatter of his own people flowed over him, quenching a thirst he hadn't been aware of.

Fragments of conversations drifted toward him. People talked easily of everyday matters: their sheep, their crops, and their children. Yet Lonewolf felt something else—a dark undercurrent of discontent and confusion.

A group of women discussed preparations for the upcoming Night Way. Clan members would travel great distances for the ceremony to see their sons and daughters initiated on the eighth night. Then one woman said that maybe she would not take her children. It was all so much trouble. Another one mumbled agreement.

Imbalance coursed through Lonewolf. He overheard a cluster of men talking of the meeting. One among them urged the others to attend his speech on officially naming the Navajo the *Diné*. Another mentioned the importance of grazing rights. The discord swelled. It crashed over Lonewolf, poured through him—a flood of disharmony.

A young man's angry voice rose over the crowd. His tense, fierce expression dared anyone to ignore him.

"You old men talk of old issues! What about your sons? If you don't worry about us, you won't *have* a Navajo Nation. Because we all will have moved away."

The gathering fell silent in stunned embarrassment at the young man's outburst. Finally, an elder spoke.

"Tell us what you think we should worry about."

The young *Diné* smirked. "You're worried about a few wandering sheep or what we should call ourselves. As if changing our name would solve all the problems."

"How would *you* solve our problems, Corbert?"

Willow's voice came from behind Lonewolf. The

young Navajo glared over Lonewolf's shoulder. "I would not arrest someone for the 'malicious trespassing' of sheep!"

"It's the law, Corbert, and you know it." Willow stepped in front of Lonewolf and faced the long-haired Navajo.

"Because they wandered onto a *bilagaana's* land."

Hatred gleamed in the man's eyes. Lonewolf took a step around Willow, his skin prickling as if he had been attacked. But Willow's calm voice held him fast.

"Do you respect the range land of another Navajo?"

Murmurs rose from the crowd which had gathered. The *Diné*'s eyes narrowed on Willow then he turned to the crowd. "Don't let her words confuse you! We respect our land, we respect each other. But we do not have control over our own destiny. Our tribal leaders gave that away."

The elder raised a hand for quiet. "We have sovereignty. We are the Navajo Nation."

"You call us a nation. But we're ruled by Washington. We have to go to them for schools, for health care."

Several young *Diné* raised their voices in agreement. The elder Navajo spoke. "We have a President. We have our own police, our own laws. Some other things take time."

"Our own laws, you say? Have you tried to get eagle feathers lately? The white man decides if and when we can have them. What will *Hataałii* use for the Night Way? Ask Officer Becenti if she would let someone go who had 'illegal' feathers."

All eyes turned to Willow. Lightning tension crackled the air.

"*Hataałii*'s feathers are legal, Corbert, and you know it. And do you think self-rule means no laws? That you can do whatever you please?"

"What about drinking or gambling if we want?" the

man shot back. ''We're at the mercy of the white man and his laws. He treats us like children.''

''If you want to drink and gamble, then you're thinking like a child. Those things don't make you a man—a free man.''

''I should have a choice! And casinos would bring us money. We need jobs, we need food for our tables.''

''Gambling your money away won't put food on your table, Corbert. And our children should not have to grow up with drunks.'' Willow spoke softly, but her words carried. ''Look around you, Corbert. We have one of the highest suicide rates. Our hospitals are a joke. Our children—'' She broke off and looked over the crowd. ''Our children are dying. What will your self-rule do about that? Where have you been when we have talked about a community center for the children? We need strong arms to help build a place for the children to go, where they'll be safe, where they can learn to be the best they can be.''

''Where you can teach them to be good little sheep?'' He spat the words out.

''We would teach them to think for themselves, to make lives for themselves. Not to depend on Washington or on the Navajo Tribe. But on themselves.''

''Then why do you take anything from Washington?''

''We take what was promised in the treaty,'' Willow said.

''Have they kept all their promises?'' The man held Willow's gaze.

''No,'' she said, finally.

''Broken promises equal broken treaties,'' the *Diné* said simply.

Willow stared back, her eyes dark and unflinching. ''So you would throw out the whole treaty? And where would that leave us?''

''With our dignity,'' he said to Willow. Then he looked at Lonewolf, his black eyes glittering like hot coals, and Lonewolf saw a warrior—a fighter like Black Horse. So desperate for freedom he would sacrifice everything.

How many Diné will die while you save your pride? The words Lonewolf had spoken to the council echoed in his head. And how many *had* died so that their descendants could stand in the sunshine, without threat of bullets or poison arrows, and still—still!—make pride the issue.

The man had already turned away when Lonewolf chose to speak. "Should the warriors of the past have fought and died to the last man, to save pride for the *Diné*?"

The young *Diné* faced Lonewolf. "Yes," he said. "I would risk our lives and our children's lives. Without our pride, the People are no longer *Diné*. We would mean nothing to the earth or the stars. Nothing."

"Then you would give away too much. Pride alone has never kept anyone alive."

The *Diné* walked away with a few others. Onlookers went back to their groups or inside. Soon, only Lonewolf and Willow remained. And, for a moment, Lonewolf reflected how—this time—after speaking his mind, he was not standing alone. The sensation was a bit unsettling, like a spinned coin coming to a rest. He took Willow's hand in his—a perfect fit, his anchor in this time. But she was more than that. He was struck by how odd it was that this moment should feel so comfortable and right.

They walked around the front of the Chapter House. "Did you find Grandfather?"

"No," she said. "Too bad, because I wish he had seen you put *your* two cents in."

"Ah, is that what I did?"

Willow looked up and smiled and Lonewolf discovered pure pleasure.

* * *

Willow had a hard time concentrating on the road. Without turning her head, she could see the bow and quiver resting against Lonewolf's thigh. His long, bronze fingers idly grazed the bow and Willow felt a jolt as if he had actually touched her.

"Did you make that?" Willow was glad the loud whine of the jeep's tires covered the catch in her voice.

"No. I traded it from an Apache."

"What did you trade to him?"

"Turquoise. From a Ute."

"The enemy?"

"He was dead."

Willow stared at the highway. Of course he had killed. Nineteenth-century Navajoland was a battleground. And before the United States Army, it had been the Mexicans. For two hundred years, warfare and survival had been a fact of Navajo life.

From the corner of her eye, Willow could only see Lonewolf's black hair whipping violently in the wind. He stared, as he had since they left Window Rock, at the passing landscape. It was nothing spectacular. Just rolling piñon hills and red-streaked sandstone.

"And you, little one, have you killed?"

His deep voice traveled on the wind and hit her broadside.

"No," she finally said. "But I would if I had to."

"It is better not to have to," he said and his voice held a note of sadness.

What an odd thing for a warrior to say. She could imagine getting sick of the warfare and wishing desperately for it to be over. But his words were those of a philosopher, a man who questioned the status quo. Willow suddenly wondered about his place in the past. How did a thinker fit in with those driven to retaliate? Not well, she would imagine. He would be a loner.

The thought curled around her stomach and clenched. She didn't want him to be alone. And maybe, if the past were so painful, he wouldn't, either. She pulled together all her courage and, staring straight ahead, asked the question.

"Will you go back, Lonewolf?"

"Yes."

The knot in her stomach twisted.

"I must," he added and Willow could tell he now looked at her.

She clenched her jaw against the pain, against the selfishness that gripped her. "Of course you do," she said. "That's where you belong." She said them aloud, though the words were meant to console her own heart.

She was right. He did not belong here. But for a moment, as he had stared at the serene landscape, he had pondered a place of no more battles, a time when Navajo warriors did not have to fight to free hostages stolen by Utes, Mexicans, and even rancheros. A time when no more Navajo children were sold into slavery.

A place where even he could find peace. He scowled at his weakness. He would be an outsider here, never a part of the whole, just as he was in the past. Lonewolf looked at Willow and wondered where she found her strength—that steely determination evident even now as wisps of her black hair floated over strong cheekbones and keen green eyes. Not quite *bilagaana* and not quite Navajo.

Even her job echoed the same conflict. She worked for the Navajo, yet she was accused of enforcing the white man's laws. How did she find the balance between the two?

Lonewolf guessed that sometimes she did not. He had felt a turmoil within her each time the visions descended. A turmoil that belied her calm, controlled exterior.

And yet, she provided an anchor for him in this time. She, who did not trust stargazers—who believed in logic, not myths and legends—she had, perhaps, more balance than he.

The jeep slowed and Lonewolf saw the hospital. Would that balance tip once Manuelito became the Starway Shaman? What would be *her* anchor?

Lonewolf's heart did a strange flip. He would not be here to help. He would have returned to the place he belonged and he would be alone, as he had been his entire life. For that was *his* balance.

Lonewolf followed Willow into the hospital. He liked watching her walk. He had decided days ago that he approved of women in pants—especially Willow. But today, she walked stiffly, without her usual grace. She did not look from side to side—and never at him.

Lonewolf could not wonder long about what bothered Willow. From the moment he entered the hospital his heart had hastened and with every step toward Manuelito, his urgency heightened.

But he could not make his legs move faster. They dragged through quicksand, each movement an extreme effort. The corridor became a tunnel, dark and stifling.

He knew, in the way of dreams and nightmares, he had entered Manuelito's world. He fought the terror of his own memory of falling forever.

Without knowing how, he found himself inside Manuelito's room. He swallowed his panting, trying to calm himself.

A man in a white coat stood beside Manuelito's bed. He looked up at Lonewolf and spoke, but Lonewolf could not hear the words.

What he did hear was the far-off voice of a small boy. ''*Nó woh di naa niná.*'' Go away.

The world turned black. Lonewolf searched the darkness for the boy. He called out. ''*Shich'i' yániti', shi yázhi.*'' Talk to me, little one.

Fragments of dying stars broke the blackness. He had to find him!

The child would hide as he had. Terrified of the shards of light, the thunder of the celestials. Then he saw Manuelito, crouched, surrounded by blackness, only his eyes wide. *"Neezgai."* It hurts.

Lonewolf's heart seized. *"Níká iishyeed, shi yázhi."* I will help you, little one.

But Lonewolf heard not his voice, but Grey Feather's. Confused, Lonewolf reached to Manuelito, but felt *himself* lifted.

Fear welled within him. *"Do tah!"* He tried to call out, but already the boy was gone and the terror within Lonewolf was unleashed. His heart pounded in his throat, hammered in his head. He tried to rise—he could not fail! Not again!—but strong arms held him. Shook him.

"Lonewolf! Lonewolf!"

"Ma'am, please move back."

Lonewolf felt a finger at his eye, then his eyelid was pressed open. The man in the white coat shone a light in Lonewolf's eye.

Lonewolf tried to blink and the fingers released his lid.

"He's not unconscious," the man said.

Lonewolf felt a hand at his wrist. He tried to shake it off, but his hand hit the floor. He shifted and found he was lying on the floor.

"Take it easy, fella."

"Lonewolf."

It was Willow and the confusion evaporated. He was in the hospital room. He had entered Manuelito's vision. He had not failed. Not yet.

Lonewolf pushed himself up on one arm and opened his eyes. Willow stared back, her eyes full of concern. "What happened? You ran past me."

"I—" Lonewolf looked at the man. "I am all right," he said.

"Let me get a nurse in here," the man said.

Lonewolf locked eyes with Willow. *"T'áá K'ad Manuelito baa deeshaa."* I must see Manuelito now. Willow nodded.

"He's fine, Doctor. It's—" She paused. "It's the altitude. He's just not used to it."

The doctor looked at Lonewolf and raised both his brows. "Altitude?"

"He's not from here," Willow said. She took Lonewolf's arm and helped him to stand.

"Still, he should sit down."

Lonewolf walked to the bed and laid a hand on Manuelito. The turmoil within Manuelito rose to Lonewolf's fingertips. *"T'áá doo bina nizidii, shi yázhi."* Do not be afraid, little one.

"Mr. Lonewolf—"

"So, you must be Dr. Voorman," Willow broke in. "I'm Willow Becenti. Officer Becenti. I'm Manny's—Manuelito's—guardian. I've been eager to hear the results of your tests."

"Are you a relative, Mr. Lonewolf?"

"He's Manny's uncle," Willow supplied.

"I see."

Lonewolf laid his palm on Manuelito's chest. The churning did not ease, but spun wildly, like a dust storm.

"Well, I'm afraid I don't have much news, Officer Becenti. We've run every test we can—from a complete blood workup to MRI of the brain to testing hormone levels. Everything is normal. Except his heart. I have recommended lidocaine for the tachycardia." He glanced at Willow. "His fast heart rate," he explained. "His seizures are neurological and we can control them with phenobarbital."

The doctor turned to Lonewolf and eyed his hand on Manuelito's forehead. "It would help if we knew what brought this on. But you say he didn't get hit on the head or take a bad fall?"

"No, nothing. We were just walking in the canyon."

Willow's voice made Lonewolf shift to see her. Her face was pale and drawn—her gaze unwavering on Manuelito. "So, basically, you don't know any more than when I brought him in." Willow brushed past the doctor and stood by Manuelito.

The doctor straightened and faced her. "Well, we know there is no apparent brain trauma. No tumors, no blood clots."

"And what you recommend is more drugs."

"Until we find out what is causing this, all we can do is try to ease the seizures and keep his body functioning."

"I see. Thank you, Doctor."

Willow laid her hand on Manuelito's forehead, her fingers a breath away from Lonewolf's. Lonewolf felt a responding tremor through Manuelito, focused, yearning, seeking. Lonewolf's gaze flew to Willow. The child searched for her. Did she feel it? A great spasm wracked Manuelito and Willow snatched her hand back.

"*Ni ni zin.*" He wants you, Lonewolf said quietly and laid his hand over hers.

Another quiver, like a shuddering breath, ran through the child and Willow's eyes darted to Lonewolf.

Lonewolf smiled, overcome with the power she held in her hands. "*K'ad á nlí'í nli. Dinilnaa niká ninádá, shi yázhi.*" *You* are doing it. He searches for *you*, little one.

She didn't smile. Her eyes filled, glistening green pools, and the anguish in them struck Lonewolf's heart.

Manuelito quieted, his breathing evened, and Willow slowly slipped her hand from beneath Lonewolf's. She clenched her jaw against the tears, trying to focus, keep control.

It wasn't in her. She wouldn't *let* it be in her. Willow wrung her hands as if she could squeeze out any remnants of what she'd felt: the turmoil within Manuelito rising to her fingers like lightning to a rod. The churning had pulled at her, spiraled within her, tossed around her emotions—and her control. The thought shook her to the ground and she leaned against the bed.

She struggled now to find any control remaining. How did Lonewolf stand it? To be assaulted like that, have every emotion whipped and tossed like dry sagebrush.

She hadn't asked for any powers—didn't *want* any. That was for others. For her father, her grandfather, for Lonewolf. It wasn't in Willow, no matter what anyone said, no matter how hard they wished. And she knew they had. Her grandfather still did.

But she didn't have the courage. Whatever they looked for in her wasn't there! Didn't they see that? Her mother had. Willow didn't even have a last memory of her. Not one of goodbye. She was just gone. And Willow had known she hadn't been enough for her mother.

Willow couldn't look at Lonewolf, knowing the message his eyes held, knowing what he would want to see in hers. But it wasn't there. And he was wrong to think she had helped with Manuelito. Wrong!

Willow pushed away from the bed and started for the door. Lonewolf's hands settled on her shoulders and he turned her to face him.

"He will be fine, Willow."

His voice, full of confidence and compassion, nearly destroyed her. She wanted to lean into him, draw on his strength. But she had no right. He deserved someone with more courage and that wasn't her.

He still held her shoulders, awaiting an answer. Willow shrugged a vague agreement, her throat too constricted to trust.

She let her legs take her out of the room, down the hallways and back into the sunshine. With a deep steadying breath, she willed the fear from her eyes, the tightness from her lips. She could *look* in control.

By the time Lonewolf fell into step beside her, her mask was complete. Lonewolf's arm slid over her shoulders and the rightness of it only increased the ache within Willow.

"Do not worry, Willow, I will not fail."

The ache grew to a lump in Willow's throat. He thought she was worried about Manuelito when all she'd thought about was herself! Willow straightened her back and willed down her fears.

"Until Manuelito is fine, I'll worry."

FOURTEEN

The barking dogs preceded them. Willow could hear their warning yips and howls before she took the last turn in the path and her headlights captured their gleaming eyes. Most Navajo dogs, like their masters, would wait warily for a stranger to approach. Not these. But then, these dogs had been raised by Grandfather.

As had she. She knew well Grandfather's philosophy of taking on the world, exploring it, enjoying life's surprises. Grandfather had made the world a great adventure.

So when he encouraged her visions, Willow had thought that too would be fun. It was, in the beginning, when she had thought it was only play. But the first time a vision grabbed her, took her past the edge of reason, Willow had gotten sick—literally. And no matter how hard she had tried—oh! how much she had wanted to please him!—she could not give her mind over to the unknown. The uncertainty and the nausea made it hard. The paralyzing terror made it downright dangerous.

But Grandfather never gave up. He'd pushed her to explore in his own relentless, impossibly patient way. And Willow's frustrations and fears had grown, until, as a teenager, they had mutated to anger. Then *she* was the one to put an end to it.

If Grandfather knew of the visions she had shared with Lonewolf, of what she had felt swirl through Manuelito and into her . . . There'd be no escape.

But she did not have to admit to the visions. She only had to ask his help in finding the chant skin. Just because

Manuelito would become the next Starway Shaman did not involve Willow. This was not about her.

Willow stopped the jeep in front of the hogan, took a deep breath, and tightened the mask she'd donned at the hospital.

Soft light and flute music emanated from the hogan.

"He's home," she said to Lonewolf.

Lonewolf stepped from the jeep into the tangle of legs and furry heads eager for a rub. Willow knocked once and entered. Only one kerosene lamp burned in the kitchen area. In the dim light, Willow could see the brief glow of a cigarette.

"Grandfather?"

"Children! Come in, come in."

Willow and Lonewolf settled at the wooden table. "Grandfather, we need your help."

"Yes, I heard you looked for me today at Kinlichee." He smiled at Lonewolf. "News on the reservation travels like an electrical storm. Especially when made by a stranger. So, Lonewolf, what did you think of Corbert Joe?"

Grandfather drew thoughtfully on the cigarette and Willow caught the gleam in his eye. "Watch out, Lonewolf. It's a trap," she said. "Grandfather *started* the whole push for self-rule."

"Granddaughter, self-rule is not a trap. *Complacency* is the trap. People should not believe everything will work out, that Washington will look out for us. That the *bilagaana* cannot possibly be so evil."

"We didn't come to talk politics." Willow heard the annoyance in her voice and tried to clamp it down. "Grandfather, have you ever heard of a Starway Chant skin?"

"Yes," he said, but he looked at Lonewolf. "Why do you ask me?"

Willow caught the question in his eyes. "Grandfather,

I know all about Lonewolf. I know he's the last stargazer."

"Good, good!" He smiled without a hint of embarrassment. "But, still—why ask me? Shouldn't you have it?"

"I did, Grandfather," Lonewolf said. "One hundred and thirty years ago."

"Where did you leave it?"

"With *Ha'tanii*. Where it has always been safe."

"At Four Hole Site," Grandfather said, his brows slightly furrowed. "And you have been to Four Hole?"

Grandfather's tone made the question sound more like an accusation and Willow remembered thinking, as she hid in the cave, how odd it was Grandfather had never shown her those particular caves.

"We searched for it this morning," she said. "We didn't find the skin."

"I saw signs of recent digging," Lonewolf said.

"Digging at Four Hole?" Grandfather stood from the table and walked to the portable stove where he knelt at the pot of water. "No one should be in that cave." His words came out like a threat.

"Why, Grandfather? Why didn't you ever take me there?"

Grandfather made his way back to the table, balancing an overfull cup of water. "Those caves are dangerous," he said and spooned instant coffee and sugar into his cup.

"They weren't dangerous when I hid from Lonewolf." Willow didn't know why she said that, what made her want to contradict Grandfather. "And the 'danger' hasn't stopped other people."

"What do you mean?" Water slipped over the side of Grandfather's cup, carrying with it specks of coffee grit. One lean, brown desert-aged finger curved to the cup and wiped it.

"I found a gun there this morning."

"A gun?" Grandfather gasped and Willow saw trembling coffee slosh over the rim.

"I've taken it in for analysis. I'm hoping it's the murder weapon."

"A gun? You found a gun?" Grandfather got up and walked with no purpose around the kitchen. "How dare they?" he said so low, Willow barely heard.

"Grandfather, Lonewolf needs the chant skin."

"And you think I should know where it is?" he snapped.

"I thought you might know something about it. You have always protected the canyon."

Instead of the pride he usually displayed at the mention of his lifelong obsession, Grandfather glared at Willow, his lips a furious thin line. "Yes," he said. "As did my father and his father. Three generations"—he looked pointedly at Willow—"have protected the canyon and its artifacts."

The old roles asserted themselves: Willow and Grandfather as adversaries. Instantly, the old feelings of anger and frustration leapt through her. "You're not the only one who cares, Grandfather." Willow pulled the sheet from her pocket and handed it to him. "Cal asked me to show you this. Someone tried to sell that pottery to Weatherbee at Red Rock, but the old trader got suspicious."

"No, this can't be."

"Do you recognize any of it?"

"Yes, it's Navajo, early eighteen hundreds." He spoke with such sadness, Willow's heart went out to him. She hated to ask the next question.

"Do you know the provenance?"

"The canyon," he said simply, then looked at her, his eyes filled with self-reproach. "They came from the canyon."

"Grandfather, no one is blaming you."

"No one?" His gaze settled evenly on her.

"I don't blame you, I never have. One man cannot protect the whole canyon."

"This is impossible." The paper trembled slightly in Grandfather's hands.

Alarm grew within Willow. She'd never seen him so upset. She reached out to touch him, to console him, but withdrew her hand. She couldn't hold the real world at bay for Grandfather.

"Grandfather," Lonewolf said. "Do you know anything about the chant skin?"

"It's hardly more than a legend—like the last stargazer." He gave a strained smile. "You'll pardon me, Lonewolf, but it's true. Why do you need it?"

"For Manuelito," Lonewolf said. "In two days, the stars will align and the ceremony must be performed."

"My God. The child," Grandfather said. "He will be the next Starway Shaman?"

"If I can find the chant skin."

"This can't be happening," he said. "First the boy, murdered; then the man, murdered; this pottery; and now the chant skin. This has gone too far."

Grandfather stared at a wall covered with a jumble of Navajo artifacts. Willow couldn't have guessed what he was looking at.

"Grandfather, I don't think the murders had anything to do with the canyon or its artifacts. I have my own theory. It's not pretty and it involves Arabs and drugs. But I think the canyon was just a hiding place."

"Arabs? Drugs?"

Willow could hardly concentrate past the confusion in Grandfather's eyes. "An Arab's home and his business—Khalib Trading—were bombed in Gallup. The man who chased me, the one Lonewolf shot with an arrow? He was also an Indian trader. Small-time, though. I think he and Khalib were dealing drugs, stashing them in the canyon, and he thought I'd found something. The boy probably died the same way—stumbling on something he shouldn't have. I figure the bombs in Gallup were someone's retribution—''

''Do tah!'' Grandfather's sharp voice startled Willow. He had never yelled at her and never at *anyone* with such force. ''You worry about all the wrong things, Granddaughter. Just like your mother. This will stop. It must stop!'' He tossed the sheet at Willow and it fluttered to her hand as he started for the door. He paused alongside Lonewolf.

''What will happen if you do not have the skin for Manuelito?''

''If I cannot do the ceremony, he will die, Grandfather.''

''Could you be wrong?''

''No.''

''Then we have to find the skin. There are some people I can talk to,'' he said, moving to the door. ''Collectors. That sort. It must be somewhere.''

The urgency in Grandfather's voice sent a trickle of fear down Willow's spine. He sounded agitated, almost desperate, as if he were the one facing death.

Something else bothered her. Grandfather had not spoken of Willow's mother in years. As far as he was concerned, the subject of her mother fell into the category of old enemies.

And he had never compared Willow to her mother. The concept was so new, Willow wasn't sure whether to be pleased or insulted. She'd often wondered what her mother was like. But there were no memories and no pictures to ponder. All Willow knew was that her mother had left the child. Whatever Willow was, was either not enough or too much for her mother to bear.

Willow felt there was something she should understand—something important that hung just past the edge of her grasp. But she couldn't conjure her mother up, not even the *feeling* of being with her.

''Why are you angry?''

The question startled Willow from her thoughts. She saw the hogan door shut behind Grandfather.

"What?"

"You were angry, then sad. Why?"

Willow thought of denying it. But Lonewolf looked at her just then and his gaze left her no escape.

"It's an old argument with old feelings. I'm sorry I let them overtake me."

Lonewolf wondered how to get the truth from Willow. Ever since the hospital, when Lonewolf had felt Manuelito respond to her touch, she had been distant. He had thought she was concerned for Manuelito. But it was more, much more.

Whatever worried her had grown over each silent mile, until it seemed to have a life—some cold presence that now stood between them. Lonewolf rose and walked to the pottery shelves. He let his fingers trace the geometric patterns; he ran his hands inside the bowls.

"You were angry because Grandfather protects the canyon?"

"He's always been the unofficial protector of the canyon and anything else within his domain. Including me."

"And you disagree."

"Yes, I disagree. He believes in the old ways, the old things—" She gestured around the packed hogan. "Those are paramount."

Lonewolf faced Willow. "And what do *you* believe?"

"I believe in Navajo minds and their abilities," she answered without hesitation. "I believe in the here and now. In living cultures, not celebrating the dead."

"The dead?"

"All this lifeless stuff made by people who are dead and gone—" She broke off. "Oh my God, Lonewolf. I'm sorry. You don't know any of these pieces, the people . . . ?"

"No, little one, you have not offended me." He

smiled. "But why are you so offended by these things?"

"Did you know there's a fortune here? Just one of these pots would sell for thousands in a store. Collectors, museums, make a whole living off things made by dead people. But tourists scream over the price of a new rug, which maybe took months to make and is the only income for the Navajo woman who has to put the food on the table. Her husband, meanwhile, is free to drink his earnings, or gamble, or spend them all on a new truck."

"So you argue with Grandfather about fairness."

"No, it's more than that." Willow walked to the portable stove, grabbed a cup, and poured hot water into it. Lonewolf noted she followed the same steps as Grandfather when she had asked him about Four Hole Site.

"It's not just the fairness, or the money," she said over her shoulder. "It's what all this represents. To Grandfather these things represent our heritage, our culture, the Navajo way that he wants to preserve."

"And for you?"

"For me, these are just things. Just a distraction from what the Navajo really are: a great people who need guidance." She stared into the slack brown liquid in her cup.

"What is it, Willow? What are you afraid of?"

Her quick glance, full of fear, confirmed his guess. But she quickly masked it. "I only wonder, how will Manuelito guide anyone? He is just a child."

"You will help him." Lonewolf walked to her and placed his palm on Willow's cheek. She was so soft, so beautiful, so afraid. He could feel the swirl of emotions through her. Yet she was so determined not to show it, her eyes glittered with the effort. How could he get past that wall? How could he ease the fears she would not admit?

He framed her face with his hands. "You have nothing to fear, *shi yázhi*. The stars will guide Manuelito, just as they have me."

The fear within her formed a lump in Willow's throat. "Why can't you just be the stargazer, Lonewolf? Why Manuelito?" *Why do you have to leave?*

Pain flooded Lonewolf's eyes with such suddenness Willow's eyes pricked.

"I failed in my time," he said. "Because of my failure, much is wrong for the *Diné*. It is not I who can make it right, but the child today gifted by the starborn ancestors."

The enormity of his confession settled in Willow's gut. He had been sent to right a wrong. To accomplish a mission. With no regard for whatever life he had or the lives he would encounter here. The stars did not care that her heart had been stolen by a nineteenth-century warrior. They did not care what it would cost her in loneliness or in the fears she would have to face.

And right now, neither did she.

"I'm sorry for whatever you've endured—being torn from your life and dropped into this time." Willow laid a hand on his chest and felt Lonewolf draw a quick breath.

"But I am so grateful to the stars for sending you." She placed her other hand at Lonewolf's jaw. So strong, so sure.

Her heartbeat matched the accelerated thump of Lonewolf's. He wanted her, she could feel it in the tenseness of his chest, the pulsing below his jaw. Her gaze fell to his mouth; masculine, firm lips. His hand pressed at her back and Willow looked up to eyes so full of desire, her knees went weak.

"I want *your* magic, Lonewolf," she whispered, as he lowered his head and captured her lips.

Lonewolf did not want magic. His needs were much more basic. He wanted Willow, in the same way a wolf wants its mate—with no thought, only a primal urge. A need so deep and driving, the wolf would fight to the death any challenger—his need for a mate stronger than his need for isolation. For when he had taken the she-wolf, with unleashed animal instincts, he made her his own.

Lonewolf knew this code. But he would break it. He would own this warrior, take her as his. Then leave, never to see her again. And never to love anyone again, because she would always be there in his soul. He knew this much. But he could not think about it. The pain within would smother him. He would live with it later, when he was without her.

Tonight, she would be his.

The rugs below were their bed; the night sky blinked and danced through the hogan smoke hole. In the heart of Navajoland, the two warriors fought their darkest fears and succumbed to their deepest needs.

Garments tore. Needy hands grasped and kneaded. Lips, desperate to fill the threatening void, pressed, sought, demanded. Nothing would make the hollow fears disappear—so they each grabbed for more.

As their wild cries of pleasure rose, Willow and Lonewolf lay spent and defeated: two halves of a whole that could not be united.

"Why didn't you just give the Feds our business card, you idiot?"

"We've sold to Red Rock before," the man said lazily, as if speaking were an effort for his huge body.

"You couldn't use your head and sell the Zuni?" Curtis tossed a Zuni dough bowl against the wall, in one quick move destroying a fifty-year-old piece of art.

"I told you I needed money." Gonzales shrugged. "You said to sell something."

"But not the Navajo. You might as well have waved a red flag. Why the hell d'you think I planted the drugs?"

"That's not my concern," Gonzales said.

Curtis reminded himself, not for the first time, that he

needed Gonzales and his connections. "I was laying a trail to the Arabs. And if you'd just thought about that—"

"Look, it was only a few pieces, which is all you've let me see." Gonzales straightened and hitched up his pants. "Where's the rest, Curtis?"

"It's safe. Trust me."

"I want to see the stash, Curtis. And so does the German. He wants pictures."

Curtis had known this moment would come. With ease, he transformed his face to look hurt. "You don't trust me. Fine." He held up a hand even though Gonzales had not protested. "I'll take you to the storage unit tomorrow morning. And you can take all the pictures you want."

Before Gonzales had a chance to answer, someone knocked on the door.

"Yeah?"

"Oh, good. Good. I'm glad you're home. We have to talk."

Damn it! Why this guy? God, he was trapped! He glanced at Gonzales, who was pacing the short, narrow kitchen.

"Who's there?" Gonzales barked.

"A neighbor. I'll take care of this." Curtis pulled the door shut behind him.

"What do you want?"

"I need to see what you've collected."

"This isn't a good time."

"You don't understand. This has to end."

"Are you crazy, old man?"

The old man's eyes hardened. "Yes, I was a fool. I thought I was doing the right thing, but I wasn't. Now it has to end."

The vise tightened. Curtis tried to remember how much money he had stashed. Not enough.

"But I haven't retrieved everything. You don't want

to leave anything there for vandals, right? I mean, that was the whole point."

"Except you have become the vandal, haven't you, Curtis? You tried to sell some pots at Red Rock."

"It wasn't me, it was my partner."

"Your partner? I hired only you, Curtis. No one else."

"We needed money and you weren't around. But it won't happen again, I promise." Curtis had the acute sense of money slipping through his hands. "We're saving history, remember? Tell you what, I'll get a list together in the next couple of days and we'll talk again. You'll feel better when you see what you've saved for future generations."

"No, no! It can't wait. I must see what you have now!"

"That's impossible. I have someone here. You know. I'm entertaining someone."

"Just tell me, did you find a deerskin with painting on it?"

"A skin? No. Was there supposed to be one?"

"You've been to Four Hole, no?"

At the mention of his main hoarding site, Curtis felt his stomach clench. "Of course," he answered nonchalantly. "Nothing there, though. Listen, I'll be going back to that site. Soon, in fact. I'll keep an eye out."

"No. No more!"

"Now look, no reason to get so upset. I'm just doing what you hired me for. What's so important about this skin?"

"You'd remember it if you saw it. It's old, painted with a planetaria."

Curtis mentally calculated the worth of the artifact and his mouth watered. This old fool didn't even know what he had. Curtis would bet on it. But Curtis knew, and he wasn't about to let loose, not now. "I'll tell you what, I'll take you to the storage tomorrow afternoon."

"I want to see the list of what you have. And then this is over."

"You're upset. I can help. We'll see what's in storage. The list is there, too."

The old man's keen eyes bored into Curtis, leaving Curtis with the uneasy feeling his thoughts had been read. He shook his head with disgust.

"Tomorrow, then?" Curtis pasted on his most sincere smile. "The Cubby Hole Storage in Chinle. I'll meet you outside the office at four."

The old man walked into the night shadows then stopped and seemed to grow taller and more erect before Curtis's eyes. Then he turned.

"Don't try to keep secrets from me," was all he said before he disappeared down the rutted path.

Curtis could hear noises from the back of the trailer. Gonzales was searching the whole damn place. As if Curtis were stupid enough to store anything there.

Or even in a storage unit. Curtis smiled. Oh, there was enough in the unit to keep Gonzales happy and keep the old man busy. But he'd stashed the best where no one would find it. Any museum would kill for what Curtis had in the cave. Not that he could sell it to them, or anyone else in the United States. Not yet. But all in good time. Curtis wasn't stupid. He had a plan.

'Course, the plan hadn't included taking out the old man. Maybe it should have. Curtis was flexible. Something Gonzales still had to learn. What the hell difference was one more dead body?

FIFTEEN

Lonewolf squinted at the perfect sky, bright and cool blue like a polished turquoise stone. Against the high blue, the canyon walls seemed taller, deeper red, the desert varnish streaking the sandstone even more brown. As always, the magnitude of the canyon, its awesome beauty, filled Lonewolf with peace.

Morning sounds of the canyon drifted to him. Some were as old as time. A red-tailed hawk glided high overhead, riding the wind that blew across the mesa. His down-slurred scream echoed off the towering cliffs. The rising wind brought also the descending trill of the canyon wrens and the nearly imperceptible rustle of carrizo grass.

But other sounds were new. From the canyon floor rose the distant laughter of Navajo women and the grumble of a jeep rumbling over rutted arroyos.

Four days ago, in Lonewolf's time, those sounds would not have existed. Instead, he would have heard horses, the shouts of warriors, the cries of hungry children. His ears strained for those familiar sounds. But they were not there.

Neither were the scars from all the battles, no blackened earth from the hundreds of council fires of the gathered warriors; no burned-out hogans or starving cattle; no blood staining the canyon floor. The only evidence of battle was an absence: the glorious grove of peach trees now gone.

Even *that* the canyon had healed with grass and flowers. Its wounds healed, with no scars remaining.

In Lonewolf's life, he had collected many, many scars. Those one could see, and those he carried within. Each wound reopened the last, until the layers of scar tissue were so thick he had become impervious to the dull ache. Unlike the canyon, his scars had not healed, only been buried.

The canyon endured, not as some monument to tragedy but as a constant source of strength and life for the People. It held the heart and soul of the People, but it was not sad. It lived. And so did the *Diné*.

And, on that new morning, on the mesa above the canyon, Lonewolf too wanted to live—taking each day as a new one without the burden of old wounds, old betrayals. Without the fear of failure.

What would it be like to live, unburdened with the past, with those failures? Departure, loss—they were so a part of him, he expected it. But he didn't want that. He didn't want a life alone. That new thought clenched his heart.

He had perceived the possibility of that as he lay with Willow. Their lovemaking, at first needy and desperate, had become something different—something more grand than the two of them. As if they completed each other.

No one before had made him feel whole. Not the Talmans, who had loved him, raised him as their own. Not Corn Flower, whom he had loved, but whose gentle spirit made his own fears seem more uncontrollable.

Willow's fears matched his own. So did her strength. They were like sand and water. Water ran through sand, over sand, each remaining basically unchanged. But then a force of nature blended the two into something more powerful—quicksand. Which nothing could escape, including the sand and the water.

That was how Lonewolf felt. Captured by Willow. A part of her. And she was a part of him. Was it possible, could he dare hope she could feel the same?

He could fight the fears within her, defeat them. By the Holy Ones, he would take them on as his own. Free her to trust him. But that was not a battle he had won before—not with her, not with the council, not with the majority of the People. He had always told himself he could stand alone. But now, by all he held sacred, he wanted to stand with Willow.

Lonewolf gazed at the canyon below. Its magnitude imbued him with strength. Here, where the greatness of the People's spirit was reflected in the canyon, anything seemed possible.

Willow woke up humming. The vibration, running up her chest and tickling the back of her throat, brought her wide awake. That, and the fact she didn't know the song.

She liked the rhythmic melody—simple yet haunting—and tried to remember where she'd heard it. She listened. Listened!

The song came from outside and she knew the source. Lonewolf. His voice, masculine and somewhat rough, drifted on the morning light, through the small window, and settled beside her, as if he were whispering in her ear.

The memory of their night of needy lovemaking flowed over her and Willow felt her body respond at the mere thought of his lips on hers, on her breasts; his fingers stroking behind her knees.

She would have reached for Lonewolf but she was alone. With only his song beside her, touching her, filling her with desire. A song she knew would haunt her as it had even as she slept, provoking a hum from unconscious lips.

He could reach past her barriers, without her permission, without even her knowledge. As if her heart were a willing accomplice. When had that happened? When had her heart learned of him? When he stood—confused, yet defiant—in the cave? Or was it when he had told Corbert that pride alone wasn't enough?

Or, simply, was it his passion, which took all her fears and replaced them with strength?

It had all accumulated, detail by detail, into this man whose song burrowed within her. Her heart knew him better than anyone else.

Our hearts know each other. Lonewolf's words and the first vision they had shared—passion in the firelight—washed over her. He had become a part of her then. And each time since, when he held her, she took more of him, letting his strength flood through her—using his strength to deny her own fears.

She told herself it was fair. In two days he would leave and she would be alone. With Grandfather and Manuelito. One who believed in the power of traditions and the other who would *be* a living legend. Panic rose within her, as if a horrible sleeping giant had awakened.

She clenched the sheets. It wouldn't matter. It didn't involve her. *She* was not the stargazer. She would not have to endure the visions.

If they came, who would she turn to? An old man? A child? Lonewolf would be gone.

Suddenly, the sound of Lonewolf was not enough for Willow. She leaned up on an elbow and looked through the small window by her bed. The yard—though there was none, just an endless expanse of juniper, cedar, and red earth—was empty. Then Lonewolf rounded the corner of the hogan, carrying a load of branches. The rising sun shone from behind him and into her eyes and, for a wild second, Willow thought he was naked—the length of him golden-brown, natural as buckskin.

Taut muscles stretched across his back and spiraled his arm as lean tendons. He shifted the load and Willow saw deerskin hugging his long legs.

Lonewolf dropped the pile of branches near a boulder and took a seat. He pulled a long branch from the top and whittled off the limb stubs with his knife. The blade glistened in the sunlight.

She could have watched him forever: his own features as tough as the wind-warped juniper he held in his hands; his long hair stark black against the perfect turquoise sky. His strong fingers wielded the knife as he peeled and shaped the once-rough branch. With skillful strokes, he created a smooth post from a gnarled limb. He laid it on the ground, picked up another branch, and began all over again.

She could walk to him, run her hands across his back. It would be sun-warmed, soothing. He would take her in his arms. She knew he would, just as he had last night. And her fears would be forgotten, as if they didn't exist. But they did. They were real and they would be there when he was gone. As they were now, slowly straining her control.

She couldn't tell him and risk losing the desire she saw in his eyes. He would never want a coward. And that's what she was, except when she was with him.

Willow's normal urge to be *doing* something finally stirred. She threw back the covers, dispelling any desire to just lie there, and pulled jeans and a sweatshirt from the trunk below the bed. She tugged on cowboy boots, ran a brush through her hair, and left her room.

Lonewolf looked up at her and stopped humming. The world tilted as if, for Willow, Lonewolf's chant had kept it right. Welcome filled his eyes and Willow's balance returned like a magnet finding its polar partner.

"Good morning."

"Yá'át'ééh," he said and smiled, warming her more completely than the morning sun.

"Are you building a bonfire?" Willow asked, gesturing at the stack of branches.

"No, a ceremonial hogan."

"Oh." The pile of wood, which had looked huge, now seemed too few. "A whole hogan? With those?"

"I need only a small hogan. Large enough to hold one."

"Manuelito?"

"No, me. When I prepare for the ceremony." His mouth curved into his crooked smile and Willow's heart leapt. She yanked in on her feelings.

"I'm going to the station," she said.

Lonewolf just watched her, still with that smile on his face, the look in his eyes that made her crazy. She couldn't help but smile back. She couldn't stop from walking toward him. Why shouldn't she? It would be right. *It is right,* her heart said. His lips on hers, his arms around her.

He would be holding a lie.

The truth stopped her in her tracks. "I'm going to the station," she said again. "I'll do what I can to find the chant skin. I'm sure that's what Grandfather is doing right now."

Willow turned away and walked to her jeep. Lonewolf watched her and mused at the battle he had seen in her eyes. She wanted him, yet she had stopped and kept her distance. It was not fear he had seen, but determination. It was the same look he had seen in her eyes last night when he had asked what she feared. That is, *after* she had masked the panic.

He heard the jeep come to life and, in a cloud of dust, Willow disappeared down the road. What was she hiding? Why did she run from him? Like a wild animal leading a hunter away from the den.

A distraction.

It was not *him* she feared, but weakening her guard. Lonewolf smiled after his skittish cougar. She gained trust slowly, but time was not something Lonewolf had. He had to know before tomorrow night if she would trust him. Because, if not, he would be better in the past, with one hundred and thirty years between them.

Patience was the preferred way to tame a wild animal, but when a hunter was hurried, he set a trap.

Willow's bad mood had a nasty edge, like jagged lightning in a thundercloud. Just her look steered most coworkers clear. Others, oblivious to the storm, crossed her path and paid the consequences. By late afternoon, she had antagonized everyone in the squad room. That they didn't deserve it only escalated her surliness.

She blamed it on the endless phone calls. She had talked to every museum, gallery, trading post, and Tribal office in the whole southwest. Every one of them listened, asked courteous questions, promised to talk to their contacts. By the time she called the merchants in Old Town, Albuquerque, some already knew of the search for the deerskin. No one had complained about spending time on the phone with a cop.

With a whole network of merchants, collectors, and curators looking, she still had nothing. So, she blamed the mood on the futility of the whole thing. It occurred to her that no one she had spoken to had mentioned Grandfather, though most of them knew Vidal. Perhaps he had had better luck.

Willow looked at her watch. It was past five o'clock. She gathered her things and stopped a night officer on her way out.

She couldn't ignore his slight flinch when he realized whose hand was at his sleeve. "Nelson, I'm expecting some important faxes and phone calls." She used the same excuse she had given all day long. "It concerns a case I'm working on. If anything comes in, call me on the mobile. Right away."

"Sure thing, Officer Becenti."

Willow heard but didn't acknowledge. She was already on her way out the door to her jeep, back to Grandfather's. To Lonewolf.

At the thought of him, the knot of tension at her neck

eased. The grip she'd held on herself all day relaxed. Thirty minutes later, fast even by Willow's standards, she pulled up to the hogan.

A tangle of legs and wagging tails accompanied her to the hogan door. After a knock, Willow entered and glanced at the empty room. One of the dogs followed on her heels.

"So, where are they?" she asked, as she absentmindedly rubbed the matted hair behind the dog's ear.

Willow walked back outside and followed the yips and barks around the corner of the hogan. There, in the clearing of juniper, stood Lonewolf. Her body responded immediately: her heart hammered and she couldn't pull her eyes away.

"Hi," she said lightly. She placed all the nonchalance she could muster in the single word.

Lonewolf turned and, in the instant their eyes met, Willow felt a hunger leap within her. Her desire was echoed in Lonewolf's eyes. She wanted to walk to him, but forced herself to stay put.

"Is Grandfather here?"

"I have not seen him since last night. And you? Did you have any luck?"

Willow shook her head. "No. But the museums take a while and they're our best hope." Willow stood there, stiff, awkward, wanting something but she didn't know what.

Lonewolf bent and picked up a branch from the pile. He laid it atop two short poles standing parallel about three feet apart, cut a cord with his knife and lashed the branch to the corners of the poles. Five other posts completed the circle, each already fastened to the next by a branch like the one Lonewolf had just tied to the last two poles. It would be a small structure, as Lonewolf had said. The materials, scrounged from the area, would not withstand much abuse.

Of course, it wasn't meant to last long. Only for tomorrow night. Willow walked the six sides of the enclosure. The framework of cleaned branches came up only chest-high and was yet to have a roof. The primitive hogan appealed to Willow.

"Manuelito would love to camp out here," she said, thinking aloud. She could imagine him with sleeping bag and pillow and the dogs curled around him; a healthy boy on a child's adventure. Her eyes pricked and she swallowed hard.

"I'm sorry," she said.

"For what?"

For everything. Because I couldn't help. Because I have disappointed you. She clenched her jaw against the threat of tears. *Because I want to walk to you and I can't.*

Lonewolf's hands settled on her shoulders. Willow looked up, startled, without time to mask her eyes. Then, she didn't care. His gaze, as always, held hers closer than an embrace.

"You worry too much, *shi yázhi.*" The deep timbre of his voice kindled the heat in her veins.

A flash of light arced through the air and landed near Willow's feet. The knife handle bobbled as the blade sank to its shaft into the earth. A finger-light touch at Willow's jaw brought her gaze from the ground to Lonewolf.

His eyes smoldered with desire and the flames caught within her. She leaned up to him, his rock-hard thighs bracketing her, his hands at her head, sliding deep into her hair, tilting her head. Then his lips captured hers in a mind-numbing kiss.

The world stopped. Her heart sped. Pure pleasure gripped her with such intensity it hurt. An arm circled her back and pulled her closer, deepening the kiss. Willow gripped his shoulders, matching Lonewolf's strength, meeting his urgency. Air, heated by their breath and passion, circled round them. Willow would let him take her right then and there, outside in daylight.

The thought tickled her brain and brought a smile. Lonewolf slid his mouth from hers, trailed kisses to her ear.

"What is funny, little one?" he whispered.

"Not funny," Willow said, her voice hoarse. The effort to talk made her heave a sigh, then try again. "I wasn't laughing. Just smiling."

"At what?" His lips grazed her temple and scattered her thoughts.

"What?"

"What made you smile?" His tongue found her ear, licked the ridge then slid in.

Willow went limp and rigid simultaneously. Her bones melted, but the cord within her—the one Lonewolf found—drew rigid. Pulled her up, made her seek more, demanded more. Lonewolf's tongue went deeper, laving, probing to some sensitive spot with a direct link to her core.

Then his hand cupped her and massaged in rhythm with his tongue. Willow thought she would die.

The tongue-caresses became kisses and Willow nearly moaned for the want of more.

"You have not answered me, little one," he whispered between kisses.

She couldn't. The sensual assault left her mindless. He trailed his tongue around her ear, down her jaw and back, melting her. All the while, his hand moved between her legs, grinding, tightening the cord within her.

Then she felt his fingers at her waist. The snap at her jeans popped. Then he stopped.

No! Don't stop!

She opened her eyes in time to see him walking away. "No," she managed to croak.

Lonewolf smiled, the look of a lover. "Do not move," he said, then was gone.

Willow wavered at the abrupt withdrawal. Her spine was nothing but jelly without his hands, his strength. A moment later, he returned, a Navajo blanket in his hands. With a flick of his wrists, the blanket blurred, then settled on the ground.

He lowered her to the blanket, his gaze unwavering—sensual, full of passion for her. The setting sun behind him blinded her. And in that instant, the waning light made it all so clear. She loved him—not the stargazer, not the warrior. But the man. When his arms closed around her, her body sighed with the rightness, the *completeness*.

Who she was, right now, in daylight, was someone better, someone stronger, someone more worthy of Lonewolf. It was the darkness that bred her fears, because visions came more easily in the night—like photographs emerging in a darkroom. With no visions, no magic, no stars—it was easy to be brave. But that bravery was ultimately dishonest.

The truth about herself fell from her heart to her lips. "There aren't any stars," she said.

Lonewolf rolled her onto her back and sat astride her. His gaze held hers and Willow panicked. She didn't want him to know her fears. Why had she said anything?

He looked at her with knowing eyes and smiled. "Ah, little one, look above you. There are always stars, even in the day."

"But the sunlight hides them."

Lonewolf quirked a mischievous grin. "They say the sun *is* a star."

His crooked smile, the squint of his eyes, his heat—warmer than the sun—he was irresistible. Willow proved it—in the glow of the evening sun.

SIXTEEN

It would be so easy. She could pretend forever as long as Lonewolf held her and talked. Willow loved the sound of his voice, like a growl from deep inside him that reverberated through her. She pressed her cheek to his bare chest and breathed him in. He smelled of daylight, cedar, and hard work. Honest things, just like the man.

He talked of stars and planets, comets and constellations—white man's and the Navajo's. All the while, Willow contemplated the miracle that he had come from another time, to her—that he desired her. If they were in the past, would she be beside him? Would she have a place in his life—defending their home, fighting the enemies, protecting their children?

Willow thought of this, nestled at Lonewolf's shoulder, his voice whispering secrets of the skies.

"Do you miss your home? Your time?"

Lonewolf stared into the darkness, his brow furrowed, as if he were looking back in time.

"Yes," he said finally.

"What do you miss?"

He gave her a half-smile. "There, I knew who were my enemies."

Willow thought he might be joking. "What would you be doing right now?"

"I do not know. I was on my way to find Rope Thrower. I suppose I would be captive. And if he would not listen . . ." Lonewolf shrugged, rocking Willow's head closer to his chest. She felt his heart beat beneath her. "I would be dead."

He had not asked for sympathy. He had stated the facts, just as she would have done. But the cold truth swept through her and brought the crystal-clear vision of Lonewolf sprawled on the ground, lifeless. Willow shuddered involuntarily. Lonewolf pressed her nearer, but the chill stayed.

"You were going alone? With no help?"

"I had no choice."

The determination in his voice barely masked the trace of loneliness. Willow knew that feeling all too well. It was the hell-bound drive of total commitment and God help the person who stood in the way.

"Would you do the same now?"

"No," he said in a tight voice.

"What? What would you do differently? The People could not defeat Kit Carson. Ever. And you could never convince them all to leave *Dinehtah*. There was no other possible ending but the one already played out."

"Not if we kidnapped Carson and negotiated a peace."

Willow touched Lonewolf's grim jaw with her finger and turned his face to hers.

"The People survived that time, Lonewolf. They survived and so did *Dinehtah*. And now, the Navajo are the largest tribe in the United States. We did defeat them."

Lonewolf's eyes gleamed with starshine. "Yes. And think how much stronger we *would* be if we had never had to endure that torture and humiliation."

"You would go back to that?"

"You once said that is where I belong."

The words stuck in Willow's throat. That's not what she had meant. She had pictured him with a life he would want to return to.

"What about your family in Abiquiu? What were you doing with them?"

"They bought me."

"Bought you! How?"

"The usual way. On the Santa Fe market. Off an auction block."

"How old were you?"

"Eight."

Willow registered that as the same age as Manuelito. But her mind was working hard to encompass the nightmare being revealed.

"How horrible. Oh, God." She shut her eyes against the evil. "What kind of people—"

"They were very good people."

"What?"

"The Talmans. They were very good to me. They raised me as their son."

"How did you end up being sold?"

"Mexican raiders killed my mother and stole me."

"Oh, my God, I'm so sorry, Lonewolf." She looked at the man beside her and tried to imagine a small boy, taken away from everything that he knew. "You must've been so scared."

"I had the stars," he said simply.

Willow didn't know what to say. She pictured the child Lonewolf—thrown across a horse, surrounded by enemies—sure of his death.

How had Lonewolf survived? What had kept that frightened child alive? She couldn't ask the questions. She knew the grown warrior would hear only pity.

Neither one spoke, as if their silence condemned the cruel past to a far-off hell. Willow groped for a way to begin the conversation again.

"The Talmans. You said they were good. But . . ." Willow knitted her brow. "I'm having a hard time picturing a loving couple who buy a kidnapped child off an auction block."

"They had come from Philadelphia to start a business and a family. But they could not have children." Lonewolf turned his head toward Willow and smiled. "They adopted me."

The love in Lonewolf's eyes for his white parents brought Willow's heart to her throat.

"I'm glad they were good to you. You must've been very lonely, though."

"At first, yes. Then I discovered their library. Books on every wall, all the way to the ceiling. I would sit in a corner and just look at the pictures—until one day Father found me and taught me to read."

"They didn't send you to school?"

"No. Mother taught me studies at home. Mother said she would not have me learn in a system that called Indians savages. She had many fights with the local officials."

Willow felt her heart warm to these people who had protected Lonewolf and given him love. They had provided for this child, so different from themselves.

"How long were you with them?"

"Twelve years."

Willow calculated in her head. "You were still living with them when you were twenty?"

"That is when they died."

Lonewolf must have seen her questioning look, for he continued. "We had moved to Abiquiu. Father wanted to open a store there."

Willow nodded for him to go on.

"Abiquiu is . . . was," he corrected, "a small settlement. It was not far from the Utes. I was nervous about being there, but Mother and Father always sought something new."

Lonewolf turned his face back to the skies, leaving only his chiseled profile for Willow to study.

"They feared nothing, my mother and father. Not new

things, not new people, not the wilderness. Nothing. I admired that.''

For a moment he was silent.

''But, they should have feared the Utes.''

His words in the night, like dark, lethal shadows, threatened vengeance. Willow could almost feel his hatred.

''After that I returned to the canyon.''

His story ended, but Willow knew the torment had not. What had life been like for this orphan, torn from his family and raised by whites for so many years? She assumed his real father had still been alive, and others would have been overjoyed to see him. It was rare that captives ever returned to the Navajo.

But he would have been different. He knew how to read and write. He knew the ways of the white man—the enemies.

His life was more like hers than she had guessed. Like her, he had walked the line between two worlds, trying to fit into both. Finally, trying to be just one. And did they ever trust him?

She knew the answer to that by the hard line of his jaw and the keen set of his eyes.

''But it was hard for you at the canyon, too.''

He didn't look at her when he answered. ''Yes.''

''But your powers. Your visions. Surely you must have been a respected stargazer.''

Willow felt Lonewolf stiffen beside her.

''No. I do not imagine I am missed, little one.''

''There is no one else?''

''My only family is Grey Feather. And he, little one, he sent me here.'' Lonewolf smiled at her and Willow felt an agony pierce her heart, that he could so calmly talk of being sent away.

''Why?''

''I think he knew what was to happen.''

Willow gazed at her nineteenth-century warrior and

knew then why she loved him. He would go back to help the people who distrusted him. Not to prove anything, but because he was the one who could see the truth.

Willow lost track of the minutes as she stared at Lonewolf, memorizing the look of him. Lonewolf pointed to a cluster of stars and joined them with his finger, drawing imaginary lines that created the Navajo constellation Talking God.

Willow let him go on. She didn't have the voice to stop him.

He finished with Talking God and moved on to Listening Woman. He showed Willow the path between the two. She looked, unseeing. The bright stars blurred to indistinct globes of light, like street lamps in fog.

"That cluster there. Those are the Seven Sisters. The lodestars."

"Lodestars?"

"The guides, the pathfinders for any journey. They will teach you the skies."

Willow's attention riveted on his words. "What do you mean 'teach me'?"

Lonewolf rolled toward Willow, his arms wrapped around her back. When he spoke, his breath warmed her cheek. "You have a gift, Willow. You know it from your visions. To deny it is only to shrink back from your powers."

Willow didn't want to respond. She would have to deny his insight, argue about the legends. But pressed to him, all Willow wanted was to drink in his scent, drift on the vapors, and not land on solid ground. Not yet.

"You are not a coward," he whispered in her ear.

"How—?" Willow's breath caught. But of course he knew. One look in those fathomless eyes—he knew everything about her. Even her secrets. "Maybe I am," Willow murmured. Lonewolf spoke like a lover would, with words to caress and cradle. Instead, his words stung.

"What are you afraid of, *shi yázhi*? The stars are here to help you. They circle, night and day, awaiting your command. They will not leave, and they will never misjudge you. The stars know you and accept you."

She could not trust the stars. They had taken her father. He had trusted their guidance. She was sure of it. She had imagined him alone in the jungle, tracked by silent, deadly enemies. He would have looked to the skies and pled for safe conduct. But no spark of energy in the sky can deliver any human needs.

If her father hadn't died, maybe her mother wouldn't have left.

Grief boiled up within Willow. She tamped it down behind clenched teeth and shook loose of Lonewolf's warm embrace.

"No, Lonewolf. The stars don't watch over me."

Willow retreated to the hogan. She shivered with waves of tremors, her mind gripped in panic.

The stars had taken her father. It was simplistic. She knew that. But that conclusion had steered her whole life. Legends, myths, superstitions . . . the old ways—they were all a threat. Only logic and open eyes kept you safe and made you strong.

She struggled to calm herself. She had nothing to fear. Lonewolf couldn't force her to stargaze. He couldn't make her do anything she didn't want to. She told herself everything was all right, then she scolded herself for being childish.

Willow's pacing brought her to Grandfather's sagging shelves of artifacts. She had the murderous impulse to swipe the ancient pots from their precious haven, send them crashing to the floor.

With forced gentleness, she gingerly picked up an old pottery dipper, painted with black geometric patterns against a dark red slip.

Ancient shell necklaces curled around chipped white pottery, which, in turn, supported primitive buckskin shields leaning against the mud wall. Willow stepped over a cradle board of brittle wicker and leather thongs. She wasn't immune to their history, nor even to their beauty. Their designs, though simple, were done with artistic care, by someone whose time for leisure was practically nonexistent. And yet, here they stood, testimony to some ancient Navajo's need to express herself.

Willow held a small wooden duck, no bigger than her palm. Two hundred years ago this duck had captured the illness of some poor Navajo and had then been buried, never to be touched again. She rubbed the smooth surface with her thumb and wondered when she had begun to hate everything old, traditional. She felt a sob grow in her throat and quickly replaced the duck on the shelf.

This was her heritage, created by her ancestors. But it held no significance for the here and now. Their silent arrogance angered her. Old pieces made by dead people. So what? What about the living?

Willow shoved her hands into her pockets, not trusting them. A paper fluttered on the floor as if stirred by a breeze. Willow glanced at the door, expecting to see Lonewolf. But no one was there.

She picked up the crinkled sheet and recognized the fax from Nelson about the confiscated pottery.

The only noise was the sound of the doll kachinas swinging from the beams. All Willow's senses came alive, heightened. Cedar fragrance filled the hogan. The beams creaked and the shelves moaned.

She heard a crash. One of the pottery bowls lay at her feet, in pieces. Willow reached for the pottery and instantly fell into a black void.

The chasm swallowed her like quicksand. It encased her in a suffocation so real, she panicked for breath. Terror pressed on her with such deadly force, she couldn't scream.

Willow struggled for reality. Suddenly the broken bowl floated before her. She held the two pieces and fit them together as one. The free-fall stopped and she landed, with a thud, on her feet.

She was in the canyon, in the Four Hole caves. Grandfather called to her. She couldn't see him, but she followed his voice deeper into the caverns. He yelled for her to hurry. Willow ran through the narrow passages.

Then, right before her, two men fought, violently. The larger one had the advantage. He leered at her, a cruel exaggeration of a human's face, even as he continued the fight.

Neither of the men was Grandfather. Where was he? She felt as if she should know.

Willow stared at the lethal battle. The larger man forced the other over the edge, strangling him with his hands.

The man on the ground looked at her, pleading.

Willow held the bowl tight, afraid to let the halves separate. Afraid to face the endless fall again.

But by holding the bowl, she couldn't get her gun. Someone was going to die. She let the pieces go and in that instant, the larger man pulled a gun and shot the other man. The blast rocked Willow. Her arms flung out and she caught the hand of the dying boy. He looked at her, his face tortured and already dead.

It was the boy found in the cave.

Willow screamed at the image. She grabbed wildly for the broken bowl, as she careened over the precipice.

She told herself she was dreaming. She commanded the nightmare to end. Yet she continued to fall in a downward rush, never ending.

Unbidden, Lonewolf's voice came to her, calm and firm. His words reached to her, slowed the fall. But something tugged at her, a thread of understanding. Something she should know. Lonewolf's persistent voice called to her. She focused on his voice, forced herself to concentrate. Slowly, she felt herself rise from the black depths, Lonewolf's voice like a solid platform beneath her.

When she opened her eyes, he was leaning over her, his own eyes frightening for their intensity. Like the surface of a black pond, absorbing all light—yet promising unseen depths—Lonewolf's eyes concealed what lay within. Willow stared, mesmerized by their calm.

This was real. Lonewolf was real.

Unfortunately, the murder had been real, too. And she had just witnessed it. How could that be?

Still speechless, Willow watched Lonewolf take the pottery pieces from her hands. Fear rose within her quick and sure.

"Don't," she murmured, her voice hoarse. She would've raised her hand to stop him, but she couldn't move.

"It is all right, *shi yázhi.*"

His knowing voice soothed her, but Willow knew, to her bones, that it wasn't all right.

"No, something is very wrong, Lonewolf."

He set the pieces down and moved close to her. Willow could smell the crisp scent of juniper on him.

"What did you see, little one? Tell me."

Willow still felt dizzy, and her mind resisted reliving the ordeal. Lonewolf laid a hand on her shoulder and Willow calmed at the sureness in his touch. She raised her eyes to his—earnest and demanding.

"I saw the murder of that boy. The one we found in Dead Man's cove." Willow kept her eyes glued to Lonewolf's. She stared into them, beyond them, and their impenetrable blackness comforted her somehow. "It was so real. I thought I could save him."

"Did you see the murderer?"

"Yes . . . no. He looked right at me, but his face wasn't real. It was distorted, a mockery." She shook her head and broke the gaze with Lonewolf.

"What brought it on, *shi yázhi*?"

"The pot." Willow nodded at the broken pieces. "It fell from the shelf and I reached to pick it up."

Lonewolf sat back on one haunch, his long hair hanging forward hiding his face as he studied the bowl.

"Why this bowl?" he asked, as if talking to himself. "It is only a mixing bowl. There are many of them."

"Not in this day, there aren't. Unless you know of a secret stash somewhere. If you do, you could be a rich man." She chuckled, but it sounded absurd, like a paltry cough.

She remembered the fax from Nelson. She searched the ground around her, then felt beneath her and found the crumpled sheet. Willow smoothed it out over her knees.

Six different pots were pictured. Each one had animal designs on it—the most rare of all Navajo pottery. So did the broken one Lonewolf was holding. The only difference was this one had cloud steps painted on the outside in black against a stark white slip. The ones in the pictures may have been white, she couldn't tell. But they didn't have the step pattern surrounding the outsides.

The haunting sense that she should know something grew more insistent. She'd seen that cloud-step pattern before.

Suddenly, it came to her—the shard she'd found near the body in the cave . . . the same murder she'd just witnessed in the vision.

The wisp of understanding that had eluded her crystallized in full form. She said it as soon as the thought occurred.

"Grandfather is in danger."

"How do you know?"

"I just do, that's all. I know it."

SEVENTEEN

"Willow, look at me. *How* do you know Grandfather is in danger?"

Lonewolf's black eyes demanded that Willow remember the vision. Her chest tightened, a wave of tremors wracked her. She forced her words past teeth clenched against chattering. "Because he called to me. His voice drew me to Four Hole Site." The quaking intensified, spreading throughout her. She vaguely felt Lonewolf's hand at her shoulder.

"Willow, listen to me. Did you *see* Grandfather in the cave or just hear him?"

Willow couldn't focus on the vision, on Lonewolf, on anything. She was desperately trying to pull together the fragments of her mind.

"Willow!"

"I don't know!" She covered her face with her hands.

Lonewolf's arms circled her and pressed her to him. "It is all right, *shi yázhi*." He rubbed her back, up and down. "Shh, now. I am here."

He held her tight, his whispered words a calming heat against her hair. Gradually, Willow relaxed. Her mind settled and she called back the vision, cautiously, without emotion, as if she were viewing a movie.

"No," she said, shakily, her words muffled at Lonewolf's chest. "I didn't see Grandfather. I only heard him."

"I see," Lonewolf said. After a moment, he pulled away.

Willow opened her eyes to see him reach for the broken pieces of the bowl. Her mind rebelled. "No!"

Lonewolf carried the pieces to the door. "Stay here, *shi yázhi*. I will find Grandfather."

His order was useless. Willow could no more stand alone in the empty hogan than she could stop breathing. She followed Lonewolf into the night and found him in the ceremonial hogan. He sat motionless, the bowl in his hands. His deep hum filled the air and the ground she stood on. It rumbled through her like an ancient song coming from the core of the earth.

She watched him, a lone figure seeking out a vision, and the sight awed her. He sought the very thing which terrified her. She had the nearly overwhelming urge to drag him from the hogan for his own safety, save him from the horror.

But, of course, he was not afraid. In the rising moonlight she could see the profile of his face: strong and sure. He sat cross-legged, the bowl in his lap, his arms extended and his palms up. All the time, his hum vibrated through her.

The tone intensified, dropping impossibly deeper. It pulled inside her, from the bottoms of her feet, as if Lonewolf commanded gravity. One of Grandfather's dogs whimpered softly.

The air stilled. All movement stopped. Willow knew without seeing that tiny animals halted in their tracks and birds listened.

What she *did* see brought a gasp. The juniper trees, stunted and gnarled, reached toward Lonewolf. The fountain grass leaned to him, a sea of trembling pinkish plumes. And above her, the stars brightened.

All things focused on Lonewolf, drawn to him and his song. Including Willow. She knew she would remember this the rest of her life—when Lonewolf held the attention of all living things: their power was his, their knowledge was his.

The moment humbled Willow—then brought the fear

burning deep within her to the surface. The vision had first come to her, spontaneously. Not to Lonewolf. The powers had sought her out, without her permission, against her will.

The awesome nature of what she battled cowed her. In her blind ignorance, Willow had thought she had a choice. Did she not have any more say in her fate than Lonewolf, or Manuelito, than the stars hanging above, or her father who had believed in them—or her mother who had left?

No! *We all have a choice!* Willow recoiled from the merciless rule of destiny. She would have backed away, but her feet were riveted to the spot. Instead, she endured, for what seemed like hours, as Lonewolf sat, transfixed.

Willow jumped at the touch on her shoulder. Lonewolf crouched before her—when had she sat down?—his eyes serious.

"I must go, *shi yázhi.*" He stood and walked by her.

"Hold on, Lonewolf! Where are you going?" Willow stumbled to her feet, her legs tingling with sleepiness.

"To the canyon, to get Grandfather," he said without turning.

"Not without me, you're not."

Lonewolf kept walking to the corral. Willow ran to keep up. "Tell me what you saw, Lonewolf."

He didn't answer, but slid the post free at the corral gate and entered. Willow stopped when she saw only Red Wing.

"Grandfather's horse is gone," she said.

Lonewolf settled the bridle over Red Wing's head. Willow grabbed his arm.

"Lonewolf, stop it right now and look at me." The intensity in his eyes took her breath away. "What is it? What did you see?"

"You were right. Grandfather is in danger." He

moved to get on the horse, but Willow blocked him.

"You're not going without me, Lonewolf. That's my horse you're getting on to look for *my* grandfather. Not to mention I'm the cop around here, not you."

"Willow, I saw Grandfather at Four Hole and something is holding him there."

"Something? Or someone?"

"I saw only him."

"But?"

"But it does not feel right." His black eyes shadowed and Willow sensed he was holding something back.

"What aren't you telling me?"

He smiled then. "I also saw the chant skin."

"With Grandfather? But you searched Four Hole."

"Not all the caves. Only where I had buried it. Perhaps Grandfather found it."

"I'm going with you," Willow said. Lonewolf paused, then, in an effortless roll, mounted Red Wing. He held out his hand.

"Don't move," Willow said and ran to the hogan. She belted her gun on and grabbed her backpack. Lonewolf stood where she had left him. He extended his hand and swung Willow up behind him.

Willow wrapped her arms around him and his hand closed over the two of hers. As quiet as the night, Lonewolf urged Red Wing toward the cliff.

They halted at the top of Bear Trail.

"There's Nizhoni." Willow pointed to Grandfather's horse, its near-black coat merely a reflection in the moonglow.

Lonewolf and Willow began their descent into the abyss. The night seemed to come from the canyon, veiling the chasm in blackness darker than the sky. Down there was Grandfather . . . and something else. Willow now felt it, too.

Willow flicked on her flashlight. The splayed light

caught a deer mouse mid-trail, its eyes bright amber like a miniature demon.

"Do tah!" Lonewolf's hissed whisper broke the mouse's trance and it bolted off the path.

"You might have the eyes of a night hawk, but I don't. I can't see a thing."

"You also tell of our approach." He took the flashlight from her, fumbled with the switch and finally turned it off.

The instant dearth of light now seemed more total and formidable. The path, tricky in daylight, became treacherous. Willow pictured it in her mind, the ancient rock trail barely discernible as it traversed over slabs of sandstone—only obvious from mid-point on as it wound between junipers with sharp turns and rapid descent, like a hawk stalking prey.

She thought of Grandfather. How in the world had he managed? He said he didn't tackle the canyon trails anymore—he was too old. Why would he come to the canyon in the dead of night? Especially when she had been right there in the hogan, available to help? What had possessed him?

Lost in her thoughts, Willow stumbled and fell into Lonewolf. He staggered and his feet slid on the steep slope, but he caught her. Lonewolf braced his leg against her and Willow felt the handle of his knife graze her shin.

"*'Aoo' yá'ánísht'ééh?*"

"Yes. I'm fine."

Lonewolf started down the trail again at a faster pace, the black night deeper with each step, as if they descended into a well. The malevolence grew, lurking, preying on Willow's nerves. On Lonewolf's, too. At the bottom, he stopped and crouched, as if anticipating an ambush.

They walked down the mud-packed escarpment to the rutted dry wash. A bat was flushed from a cottonwood with a loud scream at their trespass. The sudden noise sent sharp, prickly signals up Willow's spine.

Lonewolf stopped and turned to Willow. "I want you to stay here, while I go on ahead."

His eyes, still wide with surprise from the bat, reflected only the black night.

"Over my dead body," she said.

"That is what worries me."

"Are you saying I should fear for my life? What about Grandfather?"

"The danger may be greater than I thought. I want to be cautious."

"So you start with leaving behind excess baggage? Not on your life."

Willow pushed past him and continued up the arroyo. She listened intently, blocking out the soft scrape of their own steps. But the canyon was quiet—too quiet. There should have been sounds of night creatures, their bodies rustling the canyon brush, their wings disturbing the still air. Instead there was nothing. Deadly silence.

The sense of ambush grew. Willow instinctively crouched as they walked. She saw that Lonewolf was bent below the arroyo wall also.

They neared the Four Hole Site and Lonewolf touched Willow's back. She stilled mid-step. For a moment, they stood, still as yuccas, except for their soft breaths.

Willow recalled her ordeal four nights before when she had been making her escape. Like then, she felt stalked, spied on—but not afraid. She glanced at the man standing beside her—was it that Lonewolf was at her side? Or that her senses were more acute and she somehow knew fear had no place? She couldn't say.

For the first time in her life, she didn't analyze. She just let it be.

Together, they emerged from the arroyo. Four Hole Site hung on the canyon wall above them, its entrance the gaping mouth of a black beast.

They clambered up the talus slope to the opening.

"Grandfather?" Willow called into the seeping cool blackness.

Nothing. She began to wonder if he was here at all. If he wasn't, then why the growing sense of something very wrong? She stepped into the cave and started down the path to her right. Lonewolf's hand stopped her.

"Do tah," he said quietly. "Stay with me."

She almost told him to can the macho performance, but then she saw his face. Concern was written all over it. Her heart warmed and she smiled.

"It's okay, Lonewolf," she whispered back. "I do this for a living."

Lonewolf opened his mouth as if to say something, then closed it again and walked down the other path. Within a few steps he disappeared into the dark without a noise.

Too late, Willow remembered that Lonewolf had her flashlight. She needed it more than he did. He could probably see better in the dark than the daylight, just like any predator.

"Grandfather? Are you in here?"

Her words hit the stone walls and fell before her. Strange that nothing echoed in here, she thought. The deathly quiet was beginning to unnerve her. It was too much like being in a tomb. Her hand fell to her holster and she walked on, letting the path draw her deeper.

Willow knew when she'd crossed the threshold of the cavern. Nothing changed—the darkness or the dry still air. She just knew.

"Grandfather?" she whispered.

She heard pebbles fall over rocks and a small moan. The fine hairs on her nape stood up.

"Granddaughter? Is that you?"

"Yes, it's me. Keep talking so I can find you."

"Are you alone?"

Willow homed in on him and took careful steps in his direction.

"No, Lonewolf is searching the other caves for you."

"Good. I think we will need his help."

Her toe touched him and she knelt, finding herself next to an outstretched leg. Willow's eyes pricked with tears—with joy or relief, she didn't know.

"Are you all right?" She grazed her hands over him until she found his head, then cradled his face in her palms.

He coughed and Willow's heart lurched.

"Oh, child, I've been very foolish."

"What? Where are you hurt?" Her hands traveled over his body, more quickly than before. "Did you fall?"

Then she found it. At first she thought he'd lost a foot and she almost screamed. His leg ended beneath two boulders. His ankle was wedged under them.

She started to move one of the rocks and Grandfather hissed.

"Aiee!"

"Okay, hold on. Let me get Lonewolf. He has the flashlight."

Just then she heard steps coming into the cavern. A light flashed on her.

"Lonewolf," she said, turning toward the light. "Grandfather's leg—"

She swallowed her sentence at the sight of the huge man. Warning bells rang in her like a thousand alarm clocks.

"Shit," the man said.

Willow let her hand slide to her holster.

"What's the matter?" another man said. She *knew* that voice. Curtis appeared behind the hulk.

"Curtis! What are you doing here?" She didn't wait for an answer, but rose and reached for the flashlight. "Grandfather's hurt his leg."

"Not so fast, lady." The big man stepped back from her and pointed a gun. "What are *you* doing here?"

"That's his granddaughter," Curtis said.

"And a cop," Willow said. "What's going on here?"

"You didn't tell me she was a cop." The big man stared at Willow with a mixture of hate and fear.

"Can it, Becenti. Drop your gun and move aside."

"Stop! This has gone too far!" Grandfather called out, but he ended in a wrenching cough.

"You got it all wrong, old man," Curtis said. He stepped in front of the big man, took the gun, and pointed it at Willow. "We're the ones giving the orders. Now drop the gun, Becenti."

"Curtis, Grandfather's hurt—"

She didn't see the punch coming until a few seconds before impact—just enough time to twist a fraction away. The gun barrel caught her shoulder instead of her face. But it was her bad shoulder and a riot of pain shot through her, blinding her.

Willow feinted a stagger and reached for her gun. She slipped the gun from its holster and simultaneously turned, kicking her leg out. She caught Curtis in the thigh. He wheeled from the blow, fell, rolled with the impact and was on his feet. This time his gun was aimed at Grandfather. And hers was aimed straight at Curtis.

"Nice try. Now hand over the gun. Or your *grandfather* is dead."

"Don't do it, Willow. He'll kill me, anyway. Won't you, Curtis?"

Curtis sneered at Grandfather. "You've given me a lot of trouble, old man, that's for sure."

"Go ahead and shoot. But it won't solve anything."

Willow flicked a glance at her grandfather. What was he doing with a gun pointed at him and talking of dying? She didn't have a clue what was going on and she was rapidly losing what little control she had over the situation.

"No one is going to shoot, Curtis. Lower the gun. Now."

Curtis jammed the gun to Grandfather's temple. "Go to hell—"

He didn't get to finish. A thundering yell—primal, hair-raising—filled the small cavern. The flash of a blade appeared at the big man's throat. Curtis swung, fired, and missed. Willow kicked and, this time, Curtis sprawled. He scrambled to rise.

"Don't," she ordered, her gun leveled on him. She could hear grunts and scuffling. Lonewolf had his hands full.

Curtis snarled at her from all fours, like a rabid animal. She saw the madness in his eyes. He pulled back, ready to spring. Willow fired, hitting his shoulder. He screamed and fell back. But he still held the gun.

"Drop it, Curtis."

He looked at her bewildered, as if he didn't comprehend. His eyelids lowered, his face drooped. But Willow knew it wasn't over.

"Drop it," she said again. Her voice barely carried over a loud thud of someone hitting the ground.

Curtis looked up at her slowly, his features distorted with pain and hatred. In that instant, she knew. The pit of her stomach roiled against the knowledge. Everything seemed to move in slow motion. He was the one from her vision. The one who had killed the boy.

The next instant, Lonewolf came into her vision. Not walking, but flying through the air. He landed with a murderous scream on Curtis. The gun flew from Curtis's hand and Willow kicked it out of reach.

For a moment, the only sound was heavy breathing. Willow reached for her single set of handcuffs. She debated which man posed the greater threat and decided on Curtis. Notwithstanding the blood at his shoulder, he still looked ready to fight. He squirmed beneath Lonewolf, who looked only too ready to finish him off. She glanced at the other man, who lay unmoving in a heap. Willow checked for a pulse and wondered what Lonewolf had hit him with.

"What took you so long?" she asked, as she fastened the cuffs on Curtis.

"Why did you not yell?"

They looked at each other and what Willow saw in his eyes rocked her to her toes. A warrior—her warrior—ready to kill for her. She smiled, at a loss for anything to say, then turned to Grandfather. She had questions; lots of them. She started with the most important.

"Are you all right?"

Grandfather didn't look at her. His gaze was fixed on Curtis and Willow wondered if he'd heard.

Residual adrenaline prickled her skin. She wanted to pace, walk it off. The cop in her saw an accomplice. Willow saw the old man who had raised her, taught her values, always been there for her.

"Grandfather, it's all over. Are you okay?"

He looked away from Curtis, but still not at her.

"I'm sorry," he said.

"What was this all about? Why would Curtis want to kill you?"

"He worked for me."

The answer came and for a second Willow didn't want to hear any more. She felt her world rock and she was teetering, off balance. If anyone spoke another word, she would fall. Nothing would ever be the same.

But it was her voice that broke the silence.

"What did he do for you?"

"He stole pottery and artifacts from the canyon."

There it was. The final linchpin to a rational world. Her grandfather—keeper of traditions—a criminal? The protector of the canyon paid thieves to steal artifacts?

She looked at him. Lonewolf had freed his ankle, but he still lay there, with a look of such complete failure that Willow's heart went to him—and she almost forgot the enormity of what he'd done.

"Why?" she finally asked, still not able to believe she was questioning her grandfather.

"To save our history."

"To save history, you stole it. I don't understand."

"I didn't steal it for me. I stole it for you."

"Don't," Willow said.

"And for all *Diné*."

"What gave you the right, Grandfather? Who said you could take things into your own hands?" Anger rose in Willow.

"Who else cared, little one?"

"Stop it! You don't own this canyon. You're not the only one who cares."

"Do you?" His question, though spoken softly, fueled her fury, provoking her past mere anger, to something more devastating.

"Do I what? Care? How dare you! I care more than you do. But you don't get that, do you? I care about the living. Not the dead and gone. Not some lifeless relics."

"The relics are our life. Ask Lonewolf."

Willow wasn't prepared to include anyone else in her wrath. She couldn't even look at Lonewolf, afraid of what she'd see. He would agree with Grandfather. How couldn't he? His life was *based* on tradition, legends. The feeling that she stood alone here, misjudged by the very ones she fought for, drove her fury almost to the breaking point.

"Go ahead," she demanded. "You ask Lonewolf. Ask him if pottery and broken artifacts were more important than war strategy and storing food. His life was about survival. Making it through the day. Mine is about the future. Yours, Grandfather, is about the past."

Grandfather looked at her, his eyes sad with understanding, as if she were some pitiful creature. His look pushed her even further.

"The only thing that makes that stuff valuable now are the collectors. Museums. White men. Is that what you did it for? The money?" Willow heard her voice rise to a yell.

"Don't be a fool!" Grandfather's voice rose above hers.

Willow glared at him. "That's it, isn't it? They offered money." She gestured at Curtis. His cool look of satisfaction disconcerted her. She wanted to slap it off his face, but her anger at Grandfather consumed her. Of all the people in her life, she could not believe he was the one who had betrayed her. That's what he had done when he trusted these thieves more than he trusted the laws she represented.

"How could you do this, Grandfather? Do you have so little respect for me?"

"Everything is not about you, little one."

"But this is, Grandfather. And you know it. Otherwise, why did you say you were sorry?"

"Because I hoped I could find the chant skin. But I couldn't. Could I, Curtis?"

"I told you I hadn't seen it, old man."

He hadn't threatened. He hadn't even moved. But a shiver crawled up Willow's spine as Curtis spoke. And, for a moment, she said a silent prayer of thanks that she'd found Grandfather.

"So what was *your* interest, Curtis? Just helping out the tribe?"

"Sure, why not?" He shrugged.

"And where have you been keeping all these valuable finds?"

Curtis smiled and Willow's skin crawled.

"Who says I've got anything?"

EIGHTEEN

"Then why are you here, Curtis?"

Curtis's gaze flitted around the cave, never lighting on Willow. "I told the old man I'd look," he said finally. "Just trying to help."

A low groan filled the cavern. The big man held one hand to his head, his eyes still closed as he tried to sit up. What he didn't see was Lonewolf's knee planted on his chest.

"What the hell?"

He opened his eyes and Willow enjoyed his look of total bewilderment as he faced a gun barrel and a fierce Indian.

"Welcome to the party. Your partner and I were just having a very interesting conversation." Willow dropped her fake smile and fixed her most sobering look on the big man. His eyes flicked to Curtis.

"Curtis." His rough voice held a wealth of warning.

"She doesn't know anything."

"On the contrary. I know you boys have been very busy stealing Navajo artifacts from the canyon."

"Damn you, Curtis!"

"Shut up, Gonzales."

"Oh no, by all means, Gonzales, talk. I'd like to hear your side. For instance, what were you going to do with the chant skin?"

"Curtis, you bastard. You couldn't keep your mouth shut, could you?"

"I tell you she doesn't know anything!"

Willow watched the two of them and let her mind

pull the pieces together. She decided to play on a hunch.

"Know what I think, Curtis? I think you found lots of stuff." Willow paced, pretending to be deep in thought, but always keeping both Gonzales and Curtis in view. "So much, in fact, you couldn't move it all out of the canyon."

Gonzales was glaring at Curtis and Willow knew she was onto something.

"So you hid it here."

"You don't know what you're talking about, Becenti. Go ahead and look, if you're so sure."

Willow ignored Curtis. "You were so careful." Willow paced some more. "You didn't tell Grandfather what you'd found." She stopped and gave Gonzales a pitiful look. "He probably didn't tell you either, right, Gonzales?"

She thought Gonzales might burst, he was turning so red with anger.

" 'Course, you needed money. So you sold a few pieces now and then." She shook her head with dismay. "Bad move, Curtis. I'm sure the guy at Red Rock can identify you, or your partner here.

"But that wasn't your worst mistake, was it, Curtis?" Willow crouched right in front of him, no more than inches away. "Sammy Nez."

Curtis looked her in the eye without flinching. She stared back and saw . . . nothing. He was void—no remorse for anything he'd done. But in her mind's eye, she saw the replay of the vision, when he'd killed Sammy Nez. Willow was close enough to hear Curtis's shallow breath. She hoped he couldn't hear the pounding of her own heart.

"What happened, Curtis? Did he see you stealing some pottery? Or maybe he was even helping you and you got greedy. Whatever. He was a problem. So you killed him."

Curtis smiled wickedly and Willow had to steel herself not to move back.

"You've got quite an imagination. Go ahead, arrest me. You can't prove any of it."

"Oh, but I can, Curtis."

She stood up and brushed off her pants as if making ready to leave.

"I'm gonna kill you, Curtis! You said you had everything taken care of!" Gonzales surged against Lonewolf, but the warrior held firm.

"Shut the hell up, Gonzales! She's full of shit and she knows it! Let her take us in—she's got nothing. She's just trying to get the old man off the hook and save her job. He's the criminal here!"

Curtis tried to fling an arm in Grandfather's direction, forgetting that his wrists were cuffed. He lost his balance and fell facedown on the hard rock floor.

Willow lifted his head by the hair at his forehead. "Gonzales and I are going to have a long talk, Curtis. You killed a boy. You're going away for a long time." She let loose of his hair and helped him sit up, restraining herself from being rough.

She wanted to hit him hard. Mostly for what he'd done to Sammy—a defenseless boy whose youth and innocence cost him his life. But part of her rage was directed at Grandfather. Two people were dead. Grandfather had, in a way, made that happen. She couldn't look at him. Not without screaming at him—and that would shatter the control she held on to by a thread.

Hidden somewhere was a hoard of pottery, a lifeless pile of clay that people had died for. She felt her rage well into a bitter lump in her throat. When she found the stash, they'd all be lucky if she didn't smash it to worthless pieces.

She felt Lonewolf's gaze on her. What did he make of this? she wondered. For him, artifacts weren't legal or illegal. They were just there, like the red rock and the turquoise sky. Just another part of the canyon—immutable, constant, anonymous—until now.

She considered not trying to find the stolen pottery. She could leave it where it lay: hidden, inaccessible. And maybe, after enough time, it would be forgotten.

Not likely, she realized, with a glance at Curtis. He still thought he could get away with everything. Which meant he'd hidden the pottery and Gonzales didn't know where. What if it were right under their noses?

"You know, Curtis, you're in an awful hurry to get arrested. Or are you just in a hurry to leave this cave?"

"I haven't got anything more to say to you, Officer."

Willow looked at the one man who knew these caves better than anyone. Lonewolf. He hadn't said a word, nor moved from his post by Gonzales.

"Is there any place in these caves a hoard of artifacts could be hidden?"

"Perhaps."

She'd have to let him go alone. She didn't want to make more than one journey through the narrow cave passages with the prisoners.

With a nod of her head, Lonewolf stood and walked out of the cave. Willow saw a glint of excitement in his eyes. Why would he care about finding anything? Then she thought of the chant skin. Of course.

She saw Curtis watch Lonewolf leave the cave.

"Worried, Curtis? You should be."

"I told you, Becenti. There's nothing to find."

"Oh, but Lonewolf knows the caves better than anyone alive. He'll find your stash."

Curtis humphed. "If you ask me, he couldn't even find the right clothes to wear. Where'd you find him, Becenti? Under a rock?"

Willow just smiled.

But the kid was nervous. He needed to talk. "It occurs to me, Becenti, that you're the one who'll be answering the questions at the station. Considering it's your grandfather who hired me.''

''I appreciate your concern, Curtis. But if I were you, I'd worry about what Gonzales will say. I have a feeling he's not too fond of you right now.''

With a glance, Curtis undoubtedly saw what Willow meant, for he started talking fast to the big man. Willow listened, but her mind was really on what Curtis had said to her. He was right. About everything. She would have a lot of questions to answer. She didn't want to think about that right now. What she wanted to do was sit beside her grandfather and have him explain everything. She needed to hear some rational explanation that would justify everything that had happened. Except there was nothing he could say. He had placed the artifacts above all else. And because of him, a boy had died and another man had been shot.

No, she couldn't sit beside him. She couldn't even look at him. He seemed to know her mood, because he didn't say a word. And, for now, with her gun trained on the two men, she could pretend she was doing her job and that Grandfather wasn't even there.

The minutes ticked by. Gonzales had scooted away from Curtis, leaving the kid looking sulky and nervous. Willow wondered what Lonewolf was doing. She knew in her gut that Curtis had hidden his stash somewhere in Four Hole. That would explain his presence here and the gun she'd found. But a very big part of her wanted Lonewolf to find nothing. Then maybe all this would go away, as if it had never happened. Except Grandfather had said he hired Curtis to steal the pots. Willow couldn't make that go away.

She saw a light approaching down the passage. If Lonewolf was carrying anything, it was all over. Gonzales would squeal on Curtis—and Curtis would squeal on Grandfather.

Willow's stomach knotted. Nothing. Anything. It was all the same.

Suddenly, the beam of his flashlight filled the cavern and Willow couldn't see Lonewolf behind it. Then he turned and what she thought was a tall shadow was Lonewolf. He had something draped over his arm.

Lonewolf stepped over Gonzales and Curtis as if they were merely boulders in his way, and held out his arm to Willow.

"There is more," he said.

The disappointment in his voice so matched her own lousy mood that Willow nearly missed it. Then it clicked. He hadn't found the chant skin. She took the cloth from his arm and unfolded it. Without a word, Lonewolf took his place guarding Gonzales and Curtis.

Willow immediately recognized the fairly loose, light-weight weave of a serape. She wasn't an expert in Navajo artifacts, but she knew this couldn't be newer than the mid-1800's. After that, blankets had become heavier until they finally evolved into rugs.

Willow ran her hands over the soft blanket. The whole piece was light brown save for muted hues of gray and off-white which banded the ends. Natural sheep's wool, coarse and dirty, had been painstakingly cleaned, carded, and finely spun to make a blanket as soft as any twentieth-century one. But this weaver had known fear and hunger, raids by Mexicans and Utes. And now, only the serape remained, a testament to her talent and perseverance.

"What else did you find?" she asked, her voice clogged with emotion.

"Pots, canteens, some other blankets, bowls. Much more."

His monotone drew her gaze. It struck her that maybe he recognized some of the pieces. Maybe even this very serape. Had it been his? An arrow of grief pierced her. Not because he might know the pieces, but because she could not allow herself to become sentimental. This was only a thing. Beautiful as it may be; it didn't equal human lives. She handed the blanket back to Lonewolf. What he had found was priceless and also costly—to Curtis, Gonzales, . . . and Grandfather.

"Did you find the chant skin?" It was Grandfather.

"It is not there," Lonewolf said.

"Are you sure? Did you look through everything?"

"He said it's not there!" Willow snapped. She covered it by immediately addressing Curtis. "Get on your feet, Curtis. You too, Gonzales. I'm sure you're all rested up for the long trek to Chinle."

"We need to look through what Curtis hid. Maybe Lonewolf didn't see it all." Grandfather's calm voice grated on Willow.

"Not now, Grandfather." Willow busied herself by watching Curtis and Gonzales get to their feet.

"Lonewolf needs the skin!"

Willow ignored him. "Lonewolf, could you help Grandfather get up?"

"Willow!" Grandfather's voice was as harsh as her own thoughts. "What's gotten into you, child?"

"Don't talk to me about the skin!" Willow faced Grandfather, anger pumping through her. "Not now. Not another word!"

"Then when? When it's too late?"

"Two men are dead, Grandfather. And all because of your obsession with the artifacts!"

"You blame me for the boy's death. Maybe you're right. But what about Manuelito? Who will you blame when he dies?"

"He won't die!"

That was her last word. It was the last *anyone* said as they left the cave and slowly made their way out of the canyon.

Willow let Grandfather lead and set the pace. Lonewolf helped him. Gonzales and Curtis followed and Willow brought up the rear with her gun ready. Lonewolf had Curtis's gun, just in case. The going was slow and silent.

That was fine with Willow. She was in no hurry to reach Chinle and the police station. Each step took her closer to where she had to make a decision about Grandfather.

He couldn't kill anybody. He couldn't even deliberately hurt anyone. And she knew he didn't steal the artifacts to make money. No, he hadn't done it for profit, but for pride. Navajo pride. He could justify anything in the name of Navajo heritage.

She couldn't—and wouldn't. Navajo history would not save her people. It was their claim on the future that would make the Navajo great.

Willow wanted to scream at Grandfather, *What makes the dead and gone so damned important?*

Anger drove through her. Damn his pride that kept the Navajo shackled to the past.

Low voices drifted to her. Lonewolf and Grandfather were talking. A man from the past and a man mired in the past. That thought bothered her the whole trek back up the cliff.

"Book these two on assault with weapon, battery-officer, conspiring to steal federal property, and federal trespassing. For now," Willow added.

The desk captain nodded and made notes on the arrest forms. "Bail?" he asked without looking.

"No bail, not until the hearing. They'll fly."

"Okay." He nodded to the officer standing by and Curtis and Gonzales were escorted away. When the double doors closed behind them, the desk officer fixed Willow with a questioning look.

"What have you got going here, Willow?"

Willow didn't mind the familiarity from her old captain.

"Murder. Curtis killed the Nez boy and probably the man—Romero—we found in Bear Arroyo. I think I've got the gun."

The captain shook his head. "Hard to believe about Curtis. I know he doesn't have any priors."

"Guess he saved up all his criminal impulses."

The captain grunted; the sound of an officer who'd seen almost everything.

"So, how are you doing with the boys at the Rock?"

"Fine," she said. She couldn't put it off any longer. "There's something else."

The captain spoke over her. "And how's *Hastiin* Becenti?"

Willow focused on a picture of the Navajo President. His predecessor was serving time for embezzling funds from the Navajo Tribal accounts.

"He's here. He's under arrest, too."

"What?"

"For conspiring to steal artifacts."

"Come on, Willow. Be serious."

Willow forced herself to face the captain. He looked as if he thought she were joking. Willow herself couldn't believe what she was saying, but she had to go through with it. "I'm serious. He hired Curtis to steal pottery."

"From the canyon? He wouldn't do that."

"They both admitted to it."

Willow heard the creak of a door and turned to see Lonewolf leading Grandfather from the men's room. As he came closer, limping slightly, Willow noticed he had removed his *'atsii nazt'i'ii* headband, a symbol of honor and stature for Navajo men.

She tore her gaze from him and stared at the captain. "He has surrendered, Captain. I want you to book him for conspiring to steal federal property."

The captain stared over her shoulder. When he finally looked at her, Willow nearly reached to console him. He had the look of someone suddenly lost on a familiar path. Grandfather stopped beside Willow.

"It's all true." Grandfather's clear, strong voice rang in the silence.

"Now, Vidal, there must be some misunderstanding."

"There is no mistake. I hired Curtis to steal artifacts from the canyon."

"Why? Why would you do that?"

"I was a fool," he said simply.

He wants to be arrested. He wouldn't argue with her. Grandfather would let her put him in jail with other criminals. With Curtis and Gonzales.

The captain looked back at Willow. He looked no less confused than before. "Willow?"

"It's a federal crime, sir."

"What evidence do you have?" The captain's tone put Willow on notice.

"His confession, for one," she shot back. "And a hoard of artifacts in Four Hole Site."

"And if I do the paperwork on this, it goes to the Feds. You really want that?"

"We don't have a choice, sir."

The captain ran his hand through his thick crop of black hair. "Vidal," he said, his head still bent. "What were you going to do with the artifacts?"

"Keep them safe from—"

"That's not the point!" Willow yelled. "Grandfather hired Curtis. Curtis got greedy and two people are dead! If it were anyone else you would not be dragging this out."

"But it isn't anyone else, Willow. It's Vidal Becenti!" The captain slammed his fist on the table and the pictures behind him shook. "Because of him we have *stopped* other thieves in the canyon. He is the elder of my clan. He sang at the *Entah* for my mother and cured her heart pains, for Christ's sake!"

Willow had never heard the captain swear.

"Shash'la yádii, T'áá'akó téé."

Grandfather's quiet reassurance settled on the room like a prayer.

"Now, do your duty, son. My ankle is killing me and I need to sit down."

"Vidal Becenti, do you swear you will not leave the area? And that you will make yourself available for any questioning?"

"Where would I go?"

"Do—you—swear?" The captain blasted each word.

"Yes."

"Then, I release you on your own recognizance."

"But—" Willow started.

"I'll do the paperwork, Willow. There'll be a record. And I have your grandfather's word. That has always been good enough for me."

Willow swallowed her protest. "Fine," she said. "I'll be in touch about Curtis and Gonzales."

They rode in silence to Grandfather's hogan. The borrowed jeep rumbled, but to Lonewolf, the now familiar sound was not noisy, but a comfort—a reminder that Mother Earth lived and could bend man's tasks to her own whims: like buckling the black surface of the road. But the two souls riding in the front of the jeep did not seem open to any comfort.

From his seat in the back, he could see Willow and Grandfather. Lonewolf was struck by how alike they were. They were roughly the same size and the pitch-black night swallowed contours and blurred edges, until only their shared heritage stood out: high cheekbones, narrow noses, and long hair blowing in the wind—Grandfather's freed from the black headband.

What the night made the same, became wholly different if one closed one's eyes and sought with other senses. Lonewolf could feel the old man's anguish, an immeasurable sorrow that consumed him, as if he were a fire smothered in dirt.

Willow's essence came to Lonewolf hard and aggressive, opening his eyes. As usual, she drove fast and fearless, but now she attacked the road. Her arms stretched taut; her hands gripped the wheel. Her hair whipped wild, mixing with the night. She looked straight ahead; and, even when the path became narrow and rough, she never slowed.

He did not understand her rage at Grandfather. Whatever Grandfather had done, he had done it in good heart. Lonewolf knew that. What had he done wrong? Why would Willow have him arrested? Was it now wrong to keep those things the People had made?

Lonewolf saw the serape as he had found it: thrown carelessly among the pots and other things. He had immediately recognized it. The old woman Spider had woven it for her son; and he had worn it to Santa Fe when he and the other headmen met with the *bilagaana* to talk peace—one more time.

When Lonewolf had held the blanket, he had felt the delicate play of Spider's deft fingers, flashing across the loom. And he had smiled. He was not a sentimental man. After all, it was only a blanket. But he remembered how proud Juan had been to wear a fine blanket to meet the governor.

Grandfather was a sentimental man, Lonewolf concluded. All those things in his hogan—as if they held the spirits of those gone before. But those pots, canteens, blankets, kachina dolls—all those things—were not meant to be collected. They were made to be used. They had a purpose; like the people who had made them.

He had thought Willow would understand that, given her logical, no-nonsense approach to everything. But she had refused to even discuss the chant skin in the cave. When, of all things they had found, that would have held the most significance, for it was still useful.

The jeep lurched, chucking Lonewolf up from his seat. His eyes met Willow's in the reflection of the small mirror and, in that second before she quickly looked away, Lonewolf saw the cause of her anger: fear.

Impossibly, the jeep picked up speed, on the attack. Willow could be riding a horse, full-out, her body tense, yet at one with the motion: as if chasing an enemy . . . or escaping whatever demon possessed her.

He wondered if she even knew she was afraid; she was so consumed with anger. But that would pass.

The fear would be the hardest to defeat, because she would have to face the adversary: herself. She would not be alone, though. He had experience with battling the demons inside—the ones that threaten your inner power. And he would be there with her.

NINETEEN

The jeep bucked and lurched over the cow path. Wicked junipers grabbed and poked as the jeep struggled to pass. With a grinding heave, it broke free onto the sandstone. The lights of the jeep caught the startled glance of Red Wing and Grandfather's horse.

Lonewolf followed Grandfather out of the jeep and went around to Willow's side. He braced his hands on the rim.

"We will talk back at Grandfather's."

"No."

She sat staring ahead, her wind-tousled hair half covering her face. The reflected light from the jeep outlined the silhouette of her face: full lips pressed together, nostrils that slightly flared with every breath, the sweep of generous eyelashes that framed unblinking eyes. Each part wholly feminine, but the sum total equaled a determined, headstrong woman.

"Who are you mad at, *shi yázhi*?"

"You don't understand."

"I think I do. You are mad that Grandfather risked his life for things you wished had stayed buried."

"Two people died, Lonewolf." She faced him, her green eyes glittering in the dark. "And for what? Those things?"

"So you are mad because foolish men died?"

"Sammy Nez was a boy. He couldn't have known what he was getting into."

"Maybe he too was greedy, *shi yázhi*."

"Maybe you're right. And maybe we'll never find out. What I *do* know is that he's dead."

"Because of all the old things."

"Yes."

"So you blame them."

"Don't twist my words, Lonewolf. I don't blame 'lifeless, brainless things.' I blame people."

"I see. Then if you are not mad at those 'lifeless things,' we can talk about the chant skin, no?"

"I warn you, Lonewolf, now is not a good time to talk artifacts with me."

"Willow, I saw the skin in the same vision with Grandfather. It should have been in that cave."

"Maybe it had been. Who knows how long ago? But you saw the pile in the cave and it wasn't there."

"It was floating," he continued. "And a light shone on it."

"What do you want from me, Lonewolf? I didn't bring you here, the stars did. I didn't tell you Manuelito would be the next Starway Shaman. Thc stars did. I have contacted everyone I can think of. I can't snap my fingers and make the chant skin appear."

Willow got out of the jeep and faced him. "And another thing. If the stars are so goddamn sure Manuelito has to have this ceremony or he'll die, then why—*why*—didn't *you* keep the skin? None of this would be necessary."

"So you think you are mad at me, too?"

"Think? I'm mad at the whole blasted lot of you. At Grandfather for not trusting me. He hired thieves!" Willow slammed her fist down on the jeep. "I'm mad at the museums and traders, the collectors around the world, who place more value in a piece of clay or in a pile of yarn made one hundred years ago, than what's made today—what keeps the People *alive* today!"

"What does any of this have to do with the chant skin?"

"Oh, it's so easy for you. All you have to do is perform a ceremony, turn a boy into a Starway Shaman, and go back where you came from. And I'll be here, still dealing with people locked in the nineteenth century."

"*Shi yázhi,* tradition is the grandfather who carries us over troubled waters."

"The traditions *are* the troubled waters! The People *believe*. And where does it get them? Nowhere! Except unemployed, hungry, and uneducated. The old ways are killing the Navajo."

"Beliefs do not kill, *shi yázhi.*"

"Beliefs are exactly what kill, Lonewolf." Willow broke off, a stricken look in her eyes, like that of someone who almost told a secret.

She climbed back in the jeep and brought it to life. Lonewolf could feel its pulse beneath his fingers.

"What are you afraid of?" He raised his voice above the noise.

Willow stared ahead. Lonewolf could see her struggle for control in the clench of her jaw. When she turned to him, her eyes glistening in the moonlight, he wanted to pull her from the jeep and hug her so tight the dark place within her would be squeezed out. But her words denied him.

"You wouldn't understand."

She backed up, pulling easily out of Lonewolf's grasp. Lonewolf ran to Red Wing. The horse whinnied in surprise, but quickly responded to Lonewolf's expert kicks.

He sent Red Wing flying after the cloud of dust. Within minutes, he was right behind Willow, but he couldn't get around her. The narrow path barely let the jeep pass between the dense grove of junipers.

He heard a grinding noise and the jeep leapt before him, gaining ground. She was going faster than she ever had. Lonewolf followed close, aware that he had to press Red Wing to a faster gallop.

It was not about the skin, or even Manuelito anymore. It was about him. He was one of those superstitions she would like to blame everything on. But he was living, breathing proof that the myths were not lies. He had thought that the fear was within her. But what if *he* were the cause? Coldness spread from his stomach.

The road widened and Lonewolf was ready. He pushed Red Wing harder. The horse, never faltering, gained on the jeep with each long stride. Lonewolf angled Red Wing close enough that his legs almost brushed the jeep. Muscle and machine fought for ground, neither giving way. Soon the dirt path would turn onto the hard road and Red Wing's speed would be no match.

Lonewolf urged the horse impossibly faster, past the back window of the jeep, until he could glance down and see the fierce determination on Willow's face. Lonewolf's legs tightened mercilessly around Red Wing's belly. With one hand, he grabbed the rim at the window and placed his life in her hands.

Willow glanced at him, startled, not comprehending at first. Then she saw his hand. Lonewolf held Red Wing parallel and locked gazes with Willow.

Fury and fear filled her eyes. She could slow the jeep abruptly. She could swerve. With a slight move she could break away and send him and Red Wing to the ground. In his mind's eye, Lonewolf saw the dirt road narrow even further. Even if Willow did nothing, the chase would end—painfully.

But she was a worthy adversary. She did not panic. Gradually, almost imperceptibly, the jeep slowed. The road narrowed and juniper branches found flesh, whipping across Red Wing's breast and Lonewolf's legs. But the horse did not falter.

Then it was over. Dust swirled, carrying Red Wing's

labored breath away. Lonewolf slipped off his back and stroked Red Wing's neck as he ducked beneath his head.

The jeep door slammed and Willow came at him.

"You nearly killed my horse! What the hell do you want?"

Lonewolf grabbed her shoulders. He wanted to yell that she had nothing to fear from him, that he *had* to stop her; he could not let her get away.

Instead he pulled her to him, circled her back with his arms and kissed her. The sharp taste of fury mixed with her musky scent. His heart thumped hard from the chase and sent her essence pounding through his veins.

He pressed her to him. Her heart thudded against his chest. He needed her closer. He could not get enough. It was like seeing a comet and not being able to touch it.

A shudder passed through her and she sighed, willingly opening her mouth. His tongue sought hers, not gently, but with possessive force. Equal to him, she did not retreat. She leaned up, stretching herself, as if also seeking more.

His hands caressed her buttocks, pressing, grinding. She responded to the rhythm, her lips pulling at his tongue, sliding it in and out of her mouth. Her hands swept his back, digging into the soft leather.

He could feel her need and it matched his own. He lifted her, holding her bottom, her legs wrapped around his waist. "I want you now," he said into her ear.

Suddenly, she stilled. Her hands framed his face and she made him look into her eyes.

"Why, Lonewolf? Why do you want me?"

Lonewolf could not answer. At least, not right away. His body ruled his thoughts, took away his power of speech, his ability to reason. He was base need, and he needed Willow. She completed him. His body cried for her. He searched for the right words.

"I want you, *shi yázhi,* because you are the other part to me. It is as simple as that."

"But that's *too* simple. There has to be more, a better reason."

Frustrated, Lonewolf searched his mind for the words. But before he could find them, she spoke again.

"Why did you stop me, Lonewolf?"

The answer came from his heart. "I could not let you go."

"But you will, won't you?" Willow slipped from his arms and faced him. "Tell me something, when you see yourself in the past, do you see me? Am I beside you?"

Lonewolf saw himself alone in the past, as he had always been. When he had pictured himself with Willow, it was here, in this time. But that vision now dimmed.

"Would you want that?" Lonewolf heard himself ask. He quickly clamped a lid on the hope simmering within him.

Willow searched his eyes and Lonewolf wondered what she saw there for she took a step back and crossed her arms.

"This has never been about what I want. Not from the first time we met."

What did she want from him? He needed her. He wanted her. He had not felt this way about anyone since Corn Flower. Even *with* Corn Flower. Willow was anger to his calm, brightness to his dark. She was like a thunderstorm on the mesa with the power and energy to cower the Holy Ones, but then could turn to a quenching shower, touching all that lived to their roots.

"Then what *do* you want, *shi yázhi*? For things to go back as they were? For Manuelito to be dying and no hope for a cure? For you to return to denying your powers? For me to just go away as if we had shared nothing?"

"You sound as if I have a choice. But I don't. And

neither did you, Lonewolf. We've both been manipulated by the stars."

"When it comes to the stars and their plans, very little is simple."

"You're wrong, Lonewolf. It's very simple. The stars command and we obey. The celestial spirits brought us together for one purpose: to achieve their goal—to make Manuelito the next stargazer. Our fears, our needs, mean nothing! But that's their fatal flaw, because we're not sheep, we are human beings. I choose to live by free will. I believe in plodding along, step by step, doing the right thing for the right reason. Not because the stars tell me to, or some medicine tells me to. The 'old ways' don't work."

The truth struck Lonewolf with a bolt of understanding. "You think you have a choice between the past and the present. You are wrong. They exist together. I saw how you fondled the blanket in the cave and then shoved it into my hands. Were you afraid it might hold some power?"

"I'm not afraid of some inanimate object, Lonewolf."

"Like the chant skin?" Lonewolf held her upper arm. "You once said you would do anything to help Manuelito. Has that now changed? I thought I knew you a warrior like myself, fighting injustice against the People."

"You know nothing about me or what it takes for me or the People to survive!" She pulled her arm from his hold, stepped back and faced him. "Unlike in your day, my enemies aren't obvious—they don't wear uniforms. No, my enemies can be as close as Grandfather who is more worried about saving the past, when it's the future that should concern him! If you think you can ride in and save the day, you're mistaken. I don't need a warrior!"

"Warriors are not Navajos on horseback! A warrior is someone in balance with who he is." Lonewolf fought to remain calm, but her raging words ignited his temper and mixed with stormy passion. "Will you ever find that balance? *You* confuse the past with the future. But the future grows from the past. I am proof of that! You cannot banish the power of the past by keeping it there, *shi yázhi*."

"You're right," she said, her tone flat. "I don't have a choice. I'm cornered. I can't believe and I can't *not* believe." She looked up and Lonewolf lost a breath at the pain in her eyes. "You don't need me anymore, Lonewolf. You'll do the ceremony and Manuelito will be the next great stargazer. If the stars thought I would change, that I would give in to my weaknesses"—her voice caught—"then they were wrong. I would only disappoint you."

Willow climbed in the jeep and brought it to life. Without a look back, she drove off. In the slip of time when the rumble of the jeep faded and the mesa peace settled, Lonewolf heard his heart shatter.

Lonewolf mounted Red Wing and guided him back to the cliff to join Grandfather. But Grandfather and his horse were gone—back to the hogan, Lonewolf concluded.

He slipped from Red Wing's back and walked to the cliff. He stopped at the edge on bald sandstone, the smooth slabs an island of reflected moonlight in a sea of black. Blackness surrounded him—above him, behind him, before him. He stood, a man alone, his heart as dark as the night.

He had been wrong to think Willow would love him, that he could take away her fears. Even afraid, she was stronger than him—like a cougar who, cornered and terrified, draws courage from the threat. Willow's fears strengthened her convictions: the old ways, the old things, myths, legends—she blamed them, denied them, fought their power. The vicious circle kept her one step ahead of being consumed by her fears. It also locked out understanding . . . and Lonewolf.

He was not enough for her.

Lonewolf stared into the impenetrable darkness. He could not see the canyon. He could not see where he came from or where he was going. Aloneness such as he had never known swept through him like a cold wind.

Aloneness and fear.

Lonewolf stared hard into the darkness, over time, to the past, to the only place he could call home. He would return, though they did not want him, either.

From deep in the abyss, out of cave hollows, through ancient sanctuaries, over the rubble of crumbled ruins, the voices of the canyon swelled until a river of sound flowed over Lonewolf.

Disharmony clashed within him. The rising cacophony screamed at him, punished his ears. For the first time in his life, Lonewolf could not find the single voice that spoke to him. If it was even there, it was lost in what felt like colossal anger aimed directly at Lonewolf.

"What do you want from me!" he screamed at the unseen forces. A rumble of thunder answered him.

Lonewolf turned to the east, the direction of the Holy Ones. He felt the fury of the spirits jolt through him like lightning. But that only fueled his own rage.

"You think to scare me with that? You have taken everyone I ever loved. My mother, my father, my white parents, my wife and my son. Even, finally, the hope of ever finding love with someone."

Lonewolf raised his arms to the sky, to the stars. Fierce gusts of wind blew his hair wild, whipping it back and forth. "All I had was my power, my vision. Now that keeps me alone, separate from who I love.

"Willow was right! You manipulate with disregard."

The anger welled within Lonewolf and on its wake rode passion, hot and deadly. The warrior within Lonewolf awakened.

"On the night of the ceremony, *I* will have the power of the universe. I will return to the past and deliver on my vow to lead the People to peace."

As suddenly as it began, all the noise and turmoil ceased. On the dying wind came the screech of death's owl.

"Do not threaten me with the boy's death!" he screamed at the wind, his throat tight with rage. "He will be your Starway Shaman, but I will command the power of the celestial spirits. I will not fail!"

Lonewolf let his arms drop to his sides. "I have no fear," he said. "Because I have nothing to lose. You have seen to that."

He turned from his canyon and walked to Red Wing. No voices came to guide him. The celestial spirits were silent. His fate was to be alone. So be it. But he would be alone where he belonged. In the past, with his People.

Lonewolf stood just inside the door and let his eyes adjust to the cavernous blackness—broken only by a circle of dimmer black directly below the smoke hole. The hogan even smelled somewhat like a cave—at the base the cool, clean scent of earth, but layered with the essence of hundreds of inhabitants. The inhabitants of the hogan, of course, being Grandfather's vast collection. The final smell reaching Lonewolf's nose was tobacco. Then he saw the red glint of a cigarette.

Lonewolf followed the ember to the table.

"I think she will never forgive me." The sadness in Grandfather's voice was darker than the hogan.

"Nor me," Lonewolf said.

Grandfather glanced briefly at Lonewolf. "The people in her life have not made it easy for Willow. Me, her father, her mother, you, Manuelito. None of us have given her what she really needs."

"What do you mean?"

"Balance. She struggles with it every day. Between

the Navajo world and the white, between the past and the present, between the modern and the old ways." Grandfather studied his cigarette as he rolled the end between his fingers. "Ah, my *Naa glen ni baa.* She is born to stand and fight, but she cannot win—because she battles to defeat one side, when she needs both."

Grandfather gazed at Lonewolf and smiled. "You brought it all to a head, you know."

Lonewolf inwardly winced. "She says we were used by the stars. Brought together only to help Manuelito." Lonewolf thought of Willow's glistening eyes, deeper than any green in the desert. "And she is right."

"So? What difference does it make *why* you were brought together?"

"It makes a difference to Willow, Grandfather. She does not like being controlled."

"Baah!" Grandfather snorted. "We are all manipulated. By our feelings, our fears. By the past or our hopes for the future." Grandfather gestured with his arms. "It is a part of life."

Lonewolf contemplated that wisdom and wondered how much of his determination to return and help the People was only more celestial interference. It did not matter, the result would be the same. He would return after completing the ceremony. That is, if he could find the chant skin.

"Grandfather, when I envisioned you in the cave, I also saw the skin."

"How did it appear in your vision?"

Lonewolf closed his eyes and let the vision engulf him. "It was unnatural," he said. "It floated, and . . . glowed."

The vision was the same, nothing had changed—no clue what the image meant. Frustrated, Lonewolf pushed away from the table and paced the dark room. His shoulder brushed the bookshelf, rocking the pottery. He steadied the bowls, and his annoyance grew. No hogan should be so cluttered! It made him all the more unfamiliar.

Suddenly he stopped and turned to the shadow of Grandfather. "The image is not right. It feels at once familiar but not familiar. As if it is the cave, but not the cave. But I know it is Four Hole cave!" Lonewolf raked his hand through his hair.

"Yaadi la'óolyé! Shi'bééhózin!"

"You know it?"

Grandfather laughed aloud. "It is the same, but not!" Grandfather banged the table with his fist. "It's the cave at the museum! They re-created the cave there. The director was an old friend and asked for my help. The skin must be there, Lonewolf! Someone must have donated it."

Lonewolf thought of the museum he had visited as a child in Santa Fe. Vast rooms held huge exhibits of dead animals. Each one a perfect specimen, frozen forever beneath glass as if to protect the visitors. Lonewolf shuddered involuntarily. He had run from the museum in horror of the fate the spirits of these beautifully dead animals would exact on the unknowing.

"Then I will go to the museum and take my chant skin back."

"I suppose you'll tell them you came from eighteen sixty-three to claim it? They would love that. Next thing, they'd have you on exhibit. No, no, *shi yázhi,* we will *steal* your skin!"

TWENTY

Lonewolf hid in the mine tunnel just past the prospector with the toothless grin forever plastered on his wooden face. If Lonewolf cared to look, he would see Grandfather through the window of the saloon, standing motionless behind the bar, a glass and rag in his hands. The old man had donned a white apron and insisted on the charade. Lonewolf was impressed for, so far, Grandfather had not moved a muscle—though Lonewolf swore the glass looked cleaner.

And in the way of museums, across from the Bisbee mining town was a reproduction of de Chelly with a hogan and a Navajo woman permanently bent over a loom. Red rock cliffs, only twenty feet high, surrounded the pastoral scene.

What held Lonewolf's attention were the caves straight across from him. There were three, spaced roughly five feet apart, carved into the "canyon wall." Light illuminated an Anasazi ruin in the first; in the second, the same ruin was joined with remnants of Hopi inhabitance. The third cave showed the final native influence on the canyon—Navajo.

There, within a diorama made of wood and paint, within a brick building far from de Chelly, was the *Ha'tanii* and stars painted by Lonewolf—and the Starway Chant skin. The skin was under glass mounted on the cave wall. Of course, the shaman's cave did not have an ancient dwelling in it, but that too was the way of museums.

Lonewolf waited impatiently for the visitors to leave

and the museum to close. He glanced at Grandfather and the old man winked.

"Mommy! He winked!"

"Honey, they're not real."

"But he winked at me. I saw it!"

The child pointed aggressively at Grandfather, whose smile seemed to have widened.

Lonewolf froze behind the wooden prospector, trying not to look like a Navajo in a turquoise mine. From his vantage, he could see the little girl staring into the saloon, obviously waiting for Grandfather to prove he was alive.

"Come on, Amanda. They're about to close."

The child did not move. Lonewolf did not breathe. He wondered how much longer Grandfather could stand it.

"Amanda!" The mother sounded exasperated. "Do you want to go to the gift shop or not? They're going to close."

As if a spell had been broken, the child immediately turned from the window and left. Confirming the mother's guess, the lights in the room flickered off and on twice.

Lonewolf waited to move until the child's chatter about toys had totally faded. He shifted to see Grandfather; the old man was polishing the bar counter, a wide grin on his face.

They continued to wait, through several more flickers of the lights, through the pass of a museum guard, even after the museum went dark for good. They waited.

By the time Grandfather finally appeared at the door to the mine, flashlight shining, Lonewolf had a fairly good idea what it felt like to be a permanent part of the exhibit.

Grandfather laughed.

"What is so funny, *Naat'áanii*?"

"You. You looked like a rabbit facing a gun."

"But you are having fun?" Lonewolf stepped from

behind the miner and promptly tripped on the railroad ties.

"Might as well live up to the reputation, don't you think? I think I've found my true calling as a criminal. I'm better than you, anyway. You don't look like you're having any fun."

"I am not," Lonewolf said, but Grandfather had already left the mine and was climbing over the short wall outside the canyon exhibit.

The cave seemed higher up close and the man-made walls provided no footholds. Balancing on his toes, Lonewolf could just reach his forearms into the cave. He pressed them against the cave "floor" and levered his torso up, then his legs. Grandfather shone the flashlight on the glass-enclosed chant skin.

"You'll need this," he yelled.

Lonewolf looked over the side and Grandfather handed him a screwdriver.

"For what?"

"You'll have to take the screws out."

"Why not just break the glass?"

"For one thing, it's not glass. It's plastic. And you don't want to break it, because then they would notice the skin was gone."

"They will notice that anyway, Grandfather. Because it *will* be gone."

"Not if you put this in its place." Grandfather pulled a buckskin from under his shirt and smiled up at Lonewolf. He held the skin under the flashlight's beam and Lonewolf saw a fairly good rendition of the Mountain Chant skin with the physical and spiritual boundaries of the Navajo world laid out.

"What's that smell?"

Grandfather held the skin to his nose. "Oh, it's the felt pen. I did it fairly light and rubbed it in, to make it look older. They won't smell it once it's in the case."

Lonewolf decided not to ask what how a pen could

be made of felt. "I will need the flashlight, too, Grandfather, to see the screws."

Lonewolf walked to the case and shone the flashlight on the skin. It was his. He had had doubts that he would actually find it. But there it was, and it looked very much the same as when he had last buried it.

Lonewolf put the flashlight in his mouth, aiming the light at the screw. It turned with ease until it dropped out of a hole. Lonewolf moved to the remaining screws and only had trouble with the last, when he had to keep the case against the wall with his shoulder as he took out the screw from the bottom.

The skin which had seemed to float within the case was actually stuck on some patches of rough cloth, lined on the inside of the case. Lonewolf peeled off the chant skin and replaced it with the other buckskin. He retrieved the screws from the ground and replaced them one by one, until the case was put together just as before. Lonewolf handed the screwdriver and the skin to Grandfather, then leapt to the ground. He and Grandfather both started out of the canyon exhibit.

"You were right, Grandfather. It was easy to get the skin."

"This burglary business really works up an appetite."

Lonewolf chuckled to himself as the short, round man made it over the wall. But when Grandfather pushed open the saloon doors, Lonewolf could not believe he would actually stop now to eat.

"You cannot wait until we get back to the hogan?"

"By then you'll have to carry me out, Lonewolf." He walked to the bar and pulled out two glasses.

"I thought you said you knew an easy way out," Lonewolf managed to say calmly, in spite of his growing frustration.

"I do. When they open in the morning, we'll wait a while and then just walk out with some tourists."

"In the morning?"

"Make yourself comfortable, Lonewolf. Now, how do crackers and cheese sound?"

Willow stared at the green line blipping on the monitor. As a sign of life it was a sorry depiction. Couldn't the inventor have been more creative, more respectful? Instead of a pathetic line drawing mountains and valleys on the screen, why not bold strokes of color, painting pictures? Even a puff of smoke corresponding to each heartbeat would be better than the indifferent machine—something that reflected the fight left in the body of the small boy.

Manuelito had been calm for nearly an hour now, since the last seizure. But that one had been so bad, Willow still felt drained from the effort to contain his thrashing.

Willow reached a hand to him then stopped. Even without touching him, she could feel the tornado churning within him as if the maelstrom of emotions swirled over his body in a field of energy.

This child—afraid, alone—kept up his struggle against the unknown. Willow's throat constricted at his bravery and she reached to him again.

Pain. Unrelenting, stabbing pain. Willow doubled over and grabbed her stomach. Torturous spasms wracking her whole body. They twisted her inside out, until she wished she could die.

Then she felt arms beneath her, lifting and carrying her. A familiar scent reached her—one that held the promise of steadfast safety.

The pain hadn't stopped. It was just so all-pervasive, Willow separated herself from the awful intensity. She gave herself up to the encroaching blackness, looking for surcease. Suddenly, she was the observer. She saw a Navajo child in the arms of an elder. The man laid the boy on a mat beneath the stars. As she watched, she was also the one being carried and set down. In that surreal moment, she was both.

Stars dove and crashed around them, sprinkling the earth with rained light. The old man chanted and danced. Her body was numb; the boy didn't move. A comet streaked and a jagged bolt flew from its tail. It struck the boy in the chest. Willow felt the searing blow. Her eyes flew open at the jolt of pain.

Pitch-blackness surrounded her. For a confused moment, Willow didn't know where she was. Then she saw the green line on the monitor and remembered. She was here, safe, with Manuelito.

Yet the vision had been so real. Her chest still burned and her insides were tense from fighting pain.

With a gasp of air, she tried to calm herself. Yet the memory of the agony made her wince. Lonewolf had endured that pain. Manuelito endured it now, as she stood here.

On shaky legs, Willow pulled the chair to Manuelito's bed. Something clunked to the floor and Willow scooped up the chart she had been covertly reading and tried to refocus on it. Two sentences stood out:

"Long-term Prognosis: Unknown. Suggested Action: Mayo Rehabilitation Hospital."

They wanted to send him to Phoenix and it didn't sound as if they planned his release any time soon. She gazed at Manuelito—his small, round face nestled in the pillow; his arms, thinner now than a week ago, lay limp alongside him.

Her eyes blurred again. This time she let the chart lie where it dropped.

He wouldn't be going to Phoenix. If he lived, he would be a stargazer. A man of visions the rest of his life—and more separate than ever from the dreams she had held for him.

The ache in Willow deepened. How was it that this child, so close to her heart, was now so far out of reach?

She could blame Lonewolf. From that first electric moment when she'd faced him in the cave, Willow had known he was a force to be reckoned with. But her heart wasn't up to blaming him. He asked no more from Manuelito than Lonewolf himself had to endure—suffering the tempest within in order to guide the People. A man apart, just as Manuelito would be. And both of them out of her reach.

It seemed her destiny to lose those she loved.

Willow's throat tightened around emotions she dared not let loose.

She curled her legs beneath her in the chair and gazed at Manuelito and the slow rise and fall of his chest. The quiet hum of the machines flowed over her and joined with all the other hospital hums in chorus.

A reassuring rush of will coursed through her, overcoming her doubts and surrounding her heart. Willow felt her steely resolve return.

Others might abandon her, but she would never let Manuelito down. She had herself. It always came to that—it always would.

"It looks very much like the Mountain Chant skin," Grandfather said. "Except, of course, all these spirals, crosses, diamonds, and dots. The stars, I suppose."

"Yes." Lonewolf took a drink of the tea Grandfather had provided, then carefully placed the glass on the next table, out of reach of the skin.

"What do all the star signs mean?"

"It has to do with the order of the ceremony."

Grandfather gave Lonewolf a questioning look. "How many times have you done this ceremony?"

"Never. But I know the place on the chart where the ceremony begins. From there, the stars will guide me." He sighed heavily and admitted his biggest concern. "I was not asleep."

"You mean the coma Manuelito is in?"

"Yes."

They both sat in silence. Grandfather laid a respectful hand on the skin and gently traced one of the star spirals.

"The stars have faith in you, Lonewolf, or they would not have sent you."

"They did not tell me their reasons," Lonewolf said, and heard the anger in his voice.

"So now you too feel manipulated?"

"A warrior does not ask for his battles. He accepts them. I always did what I had to do."

"Yes, *shi yázhi*. I do understand that. Willow would not even argue with that."

Lonewolf had tried to keep his thoughts only to the skin and Manuelito and his duty. If he thought of Willow his heart demanded attention and he was not brave enough to answer it.

"Ironic that the child she has raised to take on the modern world would be the one picked by the ancients," Grandfather said quietly.

Lonewolf had the strong sensation Grandfather was prodding him toward some conclusion. But what kept running through his mind was the fact the stars had determined this time was more critical for the Navajo. If that were true, perhaps the stars would fight his return to his time.

But Lonewolf had a plan. During the ceremony, the power of the stars was his. He was more than their instrument, to be ritually used. For when the stars aligned—an unnatural, extraordinary occurrence—the universe was at its weakest. It was his strength of will that kept the dueling forces of the fractured universe in control. And then, at the moment of Manuelito's passage, for the brief slot of time before the universe found its balance, the window to the past would be his to open.

There was nothing to hold him here. Manuelito would have Grandfather to guide him in the old ways and Willow to teach him the new. And Willow would have Manuelito.

His heart hurt as if gripped in sharp pincers. Any hardship he suffered until the day he died would pale against the pain he faced of leaving Willow.

A hand at Lonewolf's shoulder stirred him from his thoughts. "Tell me what you will do when you return," Grandfather said.

Lonewolf looked into the old man's deep brown eyes and, for a moment, saw Grey Feather—the man who had raised him, loved him, taught him the power . . . then sent him away. Grandfather's eyes had the same ability to reassure and comfort, and Lonewolf, though more tired than he had ever been in his life, willingly found the energy to talk.

"What I do will depend on the time I return to. If I return before the Carson campaign has begun, I will seek counsel with the Apache and the Utes."

"They are the enemies!"

"Yes, but they will lose, too. And if the headmen will come together, think of the treaty we could negotiate."

"You will never get the Apache and Utes to sit with you." Grandfather's voice echoed Lonewolf's own doubts.

"I would not go back and await the inevitable, Grandfather."

"Then you might as well stay here, Lonewolf, because you can't change anything. The future of the People will come just the same."

They were the exact words Grey Feather had spoken to Lonewolf at the counsel. How could these two wise men, one hundred and thirty years apart, say the same thing and be so wrong?

"I just told your granddaughter that the future grows from the past. I will go back and change the past."

"Yes, but the future you are talking about changing has already happened. You *think* of it as the future. But it is already past. It is history. You think that it matters what day you arrive in the past. But it doesn't."

"How do you know? Have you ever traveled through time and tried it?"

"Let me ask you this, *shi yázhi*. If you are so sure you can make a difference, how can you be sure you don't make too *much* of a difference?"

"What do you mean?"

"What if some people live who were supposed to die? And what if some people die because—who knows, maybe they attack you and you have to kill them, but they were supposed to live? Don't you see that whole families today, maybe even entire clans, could be affected by what you do?"

"You worry too much, Grandfather. I am going to talk to people. And I will give guidance. I belong there."

"Do you? Have you forgotten that the last Starway Shaman disappeared before the Long Walk?"

"You think I belong here?" Lonewolf could not contain his temper any longer. He pushed away from the table and glared at Grandfather. "You think that 'disappearance' proves that I am supposed to be here? Have you considered that I might have died in the canyon? Or while trying to talk peace with Rope Thrower? Or maybe even killed by one of my own people?"

Grandfather stood without hurry, but when he turned to Lonewolf, the young warrior faced an old warrior—a man whose eyes commanded authority. "You fool," Grandfather said. "Haven't you realized that it is exactly as you say? That you died in the past? But that the ancient ones had a better purpose for you and so brought you here? Your place is here, Lonewolf. Guiding Manuelito. Your heart breaks for the suffering of the past. But the People had their beliefs, their traditions, and a common enemy. It is these times that will break their will and tear the People apart, until we finally surrender the very thing that keeps us *Diné*: our heritage. And you will leave a small boy to lead this battle?''

"I leave you more than you had, Grandfather.''

"And what of Willow? She will need you, *shi yázhi.* You have shaken all her convictions. You must stay and rebuild them.''

Lonewolf shook his head. "Her fears have too much strength, Grandfather.''

"Baah! She only fears the unknown. She has raised the boy to take on the modern world and you tell her he is picked by the ancients. She worries too much.''

"You said that before. When you compared Willow to her mother.''

Grandfather frowned. "I shouldn't have done that. Willow and her mother are nothing alike. Willow would not abandon a child. I wager she's with Manuelito right now.''

"Her mother abandoned her?''

"Yes.'' Grandfather's voice was colder than the unlit lamps. "With a child's logic, she blamed herself for her mother leaving. Truth is, the marriage would not have lasted. That woman behaved as if she had no relatives.''

Grandfather's judgment was the most profound Navajo insult and Lonewolf could immediately picture the woman who cared for no one but herself. Lonewolf remembered the vision of the man with the child in the peach orchard and his heart filled with grief for the orphaned child.

No wonder she had grown up relying only on herself. The wonder was that *she* had not left and sought a life somewhere else. Instead, she had adopted the whole tribe as her charges to protect and guide. Grandfather was right—Willow did not abandon people.

"Willow will find her balance, Grandfather. She will have you and Manuelito.'' But as he spoke, he could only think of her last words. *You do not need my help. I would only disappoint you.*

TWENTY-ONE

The colors shimmered in the late afternoon sun—except for the white, for which Lonewolf had used the fire's recent ashes. But the black, yellow, and blue were deep and true. Lonewolf was pleased.

The blue had been the hardest. He had found sumac but the blue clay did not come from here. Once again, he had wished for his medicine bundle. Grandfather had produced his son's medicine bundle, knowing even as he did so that Lonewolf could not use it—the power of a dead man's bundle was unpredictable. But in searching the hogan, Lonewolf had found some blue clay in the bottom of one of the pots. It was just a few pebbles, but enough.

While the piñon gum and alder bark had slow-cooked to a velvet black, Lonewolf had crushed the golden currant he had picked two days before in the canyon and let dry.

Now, he placed the abalone shells, each filled with a color, in the four directions: white and yellow opposite each other, the male black in front of him and the female blue behind him. He set the *tsin dii ni'* in the center. The smell of cedar from the fresh carving stayed on his hands. It should have been oak to make the best sound when he whirled it overhead. He could only hope that the soft cedar would make the sound of thunder when the time came.

All he lacked was water from an eagle's eye. And that he could not create. If the stars did not provide the keen vision, then all his preparation was for nothing.

Grandfather had insisted on another form of preparation. Lonewolf looked at the books stacked outside the ceremonial hogan. One book detailed the Carson campaign. Another was titled, *The Treaty of 1868*.

"It is good reading," Grandfather had said. "Even if the government treats it as fiction." Then he had set the books down.

"I will not have time to read all those, Grandfather," Lonewolf said.

"Then you take the books for the trip. I'll enjoy telling the librarian where to get them."

Lonewolf now dabbed his finger into the ashes and smeared the white around his eyes. Then he took a handful of ashes and covered his upper chest, shoulders, and his upper back. He dabbed two fingers into the black—Father Sky—and painted his forehead. With more black on a fingertip, he drew dots, crosses, diamonds, and spirals on his whitened chest. He "washed" the black off with sand and shifted to face the blue—the female. His thoughts ran to Willow and his fingers froze above the liquid color. Her face filled his mind, her gaze unwavering, challenging. He felt the immediate reaction of his body from his heartbeat to his loins. With supreme will he forced her from his mind and focused on his task.

He dipped two fingers in the paint—so blue that it rivaled the streak of sky above the sunset—and colored his cheeks, nose, and around his mouth. Black above, blue below. Male and female. Two parts of a whole.

Lonewolf's throat thickened and he plunged his fist into the sand, twisting it, fiercely washing off the blue from his hand. He turned quickly to the yellow and, with two fingers, he made jagged lines down his arms. The only task remaining was to kidnap Manuelito.

The scar on Lonewolf's chest prickled with life.

* * *

It was a conspiracy. Everywhere she turned, Willow was reminded of Lonewolf. Not that she needed any reason to think of him. He was always there—not just on the edge of her thoughts, but more like a second presence within her, through which everything filtered before it reached her.

The aroma of coffee perking across the station room transported her to their first morning together and the sight of Lonewolf letting the grounds sift through his slender fingers. She could see his back—laced with scars, yet beautiful: broad and strong. She closed her eyes and her fingertips still remembered the feel of his muscles, smooth with tautness when he had arched over her making love. He was powerful and primitive, but he never intimidated her. In fact, when she thought of the times they had argued, his presence had encouraged her, taken in her wrath and dispelled it. As a lover would do.

A slap of papers on her desk startled Willow from her thoughts.

"Looks like you got your man."

"What?" Had her musings been so obvious?

Cal stood beside her desk smiling.

"What do you mean?" she repeated stupidly.

Cal pointed to the papers and Willow saw the report on the gun.

"The prints on the gun match Curtis's. And Forensics confirm the bullets dug from the boy and from Romero came from that gun. Good work," he added.

"Thanks. Now can I have the medicine bundle?"

He slid the deerskin pouch onto her desk. "Sorry I gave you a hard time about this, Willow."

She nodded but couldn't take her eyes from Lonewolf's sacred *jish* bundle. Her hand closed around the soft leather and she rubbed it between her fingers. In one direction, the worn buckskin slid beneath her thumb—so soft, she barely felt it. In the other direction, the suede resisted and tiny nubs tickled against her palm. The sensation prickled through her veins, starting a heat, as if she were kindling a fire.

"I guess you're pretty happy since that clears your friend Jake, too."

"Jake?" Cal's voice startled Willow. She withdrew her hand from the buckskin.

"The Indian," Cal said. "Where are you this morning, Willow?"

Of course, Lonewolf. She hadn't thought of him as Jake, but only as Lonewolf. *Jake. Short for Jacob.* A man's name. Not the name of a legend or someone who magically appeared from the past. That was Lonewolf. But that name also conjured up images of the wild and a man who lived in it by himself—independent, self-sufficient, with no need of others.

But that was not the full picture of Lonewolf. He also gave of himself for others. He had the biggest heart, the most generous spirit, of any man she had ever known.

Jacob. She liked the way it rolled around her mouth.

"Willow?"

She heard the scrape of a chair and then Cal was beside her at eye level.

"Look, I know you're worried about your grandfather. But it's obvious he didn't have anything to do with the murders."

"He only hired the killer," Willow said distractedly.

"From what you told me, Willow, what he hired were young legs and two strong arms. No one thinks Vidal had anything to do with the murders."

Of course they weren't wrong. Grandfather had not shot and killed anyone. Ever.

"Also, we hauled up everything Curtis had hidden. According to the curator at Northern Arizona, there are some real gems. Chiefs' blankets, Mountain Chant masks. He's thrilled. Actually, you could say Vidal did a service. Hell, the curator even talked about hiring Vidal as a consultant."

Cal's comforting tone was meant to console Willow. Instead, a great weariness welled up inside her. She was so tired of arguing from a solitary position. No one even blamed Grandfather for stealing the artifacts.

"Thanks for the information, Cal," she said and stood. "I'm sure Grandfather appreciates all you've done."

"Also, Willow." Cal stopped her with a hand to her arm. "When you see Lonewolf, please give him my apology."

"Apology?"

"I said some pretty hard things. You know, when we met in the cave, at one point I looked in his eyes. What I saw was just so—" Cal raked a hand through his hair as if searching for words. "So intense. So proud." He shook his head and looked at Willow. "You have to admit he's not your average Navajo."

Willow nodded, not trusting her voice.

"Anyway, the conclusions I jumped to later were wrong. Just tell him that."

Speechless, Willow watched Cal walk away. She couldn't remember the last time, or the first time for that matter, that Cal had apologized to a suspect. What drove him to it, she couldn't say. But she knew the words he had been struggling to find to describe the look in Lonewolf's eyes: uncompromising honesty.

With the medicine bundle in hand, Willow left the station. Forty minutes later, she parked at Junction Overlook and walked over the smooth sandstone boulders to the edge of the cliff and sat down, dangling her legs over the canyon floor, eight hundred feet below.

This was her favorite view of the canyon. One could see nearly the full spread of de Chelly—not just the main canyon, but side canyons and fingers, a labyrinth of hiding places. From here, everything looked soft and muted: smooth, rounded sandstone walls, fuzzy shapes of sheep, and the soft mounds that were hogans.

But down there, in the womb of *Dinehtah,* the struggle of life was neither smooth nor ambiguous. Merciless elements demanded respect and exacted tolls on the undisciplined. Life-killing winters, sweltering summers, flash floods, and quicksand had shaped the canyon and forged the characters of the People who called it home.

Exquisite beauty and appalling hardship—the parents of the Navajo.

As with everything Navajo, there were two opposing forces: male and female, good and evil—all a part of every living thing. Even the gods were not wholly good. It was the duality that gave the Navajo their balance.

Like a hawk's eyes zeroing in on a mouse, Willow, with sudden perception, saw the smallest truth held the most importance: it takes both parts to make the whole. And over her life, she had tried to sever parts of herself, eliminating the weaknesses, striving only for strengths. She had fought the visions, denied the legacy of her father, condemned the old ways as crutches or even lies. And what had she accomplished? She had systematically carved herself up, holding dear only her logic. Except logic cannot explain the unexplainable. Logic could not quiet all her fears. She had left herself defenseless, all because she had not accepted *everything* about herself.

Lonewolf had been willing to accept everything. Whenever he held her, she felt her fears evaporate and strength course through her. He made her whole. *He completed her*.

And tonight he would leave. The man she was meant to be with would be separated from her with the finality of all time. And what would he take with him from her? Nothing. Because she had given nothing. She had told herself he didn't need her, that she would only disappoint him.

But he needed her, too! She was the other part to him. She had felt it in his touch, in his unbridled passion. And she had seen it in his eyes. He wanted her to believe in him. That's all he had asked. And with his stargazer instincts, he had known that if she trusted him, she would have to trust herself. They would complete each other.

The late afternoon sun painted the canyon in red, purple, and magenta. The first stars dotted the sky—day and night sharing the same moment. Willow smiled with thankfulness and drove to find Lonewolf.

He became invisible. Perhaps because he was so altogether out of place that he was beyond noticing. He wore only breeches . . . and paint: an appearance that would not be normal in the hospital. Of course it was night and his deerskin leggins made no sound in the quiet corridors.

But the secret was the approach, especially when outnumbered by the enemy, which was certainly the case in this huge building.

Lonewolf masked himself with purpose and strode straight to Manuelito's room. He cloaked his presence even within the boy's room: already he could feel the power of the shifting stars and he did not want to alarm Manuelito.

The boy seemed smaller—he was certainly thinner. Lonewolf instinctively knew the child needed more strength just to endure the trip. He laid a gentle hand on Manuelito's chest, closed his eyes, and let some of his own life flow into the boy. The child resisted, at peace within the darkness, and Lonewolf understood. He remembered his own fear facing the light.

Lonewolf added his other hand and increased his concentration. The child's defenses were up but, in a way, that was good—it showed fight. Eventually Manuelito relented. Lonewolf felt the boy's lifeblood rise to his fingertips; his heartbeat increased.

Lonewolf first detached the wires at the boy's chest. They did not enter Manuelito, but were only stuck to him. Carefully, he peeled each one away. The tube leading to Manuelito's arm was another matter: it was held tight to the boy's wrist and seemed to pierce his skin. Lonewolf pulled the knife from his leggins and swiftly severed the tube just above where it disappeared into Manuelito's wrist.

Lonewolf slid his arms beneath Manuelito and lifted him free. He pulled a blanket loose from the bed and wrapped it as best he could around the child. Manuelito curled toward Lonewolf. The stargazer felt the child's heart beat against his own.

For a moment he was overcome with the buried memory of his own child. Lonewolf felt his heart reach out to this child, also so alone. Another child's life in his hands. He felt the crack widen in his control and with fierce will closed it.

He could hear muted voices from beyond the room. One was Grandfather's. With warrior's stealth, Lonewolf opened the door, slid out, and pressed himself to the wall. He could not see Grandfather, but he could hear the old man talking. Lonewolf drew the child close to him and strode through the double doors, down the shadowed corridors, and out of the hospital.

He stepped behind a bush and waited for Grandfather to complete his mission. Several minutes passed, then the door shooshed open.

"I'm here," Grandfather said to the bush.

Lonewolf stepped out. Grandfather eyed the bundle. "I made sure she saw me leave his room. She won't check him again for a while. We should have enough time."

Lonewolf followed him to the jeep—though Grandfather called it a truck. Grandfather held the door open for Lonewolf.

"Shall I hold him while you get in?"

"No." He had a great need to hold Manuelito close.

Grandfather closed the door and got into his side. Lonewolf felt Grandfather's gaze.

"Don't worry, Lonewolf. They won't find us."

Lonewolf nodded and Grandfather brought the truck to life. Soon they would be beneath the stars and destiny would be fulfilled.

Willow parked before the silent hogan. They weren't there. She knew it in her bones.

She turned off the jeep and let the night sounds surround her. Canyon wrens trilled and rustled in the cedar trees—but no human sounds. She walked into the darkness to the ceremonial hogan. Like a skeletal mound, the open frame of the hogan sat alone. Willow turned on her flashlight and its beam caught a silvery glint. She stepped between the naked juniper supports into the hogan.

The sand sank beneath her feet, swallowing her toes. She saw the shells with paint and touched her finger to the black. It had nearly jelled—its surface resisted her. Just as she had resisted Lonewolf.

What if he left before she ever saw him again? Before she could tell him that she loved him?

Suddenly, she heard an exquisite harmony of voices. Then the harmony became one voice. It sang in her head, flowed through her veins like sweet honey. The song filled her lungs and she sang. Her voice rose—mixing with the stars. Willow heard the harmony. She felt lifted, buoyant, unafraid. She opened her eyes and saw stars, millions of them, winking at her. All the constellations Lonewolf had tried to help her see hung above her: the Pleiades, Coyote, Bear, Kokopelli. All clearly defined as if someone had drawn them.

Damn it to hell, it was beautiful!

With immediate clarity, she knew the ceremony was being performed. She ran to the jeep, started it up, and headed toward Bear Trail. Maneuvering the jeep with one hand, she pulled the radio from its stand.

"Dispatch."

"Patch me through to the hospital in Fort Defiance. This is Officer Becenti."

"I just got a call from there, Officer Becenti. Manuelito Begay is missing. And get this, one nurse swears she saw a painted Indian carrying him out."

"Call them back and tell them not to worry. I know where he is."

"Must be a bad moon tonight. I'm sure getting some weird calls."

"What do you mean?"

"Got a report from the station in Chinle. Somebody broke into the museum and stole a buckskin. Go figure. Some real weirdos out tonight."

"Just two."

"What?"

"Never mind. I'm at de Chelly. I'll radio you again later."

Burglary. Kidnapping. She thought of her grandfather, too old to climb the canyon, and Lonewolf, a man from another time. Between the two of them, they'd managed pretty well. She couldn't help but smile, then she revved the jeep even faster. It wasn't a bad moon, or even a full moon. It was a cosmic happening.

Lonewolf sensed her without looking. His eyes stayed on the Seven Sisters, rising now from the horizon. He did not falter from his song, the notes rising with the constellation. But he knew Willow was near. The air vibrated with another presence.

Manuelito lay on the canyon floor, the buckskin over his chest. Lonewolf stood beside him, his arms raised to the sky, his voice carrying the song upward.

He could feel the power of the starborn ancestors pushing the stars into place. The balance of everything seemed to shift around him and within him, pulling and pushing. He suddenly remembered the sensation from his own passage—the battle between Mother Earth and Father Sky.

The Seven Sisters aligned into a mammoth star, so near, Lonewolf felt he could touch it with his outstretched arms. Then a flash, like a comet, bolted from the glowing mass. It blinded him, rocked him on his heels. He half closed his eyes, but did not move from Manuelito's side. Sparks fell in a shower of stars.

The moment was at hand. Lonewolf felt the power and the weakness in the universe at the same time. It was now or never. He knew Willow was near. He wanted to reach for her, for one last touch, one more gaze into her eyes. But he did not dare break the circle of power that existed between him, Manuelito, and the Seven Sisters.

He sang to the stars, with more desperation than passion. He sang words he had not known that he knew, but that he recognized, as if they came from another source. He knew it was the *Ha'tanii*'s song.

He saw a spark light on the buckskin and felt the burn on his own chest. The passage was almost complete. His must begin.

He sang louder. The scar on his chest throbbed. Wind rose from a dead calm. Thunder boomed in the clear sky. Lonewolf sang, his heart breaking with every word. He felt the air sizzle, as it had when he had first traveled. He wanted to look at Willow one more time, but he did not trust his heart.

Lonewolf fell to his knees and placed his hand on the *Ha'tanii,* newly scorched into the buckskin. He screamed to the horned shaman.

The air parted, as if it were curtains drawn to reveal another view. Lonewolf reached for the space between, but his hand met an impenetrable blackness. He pressed harder, but it was like pounding on a stone wall.

"Lonewolf, I'm here."

Willow's voice sounded so good, he nearly wept. But he could not answer.

"Please, Lonewolf, look at me."

Still Lonewolf could not respond. Just a word, his heart begged, a look. You *cannot* leave the woman you love!

But his whole life had been about abandonment. This was only more of what he had come to expect. This was not his time. Willow was not his. His heart pumped in fury, but Lonewolf had discipline. It was all he had left.

"Take me with you, Lonewolf!" With each word her voice rose.

You belong here.

"Do tah!" Lonewolf yelled. Then his mind focused. It had been Grey Feather's voice! He pushed at the black wall with all his might.

"Jacob, I love you."

"By all that is sacred, go from here." Lonewolf squeezed out the words with the little strength that remained in him.

Your future is here, Jacob.

It was Grey Feather's voice but not the same words. He was telling Lonewolf to stay and, in that moment, Lonewolf knew his own grandfather was there, beyond the wall. The words sank in. The truth reached his heart. This was his time. He was meant to come here and guide Manuelito and find his own destiny—with Willow.

The ground shifted. Thunder roared in his ears and Lonewolf heard the words he had said to Willow. They were the same ones that Grey Feather had spoken before Lonewolf traveled to this time. In that instant, Lonewolf knew with horrific certainty that he was being pulled to the past—by his own words! He screamed against the mistake! He was meant to be here. But already the solid wall was evaporating, moving over him like a fog. He turned to a fading Willow and screamed, "I love you!"

Willow grabbed for his hand and caught air. He vanished, right before her eyes. Willow cried out in physical pain. The weight of all she had done wrong, of all the things she tried to do right, came crashing down on her, crushing her heart. She could die now. She had lost the one person who knew her, loved her. Grief, so heavy it suffocated her, pulled her to the ground.

In her daze, she gradually noticed that Manuelito was stirring beneath the buckskin. He was alive. She pulled him close and the buckskin slipped from his chest. There, above his left breast, was the unmistakable mark of the horned shaman.

Willow hugged the child to her, rocking and weeping.

She heard the soft crunch of leather soles on hard earth. The toes of Grandfather's shoes stopped at her knee.

''He's gone.'' The words squeezed her heart.

Grandfather knelt and ran a hand through Manuelito's hair. ''Did he succeed?''

Willow managed a nod. She shifted to let Grandfather see the small scar on Manuelito's chest. The boy stirred and opened his eyes.

''Oh, Manny, you're okay. You're okay.'' Willow smiled, but her tears didn't stop. Emotions welled within her, lodging in her throat. How could she be so full of love and sorrow at the same time?

''He's okay, Granddaughter. It's you I worry about.'' His voice soothed. It was the grandfather who loved her. He took Manny into his lap. Willow collapsed into grief, her arms hugging her sides, but all she felt was emptiness.

''He said he loved me. Just before he disappeared.'' The words caught on a sob. Willow looked at Grandfather. ''I have to find him, Grandfather. I have to go to him, or bring him back. Take care of Manny.''

Willow went to his cave—to where she had hidden from him just six days before. Oh, she had tried hard to resist him, to resist the power she had felt within him. Now, she would give everything, she would face her fears, face death itself, for a chance to see him again.

Distant thunder rumbled across the mesas above. Willow stumbled blindly through the canyon—her home, a place she knew. Yet now it was foreign to her. Her feet found no sure ground, only shifting sand and ruts she fell in. She clawed her way up the talus slope, her boots crunching ancient debris.

He had yelled that he loved her. Willow clung to that.

A clap of thunder cracked the sky. Willow stood at the cave entrance and looked across the chasm. Angry clouds blocked the stars and shot barbed bolts of lightning ripping through the blackness. Wind whined down the canyon and whipped her hair. For a moment, Willow couldn't move. She was paralyzed by the swiftness of the storm, its ferocity—and its target. As if all the violent forces focused on the canyon. An arrow of lightning streaked right above her and the hair on Willow's arm rose to the electricity. Were the powers with her or against her? With a shudder, Willow stepped into the cave.

Behind her, the storm raged, its echoes stalking her through the passageway. Was it her imagination, or did the solid walls shift, rocked at their core?

The air thinned and she fought for breath. She crawled the last feet into the chamber and to the wall of the carved *Ha'tanii*. Willow eased her hand within the painted replica of Lonewolf's palm—a nandprint he had made one hundred and thirty years before. She pressed herself to it just as she had seen Lonewolf do.

Nothing happened. The cold, rough stone seemed to mock her. Her hands fisted and she drew them to the *Ha'tanii*'s chest and pounded. *What do I do?* Desperation welled from her soul. "What am I supposed to do?" she yelled, as she slipped down the wall to the ground.

"Isn't it enough you've taken everything from him? Give *me* to him!"

Her teary gaze found the ground where she had lain with Lonewolf in his arms. At the memory of their passion, her pulse quickened and a throb beat deep within her with a yearning beyond all time.

With a furious wipe of her tears, she stood, backed from the wall, and glared at the *Ha'tanii.*

"Don't stand in my way. You may not understand me. But I know you. I know your powers are great, but where are your eyes to search my heart? Look into me! See my grief! I am sorry!" She held her fists clenched, afraid to attempt touching the handprint again. She had to make it work!

"I know I have been stupid and afraid. But I have *never* been selfish! I want the same thing you do: for the People to live free, happy, with a future. But what is Lonewolf's future? Will you condemn him to a life without love? Where is your heart?"

Willow fell to the ground and wailed at the cosmos for mercy. Physically and emotionally drained, she pulled the Chant skin around her. Her cheek to the hard earth floor, Willow could hear the storm, *feel* its fury. The powers Lonewolf had brought to bear for Manuelito now churned unleashed. A world tilting into a void, out of balance.

Unbidden, Navajo words fell from her lips, words she did not know and had never heard.

"Nízaadéé níyá. Nízaadéé níyá."

All at once became still and the roar of the world disappeared.

Strong arms pulled her from the ground. Willow opened her eyes to see Lonewolf. Her senses buckled—her joy colliding with disbelief. *Was he real?*

Willow reached a tentative hand to his jaw and Lonewolf's eyes sparked. Willow's heart leapt. "How—"

He pressed his fingers to her lips and she kissed them.

"You spoke my warrior name, little one."

Willow stepped back to search his beloved face. "What does it mean?"

"He came from afar."

He opened an arm to her and Willow walked into his embrace—the steely arms of a warrior, the sureness of a lover. The gentle hands of a shaman slid up Willow's back and she knew the power of the ways of magic.

Glossary of Navajo Terms

'Ahéhee' Thank you
'Aoo' yá'ánísht'ééh Are you all right?
Bilagaana White person
Biniinaa niká nitáá He looks for you
Diné The People
Dinehtah Home of the Navajo
Diyin Diné'e Holy Ones
Do tah Emphatic response
Ha'ish'aa Let me see
Hash yiniłyé What is your name?
Hastiin Man; Mr.
Hataałii Medicine man
Ha'tanii Horned shaman
Hwééldi Bosque Redondo
Jish Medicine bundle
K'ad á nit'i nii You are doing it
Ladrones Bad men (Spanish)
Ma'ii Coyote; Mischief-maker
Naat'áanii Headman
Naatsis'áán Navajo Mountain
Neezgai It hurts
Níká iishyeed I will help you
Ni ni zin He wants you
Nó woh di naa niná You will go (go away)
Shash'la yádii, T'áá'akó téé It is all right
Shich'i' yániłti' Talk to me
Shi'éí'táádoo biniyé hida nisin It won't do any good; never mind

Shi-siláoo yázhi My little soldier
Shi yázhi Term of endearment
Siláoo yázhi Little soldiers
T'áá doo bina niłzidii Do not be afraid
T'áá k'ad Manuelito baa deeshaał I need to go to Manuelito
Tse-ewa Fortress Rock
Tsin dii ni' Thunder stick
Yaadi la'óolyé, shi'bééhózin What you are saying, I know it
Yá'át'ééh It is good; good morning
Yinish'yé My name is

Dear Reader,

In all the vast and varied landscape of the Navajo Reservation—of all the canyons in Arizona—there is none that compares to Canyon de Chelly. This is the place of mythic Navajo Creation deities; the home to the ancient Anasazi who lived like sparrows in their dwellings high in the cliffs; the site of two hundred years of legendary battles between warrior Navajos and various enemies. A walk through the labyrinthine canyons takes you straight to the heart of Navajoland and you understand in a place deep within you why the Navajo fought to their deaths to protect it.

All the settings in this story are real, including the caves, landmarks, and planetaria mentioned in Canyon de Chelly, though, in some instances, I have compressed the distances. The numerous planetaria painted by Navajo shamans in Canyon de Chelly suggest this place holds special significance for stargazers, though the tradition of painting star charts has disappeared. And, while the skill of stargazing is revered because of the Navajo respect for the rules of the stars, there are few Navajo stargazers who still practice this unique form of divining.

I would love to hear from my readers. You can write to me at P.O. Box 23203, Albuquerque, NM 87192.

All my best,
Laura

Here Is an Excerpt from Laura Baker's Next Thrilling Romance, *Legend*:

"Clah is dead?"

Jackson heard her surprise and a hint of relief. He tightened his grip on her arm, his fingers touching around the heavy denim. She didn't flinch or pull back but merely glanced from his hand to him, her huge brown eyes steady. Jackson's pulse jumped. "You're glad he's dead, aren't you?" he accused, more harshly than he intended.

"Yes," she answered, without hesitation, still staring at him.

Her direct response surprised him. Her eyes held a swirl of emotion, yet she didn't look away—she stared, unblinking, unmoving at Jackson, awaiting his next question.

It took Jackson a second to collect his thoughts. "Tell me, why would you want to see Clah dead?"

"His lies destroy people," she answered evenly.

"Like who?"

This time, she hesitated. She glanced to the ground. "My father," she finally answered, then she raised her gaze to his.

Jackson could stare forever into the black depths of her eyes—their steadiness calming. His hand dropped from her arm. The still moment expanded within him, like a hush of all noise—clarifying, hypnotizing. He had the almost overwhelming urge to lean toward her, reach a consoling hand to her.

He caught himself just in time. Jackson took a quick step backwards and narrowed his eyes on her. He'd never been taken in so fast and so sure. Jackson shook his head. "You're good," he muttered.

She blinked. He saw the brief flash of confusion. Long

lashes swept her cheeks. The more vulnerable she looked, the more irritated he got. *Damn her innocent look*. He shook his head to restore his concentration. "Destroyed your father? How?" he demanded.

"With words, talk . . ." Her voice drifted off.

"Talk doesn't destroy people."

Her brow creased with surprise. "Words create thoughts and thoughts are power, Mr. Walker," she said, as if explaining a simple truth.

The bundle in her arms squirmed. A black nose poked out. She crouched and uncovered a small dog in her lap. "Shh, Dakota," she whispered, while stroking the dog's body and legs. Her big eyes watched Jackson, waiting for a response. He could barely take his gaze from the long fingers feathering through fur.

"Thoughts didn't kill Clah, Ms. Henio. He died painfully." He heard the irritation in his voice and couldn't stop it. "The bodies were mutilated. Slashed to shreds."

"Bodies? Slashed?" She rose, her mouth slightly open. He could see surprise—and something else—on her face.

"Especially Clah's," he said, with emphasis. "As if someone were particularly passionate about *his* murder."

Her eyes riveted on his. "What do you mean, 'slashed'?"

"Gored. Torn to ribbons."

This time he could put a name on the *something else* he saw in her eyes—fear. The kind that yelled for help, the kind that clutched your heart. His heart.

"And the others—who were they?"

"A young girl and a trader from Dinnebito."

"The thief, Newcomb," she said, her tone a final judgment. "And the girl?" The concern in her voice was echoed in her questioning eyes.

"Wynema Begay. A young girl from Whippoorwill."

"They died the same way?" Her urgency gripped him.

"The same way."

"*Yenaldlooshi.*" She whispered the word like a curse. Her voice held the *shush* of a silent terror. A terror he saw in her eyes. The terror he had caused.

He could barely stand to see it there—and he couldn't look away. It was like looking at himself—what he knew was in his own eyes when the violence from the photos, and from Clah's own blood, had swept through him.

At the thought, the memory replayed with vicious speed. Too fast to stop or avoid. With but a breath to prepare, he was plunged into the abyss of clawing terror. His mind clutched for reality.

He felt denim beneath his fingers. A velvet coil brushed his hand. A heart beat against his—slower than his, moderating his own. A warm hand framed his jaw. His own heat rose to the caress—to the touch so ligh
it stunned him.

He opened eyes he hadn't known were closed. Star
up at him, from within his arms, was Ainii, her
eyes deep, measuring.

"Your thoughts are powerful."

"My thoughts . . . ?" The words left him.

He stepped back an arm's length from Ainii, hi
on her shoulders. Her face was drawn with conc
had pulled her into his arms, unconsciously
comfort. When had he lost control? *He* was t
charge, asking questions. He was the one w
sight, the perception. He'd built a career on h
his gut instinct.

But his instincts had been set on end the
seen Ainii—simultaneously annoyed yet
Hell, his hands still held her shoulders. He

raked one through his hair and turned from the dark eyes watching him.